D0429059

KILL-DEVIL AND WATER

London: 1840. A murderer is prowling the backstreets and taverns of the capital. Pyke is in the debtor's prison but Fitzroy Tilling, head of the new Metropolitan Police Force, wants him to investigate the brutal death of a young mulatto woman, recently arrived from Jamaica and apparently working as a prostitute. Tilling's police force are concentrating all their resources on the suspicious death of an influential aristocrat, so Pyke must work alone. His investigation takes him from London docks to the sugar plantations of Jamaica, in a struggle against a ruthless enemy, as well as demons of his own.

For Debbie

KILL-DEVIL AND WATER

by

Andrew Pepper

Magna Large Print Books
Long Preston, North Yorkshire,
BD23 4ND, England.

British Library Cataloguing in Publication Data.

Pepper, Andrew
  Kill-devil and water.

    A catalogue record of this book is
    available from the British Library

    ISBN   978-0-7505-3080-4

First published in Great Britain in 2008 by Weidenfeld & Nicolson,
an imprint of the Orion Publishing Group Ltd.

Published in Large Print 2009 by arrangement with
Orion Publishing Group

Magna Large Print is an imprint of Library Magna Books Ltd.

Printed and bound in Great Britain by
T.J. (International) Ltd., Cornwall, PL28 8RW

Virtue rejects facility to be her companion. She requires a craggy, rough and thorny way.

MICHEL DE MONTAIGNE

The chiefe fudling they make in the Island is Rumbullion, alias Kill-Devil, and this is made of sugar cane distilled, a hott, hellish and terrible liquor.

ANONYMOUS

PART I

London

MAY 1840

ONE

The rope mat did little to protect Pyke from the hardness of the stone floor, and the blanket afforded him no warmth, but somehow he had slept. At first light, he opened his eyes and looked around at the other figures in the ward. No one was moving. Sitting up, he rubbed his eyes and looked at the weak sunlight streaming through the barred window. He waited, to see whether he could hear birdsong – a blackbird perhaps or better still a thrush – but the only noise was the rough snoring of his fellow inmates. Casting aside the blanket, he stood up and stretched. He had slept in his clothes, as everyone did. This was the only time of the day Pyke enjoyed; aside from the sessions on the treadmill, which he had come to appreciate – the chance to push himself to the limits of his endurance. It was quiet now, peaceful even. Soon the wardsman would wake the others up and make his rounds, shuffling from prisoner to prisoner, looking for new ways to make money from them. The lad from the bake-house would arrive shortly after nine and at ten they would be allowed outside into the yard. At midday they would be given the chance to buy their lunch and at two they would take turns on the treadmill. This had been Pyke's existence for nine months and there were times when he'd forgotten about the world beyond the four walls of the prison. But at this time in the morning, before anyone else had stirred, before the jabber of tiresome conversation and the rattle of chains filled the long, narrow ward, his head was clear enough that he could remember Emily's smile and the way his son, Felix, had looked at him the last time they had been together. In the hard times, these were the things he held on to, the things that mattered.

Later that morning, Pyke was walking in the yard, staring up at the granite walls and the inward-facing iron spikes at the very top, when a turnkey approached him and told him he had a visitor.

'Now?' Pyke cupped his hands over his eyes to protect them from the glare of the sun. He tried not to show the turnkey that he was concerned.

'A peeler.'

Pyke wondered why a policeman should be visiting him after all this time. He had done many things in his life; perhaps some other wrong was about to catch up with him. Pyke followed the turnkey through a heavy oak door, bound with iron and studded with nails, along a passageway and down some steps into the press-room, where Fitzroy Tilling was pacing back and forth. He was a tall, broad-shouldered man, about the same age as Pyke, with raven-coloured hair, swept back off his high forehead, olive skin and piercing bug-like eyes.

'So you're a policeman now?' The last time Pyke had seen Tilling, about a year earlier, he had still been in the service of Sir Robert Peel, leader of the Tory party. In fact, he had served Peel in one capacity or another for the previous twenty-five years, first of all in Ireland, when Peel had been stationed there, and then back in London.

Pyke had known Tilling for more than ten of those years, and while he couldn't lay his hand on his heart and say he really *knew* the man well, they had become something more than acquaintances and less than friends in that time, particularly after Emily's death almost five years ago. They had met up for the occasional dinner, and while they'd never *openly* pried into each other's private lives, there had been, Pyke thought, a mutual if unacknowledged recognition that they were more alike than different: two middle-aged men who, if they had made different choices, might have been friends.

'Deputy commissioner.' Tilling hesitated. 'Sir Robert wanted me to spread my wings a little.'

'I suppose congratulations are in order, then.' Pyke met Tilling's stare.

Tilling reached into his pocket and pulled out a piece of paper. 'This is a magistrate's warrant authorising your immediate release.'

Pyke continued to stare at him. 'And what have I done to deserve such good fortune?' By his calculation, he had only another month and a half to serve. Or rather, a bond that he'd taken out when he had money was due to expire then, at which point he'd be able to clear sufficient debts to secure his release.

'I need your help.'

Pyke let a short silence build between them. 'What kind of help?'

Even with the benefit of hindsight, Pyke didn't

13

know exactly when it had all started to go wrong. Perhaps it was as simple as Emily's death. Perhaps that fateful day at Smithfield when a crippled ex-rifleman had cut his wife down had been the moment it had all begun to fall apart. Perhaps Pyke still blamed himself for not having done more to ensure her safety, though it was true she'd been killed because of her crusading work for the nascent trade union movement. And she had always done whatever she had wanted to, irrespective of his fears for her safety.

But it was also perhaps too easy to blame everything on Emily's death. There had been many happy times after she'd died; times when it looked as though he and Felix might pull through with only a few scars to show for it. If anything, Felix had adapted to their new situation better than Pyke had, and after a while, he barely mentioned Emily's name. Pyke had tried to learn from his son, but he'd found it a good deal harder to move on. He didn't know whether it was fair or appropriate to blame himself for Emily's death but, in one sense, this didn't matter. He was alive and she wasn't. This simple truth never failed to impress itself on him, especially in the early hours when sleep was beyond him. Emily's premature death had, however, made him utterly determined to realise her wishes for their son – that Felix be given the chance to adopt her late father's title and claim Hambledon Hall as his own. So when one of Emily's distant cousins had returned from America to stake his claim on the family estate, Pyke had hired the best legal counsel to defend Felix's birthright; and when the case was referred to the

14

High Court of Chancery, he had not only retained the services of this counsel but also hired other lawyers to further their chances. In total, the case had lasted almost three years, and by the time the Lord High Chancellor had ruled finally in favour of Emily's cousin, Pyke had sacrificed a large chunk of his fortune, trying to hold on to a house and an estate he had never liked when Emily was alive.

Afterwards, Pyke had taken to speculating on the stock market with a recklessness that had astonished even him. No 'get-rich-quick' scheme had been too outlandish, too much of a risk. In under a year he'd squandered fifty thousand pounds for very little return, but by this point he had ceased to care. Much later, when he reflected upon his behaviour, it struck him that his actions might have been wilfully self-destructive. For much of his adult life, Pyke had laboured under the assumption that money protected you from the rank unpleasantness of existence, but in the end his considerable wealth had failed to prevent Emily's death. More disturbingly, his pursuit of money may even have contributed to it.

So when the debts he'd accrued on the stock market and elsewhere had finally come home to roost, it had almost been a relief to have been sentenced to a year in prison. At the time, he had been numb to everything; to losing his fortune, even to losing his son.

Pyke watched through the smudged glass of Tilling's carriage as his son, Felix, now bounded down the steps of his uncle's apartment in

Camden Town, closely followed by Jo, his nurse-maid, who had served first Emily, then Pyke, for the previous fifteen years. She was now in her early thirties and had proved to be a loyal friend as well, even visiting Pyke in prison. It had been nine months since Pyke had last seen Felix – he'd been adamant about the lad not visiting him in prison – and he was shocked at how different his son looked; he was taller and more gangly for one thing. For a moment, the urge to open the door and greet Felix was overwhelming, but then Pyke caught a glimpse of his torn coat sleeve and smelled his unwashed body and felt a stab of shame at his circumstances. His gaze was drawn to Jo; she was a good head shorter than him and, though by no means beautiful, her thin, angular face, dotted with freckles and her flame-red hair cut in the style of a pageboy, meant she was always noticed. At the bottom of the steps, Felix turned to Jo and held out his hand. She took it and smiled. Pyke exchanged a silent glance with Tilling; what Felix had just done had been almost an adult gesture – a man coming to the assistance of a woman. On the street, Felix fell in beside Jo and the two headed off in the direction of Camden Place.

'Aren't you going to say hello to them?' Tilling hesitated. 'I thought it was the purpose of this detour.'

'I'll come back tomorrow or the day after.' Pyke tried to swallow but there was hardly any moisture in his throat.

'Are you sure?'

Pyke frowned but didn't want Tilling to know

what he was thinking. 'I'm quite sure. We can go now.'

Tilling tapped on the roof and a few moments later the carriage jerked forward. Pyke stared out through the glass and thought about the shame that had stopped him from greeting his son.

'All right, now you can tell me what it is you want, Fitzroy. Why have you gone to all this effort to arrange my release from prison?'

'A body was found yesterday morning by a stream running alongside the Ratcliff Highway.'

Pyke digested this news without visible reaction. It still didn't explain why Tilling had freed him from prison. 'And that's where we're going now?' He looked at the passing buildings, trying to get his bearings after nine months in confinement. He knew the Ratcliff Highway. It was an ancient thoroughfare running through the East End, skirting the northern perimeter of the London Dock, and was lined with taverns, gin shops, brothels and cheap lodging houses that catered to the needs of sailors on shore leave.

Tilling checked his watch. 'We're meeting the coroner at the tavern where the autopsy will take place in half an hour.'

A moment's silence passed between them. 'You know that even if you hadn't gone to all this effort, I would have been let out of prison next month.'

Tilling's glance drifted over Pyke's shoulder. 'This way, you get to see your son a month earlier than you expected.'

The corpse was that of a young woman. At a guess, Pyke supposed she had once, or as recently as a week ago, been beautiful. Her black hair was wet and matted but her legs were long and her body, shapely and well proportioned. What was left of her face reinforced this impression. Still, none of this really registered, at least not the first time Pyke saw her. Instead, all he could look at was her skin, already eaten away by a coating of quicklime, and her eyes, or the two holes bored into her lifeless face where her eyes had once been. All that remained was a few torn vessels in the empty sockets.

'Who is she?' Pyke asked, drawing his shirt-sleeve across his mouth. They were waiting for the coroner in a room above the Green Dragon public house on the Ratcliff Highway, a few hundred yards from where the corpse had first been discovered.

Tilling pulled at his collar, seemingly uncomfortable in his dark blue coat. 'That's what I want you to find out.'

Pyke allowed his gaze to fall back to the woman's face. 'Has anyone reported a daughter or wife or friend as missing?'

Tilling shook his head.

'And no one, as yet, has come forward to claim the body?' Pyke went on.

'We've done our best to keep a lid on the matter. I don't want folk traipsing out here on a macabre pilgrimage to see where she was mutilated.'

Pyke looked again at the remains of the woman's face and her long black hair and wondered who had done this to her.

A few minutes later, the coroner arrived, put his bag on the table next to the dead body and began to prepare for the autopsy. John Joseph Hart was young, clean shaven, with a cherub-like face, and a grumpy, condescending manner that belied his years. He had a high opinion of himself and conducted himself in a prissy manner that rankled with Pyke. After shaking Pyke's hand, Hart produced a large, white handkerchief and wiped his palm clean.

They watched as he made a few incisions above her breast-bone. The sight of the scalpel slicing easily through the woman's flesh made Pyke wince inwardly.

'I can say for a fact that she didn't drown. No trace of any water in her lungs, you see,' Hart said. The coroner looked at them, as if waiting for a round of applause.

Pyke pointed at the contusions on her neck. 'At a wild guess, I'd say she was strangled.'

Irritated by Pyke's intervention, Hart sighed. 'But would you have known that for sure, if I hadn't conducted my examination of her lungs?'

'So we can put down the cause of death as strangulation, then?' Tilling asked.

'I'd say so,' Hart muttered, casting a scalding look in Pyke's direction.

'And that's it? That's all you can tell us?'

'I'm a coroner, not a mind-reader,' Hart retorted, continuing to inspect the bruises around her throat.

'Well, let's hope her landlord will be a little more illuminating.'

In the pocket of a dress which had been discovered in marshy ground a few yards from the corpse, along with a half-empty bottle of Jamaica rum, was a scrap of paper giving the address of the Bluefield, a lodging house on the Ratcliff Highway. The landlord had already been summoned.

'If you look at the bruises here and here,' Pyke said, pushing the coroner to one side and pointing at the marks on either side of her slender neck, 'those would have been his thumbs.' He removed his jacket, rolled up his sleeves and turned to Hart. 'Just stand still for a moment,' he said to the bemused coroner. Before the man could answer, Pyke had wrapped his hands around Hart's throat and dug his thumbs into the area just below the glands, keeping them there for a little longer than was strictly necessary to illustrate the point. 'That's how he killed her.' He held up his hands. 'But you can see from the size of those marks that whoever did this had bigger hands than mine.' What he'd said was purely conjectural, something to irritate Hart rather than impress Tilling, and as he said it, Pyke wondered whether he still really had what it took to undertake such an investigation.

Somehow he doubted it. After all, it had been a long time – more than ten years – since he'd regularly done this kind of work; since he'd resigned from his position as a Bow Street Runner.

Having been released from Pyke's grip, Hart made exaggerated choking sounds to indicate his discomfort. 'Really, this is the most unacceptable behaviour I have ever witnessed...'

'You can see,' Pyke said, pointing to the woman's face and chest, 'that the quicklime has eaten away the skin ... here and here.' She was lying face up on the table. 'But if we roll her over on to her front...' He paused while performing this manoeuvre. 'You'll see how clean and un-blemished her back is.' Her biscuit-coloured skin felt cold and hard to the touch.

Tilling rubbed his chin. 'So what are you suggesting?'

Rolling her on to her back again, Pyke held up one of her hands. 'In spite of the quicklime, there's hardly a blemish or a callus. Not the hands of a servant or a seamstress, I'd wager.' He looked over at Tilling, surprised at how good it felt to be using his mind. 'My question is: how did she earn a living?'

Pyke could see that Tilling was thinking what he was thinking.

'Perhaps,' he added, though Tilling hadn't said anything, 'but I don't think she was a street-walker.' Pyke glanced down at her fleshy curves and felt his stomach tighten. 'She's too exotic, too refined. And that dress would have cost a few pounds, too.'

Tilling nodded, conceding the point. 'You're suggesting she had money?'

'I don't know.' Pyke picked up one of the woman's hands and had another look. 'Of course, if she had money, why would she be staying at a lodging house on the Ratcliff Highway?'

'We don't know that for sure,' Tilling said. 'At least not until young Jenks returns with the land-lord.'

'Then we should start with what we do know. Tell me what you found out from the dram-shop owner.'

Tilling explained that the old man had come

across the corpse the previous morning while emptying night soil and had reported it to the police at once. According to his testimony, the dram-shop owner had found the body lying on the bank of a stream that trickled under the Ratcliff Highway. He hadn't touched it and therefore, if he was to be believed, hadn't seen the woman's facial mutilations. The bottle of rum and the dress had been found next to the body. The man's wife hadn't slept well that night and claimed to have heard voices, and a horse and cart stopping somewhere under their bedroom window, although she hadn't climbed out of bed to have a look.

Pyke considered what he had just been told and weighed up the likely cause of death – strangulation – against the removal of her eyeballs. He was unable to find a way of reconciling the two acts. In some ways, the murder struck him as cold and clinical. The woman had been strangled and her body tossed away like a piece of rubbish. There was no indication that she'd been beaten and there was no sign of sexual congress. But her eyeballs had been gouged out with a knife; she'd been defaced in the most gruesome manner imaginable, as if the man who'd done it hadn't merely wanted to kill her but to annihilate her.

'Why cut out her eyes?' Tilling said, reading his mind.

'And why sprinkle her face and body with quicklime but leave a scrap of paper in her dress with the name and address of a lodging house?'

Pyke bent forward and sniffed the body. He'd smelled the odour as soon as he'd stepped into the room but hadn't been able to place it. Not simply the ripeness of putrefying flesh, but something sweeter, tangier.

'You said a half-empty bottle of rum was found next to the corpse?' he said, ignoring Hart.

'That's right,' Tilling replied.

'Here.' Pyke stepped aside to let Tilling do what he'd just done. 'Can you smell it on her?'

'The rum?'

'On her body. All over it, in fact.'

Tilling offered Pyke a puzzled stare. 'What are you suggesting? That she was embalmed with rum?'

'Perhaps.' Pyke took another look at the body, particularly the colour of her skin. 'I wouldn't describe her as Negro but could we say she was mulatto?'

'For what it's worth,' Hart interrupted, 'that would be my opinion on the matter.'

'That she was mulatto?' Tilling asked.

The coroner shrugged. 'Well, look at the swarthiness of her skin here and here,' he said, pointing to her hands and wrists.

'Yes, I suppose.'

'Together with the rum,' Hart said, looking warily at Pyke, 'it could mean she had some kind of connection to the West Indies.' He waited for a moment. 'After all, those people are a law unto themselves, aren't they?'

Tilling and Pyke looked at one another, frowning.

'Well, do you honestly believe a godly white man would have done that to her?' Hart added defensively.

'Are you saying that someone with darker skin

than you or I is naturally predisposed to gouge people's eyes out?' Pyke asked.

'I didn't say that ... I simply meant that the negro race is more predisposed towards savagery. Science has proved this to be so.'

Pyke looked again at the dead woman and tried to work out whether her features were Caucasian or not.

'I've been in touch with the magistrate at Shadwell. The inquest will take place here, in this room, tomorrow at ten. After that, if no one has claimed her, someone will have to make arrangements for her burial.' Hart put his scalpel back into his bag and snapped the fastener shut. 'Otherwise the stink will become unbearable.'

Tilling thanked Hart for his work and ushered him to the staircase. 'You'll recommend that the jury deliver a verdict of wilful murder, won't you?' Pyke overheard Tilling say to the coroner.

Pyke went to cover the body with a sheet. A few moments later Tilling joined him.

'So you want me to find the man who did this to her?' Pyke asked eventually.

Tilling nodded. 'Don't tell me you're not interested. I can see it in your eyes.'

Pyke walked across to the window and stared down into the yard below. It felt strange, disconcerting even, to be free all of a sudden. 'What I am interested to know is why a man in your elevated position, and with your newfound responsibilities, would consider employing the services of a lowly convict.' He paused. 'The last time I checked, there were something like three thousand men working for the New Police.'

24

'And how many of those men do you think have been trained to run an investigation of this type? Of any type.' Tilling sighed. 'You know as well as I do that the emphasis has always been placed on prevention rather than detection. That was Peel's intention when he first proposed the force ten years ago and it still holds true today.'

This much was true. Contrary to the belief of Pyke's mentor at Bow Street, Sir Richard Fox, Peel and subsequent Home Secretaries for Melbourne's Liberal governments had argued that the role of the police was not to investigate crimes after they had taken place but to prevent them from happening by crowding the streets with policemen. For his part, Pyke had always found this reasoning to be obtuse. To prevent crime, you needed to find a way of eradicating poverty – something no politician wanted to do. Until then, all you could hope to do was go after the worst offenders and use every dirty trick and every soiled piece of information to put them behind bars.

'You're telling me that the Metropolitan Police doesn't have *any* specialist detectives?' Pyke turned around. 'I don't believe that for a minute. What usually happens when someone is murdered?'

Tilling considered this. 'I suppose you wouldn't have seen or read the newspapers in Marshalsea.'

'What do you think?' In fact he hadn't read a newspaper for more than nine months.

'Two days ago Lord William Bedford was murdered in his own bed, while he slept. He was stabbed in the stomach with a letter opener.'

'Return to sender, eh?'

Tilling stared at him. 'Do you think for one moment that's amusing?'

Pyke shrugged.

'I don't think you appreciate the pressure we're under to apprehend the murderer.' Tilling wiped his forehead and thinning pate with his handkerchief. 'Bedford is, or was, a well-respected member of the aristocracy. If we don't find his murderer quickly, we'll face public ridicule *and* political censure.'

'And because of that, you don't have the time or resources to lavish on a poor mulatto woman who had the misfortune to be murdered at the same time.'

Pyke could see he'd landed a small blow; Tilling gave him a grudging nod. 'You always did have the ability to see through bluster.'

'So who killed Bedford?'

'At present, I have no idea. But as you can probably guess, our much-lauded press has already worked itself up into a frenzy of speculation.'

'And all your best men have been assigned to the investigation.'

Tilling grimaced. 'The commissioner, Sir Richard Mayne, has taken control of the case but he's handed over the day-to-day responsibilities to two of our best detectives: Inspector Baker and this chap called Benedict Pierce. I'm told he used to be a Bow Street Runner. Perhaps you know him?'

Pyke didn't even try to hide his disdain. Pierce was an unlikely combination of Christian piety and ruthless ambition – hence the kind of man who attributed the wealth he accrued to God's race rather than his own grubby machinations.

26

'Let me guess. In the meantime, Mayne's instructed you to take care of this "lesser" problem. Or make it appear as if you're taking care of it.'

'I see prison has made you even more cynical.'

'I wonder how Mayne would feel if he knew you were offering work to a jailbird such as myself?'

'If it came down to it, I could persuade him. Mayne listens to Peel and you know you still have a friend there.'

A few years earlier, while he'd still owned his own bank, Pyke had unwittingly done battle with, and vanquished, one of the Tory leader's most feared political adversaries, and he had yet to call in the favour.

Pyke turned back to the window and stared up at the sky. It felt oddly exhilarating to see it without the imposition of bars or walls. And he had already decided to do what Tilling was asking him to do; it would be a way of trying to redeem himself in the eyes of his son. 'I'll need some money to live off and a purse to run the investigation.'

Tilling nodded but waited for a few moments. 'Five pounds a week, until the killer is caught.'

Pyke turned back to face Tilling and shook his head. 'Not enough.'

'That's more than a sergeant would earn.' Tilling crossed his arms. 'Of course, I could always take you back to Marshalsea.'

'Fifteen.'

It must have been the way Pyke said it which angered Tilling because almost at once his colour rose. 'You're acting as if I've come to you holding a begging cup. In fact, you're quite right. I could get a hundred men to do this job but I thought you might appreciate the chance to make a fresh start – if not for yourself, then for your son.' Tilling's expression softened. 'Look, Pyke, I don't see this as an act of charity. You're the best detective I've ever known. But if you sink any deeper into the quagmire, you might not find a way back.'

Pyke considered Tilling's outburst, admiring the man's doggedness but hating him for being right. He nodded slowly.

'So you'll do it? You'll find the man who did this to her?' Tilling looked at him, expectantly.

'I'll see what I can find out. I'm not making any promises.'

'None expected.' Tilling waited. 'What do you need?'

'I'll need an artist with a strong constitution and a sense of discretion who can sketch as good a likeness as is possible under the circumstances.'

'Anything else?'

'Some money to get things started.'

Tilling threw him a purse. 'There's twenty pounds. That should be enough for now.' Pyke caught the purse and pocketed it without inspecting the contents. 'Won't you get into trouble for hiring my services?'

Tilling shrugged. 'I might, but that's for me to worry about.'

Lifting up the sheet, Pyke had another look at the woman's mutilated face, but it wasn't necessary. Every curve and undulation, every blemish and bruise, had already been lodged indelibly in his mind.

TWO

The landlord's name was Thrale and he'd once been a bare-knuckled fighter. Pyke didn't recognise him straight away, even though he'd seen the man fight William Benbow ten or fifteen years earlier. Thrale told them that the woman's name was Mary Edgar; that she had rented a private room in his lodging house about a week ago and had paid in advance; and that she'd shared the room with a black man called Arthur Sobers, who, until that point, had been staying in one of the general rooms for two pence a night. Sobers, Thrale said, had first shown up about three weeks earlier, having just arrived on a ship from Jamaica. Thrale seemed to be in awe of Sobers' physical presence and he struck Pyke as the kind of man who worshipped toughness, even though his own body was now old and broken. Pyke recalled the fight he'd witnessed all those years ago. In the end, Benbow had taken Thrale apart, punch by punch, but the beaten man had refused to lie down. It was as bloody a spectacle as he'd ever seen. Thrale should have stayed down but didn't. That told Pyke something about his character.

'So the two of them, Mary Edgar and this man Sobers, were intimate with one another already?'

'I'd say so.' Thrale's nose had been broken in numerous places.

'You'd say so or you know so?'

29

'She told me she wasn't used to the cold, coming from Jamaica. He told me he was just off the ship from the West Indies. They shared a room. The rest I worked out for myself.'

When they had shown Thrale her body, he hadn't flinched, not even when he saw her face. He'd identified her immediately, and when Pyke had tried to push him – how could he be so certain, given the mutilations and the effects of quicklime? – Thrale had shrugged and said he just knew. He'd identified her dress, too. He'd seen her wearing it the night before she was killed.

'Is Sobers still staying at the lodging house?'

'Ain't seen him for a couple of days.' Thrale scratched his chin. 'You think he done it?'

'That was going to be my next question.'

'How should I know? He's a tough one, that's for sure. Apart from that, he didn't give much away, kept himself to himself. She did, too.'

'You think they were attached?'

'You mean was they fucking?' His grin revealed an incomplete set of uneven, yellow teeth.

'That's one way of putting it.'

Thrale considered the question. 'They was sharing a room not much larger than a cell. They'd have to be intimate.'

'But you don't know what brought them to London in the first place?'

'No.'

'Or which ship they came on?'

'I didn't say for certain they'd come on the same ship. He told me he was just off the ship; but he didn't mention a name. She said she was from Jamaica. That's all. I don't like to pry into

30

my guests' affairs.'

Pyke waited for a moment. 'You described him as black. Would you say she was a mulatto?'

'A blue-skin?' Thrale looked into his face. 'If I walked past her on the street, I'm not sure what I'd think. She could certainly have passed as white.'

'Anything else you can tell me about her?'

Thrale sniffed and then stared down at the corpse, now covered with the sheet. 'I ain't disparaging my lodging house or the folk who stay there. But she was nicely dressed and well spoken. She looked as out of place as a butterfly in a cage of rats.'

Pyke thought about the scrap of paper they'd found in her dress. It was almost as if the man who'd killed her had wanted them to find out who she was and that she'd stayed at the Bluefield. 'But you didn't ask her why she'd chosen to rent one of your rooms?'

'Like I said, I don't pry into my guests' affairs.'

Pyke told him they'd need to find Arthur Sobers as soon as possible and that he would have to search the room and put some questions to Thrale's lodgers about Mary Edgar. He arranged to drop by the Bluefield later that afternoon and made Thrale promise not to disturb the room – and, if he saw Sobers, not to tell him what had happened.

'He seemed like a fine chap,' Thrale said, 'but I guess, with blackbirds, you just never know.'

Pyke asked Thrale whether he'd stay until the artist arrived, so that between them they could come up with a sketch of the dead woman.

'I saw you fight Benbow, must have been fifteen

31

years ago,' he said, while they waited.

'Hardest fight of my life.'

Pyke nodded. 'At the time I thought you should have stayed down.'

'And now?'

'You did what you had to.'

Thrale looked at him with new respect. 'I'd stayed down, I might as well have ended me life then and there.'

After the artist had sketched what Thrale reckoned to be a reasonable likeness of the dead woman, Pyke took a hackney carriage back to his uncle's apartment in Camden Town. On the way he asked the driver to stop at a slop-shop in Battle Bridge where he purchased a presentable frock-coat, and on Camden Place he paid a barber to trim his hair and whiskers. He got all the way to the pavement outside the apartment before realising that he didn't have anything for Felix. Not knowing what kind of gift was appropriate for a ten-year-old boy, Pyke dithered on the bottom step and was spotted through the front window by his uncle. A few moments later, the door swung open, and Godfrey hobbled down the steps to greet him.

'Dear boy, is it really you?' He took Pyke's arms in his hands and squeezed them, as he had always done when trying to show affection. His cheeks might have been a little redder than Pyke remembered, and his hair a little whiter, but aside from that, he was the same as ever. 'We weren't expecting you for another month or two.'

At the top of the steps, Pyke was greeted by

Copper, a giant mastiff and former fighting dog that Pyke had unintentionally acquired a few years earlier when he'd shot one of its legs off with a pistol. Oddly enough, the animal hadn't held this against him. Recognising him instantly, the three-legged beast hopped excitedly towards him, tail wagging. Pyke patted Copper on his black muzzle, accepting the licks to his hand, then looked up to see Felix holding the banister. He had come halfway down the inside stairs but didn't seem to be ready to join them in the hallway. 'Felix, my lad, come down here at once and greet your father,' Godfrey called out.

Felix didn't move.

Jo appeared from the back of the apartment; she was wearing a kitchen apron and her hair was tied up under a lace bonnet. *'Pyke.'* She hurried forward and they greeted one another awkwardly, a handshake and a kiss rolled into one. Although she was technically his servant, they had nonetheless become close in the years since Emily's death. In that time, Pyke had also become aware that Felix had started to regard Jo as a surrogate mother, and he'd tried not to place too great a burden on her, but her kindness and good nature meant she had always been willing to help in whatever way she could.

'You look well,' Jo said. 'You really do.'

'And so do you.' He meant it, too, but his gaze drifted up the stairs to where Felix was still standing.

Jo noticed this and said to Felix, 'Come down here at once, young man.'

But Felix still refused to budge. Pyke took a few

33

tentative steps towards him. 'Felix?' He waited for his son to look at him but the lad's eyes were planted on his shoes. 'Do you not recognise your own father?' He tried to keep his tone light and breezy, not wanting any of them to see his bitter disappointment at Felix's apparent indifference. In his head, he'd imagined the lad bounding down the stairs and throwing his arms around him.

'Hello, Father,' Felix mumbled. Then, without warning, he turned and disappeared up the stairs.

Jo called out, ordering Felix to come back down 'this minute', a maternal firmness in her tone, but when nothing happened, she said she would go and drag him down if necessary. Pyke stepped forward and blocked her path. 'It's my fault. I should have given you time to prepare, time for Felix to adjust. Leave him for the moment. He'll come round.'

'I just can't understand it,' Godfrey said, shaking his head. 'The boy talks about you constantly. Doesn't he, my dear?'

Jo smiled but her awkward reaction suggested she didn't entirely concur with Godfrey's assessment. Pyke thought about the way she had spoken to Felix, and the way Felix had taken her hand on the street earlier that day.

'You'll stay with us, though? I'm afraid you won't have your own bedroom but if you don't mind sharing the front room with Copper...'

'Thank you, but the sooner I find my own accommodation, the better it'll be for all of us.' Pyke had intended to stay the night but the coolness of Felix's reaction had wounded him and now all he wanted to do was be by himself.

34

'At least stay for a glass of claret.'

Pyke glanced up the stairs and then bent down to give Copper another pat on the head.

'Just give him a little time, dear boy. Deep down, the lad adores you.'

Jo excused herself and returned to the kitchen. Godfrey led Pyke into the front room and said, 'Perhaps you haven't heard about the success of our book...'

'It's not *our* book,' Pyke said, glancing around the room, taking in its familiar sights and smells. 'It's your book.'

'Quite.' Godfrey smiled awkwardly. 'So tell me why they let you out so soon.' He went to pour them both a glass of claret from the decanter.

'Well,' Pyke said, taking a sip of the wine, 'an old friend wants me to investigate the murder of this woman...'

He wanted Godfrey to know what he was doing because he hoped his uncle would tell Felix; most of all he wanted Felix to know that he was more than just an ex-convict.

That night, Pyke found accommodation – little more than a garret really – in Smithfield and, with nothing to unpack, he lay down on the old mattress and listened to the rain beating against the tiles. At his side Copper, who had insisted on coming with him, snored contentedly. As he tried to sleep, he thought about the ward at Marshalsea and the fact that, to all intents and purposes, he had swapped one cell for another.

Early the following morning, Pyke went to see the old man who ran the dram-shop – the one who'd found the body. He told Pyke essentially the same story he'd told Tilling: that he had first seen the corpse while discarding the previous night's soil into the stream that ran through the land at the back of his shop; that it hadn't been there the day before or else he would certainly have noticed it; and that he hadn't interfered with the corpse in any way but had sent a lad to fetch the police.

He struck Pyke as a credible witness, or as credible as someone who sold illegal spirits with the potential to blind customers could be. But it was his wife, a stout, unattractive woman with thick, wiry hair sprouting from her nose, that Pyke really wanted to talk to. She also stuck to her story and, in the end, Pyke decided that she, too, had told the truth. On the night in question, she had been woken by hushed voices coming from beneath her bedroom window; her husband, she'd told Pyke, had been drunk and hadn't stirred. She hadn't gone to the window because she suffered from gout and hadn't wanted to move from her bed, but she'd certainly heard a wagon or cart stop near the bridge. She reckoned it had stayed there for about ten minutes.

Outside by the stream, Pyke looked for further clues but found nothing except for a broken plate, a few pieces of wood and some furniture. It was a grim spot. Climbing up to the bridge, he looked down at the place where the body had been found and tried to put himself in the mind of the man who'd dumped her there. It would have been easy enough to drag the body from the cart across the road and then shove it over the edge towards the stream. The bank was muddy and yet the body, at least when he'd seen it upstairs in the tavern, had been almost spotless. This was further proof, in Pyke's mind, that the corpse had been washed with rum. But why?

Next Pyke knocked on doors and stopped people on the street but no one admitted to having seen anything on the night in question. He showed people the drawing of the dead woman but no one recognised her.

At ten o'clock he attended the coroner's inquest just a few yards away at the Green Dragon, where the jury, as expected, returned a verdict of wilful murder.

Strenuous efforts had been made to ensure that the jurors wouldn't run to the newspapers with stories of what they had seen – the last thing Pyke wanted was a rush of pilgrims to the scene of the crime – but he also knew it was only a matter of time before the story leaked out into the public domain. Still, at Pyke's insistence, the jurors had all been warned that if specific details of the mutilation made their way into the newspapers, there would be serious consequences.

A while later, returning to the old bridge, Pyke had a peculiar feeling he had known this place as a child. It took him a good few minutes to remember the exact incident and the date.

The bridge looked much smaller than he remembered, but this was to be expected. He had been eleven, maybe twelve, and he had made the journey to the Ratcliff Highway on New Year's Eve to witness the corpse of the murderer, John Williams, being paraded in an upturned coffin attached to a wagon. Williams had apparently bludgeoned to death two families who lived on the Ratcliff Highway but had committed suicide before the court could pass sentence on him. The purpose of the parade, therefore, had been to satisfy the public's demand that the murders be properly avenged. Standing on the bridge, at almost the same spot where he had stood almost thirty years earlier, Pyke could still picture the dead man's hard, mummified face and the cold, staring eyes. Later he had followed the procession north up Cannon Street to a piece of scrubland where the body was to be buried. There, he had witnessed one of the burial party, a red-faced man wearing a billycock hat, drive a wooden stake through the corpse's heart using a sledgehammer.

At the time he had been terrified – at the sight of the corpse and of the notion that the murderer, Williams, wasn't in fact dead – and for weeks afterwards he'd dreamt that his mother, who had left when Pyke was just five, had been one of Williams' early victims.

It was odd to think that the murders of two families from the Ratcliff Highway, one of the poorest and most notorious streets in the entire city, had caused such a stir throughout the metropolis. Thirty years later, an elderly aristocrat had been murdered in his elegant Park Lane home, and this was the murder that everyone was talking about. No one seemed to be bothered about the murder of an unknown mulatto woman. Of course, there was nothing especially surprising about this state of affairs but, in the circumstances, Pyke couldn't help but think about the procession he'd witnessed thirty years earlier, and it made him wonder whether the city really was a safer, fairer place to live, as the politicians and civic leaders often tried to claim.

The Bluefield lodging house was neither blue nor situated anywhere near a field. In fact, it was located at the end of a thin, sunless court and had nothing to recommend it. The smell of fried fish and horse dung was pungent and a grey-flannelled mist drifted off the river. Inside, the ceilings were low and buckled and the plaster flaked off smoke-blackened walls. Pyke found Thrale in the kitchen. The former bare-knuckled fighter took him up the corkscrew staircase to the room Mary Edgar and Arthur Sobers had rented. They knocked but no one answered. Thrale took out some keys and tried them, one by one, until the lock turned. He let Pyke go ahead of him with the lantern. The room was empty.

After Pyke had given it a thorough search, and found nothing of interest, he joined Thrale in the kitchen.

'I'm thinking they would both have come here with luggage,' Pyke said, not posing it as a question.

'I expect so.'

'You must have seen whether they did or not when they first arrived.'

'Yes, they both had cases.'

'But you didn't see them leave with their cases?'

'That's right.'

Pyke considered this. 'Sobers stayed here for about three weeks, you said. During that time, he must have talked to some of your guests.'

'Like I said earlier, they both kept themselves to themselves.'

'But when they cooked their food, for example?'

'No one wanted much to do with a blackbird, to be honest.' Thrale rubbed his eyes and hesitated. 'Actually, come to think of it, Sobers did have a visitor, or should I say a gang of visitors, about a week ago. Almost got nasty, so I heard.'

'Tell me about it.'

'What's to tell? A couple of free-booters turns up looking for Sobers and the woman. Someone points them in the direction of the room. They bangs on the door, barges in. There's some shouting. They leave. I don't even think she was there at the time. Sobers handled them on his own.'

'You know what they talked about?'

Thrale gave him a look. 'Ain't you listened to a word I said? I respect me guests' privacy.' But a peculiar smile spread across his lips as though he knew more than he'd let on.

'How many visitors were there?'

'Three.'

'Did you recognise any of them?'

Thrale shrugged. 'Not the ones who confronted Sobers.'

'But there was someone else?'

'Aye.'

Pyke waited. 'A name?'

'Ain't you going to allow me to wet me beak?'

Taking out his purse, Pyke selected a half-crown coin and thrust it into the older man's outstretched hand.

'That it?' Thrale said, looking down at the coin.

Pyke doubled it. That seemed to improve

40

Thrale's mood. 'Jemmy Crane,' he said after a while.

Pyke thought the name sounded familiar. 'Crane?'

'You know, the pornographer.' Thrale's face glistened with excitement. 'I used to know him a bit. He'd come and watch me fight, back in the old days.'

'Do you think he recognised you?'

Thrale thought about it. 'I stepped out into the court and he was waiting there. We looked at one another. He might have nodded at me.'

'And you're sure he was there with the men who'd come to see Sobers?'

'I watched 'em all leave in a group.'

Pyke waited for a moment, trying to gather his thoughts. 'Weren't you just a little bit curious to know what they wanted with Sobers and Mary Edgar?'

'Maybe.' Thrale shifted from one foot to the other. 'Afterwards I asked the culls who shared the room next to them if they'd heard anything.'

'And?'

'One fellow reckoned they was threatening Sobers but he didn't hear nothing more than that.'

'Could I speak to him?'

Thrale seemed put out. 'He's at work. You could come back a while later but he'll tell you the same thing.'

Pyke looked at the older man's weathered face. 'Why didn't you mention this yesterday when you identified the body in the Green Dragon?'

Thrale met his stare and held it. 'What does it matter?' The skin wrinkled at the corners of his eyes. 'I am mentioning it now, ain't I?'

That afternoon, Pyke accompanied the gravediggers and the body to a grassy field in Limehouse. The sky was leaden and the air cloying and humid. He watched as the two men dug the hole, their coats resting on the coffin and their sleeves rolled up. They chatted to one another as though what they were doing was the most commonplace thing in the world. When the hole had been dug, the three of them lowered the coffin into it using a length of rope. After that, the gravediggers withdrew for a few moments, perhaps thinking that Pyke had known Mary Edgar and wanted time at her graveside to remember her. As he stared down into the hole, he thought about Emily and how it had rained on the day he had buried her. Pyke didn't know whether he was still grieving for her or not; on good days, he could shut his eyes and summon an image of her that seemed so vivid it was as if she was there in the room with him, but at others he could barely remember the colour of her eyes.

He helped the diggers shovel earth back into the grave and once they had gone, he stood there for a while listening to the crows cawing and watching the masts of ships glide past on the nearby river. His thoughts, now turned back to Mary Edgar. Her good looks and dress indicated that she moved in genteel circles and that he should perhaps concentrate his search on the West End, places such as Bloomsbury, Marylebone or St John's Wood. But her body had been found on the Ratcliff Highway and, in that sense,

Tilling had been quite right. There weren't too many jobs a woman could hope to get in this part of the city, and if one ruled out domestic service and factory work, that left prostitution as the most likely option. Though not convinced by this hypothesis – if she had worked as a prostitute, surely it would have been at one of the respectable bordellos in St James's – Pyke decided to put off calling on Crane until the next day and spent the rest of the afternoon traipsing from one sleazy brothel to the next, showing the dead woman's likeness to the pimps and madams.

As he moved along the Ratcliff Highway from east to west, tramping between brothels, slop-shops, taverns, pawnbrokers, gin palaces and beer shops, past vendors selling pies, chestnuts, ginger-bread and baked potatoes, he didn't exactly feel unsafe but he did make a point of not catching anyone's eye unnecessarily. He also kept the purse he'd been given by Tilling close to his body. It was a warm, early spring afternoon but the weather did nothing to improve the Ratcliff Highway: it had always felt like the kind of place where someone might slit your belly as easily as shake your hand.

The pavements were full, but many of the faces were alien to Pyke. Lascar and Malay sailors with their dark skin and tear-shaped eyes; bearded Jews hawking piles of old clothes; German and Scandinavian stevedores, recognisable by their uniform, biding their time before their ships sailed for home; and black dockers who could carry a hogshead of sugar on their shoulders. There were the children, too: bow-legged, malnourished, running alongside the wagons and drays barefoot.

Everyone was going about their business but Pyke couldn't help feeling that people had noticed him, noticed that he was different, that he didn't belong there. Even as a Bow Street Runner, he'd rarely ventured to this part of the city: a Runner who had tried to serve a warrant on a tavern landlord here had been dragged out on to the street and kicked to death. Pyke couldn't say with any conviction that it was either the poorest or indeed the most dangerous part of the city – St Giles and parts of Shadwell and Rotherhithe came close – but it was undoubtedly the street whose reputation cast the greatest terror into the hearts of most Londoners.

He had also heard a lot about Craddock's brothel but had never had a reason to visit it. Not that he had missed much. Its ill repute was based on the promise of its madam, Eliza, that no reasonable offer would be turned down: that a 'reasonable' offer could sometimes be as little as a shilling was indicative of the kind of customer it hoped to attract. Pyke had once been told by a woman who'd worked there that a mattress might see five or six different bodies in the space of an hour. The same woman had had her face slashed by a broken bottle wielded by a drunken sailor, but Eliza hadn't even contacted the authorities, saying it would be bad for business. Instead, the woman had been dismissed. She'd been told no one would want to fuck a girl with a scarred face. There were few businesses Pyke knew of where the laws of the market were practised with the same cold efficiency.

'So who is she?' Eliza Craddock asked, when Pyke showed her the drawing of the dead woman.

She sat behind her desk like an enormous beached whale, folds of blubber hanging off her arms and face.

'I take it she's not one of yours?'

Craddock grinned, revealing an enormous gap in her front teeth. 'Most of the bucks come in here would just as well poke a hole in the wall. But a gal like that would cause a riot.'

Pyke nodded. Her thoughts confirmed his own suspicions that the dead woman probably wasn't a prostitute, at least not one who plied her trade on the Ratcliff Highway.

Craddock had another look at the charcoal sketch. 'You reckon she might be a blue-skin, then?'

Pyke had already mentioned this. He then described Arthur Sobers and asked whether she had seen him.

'I don't know him but we see all sorts in here. I ain't prejudiced against the darkies. Even employed one for a while.' She crossed her arms and shrugged. 'You could talk to her, if you like. Popular with the Lascars and the blackbirds, she was. But I had to let her go.'

'You know where I can find her?' It was unlikely that this woman had known Mary Edgar or Arthur Sobers but it was worth a try.

Craddock held out her chubby hand and Pyke tossed a shilling coin on to the table. She scooped it into her apron and rested her arms, two mounds of flesh, on the table. 'Jane Shaw. Last I heard she'd taken a room in the old lepers' hospital on Cannon Street, near New Road.'

'Is that how it works?' Pyke felt the skin tighten

around his temples. 'You use them up and when they're beyond repair you toss them away?'

But the criticism was lost on Eliza Craddock. She stared at Pyke, as if he'd spoken to her in a foreign language, and asked, 'The girl you're looking for. Is she dead or just missing?'

'Would it make any difference?'

Craddock shrugged. 'I don't like it when a girl gets killed. Makes folk jittery and it's bad for business.'

'It's bad for the girls, too.'

She regarded him with cynical good humour. 'If there's one thing I've learned, it's that there'll always be more girls.'

The old lepers' hospital on Cannon Street had long since been overrun by rogues and vagabonds of every hue: broken-down coiners, their skin eroded by the liquids used to oxidise base metal; footpads waiting to beat up their next marks; ageing prostitutes prowling the corridors; distillers inhaling fumes that would kill them; pickpockets as young as ten emptying stolen pocket handkerchiefs into the hands of their receivers; rampsmen polishing their brass cudgels; and mudlarks picking caked mud and faeces from their old boots.

Pyke found Jane Shaw in one of the rooms right at the top of the building. There was no heat or light and he'd had to pay for a lantern to guide his way through the mass of bodies, either sleeping or staring vacantly into space. A few of them begged for money, but he kept moving, only stopping to ask where he could find the 'blackbird' and only giving a farthing or two to those who helped him. Most were drunk or, as he discovered later, pacified by laudanum.

Jane Shaw could have been thirty or sixty, for all Pyke could tell. Her hair and all of her teeth had fallen out, and when he brought the lantern up to her face and saw her ravaged nose, it confirmed what he had suspected from the first moment he had stepped into the room. She was dying of untreated syphilis.

'You the first visitor I had in t'ree months,' she said, the whites of her eyes accentuated by the inky blackness of her skin.

Pyke knelt down and showed her the charcoal etching of Mary Edgar. Wincing, she sat up so that she could get a better look at it, and as she did so, she sniffed his skin. 'You smell good, like soap.'

The room, on the other hand, reeked of human faeces and for a moment he wondered how and where she defecated.

'Her name is Mary Edgar.' He put the lantern down next to the drawing so she could see it properly.

'So?'

'I wondered if you might know her.' As soon as it had left his mouth it struck Pyke as an absurd proposition, but he needed to find a way of getting her to talk.

She peered at the etching and laughed without warmth. 'That why you come here? 'Cos I'm black and she's mulatto so we must know each other?'

Pyke acknowledged the truth of her observation with a rueful smile. 'I don't know a thing about her apart from her name and that she recently arrived from Jamaica. I thought she might have fallen into the game.'

That drew a more serious nod. 'So how did you find me?'

'Craddock.'

Jane bit her lip, or what was left of it. 'That bitch had me there to serve them Lascars and Africans but it was the whites who ask for me because I was cheap and they reckoned they could do what they liked with me.'

'And as soon as you contracted syphilis she tossed you out.' Pyke tried to keep any sympathy from his voice; he guessed it would only anger her.

'She gave me a bottle of mercury, told me that would cover it.' She touched her bald head self-consciously.

Pyke brought her attention back to the drawing. 'Have you got any idea where I might start looking for her?' He paused and then told her that Mary Edgar had been sharing a room at the Bluefield lodging house with a black man called Arthur Sobers.

Jane shook her head. 'Why are you looking for her? What she done?'

Pyke shrugged. He didn't want to tell her that Mary Edgar was dead. Nor, for obvious reasons, did he want to reveal that the woman's eyes had been gouged out. But if the murder had a ritualistic element to it, as he now suspected, he wanted to find out as much as possible about such things.

'Whether she black or white, it look like she got money. So why you looking for her in a black hole like Craddock's?' Jane snorted through her disintegrating nose. 'And why you think she want to be friends with a nigger like me?'

He felt the anger of her stare. 'To be honest, I hardly know a thing about the black community in the city.'

This much was true. Whereas forty or fifty years earlier, London had had a thriving black population, buoyed by émigrés from the United States who'd fought on the side of the Crown during the revolutionary wars and former slaves who'd earned their freedom and decided to stay and work in the capital, the effects of grinding poverty and falling numbers of immigrants meant there were now probably just a few hundred – or maybe as many as a thousand – black men and women left in the city, in a population of more than a million. Pyke was used to seeing coloured faces around the docks but these men were often sailors and merchant seamen who would spend their shore leave in and around the Ratcliff Highway before leaving for the next port.

'And you think I do?' Jane looked at him. 'I was born in Gravesend. I can point it out on a map if you don't know where it is.'

'If you were a black man or woman recently arrived in the city, where would you go to eat and drink?'

'Anywhere I could afford that would take my money.' She hesitated. 'You seem to think there's one place all black folk go to spend time with each other. That's not how it is. The only thing black people got in common is being poor and getting exploited by white men like yourself.'

Pyke absorbed her insult. 'But if I did want to speak to people who might have known Mary Edgar and Arthur Sobers...'

She studied his face for a few moments, deciding whether she wanted to help or not. 'There's a beer shop at the bottom of Commercial Road, near the docks. Ask for Samuel.'

Pyke thanked her and stretched his legs, but when he reached down to gather up the drawing, she touched his hand. 'You want to know something? That's the first time I touched another human being in a month.' She looked away sudenly, perhaps because she didn't want him to see the tears in her eyes.

Pyke went to kiss her on the cheek but at the last moment she turned her head towards him and he had no choice but to embrace her mouth. Her lips were softer and saltier than he had imagined. Momentarily Pyke closed his eyes and put the smell of faeces out of his mind. When he pulled away, he expected that she might say something, but whatever had happened in that moment passed and she was staring up at the ceiling, as though nothing had happened.

'I lie here trying to remember happier times but when I shut my eyes all I can see are the faces of the men who fucked me.'

Pyke left her without saying goodbye. He guessed that she would be dead before the end of the year.

THREE

William Maginn's face glistened like a ham that been soaked in briny water and boiled vigorously until it had turned a burnished shade of pink. He was pontificating about the merits of Shakespeare's tragedies while imbibing from a hip-flask. Around him, a coterie of admirers hung on his every word. At one time, he had been the most respected and feared journalist in the city, though this had been before he had burned his bridges at *Fraser's* magazine and spent time in prison, like Pyke, for failing to pay his debts. Godfrey told Pyke all this while fretting nervously at the edges of the circle, trying to find a way of interrupting Maginn and maybe limiting his consumption of gin, at least until after the speeches.

Hatchard's bookshop on Piccadilly was full and Pyke was momentarily surprised by the number of people Godfrey had persuaded to attend the event, until he remembered that the book they'd all come to toast had attracted more than its fair share of notoriety in the months following its publication. Figures as worthy as Dickens and Bulwer had described Godfrey's book as a 'brutally honest account of wrongdoing'. Godfrey had framed those reviews. But other critics had torn it to shreds. Thackeray, for example, had compared it unfavourably to the 'already lamentable' *Eugene Aram* and had lambasted it as a 'foul, sordid piece of writing' that should be 'consigned to the nearest cesspool' for fear that 'it might irrevocably contaminate those whose misfortune it was to turn its pages'. Godfrey had framed that review as well, claiming that a book capable of provoking such hostility had to be doing something right. Pyke suspected that beneath his bluster, his uncle cared very deeply what a man like Thackeray thought and that the review had wounded him more than he cared to admit. It had been something of a surprise, then, when Maginn had written to Godfrey to offer a cautiously favourable verdict, because Maginn and Thackeray had once been good friends, and perhaps still were.

Pyke hadn't read *The True and Candid Confession of an ex-Bow Street Runner,* nor did he have any desire to do so. He had talked at length with Godfrey, while his uncle scribbled notes, and he had been as truthful and as candid as he thought appropriate. But Pyke had known from the start that what appeared in print would bear only the slightest resemblance to his own experiences. Godfrey wasn't interested in virtue and goodness; rather his writing and publishing reflected a preference for the tasteless, sordid, low and morally repugnant. Pyke knew there were things he had done in his past that fitted this description, and that his uncle would doubtless embellish such episodes into something even nastier, but he hadn't robbed or killed to satisfy his own primal urges. He had done so only when absolutely compelled to and wherever possible he had tried to do what was right, even if this meant hurting other people in the process. But none of this would make it into his uncle's book; instead it would be a fictional tale that wallowed in its own stench with the sole purpose, Pyke believed, of offending the refined sensibilities of a particular kind of educated reader.

But Pyke wasn't interested in Maginn's stories or in helping Godfrey keep a muzzle on him. He had come to his uncle's event only to spend some time with Felix, and now he surveyed the mass of faces for a sign of his son, hoping that this encounter would be better than the last one. Perhaps Felix would look him in the eye this time or maybe even allow Pyke to take him in his arms. That was all Pyke had wanted to do when Felix had shunned him at Godfrey's apartment.

It was Jo who spotted him. When she touched his arm, Pyke spun around and found himself staring into her smiling face. Felix was holding her hand, as though his life depended on it. His hair had been brushed and he wore a clean shirt. Pyke bent down and ruffled his hair the way he used to, but Felix seemed to recoil from his touch. Pyke stood up, trying to conceal his hurt from Jo. She was wearing a plain cotton dress and a straw bonnet, tied under the chin with a piece of red ribbon.

'We've been reading *Ivanhoe* together, haven't we?' Jo said, for Pyke's benefit, while squeezing Felix's hand. She raised her eyes to meet his. 'He really is a demon of a reader.'

Pyke tried to think of something he could say about Scott's book but nothing came to mind. 'I'm sure it's a good deal more uplifting than Godfrey's book.'

'I've read that one, too,' Felix piped up.

They both looked at him. 'You've read God-frey's book?' Pyke asked, appalled by the notion.

Felix stared at him, still gripping Jo's hand. 'At the end, I thought they should have hanged him by the neck for all he'd done.'

Pyke felt dizzy. Felix had read a book purporting to be an account of *his* life as a Bow Street Runner. Would the lad have known this? Not having read the book himself, Pyke didn't know what claims it made, but knowing his uncle, he was quite sure it wouldn't make for a comfortable read.

'You understand that it's all made up,' he said, adopting what he hoped was a suitably stern tone.

'Then why does it say it's a true and candid confession?' Felix replied defiantly.

Pyke glanced over at Jo for assistance but she gave him an apologetic shrug, as if this was the first she'd heard of it. 'What I meant,' he said carefully, 'was that it's not based on any one person's real experiences.'

'But weren't you a Bow Street Runner?'

Pyke tried to hide his consternation – and anger – that his son was speaking to him in such a manner. 'That's beside the point, Felix.'

Thankfully their conversation was interrupted by Godfrey, who told Pyke he needed help. Maginn was steaming drunk and, even worse, he'd seemingly now taken against the book. God-frey delivered this last piece of news in such a grave tone that Pyke felt he had no choice but to help. He told Felix they would resume their little chat in a moment.

'I've already paid him a king's ransom to be

here and now he's savaging my book to all and sundry,' Godfrey said, as they made their way across to Maginn's growing coterie.

Maginn was still in full flow. 'This book is meretricious,' he was saying, holding up a copy of *Confessions*, as though giving a sermon, 'because it wilfully misleads its educated readers by purporting to tell the truth about low types. I say *purporting* because it never tells the whole truth, nor could it hope to because it is written by a morally suspect man about a dishonourable scamp who is equally devoid of moral purpose.' His Cork brogue was unmistakable.

'Can't you stop him?' Godfrey whispered to Pyke, a note of desperation in his voice.

'What? Hit him over the head and drag him out of here by his feet?'

'If you have to, dear boy. And make sure you hurt him in the process.'

Maginn had spotted Pyke and his uncle and he acknowledged them with a thunderous stare. 'In the tap, the slop-shop and the ken, thieves and blackguards, and to this list we should add Bow Street Runners, might display occasional moments of boldness and courage, but this does not mean they should be the subject of literature, nor should we be dragooned into caring for their cutthroat sensibilities and self-serving justifications.' He addressed this final remark to Pyke.

'And yet you have written elsewhere,' Pyke replied, 'that all successfully drawn characters are necessarily a mixture of good and evil and what motivates wickedness can be the same thing that produces the noblest of actions.'

'Ah, yes. But then I was writing about *Hamlet* or *Lear,* and you, sir, are far from being a noble prince or fallen king.'

'Perhaps in your drunken state you failed to take proper notice of the preface, in which my uncle makes it clear that *Confessions* is a work of fiction and should be treated as such.'

'Is that so?' Maginn boomed, his voice thick with condescension. 'And yet it describes a daring escape from Newgate prison; a feat, if I'm not mistaken, that you, sir, undertook with help from willing accomplices – or should I say *lackeys.*'

'So?' The skin tightened around Pyke's throat at this reference to Godfrey and, indeed, Emily, who had assisted his escape.

Maginn waved over a pale young man and put his arms around him, as if to suggest they were friends. 'Allow me to introduce Mr Peter Hunt. Perhaps the name is familiar to you, sir?'

'Should it be?' Pyke allowed his gaze to settle on the nervous young man whose rouged lips and powdered face made him seem grotesque rather than fashionable.

'His father was the governor of Newgate prison on the night of your escape.' This time Maginn's smirk turned into a grimace. 'We met earlier in a tavern and discovered we were both intending to grace this event with our presence.' He had his arm clasped so tightly around the younger man's shoulder that Hunt couldn't move.

Pyke searched Hunt's eyes but saw nothing: not fear or anxiety or hate. And the young man certainly had reason enough to hate him. Pyke looked around at his uncle and saw that he'd also grasped the precariousness of the situation. For if Hunt was carrying a weapon, a pistol perhaps, and chose to take it out, anything could happen.

'What is it you want?' Pyke addressed Hunt directly, but the younger man wouldn't look up.

'What does he want?' Maginn's roaring laugh could be heard throughout the shop. He held up his copy of *Confessions*. 'In the lily-scented world you've created, sir, his father must still be alive because the escape is achieved through boldness and stealth – picking locks and scaling walls – rather than cold-blooded murder.' The smirk on his face vanished as he rounded on Pyke. 'For, in truth, didn't you stab the governor in the neck with a dagger and then throw him out of a window?'

A ripple of astonished gasps spread quickly through the room. This was exactly the kind of thing people had come to hear. Pyke looked around, to check whether Felix was within ear-shot.

'I was cleared of any wrongdoing by an official investigation and pardoned by order of the Home Secretary himself.'

But Maginn seemed more concerned by what he had read in Godfrey's book. '*Ex parte* truth-telling, the worst kind. One tells the whole truth or nothing.'

'What is it you want?' Pyke repeated, looking directly at Maginn. 'I know for a fact you've already been paid well for attending this evening.'

'What do *I* want?' Maginn took out his purse and threw it dramatically to the floor. 'I spit on your uncle's thirty pieces of silver. I want satisfaction for young Hunt and for being led astray by this monstrosity.' He was still brandishing a copy of Godfrey's book.

'What kind of satisfaction?'

'Satisfaction.' He removed his torn shooting jacket and started to roll up his sleeves.

'You intend to fight me?' Pyke tried to keep the incredulity from his voice. Maginn was tall and rangy but his body was devoid of muscle and his arms were as thin as pipe-cleaners.

'I don't intend to fight you, sir. I intend to shoot you.' With that, he retrieved a wooden box and opened it, to reveal two duelling pistols. 'One shot in each but one shot is all I'll need.'

'You're challenging me to a duel?' Pyke looked for Godfrey, but he'd been swallowed by the crowd.

'Is that a problem?'

'Look at your hands. You couldn't hit a cow if you were standing two yards away from it.' They were shaking so badly it looked as if he were suffering from some terrible disease.

'You're afraid, sir. I can see it in your eyes. Cowards usually are. I don't expect you'll be man enough to accept.'

At twenty paces the chances of Maginn firing and hitting him were so remote that Pyke found himself contemplating the challenge. Certainly there didn't seem to be any way he could get out of it, not without losing face. What worried him more was Hunt – a man who'd lost his own flesh and blood could do just about anything, especially if he felt his actions were justified. But it had been ten years since Pyke had killed his father. Could he still be sufficiently angry to attempt some kind of revenge?

'You're not going to accept this lunatic's challenge, are you?' Godfrey said, appearing at Pyke's side.

'I don't see I have any choice.' Pyke looked around the shop but Hunt had disappeared. He wanted to find Jo, to tell her to take Felix home, but she was nowhere to be seen either.

The air was cold outside but perhaps not cold enough to sober up Maginn; having insisted that they fight there and then, he stumbled around in the dark, waving his pistol in the air and talking to himself. The whole thing was ridiculous; a parody of a duel.

Pyke had already inspected his pistol and was happy with it. In fact it was a much more carefully crafted weapon than his own Long Sea Service pistol, and the feel of polished walnut was reassuring in his hand.

'Gentlemen, are you ready?' The adjudicator called out to them both. 'On my count, you will take your first step.' They had already determined what the rules of the contest would be: ten steps, to be taken at the adjudicator's prompting, then turn and fire. Pyke hoped Maginn would fire into the air.

'One.'

With his back facing Maginn's, Pyke took his first step and looked around the deserted street. A nearby gas-lamp hissed and flared, producing a dull light that barely illuminated the area directly beneath it. At the man's count, he took

59

another step and then another, trying to clear his mind and concentrate. The whole thing was absurd, but someone was about to fire a loaded pistol at him in anger and thus the potential for danger remained. Briefly he thought about Felix and Jo, wondered whether they knew what was happening or not.

'Seven.'

Pyke curled his finger around the trigger and took a deep breath.

'Eight.' He took another step.

'Nine, and...'

When he turned around, he could barely see Maginn in the gloom. The man's stovepipe hat was the most recognisable thing about him. He heard the shot before he saw the barrel of Maginn's pistol raised towards the night sky. Carefully Pyke took aim and squeezed the trigger; he couldn't see immediately, but he could tell from the gasps of the crowd huddled in the doorway of the bookshop that he'd hit the target. Later, he would hear how the stovepipe hat had flown from Maginn's head and how the journalist had stood there, rooted to the spot, too frightened even to blink.

That was when he saw the glint of metal and heard a click. As he turned around, there was a flash of exploding gunpowder and momentarily Hunt's cadaverous face was lit up, his hiding place in a smaller alleyway revealed. Too stunned to move, Pyke felt a rush of air through his ears as he waited for the shot to tear him apart. It never happened. From less than five yards, Hunt had missed his target. Pyke sucked air through his clenched teeth, tasting the acrid sting of gunpowder at the back of his throat.

The pistol clattered on to the cobblestones and Pyke saw that Hunt had sprung from his hiding place and was running away. He decided against pursuing him.

Back inside the shop, Pyke looked for Maginn but couldn't see him. He found Jo and Felix talking with Godfrey. Most of the crowd had left by now, perhaps as a result of the argument and the duel, and Pyke tried to play down what had just happened. He wondered whether any of them had actually seen the hidden shot that had been fired, or knew how close he'd come to being killed. Perhaps Godfrey did; he was much too effusive in his praise of Pyke's bravery. Jo and Felix said very little, and when it was suggested that they call it a night and go home, Pyke offered to hail them a hackney carriage on Piccadilly.

Outside, in the gaslight, Pyke noticed that his hands were still trembling. He looked up and down the darkened street for any sign of a passing cab and noticed Maginn stumbling into a side alleyway. Godfrey had seen Maginn, too, and placed his hand on Pyke's arm. 'Come back with us to my apartment.' But Pyke could feel the anger he'd been trying to repress billowing up inside him. Maginn had challenged him on a point of principle, but all he'd really wanted to do was give Hunt the chance to shoot him dead. There was no honour in that; no honour in shooting a pistol at another man's back from five paces. Suddenly he despised the Cork man for all his piousness and his false desire for 'satisfaction'. Pyke found

61

Maginn in the alleyway; he was fumbling at his breeches. A frightened prostitute was trying to free herself from his drunken grip. Maginn had knowingly colonised the moral high ground and now here he was harassing a street-walker. The hypocrisy was too much for Pyke to bear. Maginn raised his hand to slap her, but Pyke caught it, pushed the woman to one side and swung his fist into Maginn's face, dislodging two teeth in the process. Spitting blood, Maginn tried to defend himself but Pyke landed another blow, this time to the side of his head. Maginn fell forward and Pyke brought his knee up to the man's face. The prostitute disappeared farther into the alleyway. Pyke wiped his mouth on the sleeve of his frock-coat. Maginn was lying on the ground. That should have been the end of it but Pyke's thoughts turned to Mary Edgar, who had been cut up and left to rot by the side of the road, and then to Emily, who had been killed by a single rifle shot to her neck. He took a deep breath and kicked Maginn hard in the stomach, then again. He heard a noise and turned round to find Felix standing there, speechless, his face white with terror.

'Felix.' He paused, not knowing what else to say. Maginn, still on the ground, gave a muffled groan.

Godfrey and Jo stepped into the alleyway and saw Maginn lying at Pyke's feet, with Felix trembling in front of him.

Pyke looked down and noticed that the ends of his boots were glistening with Maginn's blood. He wanted to make his son understand what had happened but the words wouldn't form on his tongue. He saw the fear and revulsion in the boy's eyes. Pyke wanted the ground to open up and swallow him.

It had always amused Pyke that Holywell Street got its name from a holy well that stood in the vicinity and that pilgrims bound for Canterbury used to drink from; it amused him because ever since the radical presses had been disbanded or moved underground and the Jewish traders had relocated farther east to Spitalfields and Petticoat Lane, the street had become the centre of the city's trade in pornography. He would have liked to have seen the pilgrims' reaction to the lewd etchings and lithographs and snuff-boxes detailing men and women engaged in obscene sexual acts.

Outwardly, little had changed on the street since Elizabethan times – it had escaped the worst ravages of the Great Fire and the lath-and-plaster houses with their lofty gables, overhanging eaves and deep bays were throwbacks to another era – but the air of gloom and disrepair had a modern countenance, as did the open manner in which some of the proprietors peddled their smut. None went as far as to display lewd engravings in their windows or place the latest 'limited edition' from Paris on the lean-tos outside the shops, but the lingering scent of grubby licentiousness pervaded the immediate environment. Pyke had even heard it called 'the vilest street in the civilised world'.

Jemmy Crane's bookshop occupied a tall, four-storey building on the north side of the street. Outside, wooden trestles supported neatly stacked piles of antiquarian books and above the door a crescent moon sign gave the shop a veneer of respectability.

'What can I do for you, sir? May I say you look like a connoisseur of bedroom scenes. Am I warm, sir?' The elderly man behind the counter had a shambling gait and studied Pyke through the monocle attached to his left eye.

'I want to see Crane.'

The man gave him a kindly smile. 'Oh, I'm afraid that won't be possible.'

'He's not here?'

'Mr Crane has asked not to be disturbed.'

Pyke pushed past him and made for the back of the shop, shouting Crane's name. He had made it as far as the staircase when a man appeared at the top of the stairs, his face displaying a mixture of curiosity and irritation.

Crane cut a dashing, rakish figure and looked younger than his forty years. His hair was ink-black and his skin was smooth and free from wrinkles. He had full, plump lips and a leering, sensuous smile that put Pyke in mind of Pierce Egan's Corinthian rakes Tom and Jerry: the kind of man who both looked down on the filth and degradation around him, yet wallowed in it, too. Dressed like a dandy, he wore a tight-fitting brown frock-coat, a frilly white shirt, blue cravat and matching waistcoat over brown trousers.

Behind Crane, silhouetted at the top of the stairs, was a much burlier, rougher creature, waiting to be told what to do.

'To what do I owe this pleasure, *sir?*' Crane spoke in a clipped, polished accent, his tone, dripping with condescension.

'My name's Pyke...'

'I know who you are.' Crane paused. 'You once owned a ginnery on Giltspur Street. I used to be an acquaintance of your uncle, Godfrey Bond.'

Pyke studied Crane's expression, wondering what Godfrey would have to say about this man. 'A week ago, you accompanied three men to a guest house on the Ratcliff Highway. Your men were heard arguing with one of the guests. I need to know why you went there and what the argument was about.'

Crane's expression betrayed nothing. 'You like to get straight to the point, don't you? I admire a man who knows his own mind.' He seemed to be the kind of man who enjoyed the sound of his own voice.

'What business did you have with Arthur Sobers and Mary Edgar?'

'It was the old man who saw me, wasn't it? I didn't recognise him at the time but later it came to me. I used to watch him fight, back in the old days, a real bruiser, but I can't for the life of me remember his name.'

'Thrale.'

'That's it.' Crane's face lit up for a moment. 'These days my tastes are more refined. I have a box at the Theatre Royal and I attend concerts at Somerset House.' His smile was without the faintest hint of warmth.

'You haven't answered my question.'

'And I'm not going to.'

Pyke could see the coldness in his eyes. He removed the drawing of Mary Edgar from his pocket and handed it to Crane. 'You know her?'

Crane glanced down at the drawing and just for a moment his mask slipped and a look of curiosity, even puzzlement, crossed his face. 'No.'

'That's Mary Edgar, the woman you visited.' Pyke paused. 'She was strangled and her body dumped a few hundred yards away on the Ratcliff Highway.'

Crane assimilated this news. 'And what is your interest in this affair, sir?'

'I'm investigating her murder.'

'Out of a sense of civic duty?' His tone was vaguely mocking.

'What took you to Thrale's lodging house that day?'

'A private matter. In other words, none of your business.'

'You don't deny you were there, then?'

'How could I? Thrale saw me. And now you're here.'

'And I'm not leaving until you've answered my question.'

'I've told you all I'm going to tell you. I suggest you leave before the situation becomes unpleasant.'

'Unpleasant for me or for you?' Pyke's stare didn't once leave Crane's face.

'I might appreciate a Beethoven symphony more than a bare-knuckle fight these days but if I give the word, Sykes here will do to you what Benbow did to Thrale. And I'll watch, as I did then.'

Pyke looked up at the muscular figure at the top of the stairs. 'Does he speak as well as glare?'

That drew the thinnest of smiles. 'I admire courage up to a certain point, but after that it becomes stupidity.'

'If you know who I am – if you know me from the old days and what I'm capable of – you'll know I'm not likely to give up until I've found what I'm looking for.' Pyke waited and sighed. 'She had just arrived from Jamaica. They both had. How would a piece of dirt like you know them?'

The skin tightened around Crane's eyes. 'My patience has run out. You can find your own way out.' He turned and started back up the stairs.

'One way or another you'll tell me what I need to know,' Pyke shouted up the stairs but Crane, blocked by his burly assistant, had disappeared from view.

At the front of the shop, Pyke passed the elderly assistant who looked at him as though he'd heard at least some or all of their conversation.

For the rest of the afternoon, once he'd ascertained that Arthur Sobers hadn't returned to the Bluefield lodging house, Pyke patrolled the sunless court outside the building asking anyone who entered or emerged from the front door whether they knew or had seen Arthur Sobers. He had no luck for the first hour or so and was just about to give up – it had started to drizzle and he needed to eat – when a fat man with whiskers shuffled out of the door.

'Yeah, I 'member the cull,' he said, once Pyke had explained who he was looking for. 'Saw him a few times with a mudlark goes by the name Filthy on account of his stink.'

'You know where I can find this man?' Pyke looked down at his bruised knuckles and thought about the scene his son had witnessed the previous night.

'Filthy? A cull like that don't have no home, just sleeps rough, wherever he can lay his head.'

'Then how can I get in touch with him?'

'How should I know? You often see him on the Highway, hanging round the docks or the river at low tide.'

Pyke tried to rein in his frustration. 'Could you give me a description, then?'

The fat man rubbed his whiskers. 'Older 'n me, wizened little fellow. Grey hair. But you'd know him on account of the patches he wears over his eyes, like a pirate, and the long bamboo cane he carries.'

'This man is *blind?*'

'Didn't I say that? He's blind. That's right. Why else would he be wearing patches an' carrying a cane?'

Pyke walked back up the hill to the Ratcliff Highway thinking about what he had just been told and whether this mudlark's condition was, in any way, linked to the manner of Mary Edgar's death.

FOUR

Even for a country teetering on the brink of full-scale economic depression, the scene outside the West India Docks on the Isle of Dogs was a re-markable one. There must have been a thousand people clamouring for the attention of the foreman and his crew; in addition to the regular porters, stevedores, coopers, riggers, warehouse-men, pilers and baulkers who had already been admitted into the docks. The explanation for the crowd, if not its size, could be seen over the top of the high brick wall that circumnavigated the docks: a three-mast ship had docked overnight and word had quickly spread that the company intended to employ around fifty casual dockers to unload crates of sugar, rum and coffee on to the quayside. The mood of the would-be dockers was anxious, and even from the fringes of the crowd, Pyke could scent their desperation. Jobs were scarcer than smog-free days and the deluge into the city of farm labourers, identifiable by their dirty smocks and kerseymere coats, and navvies, unemployed since the railway boom had faltered, had made the situation even worse. The merest whiff of a job would attract tens, sometimes even hundreds, of dead-eyed men; workhouses across the city were turning people away; petty theft and begging were on the rise; and men and women were sleeping rough in numbers Pyke had never seen before.

A horn sounded and the men surged towards the arched entrance to the docks, crushing those at the front. Hands were raised to attract the foreman's attention and coins were offered, by way of a bribe. But rather than select men by pointing at them, the foreman threw a bucket of brass tickets into the mob and stood back to admire his handiwork. Scuffles broke out as men fought each other, desperate to catch or pick up the tickets, or indeed prise them from those who'd been fortunate enough to scoop them up. Some of the tussles turned violent; one man was stabbed in the eye; another had part of his ear bitten off. It was a difficult thing to watch: men fighting for a job that would earn them just a few pence an hour and that would be paid not in coins but tokens that could be redeemed only at taverns owned by the dock company, where prices were kept artificially high.

As the crowd began to disperse, Pyke contemplated what Emily would have said about such a spectacle and how little he had done since her death to honour her legacy.

Pyke passed through the stone archway and paused to survey the scene. Directly ahead of him, bobbing gently up and down in the water, was the tall ship with three masts and a thick forest of rigging. The stevedores, who were the most experienced and therefore the best paid of the workers, brought the crates and sacks up from the ship's hold as far as the deck, where the ordinary dockers would carry them down gangplanks to the quayside. There the sacks and crates were taken by warehousemen and porters to the various storage buildings that surrounded the dock.

At the company's clerical offices, Pyke showed the drawing of Mary Edgar to a bored clerk who had introduced himself as Mr Gumm and explained that she'd recently arrived in London from the West Indies.

Gumm didn't feel able to handle Pyke's query himself, so he fetched his supervisor, Nathaniel

Rowbottom, who listened insincerely as Pyke explained why he was there. Rowbottom was a fastidious dresser, nothing out of place in his plain, sober outfit, and his beard and moustache were perfectly trimmed. He struck Pyke as the kind of man who would know, to the last penny, how much money he had in the bank.

'I'm afraid I don't recognise her,' he said, barely looking at the picture. He put his hand to his mouth and yawned.

'She might have arrived on the same ship as a black man called Arthur Sobers.' Pyke offered a brief description of Sobers.

'I still don't recognise her and I've certainly never come across a gentleman matching your description.'

'You barely looked at the drawing.'

Rowbottom glanced down at the drawing and looked up again, his face blank. 'There. I've never seen her before in my life.'

'Then maybe you could tell me how many ships from Jamaica have docked here in the last two months.'

'I'm afraid I don't have that information to hand.' Rowbottom adjusted his collar. All of a sudden, he seemed a little unsure of himself.

'But you could find out.'

Rowbottom eyed him carefully. 'Take a look around you, Mr...?'

'Just Pyke will do.'

'This is a working dock, Mr Pyke. It's not a place where passengers from the Caribbean embark and disembark.'

'But the ships that depart from, and arrive, here

71

must occasionally carry passengers.' It wasn't intended as a question.

'On the odd occasion, perhaps.'

'And given what a meticulous man you are, I'm guessing you would take a record of these albeit unlikely occurrences.'

'Perhaps, but as I'm sure you'll understand, it's against our policy to permit non-company personnel to inspect company records.' He drummed his fingers impatiently on the polished surface of his desk.

'So you're not prepared to confirm or deny that Mary Edgar disembarked from a ship that docked here?'

Rowbottom continued to tap his fingers against the desk. 'Could I perhaps enquire as to the purpose of your visit?'

'She was strangled and her corpse was dumped just off the Racliff Highway.' Pyke paused to check Rowbottom's expression, but even this piece of information failed to provoke a reaction. 'I'm in charge of the investigation.'

'You're a police officer, then?'

'Not as such, but I am working for the police.'

Rowbottom sat back in his chair, trying to show he wasn't intimidated. 'But you're not actually a policeman.'

'No.'

'In which case, I'm going to kindly request that you leave these premises forthwith.' He even managed a smile. Pyke wanted to pull his teeth out with pliers.

'Is that all you're prepared to do for me?'

'To be perfectly honest, sir, I don't much care

for the tone of your questions or your impertin-
ent manner.'

Pyke licked his lips. He could feel the heat rising
in his neck. 'You haven't even begun to see im-
pertinent.' It wasn't just Rowbottom he detested,
it was what he stood for: a whole class of men –
respectable, small minded and tyrannical in their
pettiness – who were quietly taking over the
country. You could find them in every government
office, sallow and stiff lipped, processing and
documenting the world without ever leaving their
desks, affecting people's lives with the stroke of a
pen and the stamp of their official seal, never
actually seeing the consequences of their actions
in the wider world.

'I'm going to have you escorted from the
docks.' He called out for Gumm, his assistant.
'The last thing the men here need is unnecessary
interruption of their duties.'

But Pyke took a few steps towards Rowbottom's desk. 'I can find out whether a ship docked
here from Jamaica with or without your help.'

'*Gumm,*' Rowbottom called out. He looked
flustered now, even a little frightened. 'Where are
you?'

Pyke leaned forward, all the way over the desk,
and whispered, 'And if I find out that Mary
Edgar docked here, and you knew and didn't tell
me, I'm going to come back and smash your
head against the desk until your skull cracks.'

Rowbottom's indignation got the better of his
fear, but only just. His chest swelled up and he
spluttered, 'I shan't be spoken to in such an out-
rageous manner in my own office...'

But by the time he had summoned up the courage to say these words, Pyke had already left the room.

'An artist can only think, I mean truly think, in surroundings that befit him,' Edmund Saggers said, glancing dismissively around the taproom at Samuel's. 'Do you imagine the Bard scribed *King Lear* while surrounded by gnawed chop bones, dead rats and sawdust that smelled like a hog's arse?' He tried to squeeze his giant backside into the wooden chair but it was like manoeuvring an omnibus into a space previously occupied by a wheelbarrow. 'You'd better have a damned good reason for dragging me to such a lacklustre place at this ungodly hour of the morning.'

Pyke knew of cabmen who refused to take Saggers in their vehicles on account of his gargantuan girth, fearing he might permanently damage their vehicles' axles. Their fears were not entirely misplaced, either. He wasn't a tall man, standing at less than six feet, nor were his legs particularly broad and stout, considering the load they had to transport. What made the difference was his appetite and, as a consequence, a girth of quite staggering proportions. Roll upon roll of fat hung from the man's midriff so that it seemed his whole body might sink into the ground. Feeding such a monstrosity mightn't have been a problem for someone of George IV's means but, for Saggers, who earned his living as a penny-a-liner, the task of satiating his appetite constantly preoccupied him. Because of his girth, he also had to have his clothes made for him: as a result, he possessed one outfit – tweed trousers, a tweed waistcoat and a tweed frock-coat – which he wore all the time, regardless of the weather, and which reeked of his unwashed body.

'If you do exactly as I tell you, I'll take you to lunch at the Café de l'Europe or any of those fancy restaurants on Haymarket.'

Saggers eyed him cautiously. 'Anything on the menu?'

Pyke nodded.

'Even the half-buck of Halnaker venison?' It was a cut of meat that could easily have fed ten men. 'Washed down by a bottle of their finest claret?'

'Anything.'

'Well, sir, as long as it doesn't involve me having to morally compromise a young child, I'll do it.' He patted his stomach and grinned.

Saggers wrote 'copy' for newspapers about the grubbier aspects of London life – murders, suicides, coroner's inquests, fires and all manner of calamities – and was paid one and a half pence for each line, a halfpenny rise from the sum that had given his ilk their name. A column in a morning paper might earn him thirty shillings, and he would then try to sell the same story to other newspapers, thereby tripling and some-times even quadrupling this sum. Pyke had first met him through Godfrey; the penny-a-liner had chased down some details for his uncle's book and had liaised with Pyke regarding some of his recollections. In fact, Saggers was closer to Pyke's age than to Godfrey's, but given their mutual appreciation of good food and fine wine, it was perhaps not surprising that Saggers and his uncle were friends, even if Godfrey always ended up paying for their meals. Indeed, Pyke had often wondered whether the obese journalist was merely using his uncle to indulge his colossal appetite. Still, Godfrey had always raved about the man's ability to ferret out buried truths and any whiff of scandal. 'I tell you,' he had once said, 'that fellow could walk into a temperance meeting and pick out a couple who'd been rutting on the sly with one sniff.'

'What business are we talking about?' Saggers picked his nose and licked what was on his nail without embarrassment.

'A murder.' Pyke let the word create its own effect. Murders tended to lift the spirits of the penny-a-liners; hunting down arcane snippets of information about the victim or murderer could result in significant sums of money.

'You mean the lord?' Saggers said quickly, his greed suddenly getting the better of him. The newspapers had been full of stories about the demise of Lord Bedford and any new story about the murder or the police investigation would be snapped up by any number of sub-editors.

'Not Bedford, but a murder none the less.' Pyke waited for a moment. 'And right now, not many people know about it. Me, the deputy commissioner of the New Police, the coroner, the jurors at the inquest. As far as I know, it hasn't yet been reported in any of the newspapers.'

'An exclusive, eh?' Grinning, Saggers pulled out a notepad and a length of shaved charcoal. Doubtless he was already imagining the money he would make from it and the meals that would buy.

'Of course, before I can divulge any information, I need certain assurances...'

'What kind of assurances?'

'For a start, that you'll endeavour to place the story by the day after tomorrow.'

Saggers scratched his bristly chin and considered what Pyke had just said. 'If you want to see your story published so quickly, why not go directly to a newspaper?'

'I don't want it to be published in just one newspaper. I want the story to be sold to as many papers as possible. And that's where you come in.'

If Mary Edgar had, during her brief stay in London, consorted only with the types who couldn't read or write on the Ratcliff Highway, it wouldn't have made any sense to appeal for information about her in the newspapers. But if, as Pyke now suspected, she had moved in an altogether different social class, news of her murder might compel someone who'd met her to come forward. Initially Pyke had striven to keep the murder out of the public eye, but this approach hadn't borne much fruit so now it was time to change tack.

'Capital idea, sir, *capital*,' Saggers said, his grin returning. Selling a column, or even half a column to five or six sub-editors would see him clear for the rest of the month.

Pyke placed the drawing on the table. Saggers inspected it keenly, his eyes giving nothing away. 'So who is she?' he asked eventually.

'Mary Edgar. Her naked body was found the day before yesterday just off the Ratcliff Highway.'

Pyke saw him scribble down the word 'naked' on his notepad, and then he added 'exotic' and 'beautiful'. Already the story was taking shape in Saggers' mind and, for the time being, Pyke was happy to let the journalist run with it.

'I love a good "naked body" story as much as the next man, but what else can you tell me about her?'

'She had recently arrived in London from the West Indies. Jamaica.' Pyke paused. 'I'd like to know when, where she docked, and which ship she sailed on.'

Saggers scribbled a few more words down on his notepad. 'And that's it? That's all you know about her?' He had another look at the drawing. 'So how would you describe her? Black or mulatto?'

'What do you think?'

Saggers looked up from the drawing and shrugged. 'I think she looks rich.' He waited and added, 'In which case, why was her body found on the Ratcliff Highway?'

Pyke smiled. 'Exactly my question.' He'd clearly picked the right man for the job.

Saggers gave a satisfied smile. 'I've always said, give me the right raw materials and I'll write you a veritable *Beggar's Opera*. This is good, sir. It will permit me to indulge my creative juices. I'll have it written by the time the newspapers go to bed tomorrow night.'

'I don't want tragedy, I want mystery. That's how you're going to sell the story. Readers love things that can't be explained.'

'If you buy me a half-buck of Halnaker's venison, you can have anything you want.'

78

'What I want,' Pyke explained, 'is to use the story as a way of appealing for information about the dead woman.'

'Have no fear. A work of art can operate on many different levels.' Saggers took the charcoal in his hand. 'Social utility and aesthetic brilliance may seem to be unlikely companions to the uninitiated but in the hands of a master one can feed off the other as easily as a piglet sucking on his mummy's tit.' He grinned at his own analogy. 'Where are readers meant to take their information?'

'To me.' Pyke paused. 'Or to Fitzroy Tilling at the Whitehall Division of the New Police.'

Saggers looked up from his pad. 'Is this a police investigation or are you looking into the matter privately?'

'A little of both – but that's strictly off the record. You mention my name anywhere in the piece, and I'll personally see to it that you don't receive another scrap of information.'

'Don't worry, I can fudge the issue, make it sound official without mentioning names. Yet another string to my bow, as they say. And I know where my bread is buttered.'

'And where your caked is iced.'

'Actually I'm not especially partial to cake. I find it fattening.' He patted his enormous stomach. 'One last question, sir. You said that the coroner's inquest had already taken place. What was the verdict?'

'Wilful murder.'

Saggers nodded. 'But there weren't any news-papermen at the inquest? That's curious. Usually they're like jackals feeding off a carcass.' He rubbed his chin.

'The inquest was a closed one. The jurors were warned not to talk about the details of the murder.'

'I see I've struck a nerve of some sort.'

'We found the corpse in a distressed state. We didn't want to advertise this fact. You know how the macabre tends to attract all kinds of lunatic.'

'Macabre, eh?' Saggers finished off his ale and wiped the froth from his top lip with the sleeve of his coat. 'Good Lord, sir, you know how to tease a hungry man, don't you? You leave the tastiest morsels till last and then don't bat an eyelid when you throw them down on to the plate.'

'I don't want you mentioning it in your story.'

'But blood and gore sell newspapers; that's how you're going to get a sub-editor to sit up and take notice.'

'Look, for the sake of the investigation, there are certain details about the murder that need to be kept from the public.'

He didn't want news of Mary Edgar's missing eyeballs to become common knowledge. If the exact manner of her murder was reported, the investigation would become an overnight sensation and Pyke wouldn't be able to move, or even think, for the howling of journalists looking to make their fortunes from the dead woman's suffering.

'And the more you sensationalise the story, the greater the competition you'll face,' he added.

'Fine point, sir. I can see that arguing with you is like firing a pea-shooter at a rampaging elephant.' Saggers made a point of closing his pad.

'But if we're going to be working together as a team, I'd appreciate it if you told me what we're dealing with. I have a very developed imagination, sir, and if I don't know, I shall be kept awake tonight, mulling over the gruesome possibilities.'

Pyke took a moment to consider Saggers' request. 'Her eyeballs were cut out.' He watched as the colour drained from the journalist's face.

'That's horrible, *awful.*' He shook his head. 'But it would make a tremendous story.'

'I don't want it mentioned. Is that understood?'

Saggers' eyelids drooped lazily as he contemplated Pyke's response. In the end, he just simply shrugged. 'You're buying the venison, sir, you can make up the rules.'

Later, once Saggers had left, Pyke showed the etching to the rest of the drinkers in the tap and parlour rooms. He didn't come across a single black face and no one admitted to knowing Mary. At the counter, as he waited for Samuel to serve him, he placed the drawing on the counter. 'Do you recognise her?' he asked, studying Samuel's craggy face.

'A fine-looking woman. Therefore, not likely to frequent a place like this.' Samuel's skin was lighter than Pyke's but his thick, wiry hair and flat nose indicated his mixed ancestry.

'I was told this was a place where black men and women came to drink,' Pyke said.

'Who told you that?'

'No one you'd know.'

'Since a couple of black stevedores were beaten nearly to death just around the corner, for taking jobs that could have been filled by white dockers,

81

they've been keeping a lower profile.'

Pyke noted that Samuel had referred to 'them' rather than 'us'. 'She hasn't been here, then, as far as you know.'

'That's right.' Samuel smiled, shaking his head and revealing more gum than teeth. 'And a woman like that, I'd know. Believe me, I'd know.'

'How about a man just off the boat from Jamaica by the name of Arthur Sobers?' Pyke described him as best he could.

'Ain't seen him either.'

As he prepared to leave, Samuel called out, 'You could try again one night after the sun's gone down. It tends to look a bit different then. Different folk drinking here, a whole different atmosphere.' He placed a glass of rum on the counter.

Pyke went back, lifted the glass to his lips, tipped it back and opened his throat. It was as though he'd swallowed burning oil. Gagging, he bent forward, hands on his knees, forehead popping with sweat. For a moment, his vision blurred and a flash of white exploded behind his eyes. The taste the drink left in his mouth was bitter. Pyke put the glass down on the counter.

Samuel was grinning at his reaction to the rum. 'They call it kill-devil. Most white folks drink it with a little water.'

'Who's they?'

'Former slaves in the Caribbean.'

'What does it mean?'

'Some folk reckon it has medicinal properties; reckon it can cure all kinds of disease and perhaps even ward off evil spirits.'

'Have you ever heard about the practice of

embalming a corpse with rum?'

Samuel rubbed his chin while he considered Pyke's question. 'Can't say I have, but then again, I might not be the best person to ask.'

'And who might be?'

'Come back at night, *any* night, and she'll be right over there.' Samuel offered a gummy smile and pointed to a table next to the counter. 'Buy her a few kill-devils, and she'll tell you anything you ask.'

FIVE

It was late by the time the hackney cab dropped Pyke outside his uncle's apartment in Camden Town. Felix would be fast asleep by now, and as he banged on the door, Pyke wondered whether he had planned it this way or not. It was true that he was slightly embarrassed that he hadn't tried harder to win over his son, but it was also true that he didn't exactly know how to do this; whether to give the lad a few days to get over the sight of him taking Maginn apart or to grasp this nettle as soon as possible. In the end, he'd dithered and done neither.

It was Jo, rather than Godfrey, who opened the door, and as she led the way to the front room, she explained that Godfrey was dining out. She had been sitting in the armchair next to the fireplace and an open book rested on one of the arms. Hurriedly she closed it and tried to hide it under the chair but Pyke had already recognised its leather cover. He didn't say anything, though, at least not straight away. Instead, he excused himself, found a full bottle of claret in the pantry and returned to the front room with the bottle and two empty wineglasses, which he filled to the brim. At first, Jo tried to protest, saying she didn't drink wine, but Pyke insisted that he wouldn't take no for an answer and, finally, she relented.

She was wearing a simple cotton dress and her flame-coloured hair glistened softly in the candlelight. Her cheeks were slightly rosy and, when she smiled, laughter lines framed her blue eyes. She wasn't beautiful by the standards of genteel society; for a start she was too petite, no more than five feet tall, and her hips were too wide for her to be considered slim. But she was spirited and good natured and Pyke knew he'd never find a better governess, nursemaid and companion for Felix; for her part, she seemed to love the boy as her own.

'I'm sorry, Pyke. I didn't mean for Felix to see the fight...' Jo couldn't bring herself to finish the sentence.

'How was he? Did he talk about it on the way back here?'

Jo shook her head. 'He was very quiet. He's been very quiet today, as well. But...' At the last moment she seemed to lose her nerve.

'But what?'

'He's barely ten.' There was a hardness to her voice. 'Seeing that man close up, seeing the blood, I'd say it affected him.'

Pyke thought about the way he'd beaten

Maginn, and how it must have looked to Felix. 'Did *you* see it?'

'I saw that man lying in the gutter.' She bit her lip and took another sip of wine. Her neck was flushed.

'Did you know that Maginn was harassing a prostitute, and that he'd plotted to have me killed?'

This time she didn't answer. Perhaps she was worried about criticising him. Pyke wanted to tell her that he didn't mind – that he wanted to hear what she had to say – but it didn't seem appropriate.

'Sometimes I see the way the world is and I can feel the insides of my stomach crawling.' He looked down at his boots. 'That's not true. I see what *I've* done, the way I've let people down, and I want to tear out my own throat. But I've no right to say these things to you. I'm sorry, I should go. I'm not good company.'

'You've only just got here,' she said, fiddling with her silver bracelet. 'Stay a little while longer.'

A few moments of silence passed between them. Pyke took another sip of wine. 'Did he talk about me when I was away?'

'A little.'

'In what sense?'

'I think the fact that you were in prison frightened him.' She saw his face and added, 'He was scared you wouldn't come back.'

'And yet now I am back, he won't talk to me.'

'Just give him time. Losing his mother and then losing you, it was a lot to cope with.'

'For a while, after she died, I thought he was coping quite well. I thought we all were.' Pyke looked up at Jo and remembered some of the things they had done as a threesome; the long walks in the grounds at Hambledon, plucking pheasants that Pyke had shot with a rifle, and telling ghost stories around the fireplace in the old drawing room.

'I'm sure we all still miss her terribly,' Jo said, staring down at her boots.

'But it was five years ago.'

For a moment the only sound in the room was the ticking of the grandfather clock. 'He so wants your approval, Pyke,' Jo said, as she ran her fingertip around the rim of her wineglass. 'I'd say that's why he's been reading the *Newgate Calendar.*' She hesitated. 'Rightly or wrongly, Felix believes that the stories represent the world you come from.'

Pyke had learned to read from the pages of the *Newgate Calendar,* scouring it for tales of murder, piracy, highway robbery, theft and even cannibalism, and the idea that Felix was doing the same made him feel oddly satisfied, even if the reading matter itself was upsetting.

'But now, in addition to that, Felix seems to have found a copy of Godfrey's damned book.'

Jo shrugged her shoulders. 'That wasn't my doing.' She saw that Pyke was looking at the book she'd been reading when he arrived. 'For obvious reasons, I've tried my best to keep it from Felix.'

'I'm not blaming you, but the other night he came within a whisker of accusing me of being that character.'

'I wasn't even aware he'd read it, but when I asked him why he was so interested in the *New-*

gate Calendar, he told me he'd been trying to find a story about you.'

'About me?' Pyke let out an exasperated sigh. 'But I sat him down and explained I was only going to prison because I owed people money.'

'Like I said, he's ten and he has an active imagination. I think he wants to prove himself to you, though. Show you he can be tough, too.'

It was at times like this that Pyke missed Emily the most. Somehow she had always known what to say to Felix in order to reassure him. But he guessed that Jo now performed this role with equal aplomb.

'Do you think it would help if I told Felix that I'm helping the police investigate the murder of a young woman?'

Jo looked up at him. 'Is that why they let you out of Marshalsea early?'

'In part.' Pyke shrugged. 'But do you think he'd look at me in a different way, if he felt I was trying to defend the law?'

'Spend some time with him; talk to him; tell him what you're doing. It can't do any harm. He's quite resilient these days.'

Pyke picked up the bottle of wine, and before she could stop him he had filled both of their wineglasses once more.

'I see you've been reading up on me, too.' He pointed to the copy of *Confessions* that she had tried to hide under her chair.

But instead of an embarrassed silence, his comment drew a throaty laugh. 'I thought you just said it wasn't about you.'

'It isn't, but since I haven't actually read it, I

don't know how often it skirts up against the truth.'

'You haven't read it?' She seemed intrigued.

'No.'

'Why not?'

'I don't know. Maybe because I'd be angry at the liberties Godfrey has taken with the truth. Maybe because I don't like to be reminded of my past.' He shrugged. 'Or maybe because I think I'm both a better and a worse man than the one my uncle has written about.'

'How do you know if you haven't read it?'

'I know my uncle.'

That made her smile. 'The character, he is rather ... coarse.'

'And I'm not?'

'I can see a little of you in him...'

'But?'

'But he doesn't come across as particularly intelligent. He does things, he acts, but he never stops to think about why he's doing them.'

'And I do? The man who squandered his fortune and ended up in prison.' He laughed, self-deprecatingly. 'But thank you. I'd hate for you to think ill of me.'

'Why should you care what I think of you?'

'Because you're important to Felix.' Pyke considered what he'd just said. 'And you're important to me.'

Pyke had said this instinctively and, for a moment, he wished he'd kept his mouth shut. Jo seemed flustered by this comment and buried her face in her wineglass. She mumbled, 'I was always under the impression you hardly thought

88

of me at all.'

'Why would you think that? For the last few years, you've been the rock I've come to depend on. I don't know what I'd do without you. More to the point, I don't know what Felix would do.'

'I enjoy my work.' She hesitated and bit her lip. 'And you pay me very well.'

Pyke stood up, faster than he'd expected to, and the sudden rush of blood to his head made him feel disoriented. 'I have to go.'

Jo stood up, too, and followed him to the front door. 'Shall I tell Felix you'll come and see him soon?'

He turned to face her. 'Perhaps the three of us could do something or go somewhere. The zoological gardens perhaps.' He was aware of how close she was. All he had to do was reach out and touch her hand.

'He would like that.'

At the bottom of the steps Pyke turned around, expecting Jo to have disappeared back into the apartment, but she hadn't moved and was contemplating him with an expression he couldn't make sense of.

By the time a hackney cab had dropped Pyke at the steps of the police building on Whitehall, it was eleven in the morning and the sun had risen high enough in the hazy sky for the air to feel warm on his skin. The sky wasn't exactly blue – the pall of ash and dust that lingered in the air throughout the spring and summer took care of that – but a light breeze had cleared away the worst of the particles, and for the first time in as long as Pyke could remember, he felt a lightness in his step.

'There have been some exciting developments in Lord Bedford's murder investigation,' Tilling noted with evident satisfaction from behind his mahogany desk. They were sitting in his office on the first floor, an airy room with high ceilings that was filled with imposing items of furniture and offered an impressive view across Horse Guards Parade.

'Really?' Pyke yawned, not very interested.

'We've made an arrest. Bedford's valet. A young Swiss chap called Morel-Roux. He'd only been with Bedford for five or six weeks, it turns out.'

'What's the motive?'

'Pierce and his team searched this chap's room and found a five-pound note and half a dozen sovereigns. They also found the same chisel that had been used to open Bedford's desk. So they widened their search, brought in a carpenter and a plumber, and found a ten-pound note and two of the deceased's gold rings behind a skirting board in the butler's pantry – the room used by this valet.'

Tilling stood up and wandered across to the window, inspecting the view. Something was wrong. Tilling's manner had been cold and formal from the start and yet now he was divulging intimate details about another murder investigation. It didn't make sense. And he hadn't asked a single question about the search for Mary Edgar's murderer.

'So why did this valet do it?' Pyke asked, still trying to make sense of Tilling's manner. 'I mean, why kill someone you're stealing from?'

'I don't know. Perhaps Bedford had caught him in the act, or had discovered that this chap was stealing from him. Perhaps he confronted him and a struggle ensued...'

'I thought you told me that Bedford had been stabbed in his belly with a letter opener some time during the night.'

'So what if I did?' Tilling asked defensively, returning to his seat.

'Well, if he was killed in his bed, it isn't likely that he interrupted a robbery, is it?' Pyke said. 'And if I'd stolen some rings and money from my master, the last place I'd think of hiding them would be in my own quarters.'

'Well, I'm not strictly involved in the investigation, even though I have been forced to keep Bedford's friends and associates abreast of any developments. They're already demanding the noose for this valet.'

Pyke shrugged, as though the matter didn't concern him. 'So why did you summon me here to see you?' A note to this effect had been delivered to Pyke's garret earlier that morning. 'You still haven't asked about my own investigation. I assumed that was what you wanted to talk about.'

'It is, in a way.' Tilling sat up in his chair and wiped his forehead with a fresh, white handkerchief. 'Actually, this is quite awkward.'

'What's awkward?'

'Well, it appears that Morel-Roux had been reading *The True and Candid Confessions of an Ex-Bow Street Runner.*' Tilling looked up, to check his reaction.

'So?'

'Unfortunately someone, I don't yet know who, passed this snippet of information to a journalist reporting on the investigation.'

'And?'

'Dammit, man. I've read the book. I'm sure you know *exactly* what I'm referring to. The passage where the character does what, it would seem, Morel-Roux has done. Murder an aristocrat while he sleeps in his own bed. Only in your case, you manage to concoct an elaborate and, I have to say, rather unconvincing justification for taking the man's life.'

In fact, Pyke had simply held a pillow over Emily's father's face and suffocated him, but it was no surprise that Godfrey had decided to splash the pages of his 'memoir' with sufficient blood to set the readers' pulses racing.

'If I told you I haven't read the book and that it purports to be a fictional account of a man's life, would that make a difference?'

'It's not what you or I think,' Tilling said. 'But the author is your uncle and you were once a Bow Street Runner.'

'I understand that, but why is this a problem?' Pyke tried to keep his voice light but he could already see what was coming.

'The frenzy surrounding Bedford's death has been considerable already, even before we knew about this valet. Now it's going to explode; a servant killing his master. Think about it for a minute. The wealthy will be quaking in their boots, wondering if their servants will mimic Morel-Roux's actions. Meanwhile servants, at least the ones who've been poorly treated, which is most of them, will be sharpening their razor blades; either that or they'll be cheering for this Swiss fellow. It doesn't bear thinking about. What with the recession and unemployment, the whole situation couldn't be any more precarious.'

Pyke looked around the room. 'I still don't understand why this is a problem as far as our arrangement is concerned.'

'Don't you? What if someone found out that you were working, albeit in an unofficial capacity, for the Metropolitan Police? The stink would be worse than the Thames at low tide. And you know as well as I do that someone *will* find out. They always do.'

'Then we will cross that particular bridge, if and when we have to.' But Pyke knew it wouldn't be that simple. Expecting men like Saggers to do what was right was like asking a starving wolf to walk away from an injured deer.

Tilling exhaled. 'God, can you *imagine* what Lord Bedford's friends would do with this information? If they ever found out that I'd employed the man who had likely or not given Morel-Roux the idea to murder his master? They'd demand my head on a silver platter in a matter of hours. Yours, too.'

'What are you saying?' Pyke tried to ward off the uneasy feeling in his stomach. 'You want me to just disappear?'

'I didn't create this situation, Pyke. I'm just responding to it.'

'If I didn't know you better, I'd say you were safeguarding your own interests in the process.'

'That's unfair, and you know it.'

'Do I? It's how all bureaucracies work. Defecate on those below you and pander to those above you.'

'I don't have to listen to this slander...'

'And what about the investigation? I suppose it doesn't matter that I've already made good progress. Much more important to make sure you don't look bad in the eyes of Lord Bedford's friends. After all, who cares about a dead mulatto girl?'

Later Pyke would reflect that his comments had been unkind, but he wasn't going to give up the investigation without a fight.

'This conversation is finished. You're no longer representing the police, Pyke. Accept it and find something else to do.'

'Just like that?'

'If you care about the dead woman, you'll do what's best for her. Since we've made an arrest in the Bedford case, Mayne is willing to deploy more men to her murder.'

'If *I* care?' Pyke could feel his blood rising. 'Just a few days ago, you made it clear to me that her death wasn't your most pressing concern.'

'Just as you made it clear to me that money was your main motivation for agreeing to take on the investigation.'

'That's easy for you to say with your house overlooking Hampstead Heath. I can barely afford my next meal. But I'm the one who's been traipsing around the East End, not placating the friends of some dead aristocrat.'

Pyke's anger was directed at Tilling but really

he knew that he, alone, was responsible for his current predicament. Two years earlier, he had more money than he knew what to do with but he'd squandered it and now he was almost penniless. Money was no panacea, as he'd found out, but having it meant you weren't subject to the whims of others.

'I'm grateful for everything you've done, really I am. And when Pierce takes charge of the investigation, I hope you'll tell him everything you've already found out.'

'Pierce?' Pyke blinked. He could barely credit what he was hearing.

Tilling nodded; he knew very well what this would mean to Pyke. 'Believe me, he wasn't my choice.'

'You really think I'm going to buy Pierce lunch and tell him everything I know?'

'In the long run, you'll realise you don't have a choice. If you want to see this woman's killer apprehended. One way or another, this division is taking over the investigation. Now you can keep the money I gave you, but that's all. From now on, I'm ordering you to steer clear of anything to do with the dead woman.'

Pyke licked his lips. 'And if I decide not to?'

'What choice do you have? Twenty pounds won't get you very far. As you said, you can barely afford your next meal. Running a murder investigation is not something you can do on your own.' There was no gloating in Tilling's expression but he was right and Pyke knew it.

Pyke had taken the job because Tilling had offered to pay him, but suddenly it wasn't just the loss of this income which upset him; it was not being able to perform the task he'd agreed to do; not being able to find and punish whoever had strangled Mary Edgar. He had watched as two gravediggers had, without ceremony, buried her body; no one else had. Now he felt he owed it to her to find her killer ... or killers. He couldn't just walk away, leaving Pierce to botch the investigation.

'What about wanting to help me get back on my feet? Was that just a lie?' Pyke tried to swallow his bitterness. He had hoped that finding Mary Edgar's killer might restore him in Felix's eyes, too.

'I'm sorry, Pyke. If there was any way I could keep you on, I would. But I've been through every possible permutation in my mind and none of them adds up. In the light of what's happened, you're too much of a risk.'

'And that's it?' Pyke stared at his old acquaintance, feeling empty and a little nauseous. 'I'm really out?'

'As I said, I'm sorry. I really am. But let's face it, you were never really in.'

SIX

Pyke found Edmund Saggers in the fifth or sixth public house he visited. Having been to the Old Dog on Holywell Street, the Coach and Horses, the Cock, the Back Kitchen and the Cheese, all on The Strand, he eventually found the penny-a-liner hunched over a table at the back of the Cole Hole, an inkwell and a full glass of claret next to him. From the colour of his lips, it wasn't his first drink of the day.

'There's been a change of plan,' Pyke said, sitting on the bench opposite him and taking a gulp of Saggers' wine. His anger had started to abate and he'd already formulated a plan. In spite of what he'd said, or hadn't said, in Tilling's office, he had no intention of giving up the investigation and sharing what he'd discovered with Pierce.

'What kind of a change?' Saggers asked, staring mournfully at his depleted wineglass.

Pyke could see that he'd already filled two or three sides of paper and it stood to reason he wouldn't want to alter anything. Not unless it was in his financial interest to do so. 'I want you to approach only one newspaper with this story, and when you do, I want to be there with you. And I want to negotiate directly with the editor; preferably one who cares more about sales than editorial content.'

'These days, I'd say take your pick. No one cares about the craft of writing any more. Sadly I'm a man born out of his times.' He gave an exaggerated shrug. 'Would Hazlitt or Lamb be grubbing around as I have to if they were writing today? I think not.'

Pyke decided to ignore his rhetorical flourish. 'You have someone in mind?'

'I'm an artist, sir, and I create according to my inner genius. If I permitted such base thoughts as sales and the market to enter my head, I would be ruined in a moment.'

'I want you to approach an editor and set out the terms of the campaign we're going to run.'

'A campaign, eh?' Saggers finished his claret and belched. 'Like Napoleon marching on Moscow?'

'You mean, will it be long and drawn out – and expensive for the newspaper?'

Saggers grinned. 'Truly, sir, you're a man after my own heart. The more time I spend in your company, the more I like you.' He held up his empty wineglass. 'And should you deign to refill this humble vessel, my admiration for you would stretch even farther.'

Pyke hailed a pot-boy and asked him to refill Saggers' glass, but as soon as the full wineglass materialised, Pyke stood up. 'Drink up. We're off to find an editor.'

'So you're proposing we run a leader in tomorrow's edition attacking the police for their failure to adopt sufficiently robust measures for detection in cases of murder and other violent crimes?'

The office occupied by the bespectacled editor of the *Morning Examiner* stood at the top of a flight of creaking stairs in a building in a narrow courtyard just off Fleet Street. The editor, a man called Jeremiah Spratt, had his shirtsleeves rolled up and he wore an apron heavily stained with black ink. Around him were stacks of newspapers, books still waiting to be reviewed and, on the surface of his desk, waxy pools of dried ink.

'In part, yes. *The Times* and the *Morning Chronicle* have made similar arguments.'

'In case you haven't noticed we are *not The Times* nor the *Chronicle.*' But Spratt looked around his office without embarrassment. 'You said, in part?'

'One justice system for the rich, another for the poor. That's what you lead with; that's what'll grab your readers' interest. Two murders on the same day. A team of the New Police's best detectives is instantly sent to find the killer of the aristocrat; meanwhile the corpse of the poor, mulatto woman is left to rot and, more than three days later, a team still hasn't been assigned.'

With his patrician air and his mop of slightly receding grey hair, Spratt looked more like an eccentric headmaster than the rapacious, sales-obsessed editor Pyke had been promised. Still, he hadn't yet declared himself either way, regarding Pyke's proposal, and as he pushed his spectacles farther up his nose, and glanced across at Saggers, who could barely contain himself, Pyke tried to work out what his concerns were.

'How do you know all this?' Spratt smiled awkwardly. 'That's to say, how do *I* know it's all true?'

'I know because I was approached by a senior figure in the Metropolitan Police to run the investigation.' Pyke hesitated and thought about how the story he was trying to sell would affect Tilling. 'Still, I don't want that fact to appear anywhere in your newspaper.'

'And now you've been relieved of your duties. Can I ask why?'

Pyke looked across at Saggers. 'That's personal, I'm afraid.' It was late in the afternoon and Pyke wondered what time they put the morning edition to bed.

'Yet you expect me to take your word for all of this?' Spratt ran his fingers through his thinning hair. 'And in return you want me to lampoon the police and turn them into a laughing stock?'

'I don't want you to turn them into a laughing stock. I just want you to draw attention to the different provisions made for the rich and the poor, call for the establishment of a new detective squad and lay down a challenge; in effect, that a dedicated team of your very best men – that's to say, Saggers here and myself – will hunt down this woman's murderer *before* the police do.' Pyke took a moment to arrange his thoughts. 'Think of it as an act of public service. If we're successful, a murderer will be arrested, tried and punished. And if we're not successful, the New Police will be forced to re-examine the way they privilege prevention of crime over detection. Who knows? Perhaps a new detective squad will arise from your campaign. And think of the additional newspapers you'll sell. People always love a murder, but I promise you, they'll love reading about the progress of your intrepid detectives even more, especially if we find the killer before the police do. Everyone likes to cheer for the underdog. If this thing catches on, people will be queuing at the news stands to read the latest instalment.'

'Truly, it's a monumental idea,' Saggers said, oozing insincerity. 'One of breathtaking originality that befits a great man such as yourself and a paper of this calibre.'

Pyke glared at Saggers for his syrupy intervention; they were winning Spratt over already and didn't need to resort to sycophancy.

'You reckon a leader and a daily column ought to do it?' Spratt asked, inspecting an ink stain on his fingers.

'Perhaps not a daily column. But at least every other day, or when there's something to report. And we can ask your readers to help us with our enquiries. We could ask anyone who might have known or seen Mary Edgar to contact us. A small reward could be made available.'

'Rewards cost money and money's something I don't have.'

'Then we'll just appeal to the goodness of your readers' hearts.'

That drew an approving nod.

'Of course, I'll need some money for the investigation. Twenty pounds ought to do it to start off. And for the column itself, Saggers will want to be paid twopence a line rather than the usual one and a half.'

'Twenty pounds, you say?' Spratt sucked the air in through his teeth. 'I might be able to raise such a sum but it's not a bottomless well, if that's what you're thinking.'

'You'll do it, then?' Pyke swapped a quick glance with Saggers, who looked as if he might explode with happiness.

'Indeed I will,' Spratt said, 'but on one condition.'

'Oh?'

'To give the story credibility, I'll need to include the name of this senior figure in the New Police who approached you to run the investigation.'

Pyke felt a sudden tightness in his throat. 'Why's that?'

Spratt shrugged. 'His name corroborates the story.'

'For what it's worth, he's a friend of mine.'

'Then you have a difficult choice to make.'

'It might seem odd to you but the idea of humiliating this person strikes me as wrong.'

'Then you can find yourself another news-paper.'

Pyke wetted his lips. 'What if I told you he gave me the work as a favour, because he thought – rightly as it turned out – that I needed something to do?'

'So you don't want to hurt someone who's given you a helping hand. That makes you a fine human being. Now take off your halo and see things from my perspective. Paying civilians from the public purse to do the work of the police is wrong.'

'It's your job to see things in terms of right and wrong. For the rest of us, fault isn't so easy to apportion.'

'Listen, Pyke, I don't have time to debate the ethics of journalism. Either you agree to my condition or we shake hands and go our separate ways. Which is it to be?'

Pyke stole another glance at Saggers and briefly weighed up his debt to Tilling against his desire to find Mary Edgar's murderer and vindicate himself in his son's eyes. 'His name's Fitzroy Tilling.' Pyke hesitated, still contemplating his betrayal. 'He's the deputy commissioner.'

Outside Spratt's office, Saggers turned to him and whispered, 'For a moment I thought you were going to piss our deal up against the wall for the sake of, what, a friendship?'

Pyke had to fight the urge to grab the fat man by his neck and squeeze it until he choked.

Pyke sat at the counter in the smoky confines of Samuel's taproom drinking rum and water. As the man had predicted, the atmosphere of the place was different. Perhaps it was the babble of different languages which made it so: Scandinavians drunkenly toasting each other and dark-skinned Italians smoking their pipes and cheroots. The rest of the faces belonged to Negro and Lascar sailors, each keeping to their own, the different nationalities and races in the cramped room rubbing shoulders with one another, but never mixing.

A part-time dock labourer called Johnny – a man in his forties with blue-black skin and forearms as thick as sapling trees corded with veins – recognised Mary Edgar from the charcoal drawing. He told Pyke he'd seen her in the window of a gentleman's carriage on Commercial Road about two or three weeks earlier, coming from the direction of the West India Docks. He didn't recognise anyone resembling Arthur Sobers' description but told Pyke that a ship from Jamaica called the *Island Queen* had docked there around the same time.

But that wasn't the end of Pyke's good fortune. Samuel directed him towards a woman in her sixties with dark, wrinkled skin who was sitting on her own at a table in the corner of the room. He showed her the drawing and told her the woman had been killed. That provoked very little reaction, but when he suggested that her body might have been embalmed with rum, a glimmer passed across her hooded eyes.

She picked up a glass and swallowed the drink he'd bought her in a single gulp. 'We call it kill-devil. These days I like it with a little water.'

'Is it a practice you're familiar with?'

'Not since I been living in this country.'

'But you have heard of it?'

Her glance drifted over his shoulder and her eyes glazed over. 'Folk reckoned it could ward off the duppies.'

'Duppies?'

'Ghosts. Evil spirits.'

'As in witchcraft?' Pyke waited to catch the old woman's eyes and thought about Mary Edgar's mutilated face.

'Obeah.'

'What's that?'

'Some black folk reckon Obeah men and women can commune with the dead; they have the power to curse and cause harm, as well as cure and uplift.'

'And rum is part of what they do?'

'Where I grew up, rum's a part of what every-one does. It's what kept us going, made the hard times feel better.' For the first time, she scrutin-ised Pyke's expression carefully and added, 'You sure this girl was embalmed with rum?'

'I think so. A bottle of rum had been left by the body and even though it was muddy, the body was spotless, as though it had been washed.'

'With rum?'

Pyke nodded.

'And this would have been after she was killed?'

'Does it make a difference?'

As the woman looked away, the light left her eyes, as if someone had blown out a candle. 'You kill someone, maybe you want to find a way of appeasing their spirit...'

Pyke waited for a moment, wondering whether he should say anything about Mary Edgar's facial mutilation or not. 'What if someone had cut out her eyeball?' he whispered. 'What might that mean?'

She looked up at him, unable to hide her interest. 'The whole eyeball, you say?'

It was dark when Pyke took Copper for a walk around Smithfield, though in fairness to the mastiff, Copper didn't need Pyke's sanction, or company, to enjoy the attractions of the field. It had always amazed Pyke how well the animal had adjusted to the loss of one of his legs and how nimble he was in spite of his injury. It had also surprised him how gentle Copper was around Felix – especially since he'd been trained to kill other animals. The field was almost deserted but Copper wasn't interested in traversing it, preferring instead to forage for scraps around the perimeter. While he did so, Pyke stepped into the Queen's Head on the south side of the field and ordered a gin. He drank this and then another, watching the tables of revellers without envy or self-pity. At one of the tables, he joined a game of Primero and on the third hand dealt he drew two sixes, so he decided to bet the rest of the money from Tilling's purse and what he'd been given by Spratt. A lawyer's clerk and a butcher matched his bets and when they all turned over their cards,

Pyke's two sixes beat the lawyer's sevens and the butcher's aces. That earned him between fifty and sixty pounds, enough to cover his expenses in the coming weeks. To the chagrin of his opponents, Pyke excused himself before he could give them the chance to win their money back.

At his garret, he found Copper waiting for him on the steps, gnawing a bone. The mastiff barely looked up from his prize but managed to wag his tail. Inside the door was a bottle of claret with a note attached to it – 'No hard feelings. Fitzroy'. He picked up the bottle and followed Copper up the narrow staircase, wondering why friends were so hard to make yet so easy to lose.

That night, Pyke lay in his garret, thinking about Felix, Jo and the murdered woman, though not necessarily in that order. A couple of tallow candles burned on the mantelpiece and, at his feet, Copper dozed contentedly. Unable to sleep, he took his copy of Hobbes' *Leviathan* and began to read it from the beginning. It relaxed him and helped to turn his thoughts from the events of the past few days. Even Hobbes' grim portrait of nature failed to disturb him unduly. In fact, he found himself agreeing with its sentiments; that men were engaged in a desperate struggle of all against all, and that life, as Hobbes had so aptly put it, was 'nasty, brutish and short'. So it had been for the dead woman.

SEVEN

The next morning Pyke asked for Saggers in the Cole Hole, the Turk's Head and the Crown and Anchor. He eventually found the penny-a-liner in the Back Kitchen; the morning edition of the *Examiner* was spread out on the table, together with an empty flagon of claret and a plateful of chop bones. The room was deserted, except for a few snoring drunkards, and it smelled of un-washed bodies and fried food. Saggers picked up the newspaper and showed Pyke the leading article and the column he'd penned about Mary Edgar's murder. Pyke read it and told Saggers he'd done a thorough job.

In fact, it was difficult to see how Saggers and Spratt might have done a better job. The tone of the leader was just right; a delicate mixture of con-cern, mockery and indignation: 'Prevention of crime is no longer sufficient on its own to safe-guard the interests of the citizens of this great metropolis.' Or, even better, 'The sheer incom-petence of the Metropolitan Police beggars belief.' Best of all, 'We have no doubt that a special team of committed, hardworking journalists will find the killer, or killers, of this poor black woman before the bumbling fools of the police.' Pyke noticed a brief reference to Fitzroy Tilling and passed over it.

'A veritable masterpiece, even if I say so

myself,' Saggers said, delivering his verdict.

'Any repercussions?'

'Any repercussions, the man asks?' Saggers appealed to a drunkard sitting next to them. 'Well, sir, it would seem that Sir Richard Mayne came to see Spratt *in person* this morning, after he'd seen the newspaper. I'm reliably informed that he was incandescent with rage. He ranted and raved and made all kinds of threats. I'm only sorry I didn't see it with my own eyes.'

'Mayne? In person?' Pyke hadn't expected the riposte to come from the commissioner himself. 'And did Spratt manage to hold his ground?'

Saggers' grin widened. 'Spratt was delighted he'd managed to rile a man as important as Mayne. Told him there was no way he was going to abandon the campaign and said that if Mayne wanted him to print a retraction, he'd have to bloody well find the woman's killer before we did.'

'He said that?' Pyke had witnessed Spratt's ruthless side, but now he was impressed by the man's integrity.

'Spratt might not look the part but when he gets behind something, he's won't give any ground unless he absolutely has to.'

'I'd like you to try to dig up some information about the West India Dock Company,' Pyke said, then explained that Mary Edgar had been seen leaving the docks in a gentleman's carriage.

Saggers rubbed his chin. 'What makes you think the company's involved?'

'I don't, at least not yet. But I think one of their clerks lied to me about not knowing Mary Edgar, which makes me suspicious.'

'In which case, sir, I will be suspicious on your behalf.' Saggers grinned at Pyke, then belched.

Nathaniel Rowbottom returned to his office, carrying a ledger in one hand and a quill and fresh ink in the other. Pyke waited until he had closed the heavy, panelled door, and had deposited the items on his desk before making his move. The knife was already in Pyke's hand and the terrified clerk didn't have time even to blink, let alone shout for help, before Pyke had twisted his arm, and pressed the blade into his throat. A few spots of blood appeared on his neck where the serrated edge had penetrated the skin. Rowbottom had lied to Pyke and would continue to lie to him unless he thought that his life was in danger.

'If you don't answer me truthfully, I'll slit your throat and leave you to bleed to death like a slaughtered pig. I've killed men before and I'll do it again. Nod once, very slowly, if you understand.' Pyke was standing over him, whispering in his ear, the knife still pressed against his throat.

For a moment Rowbottom was too terrified to do anything, but eventually it came, a slight tilt of his head.

'Mary Edgar docked here a little over two weeks ago, on one of the ships that arrived from the West Indies. I want two names, that's all; the ship she disembarked from and the man who met her.'

'I don't know...'

Pyke dug the blade deeper into Rowbottom's neck. 'Think *very* carefully about what will happen if you don't answer my question.'

'The *Island Queen*,' Rowbottom croaked, in

barely more than a whisper. 'That's the name of the ship. And that's all I know. I promise you.' It was the same ship the docker had told him about.

Pyke tutted under his breath and drew the blade very slightly across the clerk's throat. A faint line of crimson appeared. 'She was taken somewhere in a gentleman's carriage. I just want the name of the man who arranged it.'

'I don't know. He didn't give me his name; he just told me he wanted to meet someone arriving on the *Island Queen*. I didn't think anything of it at the time.'

'One more jerk of my wrist and I'll sever your jugular vein. And you know what'll happen if I do that? You'll be dead within five, ten minutes. No one saw me come in here and no one will notice me leaving. And you will have died for what? To protect the name of a client or associate who, if the roles were reversed, would have told me your name in a second.' Pyke licked a line of saliva from his bottom lip.

'I *can't* tell you.'

'Then you're dead.'

'No. *Please*.' Rowbottom seemed to be losing control of his bowels. The smell was appalling.

'A name. One last chance.'

'Alefounder,' Rowbottom sobbed. 'William Alefounder.'

Pyke kept the blade to his throat but eased the pressure a little. 'There; that wasn't so difficult, was it?'

A wail of despair spilled from Rowbottom's mouth.

'Who is he and where can I find him?'

The clerk fell on to his desk. 'He's a sugar trader... His offices are located in St Michael's Alley just off Cornhill ... across from the Jamaica Coffee House.'

In quieter moments, Pyke liked to think of himself as fair and even-handed in his dealings with others: someone who didn't take account of status, wealth, religion or colour but who dealt with people on their own terms. But this was not true. In fact, he had always pursued the wealthy and privileged as though they had personally done him wrong.

'Go and fetch the police.'

William Alefounder looked at Pyke from his place at the end of a polished mahogany table in what was evidently the company boardroom, then glowered at the apologetic assistant who'd been unable to prevent Pyke from interrupting the meeting. Around the table were five or six smartly attired men, in addition to Alefounder, all of whom Pyke could have beaten in a fight with one arm tied behind his back.

'Do it *now.*'

The assistant fled from the boardroom but left the door open. A couple of clerks had gathered at the threshold, alerted by the brusque, even violent, way in which Pyke had forced his way through their various lines of defence.

Pyke strode over to where Alefounder was sitting and put the charcoal etching of Mary Edgar down on to the table.

'Her name is Mary Edgar, but you already know that. She was murdered about a week ago.

Her naked corpse was found just off the Ratcliff Highway. You met her off the *Island Queen* when it arrived at the West India Docks some time before the twenty-fifth of last month.'

Alefounder's impassive stare and cool, almost translucent eyes gave little away. Pyke couldn't tell how tall he was, but his solid chest, broad shoulders and lantern jaw suggested he should not be taken lightly. In other circumstances, Pyke might even have described him as good looking. His skin was dark and smooth and his black hair, cut short, was flecked with a few grey hairs, the only indication that he was middle-aged rather than young.

The eyes of the other men gathered around the table had shifted from Pyke to Alefounder. Now it was up to the trader to explain himself and Pyke thought he saw a chink in his armour: a hint of nerves, a smile that was a little too wide and a slight quiver of his top lip.

'Yes, her name is familiar but I've never actually met her.' Alefounder glanced down at the drawing in front of him. 'You say she's been murdered?' He tried to appear unconcerned but droplets of sweat were massing on his forehead.

'She was strangled then tossed away like night soil.'

Alefounder's hands began to tremble. 'I'm disturbed you can talk about another human being in such a manner.'

'I saw her corpse. I stood over her grave while they buried her.'

'Please leave. I don't have to answer your questions, sir, or justify myself to you.'

'How did you know Mary Edgar?' Pyke asked.

'I *didn't* know her.'

In the ten years he'd served as a Bow Street Runner, then five years as a partner in his own bank, Pyke had learned to tell when someone was lying. It was what made him a decent card player, too. Sometimes it was just an instinct; a feeling that was hard to put into words. At other times you could actually see that someone was lying. In this instance, it was a little of both.

'Then why did you meet her from the ship?'

'I didn't.' Alefounder even managed a slight smile. 'I arranged for my carriage to meet her and transport her to an address in town.'

'Why?'

'As a favour to an old friend.'

'His name?'

'As I said, I don't have to answer your questions, sir. And I don't care for your tone, either.'

Pyke folded his arms. 'So whereabouts in the city did your carriage take her?'

'I had no idea until now that she was dead and I shall, of course, make myself available to the police to answer any questions *they* might wish to ask me.'

'You're saying you never laid eyes on her?'

Alefounder floundered and looked around the room for support. None seemed forthcoming.

'Just answer me this.' Pyke waited for the man to meet his stare. 'Why did you try to force a clerk called Rowbottom at the West India Dock to keep your name out of the affair?'

'I have absolutely no idea what you're talking about.' But Pyke could see very well that he did.

'Were you fucking her or did you just *want* to

113

fuck her?'

That was enough to bring the support of the room back behind Alefounder. Pyke had seen it before. Sooner or later, people rallied to their own. In this instance, it was perfectly acceptable for a man to sleep with his mistress in private, but the moment someone made a reference to sexual congress in public, the outrage on their faces was inevitable.

'So, you were consorting with Mary and your wife or someone else found out, and you decided the best thing to do would be to get rid of her.' Pyke checked the size of Alefounder's hands. They were small, like a squirrel's.

'Really, sir, your ability to cause offence to one and all...' One of the men sitting behind the table rose to his feet.

Pyke realised he'd overplayed his hand because he'd given Alefounder the chance to play peacemaker. The trader held up his hands, interrupting his associate, and turned to Pyke. 'The police have already been summoned; you should go now before you are led away in manacles.'

Pyke noticed a print hanging above the fireplace detailing a lush, tropical landscape. 'A slave owner I once had the misfortune of knowing raped one of his female slaves. Later on, he heard she was pregnant, so he waited until she gave birth and then strangled his own progeny in front of her, as soon as it had emerged from her womb. Don't you dare lecture me about manacles.'

No one even looked at him.

Pyke picked up the drawing, and as he did so, he leaned across the trader and whispered, 'If I

114

find out you're part of this, in any way, I'll make it my business to ruin your life.'

For a moment, Alefounder didn't know where to look or what to do.

Pyke stepped out on to the pavement in St Michael's Alley just as two breathless police constables appeared at the far end of the passage.

Half an hour later, and twenty shillings lighter, Pyke emerged from the Jamaica Coffee House with a much fuller picture of William Alefounder. He was forty-five, married, with no children, and he lived in a large, detached property on Richmond Green. He was generally well respected and had inherited his sugar trading company from his father. Each morning, regardless of the weather, he travelled into the city in an open-topped phaeton. The company, Pyke was told, had gone through a bad patch a few years earlier but was moderately prosperous and dealt primarily with sugar plantations in Jamaica, where Alefounder went once a year to conduct his business. There were a few grumbles about his high-handed manner and the dismal rates he paid his clerks, but most of the men Pyke had approached preferred to chat about his physical vigour – he liked to ride horses and play polo – and his charitable work for the Suppression of Vice Society, of which he was a board member. But a few of the men Pyke talked to had other, less favourable stories to tell; stories that stood in sharp relief to accounts of the charity work he did. Apparently Alefounder was also a notorious philanderer and had cheated on his wife countless times during their marriage. No one had been able to give Pyke exact details but at least two clerks had said the same thing, which was sufficient corroboration in his mind. The idea that Alefounder might pontificate about the ills of lewd behaviour in public and carry on in private attested, in Pyke's view, to his gross hypocrisy. But was he capable of murder? That was the question Pyke needed to answer.

Copper was waiting for Pyke on the steps of the ancient, dilapidated tenement that housed his garret. So, too, was Benedict Pierce. A former Bow Street Runner and now part of the Metropolitan Police's Whitehall Division, Inspector Benedict Pierce, was the man who'd been appointed to lead the investigation into Mary Edgar's death. Pierce wore his dark blue uniform as Pyke had imagined he would: nothing was out of place; the belt was neatly buckled around his waist, the coat was buttoned right the way up to his collar, and every one of the brass buttons had been polished to such a sheen you could see your reflection in it. His pencil moustache had been neatly trimmed, as had his sideburns, and his sandy-coloured hair had been slicked back off his forehead with some unguent.

Pierce looked as if he had made the transition from Bow Street Runner to New Police without too many difficulties. In fact, Pyke thought, he was probably far more at home in the New Police, with its rules and procedures, than he had been at Bow Street.

It was a damp afternoon, with dark clouds

threatening to dump their rain on the city's streets. Pierce was standing under a butcher's awning; in the window, a heap of meat sat slowly blackening under the flare of a gas-lamp. Pyke ignored him and went to pat Copper on the head.

'Come on, let's walk,' Pierce said, impatient now that Pyke had returned home.

'What brings you down here?'

'You know as well as I do I've come to talk about the dead girl.' Pierce strode forward in the direction of Smithfield. Just ahead of them, a collie was barking at a stationary cow but keeping far enough back from the animal's hind legs to avoid being kicked.

'Yes, I heard you'd been given the investigation.' It was clear he didn't yet know about Mary Edgar's connection to Alefounder, but if the sugar trader was as good as his word, Pierce and his team would soon be paid a visit.

Pierce took a couple more steps, then stopped. 'I want to know everything you've found out about the murder so far.'

'Then I suggest you read the newspapers. I'm told the *Examiner* has taken an interest in this case.' Pyke allowed himself a quiet smirk.

'We already know you're responsible for that, Pyke, and believe me, it's left you dangerously short of friends.' Pierce was, of course, referring to Tilling, and Pyke found himself wondering again how Tilling had reacted to the story in the *Examiner* and whether he had been punished for employing Pyke's services. 'You know it's a crime to withhold information about a criminal act from a police officer.'

117

'You do your job, I'll do mine. And if you stay out of my way, I'll stay out of yours. How does that sound?' Pyke looked down at a mountain of rotting animal flesh quivering in the gutter.

'The old way of doing things, your way, is over. Finished. Just crawl back to the stone Tilling found you under and stay there.'

'Do your job, Pierce. Be a detective. Go and find things out. It's what you're paid to do.'

'This is now a police matter. If I find out you've been withholding information or using your limited skills to inappropriate ends, I'll make sure you go back to prison for good.'

'You've never liked me, have you, Pierce?'

'Liked you? I've always thought you were corrupt. I despised you and everything you stood for. I still do.'

'For all your moral righteousness, I know you cut corners, Pierce. Too busy trying to impress your seniors. In this instance, I'm guessing you won't look any farther than Arthur Sobers. Find him and you've found Mary Edgar's murderer.'

Pierce tried to hide his surprise but didn't quite manage it. 'Do you know where he is?'

Pyke stepped over the rotting meat, avoiding the swarm of flies that was hovering over it. He left Pierce standing with a vacant expression on his face and joined Copper at the door of his building.

Later that evening, just as it was getting dark, and after Pyke had washed himself with a sliver of soap and a bucket full of water in the yard and changed his clothes, he set off along Cock Lane in the direction of Giltspur Street and Smith-field, where he would hail a hackney coach to take him to Camden Town. He would see Felix before he went to bed and then perhaps stay for dinner with his uncle and Jo. Whistling, he didn't notice the men appear from a side alley and creep up behind him until they were almost upon him. Spinning around, he held up his hand and tried to parry the blow, but was pushed from behind, and struck over the head with a cudgel. The last thing he remembered was falling to his knees, and worrying about dirtying his clothes.

When he regained consciousness, he discovered he'd been hooded and his hands had been tied to the back of the chair he was sitting on. Disoriented, dry-mouthed and with a headache so intense his whole skull seemed to be throbbing, he tried to work out how long he had been unconscious and where his attackers had taken him. It took him a few moments to realise how quiet the place was and a few more to sense how cold and empty it felt. Then the smell hit him; the ripeness of putrefying flesh and the metallic scent of fresh blood. At a guess, he decided, he was being held in the back room of a butcher's shop or one of the underground slaughterhouses in the vicinity of the market.

At the same time, when Pyke heard the clip-clop of footsteps and felt someone tug off his hood, he was still surprised to find himself looking up into the grinning face of one of the city's most feared criminals.

Up close, the first thing he noticed was the careful manner in which Field had groomed his

119

facial hair; his elaborate handlebar moustache was oiled and coiled, his broad, mutton-chop side-burns had been freshly trimmed and the thick tufts of red hair on top of his head smelled vaguely of perfume. Indeed, with his unnaturally red lips and long, wispy eyelashes, there was something almost feminine about Field's appearance, and it was only when you looked into his eyes, like two dark holes drilled into his skull, that you realised something was missing in him, something that you recognised in others that made them human.

There were plenty of stories about Harold Field circulating around the slaughterhouses, tripe dressers, glue-boilers and butchers of Smithfield; some were true, others were distortions. But the very fact that everyone knew something about Field and that the something they knew invariably painted him in a nefarious light meant that he had achieved an almost mythical reputation in the area. Field owned and ran a slaughterhouse on the south side of Smithfield and was a butcher by pro-fession. According to rumour, countless enemies had been killed in the vast underground chambers whose walls were covered in layer upon layer of putrefying fat; then dismembered and incinerated, to hide the evidence. Pyke's own story about Field related to a time he had been drinking in one of the man's many gin palaces. This had been a little over a year ago and Field himself had been pre-sent, counting the takings in a back room. Instead of pot-boys, Field employed young women to serve his drinks, a popular development with many of his customers, but for one man in par-ticular, a man who didn't know of Field's reputation, the temptation of so much young flesh had been too much to bear. Inebriated, he had tried to grope one of the servers and when she resisted, he'd punched her in the face. Field hadn't witnessed the incident personally but someone, of course, told him about it. Still wearing his cutting apron, stained red with sheep's blood, he'd casually walked across the room to where the man was sitting, produced a gleaming meat cleaver and swung it down on the table, severing the man's hand from his arm just above his wrist. Pyke had watched Field walk back to the counter whistling a tune, as though nothing had happened. He had passed close to where Pyke was standing, the meat cleaver in his hand dripping with blood, and when he spotted Pyke, he'd stopped, because he knew Pyke both by reputation and from a previous encounter, and began a conversation about the mild weather. But it wasn't the cleaver which had stuck in Pyke's mind most of all: it had been Field's eyes, clear, almost translucent, but without the slightest hint of life, like a frozen lake in the middle of winter.

True to this memory, Field was carrying a cleaver now and he wiped the blade on his clean white apron.

'Welcome to my humble slaughterhouse.'

Pyke took a moment to check the bindings around his wrists. The cleaver, he knew, was intended to intimidate him – but knowing this didn't make it any less intimidating. Field circled around his chair.

'I apologise for the manner in which I extended my invitation.' Field stared at him. 'I wanted to have a talk, just the two of us, with no chance of anyone eavesdropping on our conversation.'

'Do you usually tie up people you want to talk to?'

'Please excuse my manners.' Field took his cleaver and sliced through the rope binding Pyke's wrists to the chair. 'Is that better?'

'Thank you.' Pyke touched the burns on his wrists.

'Before you went to prison, you lost a sum of about one hundred pounds to a lawyer in a game of cards. Now he owes me and therefore *you* owe me.' Field fiddled with one end of his moustache. 'I'm prepared to offer you another way of paying off this debt.'

Pyke tried to cast his mind back to the card game in question. He could remember the lawyer's face but not his name. He had been drinking heavily at the time and had lost the pot on the turn of the final hand, his kings losing to the lawyer's aces. By that point, his gambling had got completely out of hand, and briefly he wondered how many other people he still owed money to.

'All right,' he said, 'I'm listening.'

'I believe you know a gentleman called Jemmy Crane. A pornographer, actually. Let's call him what he is. He would like people to think of him as a man of letters but I don't wish to bestow such a title on him.'

Pyke kept his expression perfectly blank. 'Why do you say that?'

'Don't insult my intelligence. I'm a resourceful man. I know, for example, that you recently had a contretemps with Crane in his shop.'

Pyke thought about the elderly shop assistant who'd overheard his conversation with Crane. 'Is that why you brought me here?'

'I brought you here because I was intrigued.' Field's cheeks glistened in the gaslight. 'I was told you questioned Crane about the death of a young woman.'

'That's right.'

'I'm intrigued by that, too.'

This time Pyke told Field what he knew – he didn't have a good reason not to. For his part, Field listened carefully, and when Pyke had finished, he tweaked his moustache and said, 'You believe Crane is somehow responsible?'

'I don't know. Like I said, he sent some of his men to talk to Mary Edgar and this other man, Arthur Sobers. I asked him why and he refused to tell me.'

Field digested what Pyke had told him. 'And, quite naturally, you're suspicious.'

'You could say that.'

A smile spread across Field's lips. 'Then I believe our interests might happily coincide.'

'In what sense?'

'I'm told Crane has been searching for girls to pose for daguerreotypes taken from life.' Field paused. 'I assume you know what I'm referring to.'

Pyke nodded.

'Bessie Daniels was sold to Crane by a madam in the East End. I was alerted to this fact and managed to have a chat with her before she was dispatched to him. I offered to pay her to be my eyes and ears in Crane's premises, but I've not

123

heard from her for a week or so. Suffice to say, I'm starting to get anxious.'

'Why would you want eyes and ears in Crane's shop?'

'That's not your concern.' Field's smile curdled at the edges of his mouth. 'I'm reliably informed Crane owns a property in the East End.' He pressed a slip of paper into Pyke's hand. 'That's the address. I'd like you to determine whether Crane has taken her there.'

Pyke considered this for a moment. 'And if I do find her?'

'Elicit whatever information she has to impart but leave her where she is. Above all, don't divulge my interest in Crane's affairs to anyone.' Seeing the expression on Pyke's face, he added, 'For reasons I'd rather not discuss, I can't risk one of my men being seen talking to her.'

'And how will I recognise her?'

'Medium height, blonde hair, well-proportioned figure. She'd be quite attractive if it wasn't for her hare-lip.'

Pyke looked around at the blood-splattered walls. 'What if I found a way of paying you back the money I owe you?'

'I'm afraid that option is no longer available to you, Pyke.'

'And if I decided to carry on with my life and pretend we'd never had this conversation?'

'Then you would be dead within a week. It's as simple as that.' Field put his hand on Pyke's shoulder. In another context, it could almost have been a fatherly gesture. 'It wouldn't give me any real pleasure to have you killed, but I wouldn't lose any sleep over it either. You're a resourceful fellow and I need your help. Think of it that way. I'll expect to hear from you by the weekend.'

EIGHT

Pyke must have been out for longer than he'd thought because it was almost light when he emerged from Field's slaughterhouse. It wasn't a market day and the giant field was almost deserted. Even so, the air smelled of the mephitic fumes produced by the nearby glue renderers and tripe-boilers. Thankfully it hadn't rained in the night and the ground underfoot wasn't the usual slush of mud and manure. For a moment, he stopped and looked out across the expanse of open space, a thin layer of mist rising up from the ground. This was the place where, five years earlier, Emily had died in his arms; where a rifleman's bullet had torn a hole in her throat and the blood, the life, had leaked out of her. He looked over towards the exact spot where it had happened and tried to will some kind of sentiment but none would come. It didn't seem to matter *who* was to blame any more – Emily was dead and she wasn't coming back. That was the only thing that mattered. In the distance, a stray dog trotted through the mist, its head and tail just visible above the layer of white. It was strange, in a way, that he had chosen to live only a few streets from the place she'd been killed, but somehow he felt comforted by this proximity. It was also where his father had fallen under the boots of a stampeding mob and where his ex-mistress had been stabbed in the stomach while he slept next to her. That he, of all of them, should still be breathing seemed more than wrong, and even though he didn't believe in the existence of an all-powerful deity, he often wondered whether fate had somehow conspired to let him live while those he cared for, those he loved, perished.

As the sun peeked over the roofs of the build-ings, Pyke checked to make sure the charcoal etching was still in his pocket. He closed his eyes and felt the stiff breeze against his face. In his mind, a shadowy figure was hunched over Mary Edgar's body with a cloth, liberally splashing it with rum. *He worked quietly and methodically, cleaning every speck of dirt from her dark skin. When he was done, he took a scalpel and knelt down next to her face, drops of perspiration dripping on to the purple welt on her neck. The first incision sliced into the skin around her eye, the blade lodging deep into the bone. Calm nerves and a steady hand were needed. After a few minutes, he had cut out one of the eyeballs and wrapped it up in a clean handkerchief. Ten minutes later, the other eyeball had been extracted...*

Pyke felt something brush past his leg. He looked down to see the same dog he'd noticed earlier, padding towards a gas-lamp. Perhaps he was wrong that no one else cared about Mary Edgar. Maybe Pierce was just as committed to apprehending and punishing her murderer as he was. But as the sun cast its pale light over the field, it was hard not to think he was as alone in

126

his task as Mary Edgar had been in her death. In that sense, it felt as if the two of them were joined.

Pyke was waiting on the pavement in front of Godfrey's apartment when Jo and Felix appeared, a little after nine o'clock. Felix was dressed for school and Jo wore a woollen shawl over her cotton print dress. This time Felix's greeting was a little less diffident than it had been either at Hatchard's or the first time Pyke had shown up after his release from prison. And when he suggested that his son might miss school just this once, and proposed spending the morning together, the three of them, the lad sparked into life. By the time they'd walked to the zoological gardens in Regent's Park, less than ten minutes from Godfrey's apartment, Felix had listed the numerous ways in which the malefactors from the *Newgate Calendar* had been punished by the state.

'William Gregg, traitor, hanged at Tyburn, 1708; Jonathan Wild, hanged at Tyburn, 1725; Catherine Hayes, burned alive at Tyburn, 1726; Captain John Porteous, convicted of murder but killed by the mob in 1736; William Stroud, whipped through the streets of Westminster, 1752.'

Even when they had paid their admission fee, and were moving between the various exhibits, Felix appeared less interested in the animals than in regaling Pyke with the exploits of the characters he'd read about.

'Did you know that after Sawney Beane killed his victims, he quartered them, and then salted and pickled their flesh and ate it?'

They were standing in front of the giraffe

enclosure. Pyke glanced over at Jo, who gave him an exasperated shrug.

'Come on, Felix, let's walk over to the monkeys.' He indicated to Jo that they would be back presently. She smiled and went to sit on a bench in front of the giraffes.

'So why are you so interested in the stories from the *Newgate Calendar?*' he asked, when they were alone. He put a gentle hand on the lad's shoulder.

'It was Uncle Godfrey's idea. He told me that's how you'd learned to read, when you were a boy.' There was a mixture of defiance and admiration in his voice.

'He did, did he?' Pyke kept walking. 'So tell me what you like about the stories, then.'

'I don't know.'

'Do you like the descriptions of the crimes or the fact that the bad men are always punished in the end?'

'I suppose they did bad things and they deserve to be punished.'

'But?' Pyke waited.

'I don't know. Some of them I felt sorry for. Some of them I even liked. I wanted them to get away with it. But none of them ever did. They were all hanged in the end.'

Pyke looked down at Felix whose face was rigid with concentration. He was surprised at how nuanced the boy's understanding of the stories was.

'They were all put to death to prove a point.'

'What point?'

'That crime doesn't pay; that the laws of the land need to be obeyed and that the state is all-powerful.'

'What's the state?'

'The government.'

Felix considered this and then looked up at him. 'You know what you said about the things in Uncle Godfrey's book not being true? Were you lying to me?'

'Why would I lie to you?' Pyke bent over slightly, so he could see Felix's face.

'In the book, you did some very bad things.'

'That character isn't based on me. He isn't based on anyone. He's someone your Uncle Godfrey made up.'

'Oh.' Felix dug his hands into his pockets. Ahead of them, two monkeys were climbing up the side of the cage, but Felix didn't seem to be too interested in them. 'Why did you take Copper to live with you and not me?'

For a moment, Pyke tried to think how Emily might have answered this question, but nothing came to him. The truth was actually simpler than this: she would have taken Felix with her. Briefly Pyke thought about the long, rickety staircase up to his garret, and the unsavoury figures who lived in the building, and the roughness of the general area. Clearly it was no place to bring up a child but it was also true that with the purse he'd won at the card table he could have rented a house or apartment in a better area. He tried to think of some way of explaining to Felix that he still didn't feel quite ready to take on this responsibility again; that he didn't yet trust himself to be the father he knew that Felix needed and yearned for.

'The place I'm living in at the moment is too small for all of us. But soon we'll be together again. I promise.'

Felix stared at the monkeys for a while. Neither of them spoke.

'The man I fought the other night was a coward and a drunkard. He tried to harm me, and he was hurting a woman.'

'I saw the blood on your fists,' Felix said.

Pyke couldn't tell whether he thought this was a good thing or not. He changed tack. 'A woman has been killed and I'm trying to find the man or men who killed her. That's what I do. Or what I used to do.'

'And if you find the murderer, can I watch him hang at Tyburn tree?' Felix's eyes were gleaming.

'They don't hold executions at Tyburn any more.'

'Newgate, then,' Felix added, quickly.

Pyke had wanted Felix to know what he was doing but now he felt uneasy about the direction in which the conversation was heading. He suggested that they go and find Jo, and Felix seemed to think this was a good idea.

Back at the giraffe enclosure, Pyke sat down next to Jo while Felix went to inspect the animals in the cage. 'He seems happier,' she said, giving Felix a wave.

'I know I've neglected my responsibilities...' He stopped, not sure what else to say. He didn't want to make promises he couldn't keep but, equally, he was beginning to see how his absence had affected the lad.

'You don't have to justify yourself to me.' Jo turned around to face him. Her skin glowed in the morning sunlight.

'It's funny,' he said, as though the connection between his fatherly responsibilities and *Confessions* was self-evident, 'but I never wanted Godfrey to write that damned book in the first place.'

It took her a few moments to realise what he was talking about. 'Then why did you agree to help him?'

'Because I owed him; because I gave him my word that I'd help him with his research; because he helped me when no one else would. I suppose it's what families do.' As he said this, he wondered whether Felix regarded Jo as family or not.

She studied his expression for a short while. 'You have a son who adores you. I should know. You must have done something right.'

That made him smile. He wanted to reach out and touch her, to show his gratitude, but did nothing in case she misunderstood his gesture.

The entrance to the West India Dock was heavily guarded, and when Pyke tried to pass himself off first as a docker and then as a warehouseman, he was rebuffed and told to 'get lost'. When he tried a second time, about half an hour later, the foreman was summoned and Pyke had to retreat to a nearby side street to plan a new means of gaining entry. He had heard two stevedores chatting about the *Island Queen* – which was apparently still in the dock – and this snippet of information made Pyke double his efforts to find a way into the premises.

The fifteen-foot brick wall that ran around the perimeter was too high to scale, at least without drawing attention to himself, which left the river as the only remaining route. Half an hour later, Pyke found a waterman sitting in his wooden skiff near Limehouse and he told the man he'd pay him a crown if he rowed downriver as far as the entrance to the West India's export dock.

It was a cool, clear morning and the murky brown water of the Thames was dappled with rays of sunlight so that it almost looked attractive. The gnarled waterman wasn't interested in having a conversation and rowed in silence, apart from the occasional grunt, leaving Pyke to enjoy the sensation of being out on the river, the sound of choppy water slapping hard against the skiff's wooden hull. Above them, seagulls glided and swooped in the sky, their squawks punctuating the sound of the oars moving through the water.

It took the waterman the best part of an hour to row as far as the outer entrance to the docks and, once there, Pyke had to pay the man his crown, and then another half-crown, to tie up the skiff and wait for him. From there, his route into the dock was unimpeded, and he found the *Island Queen* without any difficulty. A gang of stevedores was busy transferring a collection of wooden crates stacked up on the quayside down into the ship's belly. This was how the system worked, Pyke thought as he watched them: you plundered another country's resources, shipped whatever you could lay your hands on – coffee, sugar, rum, teak – back to the mother country and then sent those same ships back to the colonies packed with overpriced goods for the people there to buy.

One of the stevedores pointed out the ship's captain, McQuillan, and when Pyke met him on

132

deck, he was inspecting the rigging on the port side of the vessel.

'They told me you were the captain of this ship.'

'Aye, they told you right.' McQuillan put his hands up to his eyes to protect them from the sun. He was a disconcertingly short man with a wobbling chin that disappeared into the folds of fat under his neck.

'Belfast,' Pyke said.

'Sorry?'

'You're originally from Belfast, aren't you?'

'So I am.' McQuillan stopped what he was doing and looked at Pyke. 'How in God's name did ye know that?'

'I was there about ten years ago. It's not a brogue you can easily forget.'

'People here in London often mistake me for a Scotsman. No one's ever guessed I'm from Belfast.'

'Am I right in thinking you docked here on about the twenty-third of last month?'

'The twenty-fourth.' McQuillan glanced up at the sky. 'And if this breeze holds, we'll be sailing tomorrow or the day after.'

'Back to the West Indies?'

'Jamaica.' Lines appeared on his forehead. 'Mind if I ask why you're so interested in my ship?'

'I'm interested in one or possibly two passengers you brought with you from Jamaica. Mary Edgar and Arthur Sobers.' He noted the lines in the captain's forehead deepen. 'I can tell from your reaction you know who I'm talking about.'

'I'm sorry?' McQuillan said, squinting.

'Mary Edgar and Arthur Sobers. She's a

133

mulatto, he's black.'

'Am I supposed to know them?'

'I suspect you've been warned about speaking about them.' When McQuillan didn't say anything, Pyke added, 'Was it Rowbottom who approached you, by any chance? You see, he's already told me everything he knows so I don't think he'd mind if you talked to me.'

'And why would he do that?' McQuillan asked cautiously.

'Because I held a knife to his throat and told him that unless he did, I'd slit it.' It was gamble, telling him this, but Pyke didn't think that a seafaring man like McQuillan would have much time for Rowbottom.

For a while, McQuillan stared at him, as if trying to make sense of what he'd said, but then, all of a sudden, he broke into a loud laugh. 'I'd like to have seen that, surely I would.' Then he seemed to remember his instructions and his eyes glazed over. 'So what is it you want to know?'

'Did Rowbottom ever tell you why you weren't supposed to talk to anyone about Mary Edgar or Arthur Sobers?'

The captain shook his head.

'Mary Edgar's dead. She was murdered, strangled. Her body was found a few days ago near the Ratcliff Highway.'

From his reaction, Pyke could tell this was news to McQuillan. It was as though the wind had been kicked from his stomach.

'Aye, she came with us from Falmouth,' he said eventually. 'Her and the other fellow, Sobers.'

'Why? I mean, what reason did they have for

134

wanting to come to London?'

McQuillan shrugged. 'She didn't say and I didn't ask her.' He waited for a moment and added, 'I was told by an attorney in Falmouth, Michael Pemberton, to look after her and keep my crew away from her. I got the impression from him that she was spoken for, if you know what I mean.'

'But not by Pemberton?'

McQuillan just shrugged. 'I don't know.'

'And Sobers?'

'What about him?'

'How well did they seem to know each other?'

McQuillan considered this. 'They knew one another, that's for sure, but I wouldn't say they were lovers. They didn't share a cabin. In spite of his size, he seemed in awe of her. He deferred to her, rather than the other way around.'

'What else can you tell me?'

The captain sighed. 'Not a great deal. Like I said, they didn't reveal too much. I didn't ask. I was glad to have him onboard, though. He was strong and willing to work.'

'And her?'

McQuillan didn't answer him immediately. 'Mind if I speak bluntly?'

'Be my guest.'

'To be honest, I couldn't work her out. Most of the time, she'd keep herself to herself. No trouble at all. But with a little rum in her, she was a different person.'

'What kind of person?'

'Devious, I'd say. Reckoned she had special powers.' He paused. 'There's an old slave religion...'

'Obeah,' Pyke said, interrupting.

'You've heard of it?' McQuillan seemed surprised.

'It's a kind of witchcraft.'

The captain nodded. 'She reckoned she could commune with spirits. I didn't believe her for a second but this fellow, Sobers, he was terrified of her.' He licked his lips. 'I didn't mind it, just the two of them chanting away. But then some of the crew started to consult her, about old lovers they wanted her to curse, that kind of thing, so I had to put my foot down.'

'And how did she respond?'

'She'd just mimic my voice and laugh in my face. She was a good mimic, I'll say that for her.' McQuillan waited for a moment. 'She was educated, all right, and a lot of the time she was perfectly fine. But she was a tough one, that's for sure. I'd say she knew what she wanted and she knew how to get it, too.'

'Was there anyone on the ship apart from Sobers she became friendly with?' If one of the crew had developed an unhealthy interest in her, it was possible they might have followed her into the city.

McQuillan must have sensed Pyke's line of thinking. 'Look,' he said, quickly, 'I know what you're thinking and the answer's no. Sobers wouldn't let any of the crew near her and I told my lads if I caught any of 'em within ten feet of her, they'd be flogged and thrown into the brig for the rest of the journey.'

'Ten weeks at sea, perhaps longer, a beautiful woman on the ship. You can see how it might affect someone.' Pyke waited. 'For all I know, perhaps even you might have been tempted.'

McQuillan gave him a wary stare. 'Perhaps you're misunderstanding me. She might've liked the attention but she was educated, and in spite of her colour, she looked down on us, like we weren't good enough for her. Any of the men tried to do anything more 'n look at her, she would've come screaming to me in a second.'

'And perhaps you let her cry on your shoulder?' Pyke said it but somehow he couldn't see it.

McQuillan just laughed. 'Have you seen the *state* of me? You think she'd have given me a second look?' But this time, there was something in his eyes that made Pyke think otherwise.

Still, he nodded, deciding to let it go for the time being. 'Did she say anything about her plans when she got to London?'

'Not that I can recall.'

'But she must have said something. Ten weeks at sea is a long time.'

'She *did* ask a lot of questions about London; whether it was as cold and dangerous as she'd been told,' McQuillan said, frowning. 'I got the impression she was planning to settle here.'

'I understand,' Pyke said, frustrated. 'But I suppose what I'm asking is whether she had any specific questions about particular parts of the city.'

McQuillan scratched his chin. 'Not exactly, but she did mention Mayfair a few times, wanted to know what kind of a place it was.'

Mayfair? Why had she asked about Mayfair and then taken a room on the Ratcliff Highway?

'Did she say why she was interested in Mayfair or whether she knew anyone who lived there?'

'I don't know.' McQuillan thought about it for a moment. 'But what I do remember was what happened when we docked. There was a carriage waiting for her by the quayside. I thought she'd be pleased that someone had come to meet her but this fellow and her had a right to-do in front of the carriage. She didn't want to go with him and told him that in so many words. She had a tongue on her, that's for sure. But he was insistent and in the end she agreed to go with him.'

'Can you describe him?'

'The fellow?'

Pyke nodded.

'About your height and build, your hair colour too except slightly greyer. Attractive, I suppose. Well dressed, olive skin. Slightly full of himself, I'd say.'

Pyke felt a spike of excitement rip through his stomach. McQuillan had just described Alefounder.

'Did you hear her call him by name? William perhaps?'

'No, afraid not,' McQuillan said.

'But you're certain about the description?' It would be something to throw back in the trader's face.

One of the crew appeared on deck and McQuillan waved him over. They had a brief conversation, hushed so Pyke couldn't hear them, and then the young man ambled off towards the gangway. McQuillan joined Pyke and apologised for the interruption. 'Now, where were we?'

'William Alefounder? Does the name ring a bell?'

The captain rubbed his eyes. 'No, I'm sorry.'

'What did Sobers do while all this was happening on the quayside?'

'That's the thing. He didn't budge. The whole trip, he was protective of her. Some of the men got angry about it. Called him an uppity nigger and threatened to cut him. Then she gets into this big argument in front of everyone and he doesn't lift a finger to help her.'

'And when she went off in this carriage, what did he do?'

'Took his case, said goodbye and wandered down the gangplank like nothing had happened.'

'Anything else you can remember about them? However unimportant it might seem?'

McQuillan waited for a moment. 'I did overhear them mention the word kill-devil on a few occasions. I asked her about it once. She told me it was the name folk give to rum.'

'It is, isn't it?'

The captain just shrugged. 'I got the sense it was something more. Like it was code for something.'

Pyke heard something in the distance and turned around. McQuillan looked, too, and said, 'Seems you brought out a welcoming party.'

There was a pack of men, led by Rowbottom and the foreman, heading in the direction of the ship. Pyke thanked the captain for his help, but by the time he'd crossed the deck and negotiated his passage back to the quayside, they were nearly upon him. Looking around, Pyke picked up a piece of wood and turned to face his pursuers. Up close he saw that Rowbottom's neck was bandaged where he'd pressed his knife into the flesh. There were ten men including Rowbottom and the foreman. None was armed, as far as he could tell, but Pyke didn't doubt that if things didn't go their way, there would fifty or a hundred men ready to step into the breach. No one liked to see blood spilled as much as a docker. He swung the piece of wood at one of the men and looked around for a possible escape route. None was forthcoming. Behind him was the ship and the water. The foreman grinned, as a hunter might do, snaring a wild beast. He took out a cudgel and wiped his mouth with his hand. 'The cull here's due a terrible beating.' Tapping the cudgel against his open palm, he took a step forward; the others, except for Rowbottom, did likewise. They had almost surrounded him. Pyke looked behind him and saw McQuillan and some of the crew watching proceedings from the ship's deck. They weren't hostile but he knew he couldn't count on their support. If it came down to it, they would be as quick to fight him as the dockers. He swung the piece of wood and forced the foreman back a step or two.

'This is private property,' Rowbottom said, 'and you're trespassing. We're within our rights to defend ourselves as we see fit.' Surrounded by his men, he was no longer the terrified clerk Pyke had encountered in his office.

Pyke did the only thing he could and retreated back up the gangplank to the deck of the *Island Queen*. Two men tried to follow him but he pulled the plank from under their feet and watched as they fell into the water. Rather than confront the remaining eight, Pyke ran along the length of the deck and clambered down the rigging back on to the quayside. The rest of the dockers were ten, maybe fifteen yards behind him; Pyke could hear them panting; he could hear their shouts. Other dockers heard the shouts and stopped what they were doing. Some tried to block his path. Pyke ran around the quayside as far as it took him and ducked into one of the warehouses. He had to push through a group of stevedores, one of whom tried to rough him up, but Pyke pushed the man backwards into the others.

It was a rum warehouse; row upon row of rum casks stacked on shelves that extended right up to the roof. Clambering up to one of the giant barrels, he waited until the stevedores had picked themselves up, and some of his original pursuers had entered the warehouse, before rolling the barrel on to its side and letting it fall to the ground to crush the men unlucky enough to be beneath it. The barrel cracked against the stone floor, a sweet, pungent smell filling the air. Pyke did likewise to the barrel next to it and then took out a box of matches, lit one and let it fall on to the liquid. The reddish flames raced across the floor, preventing any of the men from following him. Seizing the chance to put some distance between himself and his pursuers, Pyke retreated farther into the warehouse, paying no attention to the fast-spreading fire, and found a window that he was able to crawl through at the back of the room. From there, he clambered down on to the quayside again, where he was spotted by the foreman and a couple of his men. They chased him towards the high brick wall that surrounded the entire dock area.

The first man came at Pyke with just his fists. Pyke ducked inside the first punch and swayed back to avoid the second. Then he landed two of his own, a left-right combination to the man's head, which put him down. Another man came at him but Pyke surprised him with a sharp kick to his shins; the man's head fell and Pyke brought his knee up into his face. Then it was just the foreman and his cudgel. Others would arrive soon if Pyke didn't finish this quickly. The foreman lashed at him with the cudgel, missing his cheek by a whisker, but Pyke caught him by the wrist, twisted it and forced the cudgel from his grasp. The blunt implement fell into Pyke's outstretched hand and in the same movement he smashed it against the foreman's mouth and felt the man's jaw dissolve. He fell to the ground holding his mouth, blood rushing down his chin.

To no great surprise, Pyke discovered that the waterman had long since abandoned his post. The dockers had regrouped and Rowbottom was pointing them in Pyke's direction. He couldn't risk fighting his way through to the main entrance and he didn't doubt that if the injured foreman got hold of him now, the man would kill him. He stared out at the vast expanse of river. A few seconds later, as he hit the cold, dirty water, feet first, the air rushed from his lungs and he felt himself sink under the surface.

Struggling to remain afloat, Pyke wriggled out of his coat and trod water for long enough to remove his boots. Above him, on the wharf, the men had arrived and were peering over the edge, but Pyke had already swum thirty yards out into the Thames and had drifted another hundred with the current. Keeping his mouth closed, because he didn't want to swallow the foul-smelling water, he put his head down and kicked with his legs, wondering whether he had enough strength left to make it to the other side.

NINE

At five o'clock that afternoon, Pyke presented himself to one of the uniformed clerks inside the 'A' Division building in Whitehall and was led immediately up the stone steps to an airy, high-ceilinged room on the first floor where Fitzroy Tilling, Sir Richard Mayne, Benedict Pierce and, as it turned out, William Alefounder were all waiting for him.

They couldn't have heard about the fire at the West India Dock already. Anyway, his landlady had told him that the note from Tilling, summoning him to this meeting, had been delivered to his garret some time that morning.

They barely looked up as he crossed the room to the only available chair, as though his presence were an irritation that had to be tolerated. Tilling ignored Pyke entirely. Pierce sat between Tilling and Alefounder with his arms folded. All of them were facing Mayne, the commissioner, their chairs arranged in a semicircle around his desk, as if they needed to be reminded who was in charge.

'Gentlemen, perhaps we could make a start,' Mayne said, glancing down at his watch and then in Pyke's direction for the first time. 'I believe we all know each other so I'll dispense with the formalities.' He turned to Pyke. 'I thank you for coming, sir, and I shouldn't need to add that you've been invited as a courtesy, a goodwill gesture, in the hope that we can resolve whatever differences exist between us and put an end to all the nonsense.'

Mayne was a suave, distinguished man in his middle forties, with a full head of dark hair, a pair of mutton-chop sideburns, a lantern jaw, and a patrician air that suggested he didn't suffer fools gladly.

'I don't want anything from you.' Pyke cast a quick glance at Tilling. 'I just want to be left alone.'

'Left alone to peddle these ridiculous stories in that rag of a newspaper?' Mayne shot a stern look at Tilling. 'Look, Fitzroy made a mistake contracting your services but at the time our resources were being pulled in a different direction. That said, having discussed you at length with Sir Robert Peel earlier today, I can understand why Fitzroy turned to you. To my surprise, Sir Robert made a compelling case in your defence. So now I want to put it all behind us and press ahead with the important business of finding out who killed this woman. And I want to reassure you that we are more than able to conduct the investigation ourselves.'

For now it was all smiles and kind words, but if

Pyke persisted in his current course of action, he was sure the smiles would disappear.

'I'm listening.'

'Splendid,' Mayne said, directing his remarks at Tilling. 'You see? We've made progress already.' When Tilling didn't answer, Mayne continued, 'I'm sorry to say an unfortunate incident was reported to me yesterday. It seems you made some rather wild, and entirely unfounded, accusations against Mr Alefounder and I want to put an end to that as well.'

'And that's why you've summoned Alefounder to your office, to interrogate him?'

'*Mr* Alefounder came of his own accord, as soon as he'd learned from you that a crime had been committed, but no one will be *interrogating* him, as you so colourfully put it.'

'So you want to reassure me about Alefounder's good character...'

'Indeed,' Mayne said carefully, trying to work out whether Pyke was mocking him. 'And warn you about the very severe consequences, should you continue to pester him or, for that matter, besmirch his good name in the press.'

'If he's as innocent as you claim he is, what reason would I have for trying to besmirch his name?'

Mayne looked at Alefounder and offered a reassuring smile. 'I have it on impeccable authority that Mr Alefounder's character is second to none.'

'Then perhaps you could tell me why he knowingly lied to me yesterday in his office in front of a room full of witnesses?'

That took the wind out of the commissioner's sails. 'Eh?' It was as though he hadn't actually

145

heard what Pyke had just said.

'Yesterday he told me he'd never set eyes on Mary Edgar. But then I found out that he went in person to meet her ship when it arrived at the West India Dock on the twenty-fourth of April. He even argued with her on the quayside in front of the whole crew.'

Mayne's stare was opaque. He wetted his lips and looked across at William Alefounder. 'This man isn't a suspect. What he may or may not have told you yesterday has no bearing on the murder investigation.'

This time Pyke addressed Alefounder directly. 'You knew Mary Edgar well enough to meet her ship and argue with her in public. That makes you a suspect, irrespective of whether you lied to me or not.'

But it was Mayne who answered. 'I want to make something quite clear, Pyke. We have questioned Mr Alefounder at length about his involvement in this matter and we are perfectly happy to rule him out as a suspect. That is all you need to know.'

'Where did you go after you left the docks?' Pyke said to Alefounder, ignoring Mayne's warning. He knew he was pushing his luck but he simply didn't care.

'I've said all I'm going to say to these gentlemen,' Alefounder said, pointing at Pierce and Mayne. He didn't seem to be including Tilling in this coterie, and Pyke wondered what this said about Tilling's status as a result of the piece in the *Examiner*.

'One way or another I'll find out why you lied to me, Alefounder.'

'Didn't I make myself clear?' Mayne interrupted. 'This man doesn't have to answer or justify himself in any way to you; I'll ask you to refrain from making threatening remarks as well.'

'It stinks that you're absolving him of any responsibility in this matter just because he's wealthy and has connections.'

'That's it,' Mayne said, looking at Tilling. 'Get this man out of here and escort him from the building.'

Tilling gave Mayne a look that said: *I told you so*. Alefounder said nothing and wiped his forehead with a handkerchief.

Outside, in the corridor, Pyke felt a tug on his arm, and turned around. Fitzroy Tilling's face was as tight as a drum. 'Bravo, Pyke, I thought you handled yourself with enormous tact.'

'Alefounder lied and he's been given a pat on the back. If he was poor or a valet, he'd be rotting in prison by now.'

'I can't make sense of you. You've spent most of your life cheating and swindling to fatten your own purse and yet you despise people who have money.'

'I don't hate people with money. But when I see a man like Alefounder dismiss the murder of a poor, black woman as though it doesn't even merit his consideration, I want to drive a stake through his heart.'

'And that's normal? God, Pyke, can't you see how much your anger blinds you to the truth?'

'What's that supposed to mean? Alefounder escapes censure or interrogation just because of who he knows.'

'Do you think you're the only one who cares about Mary Edgar?' The blood had risen in Tilling's face.

'Forgive me if I don't think Mayne and the others took her death quite as seriously as they did that of a murdered aristocrat.'

'By others you mean me?'

'What do you want me to say? Bedford is murdered. Within hours of his corpse being discovered, fifty men have been assigned to find his killer.'

'You still don't understand, do you?'

'Understand what?'

'I could have assigned twenty men to investigate Mary Edgar's murder but I thought of you because I could see you needed help.' Tilling shook his head. 'I even arranged for your early release from prison, and how do you go about repaying me?'

'But that's exactly my point. It wouldn't have happened if she'd been rich and white. You wouldn't have been allowed.'

'I made a decision to employ you without consulting my superiors. Now that decision has come back to bite me. Perhaps it *was* my fault, but now they're baying for your scalp. I can't help that.'

'So I should roll over and die like a whipped dog?'

Tilling turned to walk away but hesitated at the last moment. 'I used to think I knew you; that I knew who you were and what you stood for. And in spite of some of the things you did I respected you, too. Now I look at you and all I can see is a man on the verge of drowning. I want to help, but

I don't know how. I throw you a line and you throw it straight back in my face.'

It was Tilling's pity more than his anger which cut the deepest.

'It wasn't your gift to give. If it was, how could Mayne snatch it away from me so easily?'

Tilling shook his head. 'This isn't about Mary Edgar or wanting to find whoever killed her. You just want to make us look bad.'

'Can't you simply accept I might want to do something ... *good?*' He couldn't find a better word and stared at Tilling, not knowing what else to say.

'When it comes down to it, Pyke, you're a selfish creature. You are now and you always have been. If you were honest about it, I might be able to forgive you. But you're doing what you've always done: constructing a spurious morality to fit the circumstances you find yourself in.'

Pyke could feel his pent-up anger burning the tips of his ears. Tilling was already walking away from him along the corridor, his heels clipping in a tight-lipped fury. Then Pyke was alone in an unfamiliar building, and more than anything he wanted to run to the nearest apothecary and lose himself in a tincture of syrupy laudanum.

'I'm worried about him, Pyke. I think you should be, too.' Godfrey stood at the window of his apartment. It was the following afternoon and Felix was talking with an older, scruffily dressed boy below them on the street.

'Then you shouldn't encourage him to read things he's not ready for.' Pyke turned to face his

149

uncle. 'I never wanted you to write that damned book in the first place. I certainly never expected that my own son would read it.'

Godfrey reddened slightly. 'I'm not his father, Pyke. It's not my responsibility to tell him what he should and shouldn't be reading.'

Pyke bowed his head. 'I'm sorry. You're right. I shouldn't have said that.'

'Apology accepted.' Godfrey paused. 'Did you know that he was caught playing truant from school today?'

'That's probably my fault. I ambushed him and Jo yesterday morning on their way to school and persuaded them to accompany me to the zoological gardens.'

Pyke had joined his uncle at the window. He watched his son with a mixture of pride and consternation, amazed at how tall he had grown and how different he looked. Older, almost a man.

'For a while he hardly left his room. Now he's taken to spending more and more time outdoors.'

Pyke studied the lad Felix was talking to. It looked as though they were deep in conversation. 'Do you know who the older boy is?'

Godfrey pushed his spectacles up his nose and frowned. 'Never seen him before.'

'I know you mean well,' Pyke said, 'and I don't mind the lad poring over the *Newgate Calendar*, but could you please make sure that he doesn't read another word of *Confessions?*'

'Point taken, dear boy.' Godfrey cleared his throat. 'But if you were to find somewhere large enough for you, Jo and Felix to live, you wouldn't have to worry about the lad finding something

150

morally degrading here in my apartment.'

Pyke had no answer to that, so he turned and went outside. As he walked down the steps, Felix looked at him. The older boy did, too, and then ambled across the street in the direction of Camden Place.

'Is he a friend?'

Felix stared down at his boots. 'I just met him.'

'What were you talking about?'

'Just things.'

Pyke looked at the older boy, who'd turned around and was grinning. 'I don't want you to talk to him again.'

'He admired my coat.'

'I said I don't want you to see him again. Is that understood?'

Felix looked up at him defiantly. 'I'm not a child any more.'

'I know.' Pyke waited. 'But child or not, you shouldn't play truant from school.'

'They don't teach us anything worth learning, so why should I go?'

'Because I say so.' It was an inadequate response, but Pyke couldn't think of a better one.

Felix dug his hands into his pockets. 'Have you found us a place to live yet?'

'Is that what you really want?'

Pyke hadn't wanted to ask this question for fear that Felix might, when it came down to it, prefer to remain at Godfrey's. As it happened, Felix just shrugged and mumbled that of course it was what he wanted.

'I'm looking for somewhere. Really I am. But you have to be patient.' Pyke hesitated, wondering whether to say what was on his mind. 'In the meantime I'm trying to do something that will make you proud of me.'

That got Felix's attention. 'Why do you want *me* to be proud of *you?*'The idea seemed difficult for him to grasp.

'For one thing, I don't want you to think of me as that character in Godfrey's book.'

A brief silence passed between them. Felix scrunched up his face. 'That person stole from time to time and he even killed a few people.'

'Like I said, he's a made-up character.'

'But that man in the bookshop accused you of killing the other man's father.' Felix's face was hot with fear and indignation.

'There are some things you're not old enough to understand.' Pyke looked up and saw that Jo was in the front window, watching them.

'So it is true, then.' Felix's eyes were bulging. 'He said you stabbed the other man's father in the neck and threw him out of a window.'

Pyke could feel the heat under his collar. What was he supposed to say? What *could* he say? 'That man was a liar and a drunkard. You shouldn't believe him over your own father.'

'So why did you agree to fight him in a duel?'

Flummoxed, Pyke tried to think of different ways to answer Felix's question. He tried to think how Emily might have answered it but she had known Felix only as a young boy; now he was maturing rapidly. She would have been so proud of him, Pyke decided. But she still wouldn't have known how to answer all his questions.

In the end, Pyke told Felix it was nearly dinner

time and made him promise not to miss any more school. Reluctantly Felix agreed and followed Pyke up the steps to the apartment and then went on to his bedroom.

'What do you know about Jemmy Crane?' Pyke asked Godfrey, once he was sure they were alone.

'Crane?' Godfrey's face was suddenly creased with worry.

'He said he knew you.'

'We used to know some of the same people back in the old days. Why do you ask?'

Briefly Pyke told his uncle about the murder investigation and his suspicions regarding Crane, and also about Field's interest in Crane.

'He's a nasty one, that's for sure. Ruthless, too. He used to be an associate of Dugdale's back in the twenties. The market for free-thinking tracts on religion and politics died away and men like Crane and Dugdale turned to pornography. Dugdale clung on to his radical beliefs but Crane never had any such beliefs in the first place.'

'You haven't come across him for a while, then?'

'Not for years. But I don't doubt he's the same as ever. A man like that wouldn't think twice about slitting your throat if there was a profit in it.' Godfrey hesitated. 'But then again, you could say the same about Field.'

'Field once poured lamp oil down another man's throat and lit it with a match. He read the newspaper while the man choked to death. I'm sure you've heard the stories.'

'A rock and a hard place.'

Godfrey considered what Pyke had just said. 'Of course, you could just walk away from everything. Spend some time with your son.'

Pyke let this last remark pass without an answer.

As he waited for a hackney carriage, Jo emerged from the apartment and joined him on the pavement. 'I just wanted to say how much I enjoyed our trip to the zoological gardens.' She shifted awkwardly from foot to foot.

'Except it seems I've encouraged Felix to play truant from school.'

Her brow creased with worry. 'I told Felix you'd be angry when you heard about it.' She took off her bonnet and scratched the top of her head. It gave Pyke the chance to admire the colour of her hair. 'I hope I didn't assume too much.'

'Not at all,' he said, smiling. 'Use me as much as you want to. If it helps, that is.'

Jo fiddled nervously with her hair. 'Actually the reason I came out to speak with you is that Godfrey will be dining out on Wednesday...' She paused, perhaps flustered at the way this had come out. 'What I meant was, Felix wanted to help cook a meal for you, and he, or rather *we*, wondered if you might come here to dine that evening.'

Pyke stared into her blue eyes and what felt like the briefest spark of attraction passed between them. 'I'd be delighted to,' he said, even before he'd had time to think about it.

'Around seven?'

He nodded. 'Until the day after tomorrow, then.'

Pyke watched her as she gathered up her skirt and climbed the steps to Godfrey's apartment. As he did so, he wondered whether the idea for dinner had been hers all along.

TEN

Early the next morning, when the air was still cool, it took Pyke fifteen minutes to walk from the Whitechapel Road to the row of decrepit houses that Field had told him about – across from a scrubby field and a lake of stagnant water. The dwelling in question was a ramshackle cottage standing on its own at the far end of the lane. Pyke circled the property from a distance, trying to determine whether it was occupied, then crept up to each window, listening for voices or the sound of footsteps. From what he could tell, there were two or perhaps three men occupying a room at the back of the cottage – he could hear them talking. Making as little sound as possible, he tried the front door, Unsurprisingly it was locked and, using the jemmy and picklocks he'd brought with him, it took him the best part of five minutes to gain access to the front hallway. Once inside, he stood and listened, and when he was sure no one had heard him, he shuffled up the creaking staircase and tried the rooms immediately adjoining the landing. Both were unoccupied so he moved along the passageway. He was sweating slightly, and could feel his heart thumping against his ribcage. It was true that stumbling upon intruders was a terrifying experience for those whose houses were being invaded, but carrying out a burglary was just as unnerving.

The door at the far end of the passageway was unlocked, and when he opened it, Pyke had to pause and blink, to adjust to the sudden excess of light. Part of the roof was missing; initially he thought that the wind must have been responsible, but later he realised that the hole had been cut deliberately, to allow light to flood into the room. But Pyke's gaze was drawn not to the hole in the roof but to the figure draped over a sofa in the middle of the room and the camera obscura resting on a wooden stool in front of her. She was perfectly naked. He stood there for a few moments but she neither moved nor reacted to his intrusion. It wasn't until he crossed the room and shook her that he realised she was full of laudanum. Bessie Daniels, for it was undoubtedly her, stirred and looked at him through heavy-lidded eyes; when she tried to speak through her hare-lip, her words were slurred to the point of incoherence. Pyke found a sheet and threw it over her, then inspected the camera.

He had read about the process, invented by a Frenchman, Louis Daguerre, but this was the first time he had actually seen up close how it worked. Light – as much as possible, hence the cutting away of the roof – flooded through the camera lens and the resulting image was captured on a copperplate which had been exposed to an iodine solution, forming a light-sensitive silver iodide. The plate would then be developed over heated mercury, which would amalgamate with the silver, and finally the image would be fixed in a solution of salt water. The exposure took fifteen minutes, during which time the subject had to remain still; something that perhaps explained why Bessie had been drugged.

'Bessie.' Pyke shook her arm and in the process noticed an amethyst ring on one of her fingers, a serpent motif carved into the bright purple stone.

She stirred again and gave him a bewildered stare. 'Eh?'

'Harold Field sent me.' He waited for a reaction.

She looked at him, confused. Pyke could smell gin and laudanum on her breath. For a while, he wasn't sure she'd understood what he'd said, but then she fell back on to the sofa and giggled. 'Tell him...'

Pyke waited. 'Tell him what?'

More giggling. Down below he could hear voices. Footsteps, too.

'Tell him what, Bessie?'

'Morel-Roux.'

That made him pay attention. 'The valet? What's he got to do with it?'

But she wouldn't answer him.

Pyke decided he could leave her where she was – and come back and talk to her later, when she was sober – or he could take her with him. He opted for the latter. Scooping Bessie up in his arms, he staggered to the door and heaved her up over his shoulders. She was as limp as a corpse. At the top of the staircase, he steadied himself and gripped the banister. He had made it halfway down when a door opened below him and he heard someone say, 'Is it time?' There was no-where to run. Pyke tried to take the final few steps two at a time but they were on to him before he'd reached the bottom, two of them, one armed with a pistol.

'Put her down slowly and raise your hands.' One of the men, with a hatchet face, called out to Crane. Pyke did as he was told. Bessie Daniels giggled as Pyke laid her down on the floor.

Crane appeared in the hallway. 'Give me one good reason why I shouldn't tell Sykes to pull the trigger and blow a hole the size of my fist in your chest.'

Pyke took a moment to run through his options. He could always try to bolt for the door but Sykes would surely fire the pistol and, at such close range, he would probably hit his target.

'Make your choice, sir. Tell me why you came here or prepare to meet your maker.' Crane smoothed back his hair and wiped his hands on his trousers.

Pyke stared down at Bessie's comatose body. 'I was asked to find this particular woman.'

Crane seemed amused by this notion. 'By?'

Pyke waited, deciding that only the truth would do. 'Harold Field.' It was a huge risk, giving up Field's name, but Pyke knew that most people were afraid of him and mentioning Field might make Crane more likely to talk.

As expected Crane's whole demeanour changed. His shoulders tightened and his forehead creased with worry. 'What does *Field* want with her?'

'I don't know. I didn't ask. I owed Field money. This was how he demanded I repay my debt.'

They stared at one another for a few moments. Less sure of himself, Crane told Sykes and the other man to leave them alone – but also to remain close by in case Pyke tried to make a dash for it.

'Are you telling me you have nothing invested in this little action?' Crane said, once they were alone.

'That's right.'

'And that it has nothing to do with the matter you came to talk to me about the other day?'

'Field heard I'd been to your shop and decided I was the right man for this job.' Pyke hesitated. 'He didn't want to send one of his men in case you recognised them. If he finds out that I've told you this, he'll kill me, no question. He doesn't want you to know he's interested in your business.'

Crane's stare was like a lizard's. 'And why do you think he is interested in my business?' He glanced down at Bessie Daniels' semi-conscious form.

'I don't know. He wouldn't tell me. He just ordered me to bring her back to him.'

'You don't know, eh?' Crane ran his teeth over his bottom lip, eyes narrowing to slits. 'But you could find out, couldn't you?'

'Perhaps.'

That made Crane smile. 'Well?'

'Are you suggesting I switch horses halfway through the race?'

'I could be.'

'What would be in it for me?'

That seemed to be what Crane expected, and wanted, him to say. He grinned. 'I like a man who knows how to think for himself.'

A silence passed between them. 'I'll tell you what,' Pyke said. 'If I find out why Harold Field is interested in this woman, you can tell me why you went to see Mary Edgar and Arthur Sobers at Thrale's lodging house.'

'Back to that, eh?'

'That's what I'm offering. Take it or leave it.'

'I'm the one with the pistol and *you're* trying to make a deal?' Smiling, Crane shook his head, as though both irritated and impressed by Pyke's bravado.

Pyke looked into his flinty eyes. 'Do we have an agreement?'

'How will I know you're telling me the truth, not just making up any old story?'

'I suspect you know exactly why Field might be interested in your affairs. But what you don't know is how much or little *he* knows – and you need to know because Field is not a man to be taken lightly.' He hesitated. 'And if that's the case, you'll know if I'm telling the truth, won't you?'

This time Crane's smile appeared genuine. 'You're really quite remarkable. A few moments ago I was ready to kill you.'

But Pyke wasn't quite ready to shake the man's hand. 'We still haven't decided what to do about her.' They both looked down at Bessie.

'She stays with me.'

Pyke shook his head. 'I want to take her with me.'

'And hand her on a plate to Field, pay off your debt, just like that?'

'I don't doubt you've already had your money's worth from her.'

Crane folded his arms. 'She stays here for the rest of the day. Tomorrow I will pay her what I owe her and let her go home. How does that sound for a compromise?'

Pyke looked into Crane's face for signs he

might be lying. 'I have your word on that?'

'You have my word.'

As they shook hands, Crane smiled slightly, an act that later seemed both mocking and sincere.

Harold Field was playing whist in an ostentatious private room adjoining a gin palace he owned in Holborn; the thick red carpet, red velvet curtains, striped flock wallpaper and the gilt-panelled ceiling put Pyke in mind of a Roman bordello, the kind of place where Caligula might have abused little boys while being fed grapes by half-naked prostitutes. Across the table from him, Field's partner, a fat, bald, pig-like man whose face was slavered in his own sweat, was deliberating on which card to put down. On either side, their opponents shielded their hands and waited for the fat man to make his move. They swapped a brief look but their expressions remained inscrutable. Field placed his hand face down on the table and whispered something into the ear of one of his mob. Pyke couldn't tell whether Field had noticed him or not as he'd made no effort to acknowledge his presence. From the gin palace, Pyke could hear the shouts of drunken revellers over the wailing of a badly tuned fiddle. On the table itself was a pot that looked to be in excess of a hundred pounds, if the growing pile of coins were all sovereigns, as they appeared to be. Briefly Pyke entertained the thought of someone walking in and trying to steal the pot at gunpoint, and of Field's reaction, and he wondered whether there was anyone in London brave or stupid enough to attempt such an exploit. His attention was brought back to the game by Field's partner, who had tentatively laid down the queen of hearts, to a murmur of disapproval from Field; the fat man's mistake in playing the wrong card was obvious to everyone in the room. One of the opponents picked up the card and laid down his hand, taking care not to appear too triumphant. Both players eyed the pot but neither dared touch it. Field looked at the one who'd laid down his hand and whispered, 'Go ahead. Take it,' then stood up and stretched his legs. In the chair opposite him, the fat man's face was flushed and his eyes darted wildly around the room. He seemed desperate to explain himself, yet too afraid to speak.

'Take it.'

Field walked across to the mantelpiece, where one of the candles had just burned out; and, taking care not to scald himself he picked the stub out of the brass candlestick, tossed it to the floor, and barked at one of the servers to fetch a replacement.

No one in the room spoke.

One of the players gathered in the pile of coins and Field nodded, as though gratified by this development. The server returned with a candle but Field insisted that she give it to him, rather than placing it in the candlestick herself. Field then took the tall brass object in one hand, the candle in the other, and wandered back to the table. Carefully he placed the candle down on the card table and smoothed his ginger hair. The fat man gave him a pleading look and was about to say something but Field put a finger to his mouth and shook his head. The fat man held his silence and watched as Field circumnavigated the table, still carrying the brass candlestick.

He put it down on the table and retrieved his partner's hand.

'If you'd actually been concentrating and played this card,' Field said, holding up the seven of diamonds, 'then we wouldn't be having this conversation.' He shook his head. 'It's funny, isn't it, how something apparently quite trivial can have grave consequences.' The fat man nodded dumbly, unable to bring himself to meet Field's gaze.

Without saying another word, Field retrieved the brass candlestick and, in the blink of an eye, he swung the heavy end through the air and slammed it against the side of the man's head, which seemed almost to disintegrate under the force of the blow. Holding the instrument with both hands now, Field raised it above his head and brought it down against the top of the fat man's already shattered skull. The man slumped forward on to the table, and was quickly surrounded by a pool of his own blood.

Field wandered over to the mantelpiece and put the candlestick back where he'd found it. 'You can all go now,' he said in barely more than a whisper.

The room cleared almost immediately. Field's opponents opted to leave their winnings on the table.

Only Pyke and another man remained. He was tall and boyish with a smooth complexion and dimples on his cheeks but he was staring at the blood spilling from the fat man's head with curiosity rather than revulsion. Field looked over at Pyke, acknowledging his presence for the first time.

'I'll need you to clear this mess up,' Field said to his younger assistant. Then, turning to Pyke, he added, 'I'd like to introduce you to Matthew Paxton. He used to cut meat for a living, as I once did.'

Pyke and Field's assistant regarded one another warily, like two animals squaring up for a fight. Paxton wasn't afraid of Field – Pyke could see that much – and Field's introduction, as florid an account of another human being as Pyke had ever heard coming from the man's lips, indicated that he both trusted and respected Paxton. Pyke could smell the younger man's ambition.

'Looks like you need a new whist partner,' Pyke remarked, once Paxton had left them.

'I appreciate your effort, however misguided, to lighten the atmosphere.' Field smiled weakly. 'That being said, I hope you have good news for me.'

'I went to the address you gave me but the property was deserted.'

Field assimilated this piece of information without visible reaction. The pool of blood had spread across the table and had started to drip on to the carpet. 'Can I ask you a question, Pyke?'

'Do you imagine I'm going to say no?'

'If people ever stopped fearing me, I might as well kill myself because someone else would soon do it for me.' It was said, Pyke thought later, as a simple declaration of fact rather than as an explanation for what Field had just done.

164

'Then, rest assured, you stand to live for a long time yet.'

That drew the faintest trace of a smile. 'Come and work for me. I'll make it worth your while.'

'Next you'll be inviting me to play cards with you.'

Field shrugged. 'Do you think I'd have done that, if he'd been of *any* practical use to me?'

'That puts me greatly at ease.'

'I'm not such a philistine that I can't detect the irony in your voice, Pyke. I also suspect you don't much care for me and you certainly don't respect me. I sometimes wonder whether you even fear me, but I find the idea that you don't hard to fathom.' He held up his hand, to stop Pyke from replying. 'Allow me to finish. Personally I find you arrogant and entirely untrustworthy. I don't like your manners or your easy charm. But at the same time, and in spite of myself, I have to admit a sneaking admiration for you. Isn't that strange? Doesn't that strike you as strange?'

Pyke remained silent.

'Now please don't insult my intelligence.' Field wetted his fingers and smoothed the ends of his moustache. 'What did you really find at the place in Bethnal Green?'

For a moment, Pyke considered continuing with the lie. 'I found her. She was addled on laudanum – posing nude for one of Crane's copperplates. She didn't know her own name let alone what day it was. I heard footsteps. Someone came into the room. I had to fight my way out of there.' He considered telling Field about Bessie Daniels' reference to the Swiss valet but decided against doing so, at least until he'd had a chance to work out in his own mind what it meant.

Field leaned back in his chair, took out a cigar from his pocket and lit it on one of the candles. 'So why didn't you tell me that to begin with?'

Pyke looked towards the door. He didn't doubt that if Field clapped his hands, there would be five or more men in the room, all willing to do whatever Field asked them. 'I didn't want you to think I'd failed you.'

'You'll go back there tomorrow.' It wasn't put as a question.

'I tried to ask her what she knew but she didn't seem aware of what I was talking about. If I knew a little more about your interest in Crane's affairs and what I should ask her...'

Field put the cigar into his mouth and took a few puffs. 'You'll be told only what I want you to know. Is that clear?'

Pyke remained silent.

'Right at this moment I'm trying to find a reason why I shouldn't have you killed.' Field blew a smoke ring into the air and watched it drift upwards and dissolve.

'She was laid out on Crane's sofa, naked, like a slab of meat.' Seeing her like that had made Pyke think of Emily, who had devoted her life to fighting exploitation in all its guises, and had died, or been killed, for it. And yet what had *he* done? He'd left the woman in Crane's 'care'. Trying not to think about what Emily might have said to him, Pyke refocused his attention on Field.

'Are you trying to rile me?'

Pyke waited for a moment. 'Neither of us likes

men who exploit members of the fairer sex for their own profit.'

Field's irises contracted and his expression became very still. 'Do you know what I'm going to do?' As he puffed on his cigar, the hot ash glowed an intense red. Field waited for the smoke to dissipate. 'I'm going to tell you something I've never told a living soul.'

Pyke licked his lips but didn't say a word.

'My mother was killed by violent men when I was just a babe. I'm told she was beaten and raped before they strangled her and left her body in a cattle trough.'

Field sat there, his expression implacable. Finally he opened his eyes and rubbed them. 'There must be a hundred pounds there on the table,' he said, dismissing it with a wave of his hand. 'Take it. It's yours.'

Pyke looked at the coins and banknotes on the table. They were covered with the fat man's blood.

'What? You think those two cowards who won it, fairly and squarely I should add, would dare set foot in this room again? Go on. Take it.'

Pyke went to pick up one of the gold sovereigns. He got as far as touching it, the gold slick with blood. In the chair next to him, the fat man's body had slumped farther forward.

At the door, he turned around and studied Field's expression, which was a mixture of incredulity and interest.

'Can I just ask why you decided to throw what I offered you back in my face?' The coins and notes were on the table where Pyke had left them.

'I owe you enough as it is without wanting to

167

add to my debt.'

Field shook his head. 'You do know that if you'd answered that question differently, I would have killed you with my bare hands?' He motioned for Pyke to go and added, 'You still have a job to do for me. I'll expect to hear back from you by the end of the week.'

But Pyke's long, exhausting night wasn't quite over. When he got back home, he found Saggers waiting for him. Copper lay sleeping at his feet. As soon as he saw Pyke, Saggers rose, his cheeks damp with excitement.

'There's another body,' the penny-a-liner kept on saying, 'there's another body.'

ELEVEN

The next day was the first really hot one of the year and even by nine in the morning the air was warm and filled with insects and the sky was hazy with soot. The sun was well up above the warehouse roofs and church spires, although it was hard to see it through the miasma of dust, and the surface of the river at Shadwell shimmered in the light breeze. In the distance Pyke could see people picking through the viscous sludge left by the river at low tide, looking for pieces of rusted iron, frayed rope and lumps of coal. Their poverty was an abstraction, something Pyke could not begin to appreciate in spite of his own precarious circumstances. But it wasn't what they were doing which

168

appalled him; it was the stink of the river produced by the sewage that gathered on both banks. Pyke loved the river, the sheer size of it, how it made him feel when he came upon it after the narrowness of the nearby streets, but he never got used to the smell, so he told Saggers he would wait for him in the Bunch of Grapes. There, he ordered and paid for a mug of ale rather than his usual gin because he was thirsty. He was surprised at how busy the place was at this hour in the morning. He sat at a table next to the window and watched the light streaming through the smudged panes, but there was no getting away from the stink. The floor had been sprinkled with sprigs of rosemary as well as sawdust, and baskets of lemons hung above the counter, yet all he could smell was the raw sewage from the river.

Pyke had just finished his second ale when Saggers joined him, this time accompanied by a mudlark, Gilbert Meeson, who from the look and smell of him had just waded out of the sludge, and a nervous coal-whipper who shook Pyke's hand and introduced himself as George Luckins. Pyke bought drinks for all of them and Saggers helped carry them back from the counter.

George Luckins, it turned out, had read the column about Mary Edgar's murder in the *Examiner* and had got in touch with Saggers through the newspaper. His own story was as sad as it was unexpected. The previous year, his daughter, who had worked as a servant and seamstress and who, as he later revealed, had also been arrested a few times for street-walking, had gone missing just as it seemed she was pulling her life back together.

Someone had helped her to find a job, working in an East End factory as a seamstress, and she'd sworn to Luckins that she would never again sleep with men for money. A week after her disappearance, Luckins had been to see the police, who told him that since a crime hadn't actually been committed they couldn't help. After a month, he had become desperate. That was when he took up the search for his missing daughter himself. For another two months, in between loading and unloading crates of coal, he had searched for her in vain. He had looked everywhere: brothels, taverns, gin palaces, lodging houses, hospitals, even the Bedlam asylum for the insane. Nothing. He had been on the verge of giving up when a friend told him about a mudlark who'd apparently found a corpse in the river near St Katharine's Dock. Luckins had paid the mudlark – Gilbert Meeson as it turned out – a visit, to discover that Meeson had sold the corpse to a surgeon from St Thomas's hospital. But from the mudlark's description of an unusual birthmark on the corpse's neck, Luckins had been able to identify the body as his daughter.

Saggers had told Pyke Luckins' story, and throughout it the coal-whipper just sat there, mute and unmoving, his eyes not blinking and his lips cracked and blistered.

'If I'd known who she was, I wouldn't have gone and sold her to the doctor.' Gilbert Meeson's skeletal face was criss-crossed with thick, purple veins and covered by warts the size of shilling coins. 'But by the time I fished her out of the water, to be honest, there weren't a whole lot left of her.'

Luckins stared down at the ground, as though the subject of their conversation was too painful for him.

'But you're certain she'd been strangled?' Pyke asked.

'I'll tell yet what I told Mr Saggers 'ere.' Meeson glanced over at the penny-a-liner and nodded. 'I saw the marks around her neck. There was no question about it, and when the doctor seen it, he said the same.'

'But we want to know about the *eyes*,' Saggers said, breathless with excitement. 'Tell him about the eyes.'

Meeson sniffed and wiped his nose on the sleeve of his jacket. 'There weren't none.' He said it so matter-of-factly that it took Pyke a moment to comprehend what he'd just been told. Luckins, meanwhile, started to hum, a low tuneless noise that Pyke couldn't help but feel was the last defence of a man who'd already succumbed to his fate.

'What do you mean, there weren't any?'

'Like I said.' Meeson glanced over at Luckins, who was still humming. 'The doctor took one look at her body and told me they'd been cut out with a scalpel.'

'But he was still prepared to pay for it?' Pyke's palms were moist. A gust of wind rattled the frame of the window and they all looked at it, startled.

'Not much, seeing as how bloated it was, from all the time it spent in the water. But he weren't so worried about the eyes. You see, he told me he was in the business of cutting off folk's limbs.'

'What was the doctor's name?'

Meeson looked at Pyke and blinked. 'He wouldn't want me telling yer that.'

Outside, Pyke could hear the squawk of hungry gulls. 'You'll tell me his name because it's the least you can do for this man sitting next to you. You made a profit from his daughter's murder.'

The mudlark stared down at his muddy boots. 'Since yer put it that way, his name was Mort.'

Pyke's throat felt scratchy but he knew drinking more beer wouldn't do it any good. He made a mental note of the doctor's name. 'Mr Luckins?'

The coal-whipper stopped humming and looked up at him, his eyes hard and clear. 'Sir?'

'You told this man here that someone helped your daughter find work as a seamstress.' For some reason, Pyke raised his voice, as though Luckins were either a simpleton or partially deaf.

'I did, sir.'

'Can you remember the name of the man who helped her?'

'His name?'

Pyke nodded his head and waited.

'I saw 'im once, just briefly. But I never found out his name.'

'Is there anything at all you can tell me about him, or about your daughter, that might help me find the man who killed her?' Pyke could feel the sweat trickling down the small of his back.

'I 'member her telling me he worked for a society what had the word vice in the title. I can't think of the whole thing.' He shut his eyes and put his hand up to his forehead.

Pyke looked up at him, dry mouthed. 'Do you mean the Society for the Suppression of Vice?'

172

'That were it.' Luckins hesitated. 'Why? Is that any help to you?'

'Would you recognise this man if you saw him again?'

The coal-whipper's eyes glazed over. 'Perhaps. I don't know. Yer see, I didn't see him for long.' His expression was both apologetic and suggestive of a pain Pyke remembered only too well and hoped he would never have to face again.

As they prepared to leave, Pyke took the mudlark to one side and asked him whether he knew or had heard of a blind man who sometimes scavenged on the river.

'The one they call Filthy?' Meeson said, his face screwed up.

'That's him. Do you know him or where I can find him?'

'I just heard of him, sir. I ain't never seen him, let alone talked to him.'

'You don't have any idea where I might look for him?'

Meeson stared down at his boots. 'He don't work this part of the river, that's all I know.'

Outside, they watched the mudlark trudge disconsolately back towards his place in the sludge. The sun was hot and a group of bare-footed children was playing near by in puddles of mud. Pyke brought his hands up to his eyes to protect them from the glare of the sun off the water. Saggers stood at the edge of his vision, shuffling from one foot to the other.

'If it's true, if the mudlark is right, it must be the same man.' Pyke waited, not sure whether he was excited or disappointed by this notion.

Saggers nodded vigorously. 'Same cause of death, same facial mutilation, same part of London.'

'The only difference this time is that the victim, Lucy Luckins, was white.'

'Who cares? I'll not go hungry for a whole year on the money I'll make from this one.' Saggers looked at him. 'You still owe me a venison supper at the Café de l'Europe. Don't think I've forgotten, sir.'

'You can think of your stomach at a time like this?'

Saggers tried to appear hurt. 'Imagine it, sir, as my stomach thinking about me. Do you suppose I *like* being subject to the whims of this monster?' But he patted his stomach gently, as though proud of it.

'So the man we're looking for is indiscriminate about who he kills, black, white, it doesn't matter to him,' Pyke said, trying to keep his mind focused.

'You sound disappointed.'

'I'm not disappointed. I just can't reconcile it with some of the other evidence.'

'Such as?'

Pyke paused, aware he hadn't told the penny-a-liner about the bottle of rum and what he'd found out about Mary Edgar's flirtation with Obeah.

'Far be it from me to suggest you're being parsimonious with the truth, sir, but I do get the sense you're keeping certain morsels of information from me.' Saggers wiped spittle from his chin. 'As an example, perhaps you'd like to explain why you were so interested in the Vice Society?'

'I had an idea that the women might have dabbled in prostitution, that's all.'

'And do you think they did?'

Pyke shrugged. He didn't want to tell Saggers about his suspicions regarding William Ale-founder just yet. Maybe it was coincidental that he sat on the board of the same society whose agent had tried to help Lucy Luckins. Maybe this person really had tried to help her and was wholly innocent in the matter of her disappearance and murder. But Pyke had always been distrustful of coincidences, believing instead that there was usually, or nearly always, a rational explanation for instances that seemed, from the outside, to have been conjured solely by fate.

'I'm going to take this story to Spratt and he'll publish it on the front page of the *Examiner.*'

Pyke kept his gaze aimed at Saggers, though he had to squint. 'Including the part about the eyes?'

'I can tell you don't want me to.'

'You'll bring a whole lot more pain into the life of George Luckins and anyone who's close to him.'

'But not writing the story isn't going to bring his daughter back, is it?'

Pyke acknowledged this with a single nod of his head.

'So you have another objection?'

'If you sensationalise an investigation like this you'll lose control of it. Suddenly everyone will want to be involved. Overnight you'll have a hundred journalists fighting you for the story. Pretty soon, rewards will be offered. That will attract the scavengers and fortune-seekers who will, in turn, fabricate stories either for the money or just to be part of the thing. Before you can stop it, there's too many people involved, too much information out there, and the truth will slip by unnoticed.'

But Pyke could see the gleam in the fat man's eye. This was his chance. He didn't care about the sanctity of the investigation. He would do what he wanted to do, regardless of what Pyke said.

'Just promise me one thing,' Pyke added. 'Before you take this story to Spratt, confirm what the mudlark said with this doctor, Mort.'

Later, after Saggers had left him, Pyke turned back to face the river and thought about Emily; what she would have made of the mudlark's story and what she would have done to assist women like Lucy Luckins or, for that matter, Bessie Daniels.

It took Pyke just under an hour to walk to Crane's cottage in Bethnal Green, but the place was deserted; there was no sign of Bessie Daniels, Crane or any of his assistants.

This time, in the upstairs room, Pyke noticed that some chairs had been arranged in a semicircle around the sofa and on the floor he found a couple of cigar butts. It was almost as if someone – perhaps more than one person – had sat there and watched whatever had taken place on the sofa.

On his way to a luncheon appointment with Godfrey, Pyke paid another visit to Crane's shop just off the Strand. Crane arrived shortly afterwards and swore blind he'd paid Bessie and she had left of her own accord. Later, as he approached the public house on Bow Street where he'd arranged to meet his uncle, Pyke was still pondering whether Crane had told him the truth.

'The older lad who was hanging around outside my apartment the other day,' Godfrey said, once they'd finished eating. He was mopping up the rest of his steak and kidney pudding with a hunk of bread. 'I saw him chatting to Felix again yesterday. I don't like him, I don't like him one bit.'

They were sitting next to the window at the front of the Brown Bear, just across the road from the Bow Street magistrate's office.

'I told Felix he wasn't to have anything to do with the lad.'

Godfrey finished chewing. 'Whatever you said doesn't appear to have sunk in.' He paused to take a sip of claret. 'You see, if you were there, with him, all the time, you could discipline him as a father is meant to.'

Pyke waited for his uncle to look up at him. 'You never disciplined me.'

'Exactly my point. And look how you've turned out.' Godfrey chuckled to himself but quickly his face turned serious. 'This mulatto girl, whoever she was, is dead. Can't you see that? Your son is alive and he needs you, Pyke.'

'I know he needs me but what am I supposed to do? I think about Mary Edgar's corpse, what they did to her, and it makes me want to scream.'

'How terribly morbid, dear boy. Sometimes I wonder where the dashing, cavalier chap I wrote about has gone, I really do.'

'The figure in your book?'

'Friend to the people, enemy of the well-to-do.'

'I was never that.'

'Riling the great and the good.'

'I'm just trying to do a job.'

'Leave it to the police. It's what they're paid for.'

'I've been rotting in a prison cell for the last nine months. I want to do something that will make Felix proud of me. Something *I* can be proud of.' Pyke paused, aware that he was raising his voice. 'And anyway, the person in the book isn't me.'

The real reason Pyke and Godfrey had met for lunch lay just across the street from the Brown Bear. The Swiss valet accused of Lord Bedford's murder – Jerome Morel-Roux – was being held in the cells under the Bow Street magistrate's office and he had written to Godfrey begging for an audience with Pyke.

Crossing the street, Godfrey commented, 'Do you know what Morel-Roux's admiration for *Confessions* has done for sales? You can't find a copy of it anywhere in the capital or, I'm told, the provinces.'

As the gaoler, whom Godfrey had paid a king's ransom to smuggle them into the cells, led them down a steep flight of stone steps Godfrey whispered to Pyke, 'If he confesses to the murder, remember to get him to sign something.'

For ten years, until he'd retired from the Runners following his marriage to Emily, the gloomy rooms of the Bow Street magistrate's office had been a home from home to Pyke. Now, more than ten years later, he was back, and the smells of the building, mildew and floor polish, were just the same. For a moment he was

178

transported back to an earlier moment in his life.

The gaoler unlocked the door to Morel-Roux's cell, slid back the iron bolt, and pushed open the door. He told Pyke he had ten minutes. Pyke stepped into the tiny cell and waited for the door to swing closed behind him. It took his eyes a few moments to adjust to the darkness.

Morel-Roux was sitting on the stone floor, his back against the far wall. He was twenty or twenty-five, Pyke guessed, and in other contexts he might have been considered handsome. His face was gaunt and angular, with a strong jaw, prominent nose and piercing green eyes that followed Pyke around the cell.

'It seems you've caused quite a stir. I've heard stories about masters going to bed with their lanterns still burning.'

'I presume you're Pyke.' For some reason, the valet sounded disappointed.

'I'm not what you expected?'

Morel-Roux shrugged. 'I just thought you'd be younger, that's all.' He spoke in a soft, almost effeminate voice, without a trace of a foreign accent. 'I wanted *you* to know I didn't kill my master.'

'I'm flattered, of course, but you should really talk to the police.'

That produced an angry frown. 'Do you think the police care about my guilt or innocence? A crime's been committed and I'm their sacrificial lamb. I'm poor and I was born in Switzerland. No one will weep when I hang.'

Pyke looked around the small, cold cell. The valet had made a fair point. 'But there has been an investigation. Evidence has been gathered.

179

And without proper evidence, the prosecutor will never be able to convince a jury of your guilt.'

'I've read your book,' Morel-Roux said. 'Your faith in the fairness of the legal process surprises me.' For the first time, Pyke thought the valet sounded his age: stamping his foot about the unfairness of the world.

'For a start, it's not my book. And secondly, whether the evidence against you has been fabricated or not, you can't be convicted without due process.'

'Then we should start with the evidence.'

'I'm listening,' Pyke said.

'Some of my master's possessions, including an antique gold ring and two banknotes, were found behind the skirting boards in my room.'

'You're suggesting you had no idea they were there?'

Morel-Roux gave Pyke an icy stare. 'If I'd stolen them, would I have hidden them in my own quarters?'

Pyke had posed the same question to Tilling and had received no satisfactory response. This time, however, he shrugged. 'People are stupid, careless or complacent.'

'I'm not,' the valet said.

'Let's assume, for the sake of argument, that you were stealing from Bedford and he caught you red handed...'

'In the middle of the night?'

'You were there in his room, to steal from him, and he woke up and saw you.'

'If I'd startled the old man, if he'd caught me in the act, he would have cried out. Think about it.

And do you think I'd have been able to stab him without disturbing any of the other servants?'

'I don't know the house. But if you'd surprised him and stabbed him before he'd had a chance to shout for help, it might have been possible.'

'Well, I didn't and that's that.'

'Not a defence that will get you far in court, I'm afraid,' Pyke said. 'And when it comes to the trial, they will paint you as an angry, spiteful man who hated his master, whether that's true or not.'

'I had nothing against the old man. It was the other servants I hated,' Morel-Roux said, folding his arms. 'You know what the most damning piece of evidence was? No sign of forced entry. That meant it had to be one of Lord Bedford's servants, at least according to the police investigation. I was the newest member of the household and hence the most expendable. The others ganged up on me to save their own necks.'

'Are you trying to claim one of them killed him?'

'Of course not.' Morel-Roux exhaled loudly. 'The simple truth is, I don't have any idea who killed him. But I know for a fact it wasn't me.'

'Men facing the scaffold always protest their innocence.' Pyke watched him, unable to decide whether he thought the valet had done it or not.

'And the law always protects the innocent and punishes the guilty?' Morel-Roux shook his head scornfully. 'I *know* you don't believe that.'

'Because you've read a book that you *think* is about me?' Pyke tried not to let the valet see his incredulity.

'You're here, aren't you?'

'I'm here at the insistence of my uncle, the

author, who was hoping you might want to confess your crime to me in order to further publicise his book.'

'But if I *were* innocent,' Morel-Roux said, choosing to ignore Pyke's last comment, 'you wouldn't want to see me hang, would you?'

'There are a lot of things I don't want to see that happen anyway.' Pyke looked at the valet and felt his resolve weaken. Morel-Roux was right about one thing: if he was in fact innocent, Pyke wouldn't want him to die. 'Listen to me: the only way you can *absolutely* prove your innocence is to prove someone else's guilt.'

The valet nodded glumly. 'Lord Bedford was a sweet man. As far as I know, he didn't have any enemies.'

'Can you think of anything unusual that happened in the last weeks that you served the man?'

'I don't know it for a fact, but I'm fairly sure he had a mistress. In any case, there was someone staying with him the week before he was killed.'

'A mistress?' Pyke was mildly curious now. He hadn't read anything about a mistress, nor had Tilling mentioned one.

'I think so. No one was supposed to know about her. She was staying in the apartment attached to the mansion. I heard Bedford and the butler talking about her.'

'But you're certain she was his mistress?'

The valet shrugged. 'You spend a few nights in a place like this, you can't be sure of anything.'

Pyke offered a sympathetic nod. 'Do you know a man called Harold Field?'

Morel-Roux stared at him blankly. 'No. Who is he?'

'How about Jemmy Crane?'

'I haven't heard of him either. Why do you ask?'

Pyke thought about what Bessie Daniels had murmured in her addled state but decided against telling Morel-Roux about it.

'I just want you to find the man who really killed my master.' Morel-Roux's tone was pleading, desperate.

'And why would I do that?'

'Because to see a poor man go to the scaffold for something he didn't do would be an affront to your nature.'

Pyke looked at the valet's pale, sunken face and felt a stab of compassion. He had been in Morel-Roux's position once; he knew what it was like to face the scaffold. He didn't know whether Morel-Roux was guilty or not. *He* had been innocent and Godfrey and Emily had come to his rescue. If Morel-Roux was, in fact, innocent, as he claimed to be, who would come to his rescue?

'I'll look into the matter, see what I can find. That's all I can do.'

Morel-Roux flung himself at Pyke's feet and wept with gratitude.

Pyke spent the afternoon looking for Arthur Sobers in the taverns, beer-shops, bake-houses and slop-shops of the Ratcliff Highway, to no avail. The possibility that they were now searching for a man who had killed twice – killed and mutilated two women in an identical manner – disturbed him more than he cared to admit, not least because it threw into doubt his notion that Mary Edgar had known her killer.

Sobers might be able to shed important light on Mary Edgar's last days and, as such, Pyke needed to talk to him before the police did.

He had been labouring under the assumption that Mary had been killed because of something she'd done or someone she'd known, but perhaps she'd just been selected at random by the same man who'd killed Lucy Luckins. This possibility suggested that those who had known Mary – such as William Alefounder – must be innocent of her murder. He certainly needed to find out more about the sugar trader's private life, and the work he did for the Vice Society. The fact that an agent from the Vice Society had tried to rescue Lucy Luckins from a life of prostitution could, of course, be a coincidence, but this link, or rather Alefounder's possible involvement with both women, was, at present, the only thing that connected the two murders. One thing was clear: Lucy Luckins had been killed long before Mary Edgar. The mudlark had found her corpse floating in the Thames about six months ago.

Pyke ended his search for Sobers in Samuel's place near the West India Docks, but from the look of it someone had already beaten him to it. Tables and benches had been overturned and broken, the counter had been pulled away from its fixing and bottles and glasses had been smashed. He found Samuel sitting on his own, bewildered, trying to make sense of what had happened.

'The Peelers came here looking for the same man you asked about,' Samuel said, when he saw

Pyke standing there.

'They did all this?'

'Thought I was lying when I told 'em I didn't know Sobers or where to find him.'

'How many of them?'

'Ten, twelve. Tore the place apart.' He looked around the room and shook his head. 'Don't need me to tell you that.'

'They find anything?'

Samuel shook his head. 'I told you I don't know this Sobers fellow. Who is he anyhow? What's he done?'

'I'd say the police reckon he killed the woman I was asking you about.' Pyke noticed the bruise on Samuel's cheek, a purple welt already the size of an orange. 'Do you know the name of the man who did this to you?'

'I heard one of 'em call him Pierce.' Samuel frowned. 'Why? You know him?'

'Oh, I know him.'

'Go on.'

'I think he's an arrogant, ambitious fool.'

Samuel took a swig of rum and passed it to Pyke. 'In that case, I should buy you a drink.'

Pyke found Pierce in the atrium of the police building on Whitehall. He had just been talking to an elderly, smartly attired man in a high-chair. Pyke waited until the two porters had carried the old man out of the building before he approached the policeman.

'Who do you want, Pyke?'

'I hear you tore up Samuel's place.'

Pierce regarded him with renewed interest.

185

'You were there?'

'You're looking for the wrong man. Sobers didn't kill Mary Edgar.'

'You know that for a fact?'

Pyke looked at the clerks and police constables shuffling past him in the direction of the watch-house. 'Did you know Lord Bedford had a mistress?'

Pierce stared at him, blood vivid in his cheeks. 'What? Now you want to take over that investigation, too. Is there no end to your arrogance?'

'I asked a straightforward question.'

'You want a word of advice, sir?' He moved closer and whispered, 'Forget about your absurd little theories, go home, put a pistol in your mouth and pull the trigger.'

'Ask the butler.'

'Ask him what?'

'Ask him about the mistress.'

'Are you trying to tell me how to do my job?'

Pyke met his stare and shrugged. 'Someone needs to. Might as well be me.'

Later that night, after Jo and Felix had cooked him a roast beef dinner, and Pyke had read Felix a chapter of *Ivanhoe* while Jo cleared the table, Pyke joined Jo in the kitchen and helped her wash the dishes.

'That was a delicious meal,' he said, taking a wet pan from her and drying it with a cloth.

'Thank you.' Godfrey employed a maid to clean the apartment but Jo hadn't wanted to burden her with additional work.

'I think Felix enjoyed himself.'

186

Pyke waited until Jo turned to hand him one of the pots and said, 'And you?'

'I had a good time, too.' He had expected her to be flustered but she held his gaze and even smiled.

Pyke had once tried to kiss Jo, many years earlier, when she had been Emily's servant and before he and Emily had married. Then his act had been foolish and impetuous, the product of his arrogance and loneliness, and she had rightly run away from him, though he suspected she had never told Emily.

'For a while, after Emily died, and we still lived in the old hall, we were happy, weren't we, just the three of us?'

'And the servants.'

Pyke couldn't help but smile. He had never liked the servants, the ones who'd revered Emily's late father. He had never treated Jo as a servant, though. Not consciously, at least, and especially not after Emily's death.

'I thought about that time while I was in prison. It's funny, you don't realise something for what it is until it's gone.' He'd had a glass or two of wine with dinner and felt a little light headed.

Jo put down the glass she was washing and turned to face him. 'I could see the problems you were getting yourself into, with the Chancery case and then some of the business ventures. You were reckless and you almost seemed to have given up. I didn't say anything at the time, I didn't speak my mind, and I've regretted it ever since. I still regret not being more of a support to you.'

For a moment Pyke was surprised by her boldness.

'I don't blame you for holding your tongue. In the mood I was in, if you'd tried to say anything to me, I would probably have dismissed you on the spot.'

He'd meant it as a joke but realised, too late, that he'd reminded her of the social gap that existed between them – and perhaps always would.

When she didn't reply, he smiled and added, 'I didn't mean anything by that. I'm just a boy from the rookery.'

But whatever had been lingering in the air between them evaporated in that moment and Jo's manner suddenly became more formal. 'Please forgive me for speaking so bluntly to you,' she said, stiffly.

'Jo, I like it when you speak to me that way. I welcome it. Let's go through to the front room and have another glass of wine.'

'I'd like to,' she said, not meeting his eyes, 'but I have an early start tomorrow and I'll need a clear head for it.'

TWELVE

It took Pyke almost two hours to travel down to Richmond by hackney coach and by the time he was dropped off on the green, the clouds had cleared and the sky was an unbroken vista of varnished blue. Now they were ten miles out of the city, the air felt clean and birds darted among the oak and birch trees that lined the green. A butcher's boy carrying a tray of meat directed him towards the Alefounder residence, an impressive Palladian mansion on the east side of the green surrounded by an iron fence. By the front gate, a weeping willow had just blossomed and the air was perfumed with a scent that reminded him of a woman he'd once known.

Pyke found Harriet Alefounder tending to her flowers in a greenhouse at the back of the main house. She was a tall, distinguished woman, perhaps a couple of years older than her husband, her greying hair concealed under a straw bonnet. Her gaunt shoulders were covered by a woollen shawl and she was wearing gardening gloves. When Pyke explained why he was there – that he was investigating the 'unexplained' deaths of two women and needed to talk to her about her husband – he expected her to call out to her butler and have him removed from the property. But instead she took off her bonnet, rearranged her hair, which had been tied up in a knot, and said that in that case they had better retire inside where they would be more comfortable. As they made their way from the greenhouse to the doors at the rear of the house she added, 'You have to understand my husband isn't a *bad* man,' as though such an explanation were necessary. And then, 'Of course, you know that William and I no longer live under the same roof.' Pyke hadn't known this but nodded as though he did and followed her into the house.

Given what Pyke had already been told about Alefounder's roving eye, his wife's story was, in one sense, entirely without surprises. He'd had a

189

string of affairs in their nineteen-year marriage and she, for the most part, had either turned a blind eye or allowed him to do what he needed to do, apparently secure in the belief that he loved her and would never leave her. This proved to be true until he met a woman called Elizabeth Malvern. The wife explained that she hadn't known about the affair at the time and had only found out about it when William asked her for a divorce.

Until this point in her story, Alefounder's wife hadn't struck Pyke as a particularly bitter or spiteful person, but when she started to talk about the affair, and about the other woman – the *harlot* as she called her – her whole demeanour changed and the reason why she'd agreed to talk to him became apparent. She was angry and wanted the chance to vent her spleen. Pyke could well understand the source of this bitterness – her husband's head suddenly being turned by a younger, prettier, flirtatious rival – and he was surprised to learn that Alefounder had, in the end, agreed to end the affair and return home. Their domestic life was good after that, she explained, for another year or so, and as far as she knew, he hadn't tried to continue seeing 'the Malvern harlot'. Everything was fine, until the most recent trip to Jamaica – apparently he undertook these annually to arrange the purchase and shipment of sugar directly from the plantations. When he returned, his whole manner had changed. He was cold, moody and distant, she explained, and refused to talk about the problem. This continued for a number of months and things had finally come to a head within the last month. Without explanation, he had moved out of the house, taking an apartment in the city, and then had demanded a divorce, which she'd refused to give him. That conversation, the last time they'd spoken, had taken place about three weeks earlier. But Harriet Alefounder's story had one final twist.

Hurt, angry and bewildered, she had followed him in a carriage from his place of work to an apartment on The Strand. After waiting for a period of time, she followed him into the building. She'd found his apartment easily enough. All she had to do was ask one of the other residents. At the door she'd listened and heard a female voice laughing. It was the laughing which had cut her the deepest, she explained. She had paced up and down the pavement outside the apartment building for the rest of the evening. Eventually the front door opened, and that was when she saw them, arm in arm: her husband and a pretty mulatto girl. She'd fled The Strand without being spotted.

Outwardly Pyke tried to remain calm, but inwardly his heart was hammering against his ribcage. This was the confirmation he'd been looking for and it had come from the unlikeliest of sources. Of course, it didn't prove anything more than that Alefounder had been sleeping with Mary Edgar, and perhaps had been since his last visit to Jamaica, but it gave Pyke enough to warrant another conversation with the trader.

He noted down the address on The Strand that Harriet Alefounder had mentioned and waited. 'That woman – Mary Edgar – was murdered. Her corpse was found last week on the Ratcliff Highway.'

Stiffening her back Harriet Alefounder looked

at him, dry eyed, and sniffed. 'Do you expect me to say I'm sorry?'

'She was strangled and then her eyes were gouged out.' It would be in the newspapers soon enough and Pyke wanted to force some kind of reaction from her, but she barely even blinked.

'You can't expect that William could be involved in such a business?'

'I don't know what to think.' He stared into her proud face and wondered what she'd had to sacrifice to attain such a level of hardness.

'You mentioned two women had been killed,' she said, as if they were chatting about recipes for jam.

Quickly he told her about Lucy Luckins and her possible connection to the Society for the Suppression of Vice.

'That was how he *claimed* he first met the Malvern woman.' Harriet Alefounder's voice quivered slightly as she said the name.

Pyke considered this new piece of information. 'If I wanted to talk to her, do you know where I might find her?'

'Her father owns a big mansion in Belgravia – he made his money from sugar in the West Indies. As I remember it, she owned a much smaller house near Hyde Park.' She shut her eyes. 'Curzon Street, I think. I remember following my husband there, too.'

Later, as Pyke prepared to leave, she followed him to the front door and stood there for a moment, contemplating the willow tree through the window. 'You must think me a heartless, disloyal creature but in my own way I still care for him deeply. And to answer your question, I don't believe he's capable of hurting anyone, certainly not in the manner you suggested.'

Pyke had his hand on the brass door handle when she added, 'But you know what hurt me the most, when I saw the two of them walking arm in arm along The Strand? I was a long way away and my eyesight isn't what it used to be but I swear there was a little of *her*, of the Malvern woman, in this mulatto girl.' And when he looked up, her lips were trembling and her eyes had filled with tears.

The following afternoon, Pyke found Felix and the older boy on the pavement outside Godfrey's apartment.

The older lad was teaching Felix a game using three coins. He had a malnourished face, with red rims around his eyes and yellow skin from a poor diet. When he saw Pyke, he adjusted his billycock hat, pulled up his knee-breeches and put the coins into the pocket of his monkey coat. He didn't seem surprised to see Pyke and even managed to hold his gaze for a while.

'Go back into the apartment and leave us for a while,' Pyke said to Felix.

'Eric was just teaching me a trick...'

'Go inside now and wait for me there,' Pyke said, looking at the lad, Eric, rather than at Felix.

'You can't tell me what to do,' Felix said, his voice quivering with defiance.

Pyke turned to him and immediately Felix scuttled across the pavement and up into the apartment. 'I want you to leave my son alone,' he said, refocusing his attention on Eric.

'I can come and go as I please, cully,' the boy. said with a sneer. 'You don't own the street.'

'I see you outside my uncle's apartment again, I'll come and find you, and when I do, you won't even be able to hobble home.'

But Eric didn't appear to be cowed. 'Your boy's a bit green, ain't he? Wouldn't last a week on the street.'

Pyke took a step towards him. 'Anything happens to my son, God help me, I'll rip your head from your neck with my bare hands.'

'Why should I listen to a pathetic old jailbird like you? Felix told me 'bout you. Put inside for not paying your debts.' He stood his ground but his face had turned white and his hands were trembling.

'Did my son tell you that?' Pyke could feel the anger gathering inside him.

Eric saw he'd unsettled Pyke and grinned. 'That and a whole lot more about what a rotten father you are.'

For a moment it felt as if he'd swallowed a handful of nails. Pyke didn't look up at the window of the apartment but he could sense he was being watched.

'I'm going to count to five and if you're not gone by the time I finish, I won't be held accountable for my actions.'

But Eric folded his arms and remained where he was. 'Who knows? In time, and with the right guidance, maybe Felix would make a good dipper.'

Pyke grabbed him by his throat and lifted him up off his feet. Choking, Eric tried to wriggle free

194

from his grasp but Pyke held firm. He heard someone rapping on the window and looked up to see Godfrey and Jo. Then one of the neighbours appeared from their apartment and ordered Pyke to let the boy go. Pyke opened his hand and Eric fell to the pavement, holding his neck as though it were broken.

'Given I'm used to eating horse or very possibly mule, this is a most welcome change indeed, sir,' Saggers said, his mouth half open so Pyke could see the chunks of meat churning around inside. In front of him was the remains of a beefsteak that a few minutes ago had been as big as the plate itself. They were sitting at a table in the corner of the Café de l'Europe on Haymarket, well away from the rest of the early evening diners, as if to underline the fact that they didn't belong in a place where the starched linen tablecloths were a brilliant white and the cutlery alone was worth more than Saggers earned in a month. 'It's not Halnaker's venison but it's a most acceptable cut of meat,' he said, picking up the steak with his hands and gnawing the last bits of meat from the bone.

Pyke poured him another glass of claret. Saggers had already told him that Spratt, the editor, had refused to publish the story about the second body without corroboration from the surgeon, Mort, but that as yet he hadn't been able to track the man down.

'I tried to get George Luckins to go on the record about his daughter and even offered him a few groats for his effort but the man turned me down flat, said he didn't want to profit from his

195

daughter's murder.' Fat dripped down his chin. 'Can you believe some people?'

Pyke didn't know whether to laugh or despair. 'So tell me what you've managed to find out about the West India Dock Company.' This was the real reason Pyke had agreed to take Saggers to dinner.

'Ah, yes.' The fat man swallowed half the claret in a single gulp, his giant Adam's apple bobbing up and down in his throat. 'Most interesting.'

'In what sense?'

'The company is struggling but I suppose that's no secret. Sugar revenues have been falling for some time now and with the end of apprenticeship and increased competition from French and Spanish colonies investors are beginning to look elsewhere. India, for example. I'm told the East India Company is flourishing.'

'Go on.'

Saggers sat back and let out an enormous belch that filled the room and stopped the other diners in their tracks. 'One of the reasons they're so keen to distance themselves from our horrible little murder is they're just about to try to raise fresh capital, and any whiff of scandal might deter potential investors.'

'Why do they want to raise capital?'

'The short answer is that they're considering joining forces with the East India Dock Company to build a new, much larger dock farther down the Thames towards Tilbury.'

Pyke considered what he'd been told. 'Did you get me a list of major shareholders?'

With a theatrical flourish Saggers produced a

crumpled piece of paper from the pocket of his tweed coat and shoved it across the table. 'The single largest shareholder is a man called Silas Malvern.'

'Malvern.' It took him a few moments to place the name. Elizabeth Malvern had had an affair with Alefounder. Could this be the wife or daughter?

'I thought you'd be interested in him so I did a bit of digging. He sold up his interests in the West Indies a few years ago and bought a mansion in Belgravia. I'm told he's paralysed down one side of his body and has to be carried around in a high-chair.'

Pyke's thoughts turned to the old man he'd seen talking with Pierce in the atrium of the police building. 'Any family?'

'I didn't ask,' Saggers said. 'Why?'

'It doesn't matter.' Pyke took out his purse and threw a couple of sovereigns on to the table to pay for the dinner. 'It's been a pleasure, as always.'

'You're leaving so soon?' Saggers tried not to show his disappointment. 'But we haven't even perused the dessert menu or smoked cigars or sipped the finest cognac from cut-crystal glasses.'

'There'll be enough there to cover whatever you want.'

'But who shall I entertain with my repartee?' Saggers shifted to one side of his chair and let out a deafening fart.

Pyke glanced around at the stony faces of the other diners. 'Carry on like that, you'll have to beat off your admirers with a stick.'

It was too late to make the trip out to Belgravia that night but the next morning Pyke caught a hackney carriage from a stand at the end of his street and asked the driver to take him to Eaton Place via Curzon Street, near Hyde Park.

Just by asking, Pyke found the house easily enough, though it wasn't on Curzon Street as Harriet Alefounder had thought. It was a pretty, Georgian terrace on Pitts Head Mews. It was early, before ten, but the air was already warm, and as Pyke told the driver to wait for him, he removed his jacket and wiped his brow. The shutters were drawn and he couldn't see any sign of life inside the house. He banged on the door and disturbed one of the neighbours, an elderly man with a cane and a slight limp, who told him in a hushed tone that Miss Elizabeth had very recently sailed for the West Indies and wasn't expected back for a number of months.

As Pyke returned to the waiting carriage, he had one last look at the house and noticed movement in one of the upstairs windows, but as soon as the person – whoever it was – realised they'd been spotted, the curtains ruffled and the face disappeared from view. Later it struck him that he should have investigated this matter more closely, but he was eager to question Silas Malvern and he used the rest of the journey to prepare his thoughts.

The dazzling white stucco of the grand terraced mansions on Eaton Place in Belgravia screamed of their occupiers' wealth. This, Pyke had heard someone say, was the most desirable address in London and, compared with the rest of the city, it was eerily quiet. These were the white, modern palaces of the parvenu rich, neoclassical in style with columns and porticos on the outside, vast windows of plate glass and rich cornices on the inside.

Having presented himself at the front door, Pyke was told to wait in the marble-floored entrance hall while the butler went to see whether 'Mr Malvern' was receiving visitors.

Malvern was sitting in a greenhouse attached to the back of the property overlooking the garden. He cut a frail figure surrounded by the tropical plants he'd doubtless imported from the West Indies to remind himself of his former home, but whereas the jasmine, honeysuckle, lilies and orchids probably smelled fragrant and alive in their native habitat, here they produced a sweet, sickly stench that was so overpowering Pyke had to cover his mouth with a handkerchief.

'Excuse me, sir, but I told you to wait in the entrance hall,' the butler said, when he saw Pyke step into the greenhouse. He turned back to his master. 'I'll show him to the door, sir. Rest assured, you will have your peace and quiet restored.'

Malvern looked up at Pyke, his eyes as small and hard as shrivelled acorns. 'No, I'll see him. Tell the blackguard to come and sit next to me.'

The butler bowed his head and approached Pyke, still glaring. 'Mr Malvern will see...'

'I heard.' Pyke pushed past him and pulled up a chair next to the old man.

'Will there be anything else, sir?' The butler hesitated. 'Would you like me to stay here with you?'

But Malvern dismissed him with a wave of his bony hand. For a while he studied Pyke's face without speaking. 'What's your name, and why have you interrupted my morning sleep?'

'My name's Pyke, but I suspect you already know that.'

'How would I know? We've never met before, as far as I'm aware.' But his expression suddenly betrayed his wariness.

'I saw you the day before yesterday talking to Inspector Benedict Pierce of the New Police.'

'Is that a crime, sir? And what business is it of yours who I damn well talk to?'

'Given you're the major shareholder in the West India Dock Company and Pierce is leading the investigation into the murder of a woman recently arrived from Jamaica on one of your ships, I'd say you have some questions to answer.'

'I don't have to justify myself to a guttersnipe like you. I'll ask you to leave me in peace.' He rang a bell and looked expectantly towards the door.

'I paid a visit to the West India Docks recently and was forcibly removed from the premises. That suggests to me I've hit a raw nerve.'

This elicited the older man's attention. 'Are you the brigand that set fire to one of the warehouses the other day? The company lost over thirty barrels of rum. I'm told they intend to prosecute you to the fullest extent of the law.'

'If they do, you can be sure I'll drag your family's good name into the mire surrounding Mary Edgar's murder.'

As Malvern stared at Pyke, perhaps trying to gauge the threat he posed, Pyke added, 'The clerk

I talked to didn't want me to know Mary Edgar had been met from her ship by a sugar trader called William Alefounder. I take it you know him?'

'*Smith*, dammit, where are you, man?' The old man's voice didn't carry very far and he rang the bell again.

'I'm guessing you must know him because until quite recently I'm told he was intimate with your daughter.' The shock on Malvern's face seemed genuine. 'Elizabeth is your daughter, isn't she?'

The butler appeared in the doorway, glancing nervously in Pyke's direction. 'Yes, sir?'

'Tell this gentleman to leave and if he refuses to go, send one of the lads to fetch the police.'

'I want to talk to her.'

Malvern stared up at him, his cheeks hollow and his eyes lifeless. 'That would be rather difficult to arrange in the current circumstances.'

'Why? Because she's sailed for Jamaica?'

The fact that Pyke knew this was another blow to the old man's defences. He gripped the edge of his chair to stop his hands from trembling. 'Get him out of here,' he barked at the butler.

But Pyke had got what he wanted: confirmation that Elizabeth was out of the country. Ignoring the butler, he crouched down next to Malvern and whispered, 'Did you know Mary Edgar by any chance?'

'I've said all I'm going to say.' Malvern folded his arms and looked across at his butler. 'Fetch the police.'

'Guilt can be a powerful agent, can't it?' Pyke pushed the butler to one side and made for the

201

door. 'I bet late at night when everything else is silent, you can hear the screams of the slaves whose lives you destroyed.'

THIRTEEN

Carriages were backed all the way down Alder-manbury from the Guildhall, the venue for the Lord Mayor's banquet, as far as Milk Lane and even Cheapside: a multitude of vehicles, but all reflected the wealth and privilege of their owners. In the heart of the City of London, horses stood, blowing air from their nostrils and shitting on the cobbles, while footmen and drivers dressed in their finest livery conversed with old friends in hushed tones. It was a night when men came to slap one another on the back and congratulate themselves for their success. Alefounder would be in there and Pyke intended to put some difficult questions to him. From the beginning, the trader had shown scant regard for Pyke's investigation – treating it as an annoyance or even an irrelevance – and he had used his contacts to ensure that his affair with Mary Edgar remained a subject beyond discussion. He'd assumed his position was a sufficient bulwark against the vagaries of a murder investigation and that, in spite of Mary Edgar's death, his life could continue as if nothing had happened. Pyke intended to disabuse him of this notion.

There were two liveried major-domos at the

main gates checking the invitations of the guests; most had already passed through and were, doubtless, starting to take up their seats in the hall. Pyke withdrew as far as Lad Lane, which ran into one end of Aldermanbury, and waited. Fortunately he didn't have long to wait.

Lad Lane was a narrow street that connected two larger thoroughfares and was used as a cut-through from one to the other. Within five minutes, two well-dressed gentlemen who'd had to jettison their carriage on Wood Street because of the congestion outside the Guildhall entered the lane. They didn't see Pyke suddenly emerge from a doorway about halfway along, and were powerless to stop him knocking them unconscious with a plank of wood. Dragging them into an even smaller alleyway, Pyke picked the one who matched his height and build, stripped him naked and changed into the clothes. A minute or so later, he emerged from Lad Lane on to Aldermanbury with a top hat in one hand and the Lord Mayor's invitation in the other.

He presented the invitation at the gates and was ushered through immediately. The two major-domos barely looked at him. Having mounted the steps leading up to the portico, two at a time, Pyke passed unchecked through the entrance, followed the line of well-fed, silver-haired men and eventually found himself in the banqueting hall. There, more liveried servants were waiting to guide the guests to their allotted seats, but Pyke slipped past this net and started his hunt for Alefounder.

The hall itself was cavernous; statues adorned

the walls on one side of the room and a series of giant silk damasks hung on the wall opposite. Around the very top of the hall, a series of flags, including the Union Jack and several coats of arms, hung from their poles and from the panelled ceiling, and three giant chandeliers cast their light on to the guests below. There were three long rows of tables, all dressed with the finest linen, each row broken up into three smaller tables. At the very front of the hall was a raised 'top' table, where the privileged few looked down on the rest of the diners. Pyke did a quick calculation; there had to be somewhere in excess of two hundred men in the room, not including the vast army of servants whose job it was to cater to their every whim.

Some of the guests, Pyke noticed, were wearing wigs, powder and the gaudy trappings of a former era; others, perhaps the majority, wore more sensible attire: frock-coats, waistcoats, frilly shirts, neckcloths and silk cravats. Pyke didn't look out of place in the clothes he'd stolen, nor did anyone pay him much attention as he strolled down one side the room, past the guests already assembled at the tables. Still, it was hard not to feel intimidated by the sheer scale of the venue and the collective wealth of the guests. He'd once owned a bank that made annual profits in the thousands, but he'd never even come close to being invited to such an event.

He found William Alefounder sitting at one end of a table situated in the middle of the room. The sugar trader, who was oblivious to his presence, was chatting to a man next to him. He seemed comfortable in this setting and was regaling his dining companion with a story that required exaggerated gesticulation of his arms.

From behind, Pyke grabbed a handful of Alefounder's frock-coat and pulled him to his feet. For a moment the trader struggled to comprehend what was happening to him, and it was only when Pyke whispered, 'Come with me quietly or I'll humiliate you in front of these people,' that he began to grasp his predicament. His companion and some of the other guests frowned at the rough manner in which Pyke had elicited Alefounder's attention, but when they saw that the trader was following Pyke out of the hall willingly, they reverted to their conversations.

The first door Pyke could find led to the kitchens. He didn't care where it took him; he just wanted to get Alefounder away from the prying eyes of the other diners.

'I want to know how well you knew Mary Edgar and when you last saw her.'

The kitchen was a large room that extended all the way to the back of the building, so most of the cooks and servants were well out of earshot.

'I don't have to answer your questions, sir.' But for the moment, Alefounder's cocksure manner had vanished.

It was hot from all the coal-fired ovens and pans of boiling liquid, and Alefounder went to loosen his neckcloth.

'I want to know when you first met Mary Edgar, when you first started fucking her and why you strangled her and dumped her naked corpse on the Ratcliff Highway.'

But if Pyke thought that the trader would

205

crumple, he hadn't counted on the arrogance of wealth.

'I've said all I'm going to say to the people who matter.'

And when Pyke laid a hand on Alefounder's arm, the trader went to brush it away, as if it were some kind of annoying insect.

'If you touch me again, I'll make sure you spend the night under lock and key.' The skin on Alefounder's face was as taut as a drum.

Pyke took a deep breath and allowed his chest to swell to its full girth. Alefounder was unprepared for Pyke's first punch, which ripped against the side of his face, and was knocked to the floor by the second, a hammer blow that Pyke put his whole body behind and which caught Alefounder flatly on the chin. But if Alefounder believed that that was the end of his difficulties, he was badly mistaken. Pyke pulled him to his feet and dragged him across to a row of metal pots lined up on top of a large stove. There, he took the trader's hand and held it over a pot full to the brim with bubbling liquid.

'I'm giving you one more chance to answer me truthfully. Why did you meet Mary Edgar from the ship? And where did you take her?'

Dazed from the blows to his face, Alefounder struggled to remain upright, but still he didn't respond to Pyke's question.

'Do you know a woman called Lucy Luckins? She was saved by the Vice Society, only to turn up dead a few months later.'

Alefounder offered Pyke a bewildered stare. The fight seemed to have left him. 'Lucy who?'

Pyke forced the trader's arm down towards the soup pot. 'I asked you a question. Why did you meet Mary from the ship?'

Alefounder tried in vain to wrestle his arm from Pyke's grip. 'You have no authority over me, sir.'

Keeping his own hands out of the scalding liquid, Pyke forced Alefounder's arm down into the soup and held it there for a moment. Alefounder's agonised scream carried not only to the depths of the kitchen but also as far as the banqueting hall. Letting go, Pyke watched as the sugar trader fell to the floor, clutching hold of his arm, which was now covered with soup. A small audience had gathered around them, cooks, servers and even one of the major-domos. Their eyes switched between Alefounder, writhing around on the floor, and Pyke; their pity for the trader's plight quickly turned to anger over the assault that had just taken place.

Pyke hauled the trader up. 'If you don't answer my question, it won't just be your arm in that pot...'

But now one of the cooks stepped out of the crowd and pulled Alefounder from Pyke's grasp. Others began to shout for help. Instinctively Pyke knew that his moment had passed and he would leave the banquet hall empty handed. It felt as if he'd failed; as if Alefounder had beaten him. Turning around, he pushed his way through the crowd of bodies. No one tried to stop him, but the sting of failure stayed with him long after he'd found a way out of the building.

The first gin barely touched his throat, the clean

aroma of the drink filling his nostrils. The second went down just as quickly. By the fifth he couldn't feel his face, and it was only when he'd lost count of the gins he'd drunk that he remembered his promise to Jo. Outside on the street, he watched as a hackney carriage rattled past him; he made no effort to flag it down. She would be waiting for him, wondering where he'd got to. The feeling was a disconcerting one. From the tavern he'd been drinking in, he stumbled across St Paul's Yard, in the shadow of the great cathedral, to the top of Ludgate Hill, where he found a young woman with dark hair and big hips. Thrusting a five-shilling coin into her palm, Pyke led her into an alleyway that was so dark he couldn't even see the colour of her eyes. Wordlessly he unhooked his braces and let his trousers drop to his ankles. She had pulled up her layers of petticoats and as she guided him with her hand, he mumbled in her ear, 'Can I call you Mary?'

That drew a throaty laugh. 'You paid your money, you call me anything you like.'

Later, when it was finished and Pyke was pulling up his braces, she touched him on the face and asked why he'd been crying. He had already paid her and her expression was merely curious. Pyke stared at her, not even aware that he'd been upset.

'You asked if you could call me Mary.' She was peering at him through the gloom. Pyke nodded vaguely. 'So why did you keep saying you were sorry over and over to a woman called Emily?'

As the shame scalded Pyke's cheeks, he turned around and retraced his steps back to the street.

In the morning Pyke bought a baked potato and a mug of sludgy black coffee from a street vendor near the market and ate the potato sitting on the pavement. He could still taste the gin in his mouth and even the thick coffee did little to take the taste away.

The market was thronging, and the noise and stink – of animal dung and meat left too long in the sun – was sufficient to make him retch. Producing nothing but bile, Pyke wiped his mouth on the sleeve of his shirt and waited for the feeling to pass. Ahead of him in the field, long-horned Spanish cattle were being herded into drove-rings, each linked by wooden tracks, by drovers and their dogs. The cacophony of barking, grunting and lowing was almost too much for him to bear. Even worse was the plague of black flies which hovered and buzzed around the animals. The ground had dried in the sun but this, in turn, had produced its own problems. As the cattle moved across the field, they kicked up clouds of earth and dust into the air so that it was difficult to see more than a few yards in any direction.

He had slept in his own bed – he had been too inebriated to consider going anywhere else – and was surprised, given what he'd done the previous night, that no police officers had roused him during the early hours and dragged him off to answer Alefounder's charges. Nor were there any officers waiting for him when he returned to his garret after breakfast.

With Copper, Pyke spent the rest of the morning traipsing along the Ratcliff Highway, still looking for Arthur Sobers. He moved cautiously through the dense warren of narrow, windy lanes, always looking behind him for footpads and stopping only to ask people about Sobers – and the missing mudlark – when he was sure that all those in the immediate vicinity had heard Copper growl and seen the size of his jaws. Underfoot, and in spite of the hot weather, the ground was spongy and damp. On either side of the street, in the broken windows of buckling, timber-framed houses, white eyes and smudged faces stared back at him as he walked past. At one corner, he passed a man openly defecating in the street; at another, twin boys barely older than Felix, their limbs bowed from rickets, held out their hands for money.

Aware that he'd made no progress in his hunt for Sobers or the blind man known only as Filthy, Pyke left Copper back in the vicinity of Smithfield and, still curious as to why he'd received no visit from the police regarding his treatment of Alefounder, quietly asked after the trader both at his place of work and the apartment Harriet Alefounder had told him about on The Strand. At the former, he was told Alefounder had not come into work that morning. At the latter, there was no answer. With nothing else to do, and no further clues to chase, Pyke hailed a carriage and told the driver to take him all the way down to Richmond.

'You've just missed him,' Harriet Alefounder said, red eyed and slurring her words slightly, even though it was still the afternoon.

Pyke looked around the well-furnished drawing room. 'So he was here?'

She gave him a peculiar stare. 'Oh yes. He was here.'

'I need to speak to him.'

'That might be difficult, I'm afraid,' She gave a hollow laugh.

'Why? As I told you before, I suspect he might be involved in the murder of a young mulatto woman.'

What sounded like a snort emerged from her mouth. 'In that case he's slipped through your fingers, sir.' Pyke couldn't work out whether she was pleased or upset by this notion.

'Do you know where he's gone?'

'He came here from some dinner he'd attended, packed a suitcase with some of his old clothes, and left in a carriage bound for the West India Docks.'

'He's going to *Jamaica?*' The skin tightened around his temples.

'Yes,' she said, irritated. 'Where else would he go?'

Pyke contemplated this for a moment, trying to adjust to the shock. 'You know Elizabeth Malvern has recently sailed for Jamaica too.'

From Harriet Alefounder's expression, Pyke could tell she hadn't known, and upon hearing this she fell on to the sofa and began to sob.

He watched her, not knowing what to do, whether to try to comfort her or just leave. 'I am sorry...'

Still sobbing, she looked up at him and spat, 'Get out of my sight.'

'Do you know which ship he's due to sail on?'

Her eyes glowed like lumps of hot coal. 'The way he was talking last night, the ship was due to leave first thing this morning.'

'The *Island Queen?*'

'Yes, that was the name he mentioned, I think.'

Harold Field's home occupied four storeys of a Georgian town house at the northern end of Harley Street, and when Pyke presented himself at the front door, the following day, he was escorted up to a room on the third floor and told to wait for Field there. It was a far more refined home than Pyke had expected and, to pass the time, he studied Field's book collection, whose treasures included all twelve volumes of Plato's *Republic* and *Meditations by* Marcus Aurelius. In fact, with its sofas, thick striped wallpaper, high ceilings, gilt mirrors and large bay window overlooking the street, the room could have belonged to any well-to-do English gentleman.

'To what do I owe this unexpected pleasure?' Field was immaculately dressed as usual, in a knee-length, dark blue frock-coat, a fawn waistcoat and matching trousers, and a white satin cravat tied loosely around his neck.

'I thought I'd let you know that I intend to travel to Jamaica. A suspect in the murder investigation I was telling you about has absconded there, perhaps to join his mistress.'

Earlier that morning, Pyke had found out from the Admiralty that a steamer was due to depart from Southampton for Kingston at the end of the week.

'And what? This is simply a courtesy call to inform me of your decision?'

'I went back to see Crane. He assured me that he'd let Bessie Daniels go home.'

Field assimilated this piece of information. 'She hasn't been in contact with me.'

'Would she have done so, if Crane had let her go?'

Field's stare told him all he needed to know.

'In which case, I'll go and see him again,' Pyke said. 'Demand to see her.'

'And what?' Field raised his eyebrows. 'Then you will have paid off your debt to me?'

'Whatever we decide, you'll not stop me from going to the West Indies.'

Field considered Pyke for a few moments. 'Try as I might, I find you a difficult man to comprehend.'

'In what sense?'

'For a start, why do you care what happened to some faceless mulatto girl?'

Pyke shrugged. 'I don't know; perhaps because no one else does.' There were other reasons, of course, but in the circumstances this seemed as good an explanation as any.

'Don't misunderstand me,' Field said, smiling. 'I find your dedication to this particular task admirable.'

'But?'

'But you still have a job to do for me.'

A moment's silence passed between them. 'Last week, before we were interrupted and I had to make my escape, Bessie Daniels gave me a name.'

Field's irises contracted slightly. 'And you

decided to wait until now to inform me of it?'

'I didn't think anything of it at the time. Or I didn't know what to think.'

'But you still kept it from me,'

'Jerome Morel-Roux.'

'Just that?'

Pyke nodded. 'That was all she said.' He waited. 'You know he's the valet awaiting trial for the murder of Lord Bedford?'

'I'm aware of that fact.'

'Do you know why Bessie Daniels might have wanted to pass on this name to you?'

'I have absolutely no idea.' But something about the way Field said this told Pyke he was lying.

Pyke looked around the orderly room, still trying to reconcile it with his sense of Field. 'I've done what you asked me to do.'

The only noise in the room was the rattling of iron-shod wheels and clip-clop of horses' hoofs outside on the street.

'What's this man's name?' Field asked, fiddling with his moustache. 'The one who's absconded.'

'Alefounder. William Alefounder.'

'And the mistress?'

'A woman called Elizabeth Malvern.'

Field looked up at him. 'Could you repeat that name for me?'

'Elizabeth Malvern.'

'That's what I thought you said.'

Pyke looked into Field's eyes. 'Do you know her?'

'No, not personally,' Field said, waving off a fly. 'But if you were to ask Crane the same question, he might well give you a different answer.'

It took Pyke a few moments to comprehend what Harold Field was trying to tell him,

'Where's Bessie Daniels?'

Pyke had followed Crane through the shop into a dirty yard and then on to a dilapidated printing room. There, they were joined by Sykes and another man Pyke had never seen before.

'As I've told you before, I let her go.'

'She hasn't returned home.'

'You know that for a fact?'

'What have you done with her?'

'I'm getting a little tired of repeating myself.' Crane shared a brief look with the hulking Sykes.

Inside his pocket, Pyke brushed his finger over the sharp end of his sheath knife. 'Field thinks you're involved in some kind of political action relating to the trial of a Swiss valet, Jerome Morel-Roux.' This was just a guess – and a wild one at that – but Pyke couldn't think of any other reason why Crane would be connected with the plight of the Swiss valet.

Crane's hooded eyes glittered. 'A political action, eh? Like storming the barricades?'

'So you don't deny the basic truth of what I just said?'

'I'm certainly intrigued to know *how* he reached this particular conclusion, even if it is utterly wrong.'

'It's not true, then?'

Crane just shrugged. 'I can't see why a criminal like Field would be interested in a squalid little political ... what did you call it? Political action.'

'At least Field knows what he is.'

'And I don't?' Crane seemed amused by this notion.

Pyke took a step towards Crane and saw Sykes and the other man stiffen. 'I've upheld my end of our agreement. Now I want to know what took you to Thrale's lodging house.'

Crane wetted his lips. 'But have you? For all I know you've just plucked something out of the air.'

'Why did you go and see Mary Edgar and Arthur Sobers?'

'It was nothing really. Sobers had been harassing this woman he'd slept with. The brothel owner, and a friend of mine, asked for my assistance in putting him straight.'

'And that's it?'

Crane's stare was empty of sentiment. 'I'm sorry if you were expecting something more dramatic.'

'You're quite sure about that?'

'Quite sure.'

'In which case,' Pyke said, holding out his hand, 'perhaps we should shake hands and go our separate ways.'

Crane exchanged a glance with Sykes before offering his hand. It took Pyke just a few seconds to twist Crane around, retrieve his knife, put his head into a lock and hold the serrated edge against the pornographer's neck. 'One move and I'll slit your throat, and not give it a moment's thought,' Pyke whispered in Crane's ear.

The quickness of Pyke's move had caught Sykes and the other man by surprise and neither seemed to know what to do.

'That understood?' When Crane didn't say anything, he added, 'Is that understood?'

'Yes,' was all Crane managed.

'Now tell your two apes to back off and not attempt anything rash.' He dug the blade into Crane's neck and drew a few spots of blood. '*Do it.*'

'Do what he says,' Crane hissed. The two others did as they were told.

'Now tell me what really took you to Thrale's lodging house.'

Crane squirmed a little in his grip but Pyke kept the knife to his throat. 'You're a dead man, Pyke,' he whispered. 'You kill me, you're a dead man. You don't kill me, you're a dead man.'

Pyke dug the edge of the blade deeper into Crane's neck. 'I just want the truth.'

'I did it as a favour for a friend. They wanted to frighten Sobers and Edgar into leaving the country.'

'Your friend's name.'

'You'll have to kill me before I tell you that.'

'Elizabeth Malvern.' Pyke felt Crane's body stiffen. 'I'm right, aren't I?'

'If you knew that already, why are you even here?'

'I need to know *why* she asked you to try and intimidate Sobers and Mary Edgar.'

'I don't know. You'll have to ask her.'

'Don't worry, I will.' Pyke could smell the acrid scent of Crane's body odour. 'But right now I'm asking you. Where can I find her?'

'She's not here.'

'So it's true she's gone to the West Indies?'

'If you know all about her, why do you need me?'

'Why did she go?'

'Something to do with her brother. That's all I know.'

'What's someone who volunteers for the Vice Society doing with a pornographer like you?'

'You may as well cut my throat now,' Crane whispered, 'because that's as much as I'm going to tell you.'

Pyke could see that Sykes was preparing to take matters into his own hands. Wheeling Crane around so that they were blocking the door, he released his grip around Crane's neck and pushed him into Sykes's path. As they collided, Pyke bolted for the entrance and was all the way across the yard before Sykes could raise the alarm.

'Don't you understand, Pyke? Your son was caught trying to pick a gentleman's pocket on Camden Place. If I hadn't been in the vicinity, and hadn't spoken on behalf of the boy and offered to make amends to the injured party, they would have hauled him before a magistrate, perhaps even sent him to prison.'

Pyke stared at his uncle, still trying to take in this news. 'Is he here?'

'Upstairs in his room. He wouldn't say a word to me. Jo's tried to talk to him but he won't talk to her, either.'

'I'll try.' His words sounded hollow.

Godfrey shook his head. 'Your place is here with him, Pyke. Now more than ever. Not gallivanting off to the West Indies in pursuit of this phantom.' He stroked his white mane and looked across at Jo, who had just entered the room. She and Pyke exchanged an awkward glance. 'How is he?' Godfrey asked.

'He still refuses to say anything.' She looked at Pyke. 'I think we can assume he was led astray by the older boy you saw him with the other day.'

Until now Pyke had assumed that travelling to the West Indies in pursuit of Alefounder, and perhaps Elizabeth Malvern, though arduous and potentially costly, would not harm his own interests. Without really thinking about it, he knew instinctively that it was something he had to do. But here was the clearest of indications that his absence might do more harm than good. For how might Felix react if he knew what Pyke was planning? Perhaps Godfrey was right; perhaps the sensible thing to do would be to abandon his plans to travel to Jamaica. After all, he would have to bear the cost of the trip himself. He considered this, as he watched Godfrey and Jo. Yet he knew that he couldn't give up the investigation. He had come too far; he had given his word. It was true – no one else cared about Mary's death.

Addressing Jo, Godfrey said, 'Have you heard about Pyke's plan to travel to Jamaica? Now of all times.'

Briefly Jo met his gaze and then looked away. 'No, I wasn't aware of that.'

'I'll only be gone for a couple of months.' It might and probably would take him longer, but he didn't like to admit this. If he travelled by steamer, he'd been told the crossing could take as

219

little as three weeks.

'Don't you see how much your son needs you? What he did today was stupid but it was a cry for help. And now you're going to abandon him *again*.' Godfrey's face had turned the colour of beetroot.

'I'm sorry, Godfrey. I just can't let this thing go. I have to see it through to the end.' it was an inadequate answer, but it was the truth, too.

'Look, don't misunderstand me, dear boy. I'm sorry this mulatto woman was murdered but isn't that the point? She's dead. Your son isn't and he needs you here.'

'Don't you see – I'm doing this for him. In part, at least. So I can look him in the eye and say this is what I did. So he can see what I do and be proud of me. I can't just walk away from it now.'

'Let the police sort the matter out,' Godfrey said, sighing.

'I was there when they buried her.' He hesitated. 'It was just me at her graveside; me and the two gravediggers.' Pyke stole a glance at Jo, wanting her to see that he was capable of such feeling. 'I close my eyes at night and I can see her face, how it was mutilated.'

Godfrey regarded him with a mixture of pity and frustration. 'Your wife is dead, Pyke, and nothing you do now is going to bring her back.'

'And that's what you think this is?'

'Isn't it?'

They stared at one another awkwardly. Out of the corner of his eye, Pyke could see Jo squirming. But Godfrey hadn't quite finished. 'What if you're laid out with yellow fever or your ship is attacked or goes down in a storm. What will I do with Felix? I'm an old man.'

'Two months; I'll be back in two months.'

'I can't get through to him,' Godfrey said to Jo. 'He just refuses to listen. See if you can talk some sense to him.'

'Felix is almost ten,' Pyke said, trying to rein in his frustration. 'I lost my father when I was barely eight; he needs to learn to stand on his own two feet.'

'I shan't give you a penny. You won't get a single penny from me to fund this absurd venture.' Godfrey left the room muttering. 'Pig-headed man.'

Pyke waited until he was gone before saying to Jo, 'Do you think I'm as reckless and pig-headed as Godfrey seems to?'

For what seemed like minutes she stood there, her arms folded, refusing to answer the question.

The hackney carriage dropped them by the Theatre Royal on Drury Lane just as it was getting dark. Just him and Felix. The boy hadn't wanted to go with him at first but Pyke had forced the matter. The light was fading and the lamp-lighters were strung out along the street. The odour of rotting food and faeces was pungent in the breeze. Pyke took Felix's hand and told the lad to hold on to him 'at all costs'. Felix hadn't uttered a word to him during the short ride from Camden. They entered a narrow alley just past the Theatre Royal not wide enough for carriages to pass along. Two roughly dressed men stumbled out of a brothel. Through the door,

Felix caught a glimpse of the interior, lit up by the red, smoky flame of a grease lamp. He seemed transfixed by it. They passed a swag and slop-shop, tailoring hovels and a gin shop; a man was lying face down in the gutter outside. They stepped over him and continued into the heart of the rookery.

At the next corner, they came across a man dressed in a monkey jacket and oilskin cap who was whipping a donkey. Felix wanted to stop but Pyke tugged on his hand and pulled him onwards. On either side of the alleyway, disembodied faces stared at them through shattered window panes; in doorways, barefoot children watched them pass. Some uttered obscenities, their harsh, guttural accents echoing down the intricate web of alleyways and courts; but most were silent. Pyke felt Felix's grip tighten around his hand. At the next corner, they stopped for a moment outside the door to an underground slaughterhouse; Felix stared down at a mound of quivering entrails. Next door, a stream of liquid refuse from a tripe scraper and scum-boiler leaked into an open cess trench. The rookery was where Pyke had grown up, had been his home until his uncle had rescued him, and he wanted Felix to see it in all its unvarnished nastiness. They passed a toothless man who stood half naked in the street. He giggled as they stepped around him and then followed them, his trousers around his ankles, hands outstretched for coins.

At the heart of the rookery was a dilapidated building that stood on the foundations of an old leper hospital. It was called the Rat's Castle and its walls were buckled, its windows patched with rags and paper. At one of the entrances, paupers fresh from oakum picking and bone grinding tugged on Pyke's coat sleeve, begging for money; Pyke pushed them to one side and led Felix into the darkened interior. A long passageway took them into the bowels of the building, past rooms where men and women scolded, fought, swore and copulated with one another. At the top of a corkscrew staircase, a man wearing a torn shooting jacket and a billycock hat jumped out of the shadows. Felix recoiled but Pyke pushed the man backwards; pushed him so hard he toppled on to his backside.

They continued along another passageway; eventually it opened up into a much larger room where children as young as six or seven, orphans and runaways mostly, lay head to toe on the rotten floorboards, with not even a rag to sleep under. One boy was sobbing; another was being sick. A man and a woman were openly copulating in front of them. No one paid the newcomers much attention at first, but then an older boy, perhaps thirteen or fourteen, sidled up to them and asked Pyke how much he wanted 'for the boy'. He inspected Felix as if he were a slab of meat. Grabbing his son's hand, Pyke led Felix back along the passageway, ignoring the older boy's protestations. At the stairs, a couple of men were waiting for them; Pyke could see from their eyes they meant business. With his free hand, he withdrew his Long Sea Service pistol from his belt and brandished it in their faces. They fell back and let them pass. Outside the building, they retraced their path out of the rookery. Felix didn't say a single word to Pyke until they were safely ensconced inside a hackney carriage bound for Camden Town.

'That was all I knew until Godfrey offered to take me into his home.' Pyke waited. 'I don't want that life for you.'

From the bench on the other side of carriage, Felix just nodded.

'What you did today was foolish but, worse than that, it was unnecessary. Those people we saw just now; they steal because they have to. If they don't steal, they starve. We should never forget how lucky we are.'

Felix stared down at his boots. 'I'm sorry,' he mumbled.

'Reading stories can give you *some* insight into other people's lives but they never give you the whole picture.' Pyke paused to gather his thoughts. 'People tend to do things because they have to; when they don't have a choice. Often it isn't about right or wrong. It's about surviving.'

Felix seemed to consider this. 'Is that why you did some of the things you did?' he said, in a quiet, deliberate voice.

'In Godfrey's book, the character is presented in a certain way to shock and appal the readers, or at least that's what I'm guessing because I haven't actually read it.'

Felix stared at him, open mouthed. '*You* haven't read it?'

'All I'm saying is that there are always reasons why characters are drawn in the ways they are. They're there to teach us, scare us, entertain us.

224

It's not the same as what you saw just now at the Rat's Castle; there, people do what they have to in order to live. Do you understand what I'm trying to tell you?'

Felix looked through the glass at the darkened street but didn't say anything. They rode in silence for a few minutes, the clatter of wheels on cobblestones filling the carriage.

'I have to go away for a while,' Pyke said quietly.

He waited for Felix to react but the boy just sat there, then nodded. 'I heard you talking with Godfrey.'

'And what do you think?'

Felix looked up at him. There were tears in his eyes, but he was trying not to cry. 'How long will you be gone?'

'Two months, maybe a little longer.'

'Where are you going?'

'Jamaica.'

'Why?'

'I need to find the man who killed that young woman.'

Felix turned for a moment and looked out of the window in silence. 'I won't ever steal again, unless I have to.'

Pyke reached out and ruffled Felix's hair, the way he used to do when he was much younger.

Later, after Pyke had put Felix to bed, he joined Jo in the front room. His uncle had already turned in for the night. Collecting a half-full bottle of claret from the kitchen, he poured out two glasses. Jo took one reluctantly. They sat

225

down on either end of the sofa.

'Do you think I'm abandoning my son?' He stared into the empty fireplace, then turned to face her.

'Why are you asking me?' Her tone was gentle but measured.

'Because I value your opinion.'

Her expression remained inscrutable. 'But nothing I say will make you change your mind, will it?'

'So you *do* think I'm abandoning Felix.'

'I didn't say that.' She took a sip of wine and then put the glass down on the floor and retrieved what turned out to be a purse from the folds of her skirt. Putting it down in between them on the sofa, she added, 'Here. Take it. Pay me back when you get the chance.'

Pyke looked down at the bulging purse and then up at Jo's face. 'You'd really do that for me?'

She shrugged, as though the offer wasn't a generous one. 'There's seventy pounds. If you need it, it's yours.'

'I can't.' Pyke tried to swallow. 'I couldn't possibly take your money. But I'm touched more than I can say. That you'd even think about offering me your life savings is...' He couldn't think how to finish the sentence.

'Felix will be all right. Godfrey and I will keep a close eye on him. I *promise*.' This time, when she looked at him, her eyes were glistening in the candlelight.

He picked up the cloth purse and held it out for her to take. As she did so, their fingers brushed against each other. It was just the faintest of touches. Pyke didn't dare look into her face but noticed that she hadn't withdrawn her hand. She let the purse fall back on to the sofa. Neither of them moved. Finally he raised his eyes to meet hers. He felt a pull in his stomach. Extending his fingertip, he touched one of her knuckles. She didn't flinch.

'Pyke...'

Their fingers were coiled around one another; he could feel his heart thumping. 'Yes?'

'What's happening?'

He edged towards her, close enough to smell her sandalwood musk, and see the line of her creamy smooth neck. 'I don't know. Do you?'

She shut her eyes and allowed him to touch her cheek. 'No.'

Leaning towards her, he kissed her on the cheek and whispered, 'I don't want to lose you.'

'You won't.' Jo hesitated. 'You couldn't.'

'But it will complicate matters, won't it?'

This time Jo put her hand around his neck and pulled him into an embrace. 'From where I'm sitting,' she murmured, 'it's already complicated.'

Pyke opened his mouth and allowed his tongue to touch hers. Jo let out a slight gasp. 'Yes, how did it happen?' But he was already too far gone to think about the wisdom of what he was doing.

PART II

Falmouth, Jamaica

JUNE 1840

FOURTEEN

The captain of the two-mast brig had to wait until early afternoon for the right wind in order to negotiate a path through the treacherous channel between the adjoining reefs, but finally, they docked safely at the wharf at Falmouth. It was hot by then, hotter even than it had been at midday, and the sky was cloudless, a brilliant glazed blue that merged at some indistinguishable point with the gin-clear, turquoise waters. Ever since they had first entered the tropics, about a week earlier, the days had become hotter and hotter, and now Pyke felt as if he'd stepped into a giant brick kiln. In the distance, the shoreline, covered with mangrove swamps, shimmered as though it were not really there.

The steamer had docked in Kingston late the night before, after less than three weeks at sea, and at dawn Pyke had transferred to a much smaller brig, which, making use of favourable trade winds, had managed to negotiate a path around Morant Point and along the north coast of the island to Falmouth. The scenery had been spectacular – waterfalls tumbling from lush, mountainous terrain on to white-sanded coves – but after the greyness of London it was almost too much for Pyke's senses to take in. The sky was *too* blue, the sea *too* clear, and somehow none of it seemed real.

There were a couple of tall ships anchored

beyond the reef but neither was the *Island Queen*. Nor did Pyke expect to see that particular vessel for a week or two, for although the winds had been favourable for both vessels for much of the journey across the Atlantic, there had also been lulls where the wind had dropped to almost nothing. On those occasions, the steamer had turned to its giant paddle wheel and proceeded at pace, while the *Island Queen* would have been left idling, with nothing to do but wait for the wind to return. Alefounder would not set foot in Jamaica for at least another week, possibly two, which would give Pyke time to prepare for his arrival.

As they neared the shoreline, buildings came into view, a mixture of one- and two-storey dwellings built mostly from wood in the Georgian style with gingerbread fretwork, hip roofs and sash windows. Soaring above these was the occasional cabbage palm, a church tower in the far distance, and what appeared to be the town hall or courthouse, an impressive edifice with four Tuscan columns supporting an ornamental portico and pediment. 'The most fashionable port in the New World,' one of his travelling companions from Kingston had claimed. Pyke had told him that he'd reserve judgement until he saw the place for himself.

The whole town, it seemed, had come to meet the brig, for as soon as Pyke stepped off the gangplank, he was surrounded by a swarm of children fighting for the privilege of carrying his solitary suitcase. Pyke swatted them away and took a deep breath; if anything, it was hotter on land than it had been on the ship. There, at least, a stiff sea breeze had kept them cool but, here on terra firma, there was a barely a puff of wind.

Taking out his handkerchief, he mopped his brow and looked around the dusty wharf, where people and animals – mostly dogs, goats and fowl – were milling around on ground baked hard by the fierce sun. Workers, with their sleeves rolled up and floppy hats pulled down over their eyes to protect them from the glare of the sun, had already started to unload crates and sacks from the hold of the brig.

Someone had recommended a guest house on Seaboard Street, run by a jovial Scottish widow called Mrs McAlister, and having taken instructions, Pyke needed only a few minutes to find his way there. The street was dusty and deserted, and the guest house, a freshly painted, two-storey brick and timber building, looked directly out over the sea. Pyke put down his suitcase on the covered veranda and called out, 'Hello?' He'd taken off his coat, which was slung over his shoulder, and had unbuttoned some of his shirt. Pools of sweat were clearly visible under each armpit but he didn't care. A plump, matronly woman who introduced herself as Gertrude Mc-Alister greeted Pyke a few moments later and led him to a room on the upper floor with a veranda overlooking the road below and the ocean. A young woman with braided hair and glistening, blue-black skin, brought him a glass of fruit punch, which he drank down in one gulp.

About an hour later, after Pyke had bought a light cotton jacket and matching trousers, together with three cotton shirts and a straw hat, and had bathed in a copper tub in the deserted yard of the guest house, he decided to have a walk around the town, to the dismay of his host. She tried to dissuade him from venturing any farther afield than the veranda but wouldn't give a reason, alluding only to 'trouble' that might take place later that evening.

When Pyke asked whether the town had a newspaper, the landlady's chest puffed up and she told him it boasted three or perhaps four newspapers, if you counted the *Baptist Herald,* which she didn't because it was published only monthly and she didn't care for its tub-thumping agenda. Only marginally better, she added, was the *Falmouth Post,* which was still new and was agitating for further reform – 'as if there hasn't been enough upheaval already', she said, shaking her head. No, if he wanted a newspaper that reflected the concerns of respectable folk he should consult either the *Cornwall Chronicle* or the *Cornwall Gazette,* both of which were solidly committed to defending the Crown. Pyke asked her where he could find the offices of the *Falmouth Post.* She told him, of course, but admonished him under her breath.

The orange sun was low in the sky by the time Pyke ventured out, and the air felt a little cooler, though it was still balmy. He wandered along Seaboard Street as far as the courthouse and, from there, made his way up to the main square. The town, as far as he could tell, had been constructed according to a grid pattern, with streets running parallel and perpendicular to each other, making it easy to navigate. It was also surprisingly clean and the houses were, on the whole, respectable and well maintained. Most of the people he passed on Seaboard Street and on the main square were white, but as soon as he ventured farther afield, even by a block or two, the houses were smaller, and the faces in the doorways and windows were predominantly black. Though Pyke didn't feel unsafe, he didn't feel comfortable either. On the steamer from Southampton he'd been told over and over that Jamaica was an extension of the 'mother country', but in these hot, dusty streets, surrounded by alien faces and accosted by unfamiliar scents, he felt a long way from what he considered to be home.

The offices of the *Falmouth Post* occupied a timber and brick building on Market Street. Pyke found its proprietor, a tall, heavy-boned man with curly, black hair and light coffee-coloured skin, who introduced himself as John Harper. He was busy instructing his younger assistant in the craft of typesetting.

'Now, how can I help you, sir?' Harper eyed Pyke cautiously as he pushed his wire-framed spectacles farther up his nose. They had moved into his private office.

'Call me Pyke.'

'How can I help you, Mr Pyke?'

'Just Pyke will do fine.'

Harper nodded.

'Do you know a man called Michael Pemberton? I'm told he's a lawyer here in town.'

It was the name Pyke had been given by Mc-Quillan, captain of the *Island Queen;* according to him, it was Pemberton who had arranged Mary

Edgar's passage and seen her off at the wharf. Pyke felt that a newspaper was as good a place as any to start asking questions about the town's dignitaries; and a newspaperman committed to a reformist agenda might be more willing to talk candidly than one set on maintaining the status quo.

Harper's expression remained wary. 'He's an attorney here all right, but he spends most of his time up at Ginger Hill.'

'Ginger Hill?'

'It's a plantation about two hours' ride from here, up in the mountains.' Harper spoke in a deep, clear voice that suggested only the faintest trace of an accent. 'He's the estate manager.'

'But he has an office in the town?'

'You can sometimes find him at his house on Rodney Street, and he also owns a small plot of land a few miles south of here, just outside Martha Brae.' Harper studied him carefully, perhaps trying to work out Pyke's interest in the attorney.

'What kind of a man is he?'

'That would depend on who you're asking.'

'I'm asking you.'

'To a complete stranger, I'd say he was ambitious and hard working.'

That made Pyke smile. 'I think I understand.' He sat forward on his chair. 'What about Mary Edgar?'

Harper's expression remained unchanged. 'What about her?'

'You do know who I'm talking about, then.'

The big man's eyes never once left Pyke's face. 'This is a small community, sir. People tend to know each other.'

'But did ... *do* you know her in particular?' Pyke waited, hoping Harper hadn't noticed his slip.

A short silence hung between them. 'Perhaps I should ask why you're so interested in these people.'

Pyke considered telling him the truth but didn't yet know whether he could be trusted. 'If I said I was an old friend, would you believe me?'

'No, but I'm curious none the less. You do know Mary Edgar sailed for London about three months ago?'

'And Pemberton arranged her passage.'

The newspaperman frowned. 'Pemberton?'

'I'm told he saw her off at the wharf.'

'Pemberton might have made the arrangements but Charles Malvern would have been there to see her off.'

Pyke tried not to show too much interest but felt his skin prickle with excitement. 'So Charles Malvern and Mary Edgar are attached?'

'Engaged to be married, as far as I know,' Harper said.

'And Charles is Silas's son?'

'That's right.'

Briefly he assimilated this new piece of information. He wondered whether it explained why Elizabeth Malvern had sent Crane and his men to try to frighten Sobers and Mary Edgar into fleeing the city. He certainly couldn't see Silas Malvern welcoming Mary into his family with open arms. But it raised other questions, too. If Mary had been engaged to Charles Malvern, why had she taken a room in a lodging house on the

Ratcliff Highway? And why had she been dallying with Alefounder?

'I was told Silas's daughter, Elizabeth Malvern, had sailed for this part of the world.' By Pyke's calculations, she would have left two or possibly three weeks before him, and if she'd come by steamer, she should have been there for a number of weeks already.

'Not as far as I'm aware.' Harper's elbows were resting on the desk. He was trying to appear relaxed but Pyke could see the tension in his shoulders.

'Are you certain about that?'

'You want her, ask for her up at Ginger Hill.'

'I'll do that,' Pyke said, still trying to work out whether he liked the big newspaperman. 'It can't have been easy for people to take, a mulatto girl being engaged to a rich white planter.'

'I suppose not.'

'I'm guessing his family have objections, too. The father, for example. You knew him when he was here?'

'Not personally.' Harper's eyes narrowed.

'I wouldn't think you'd be one of their supporters.'

'Who said I was?'

'Then what's to stop us from having a private chat?'

But Harper was rubbing his chin and looking at Pyke with ill-concealed suspicion. 'You know something? This conversation is beginning to make me feel uncomfortable. So either you tell me what you want and why you're here or I ask you to leave.'

238

Pyke nodded. 'All right.'

From his desk, the newspaperman produced a bottle of rum and two glasses. He filled them with the murky spirit and pushed one of them across the desk. Pyke took it, closed his eyes and swallowed the rum in a single gulp. The fiery liquid burned the sides of his throat. Harper laughed when he saw Pyke shudder. 'Most white folk take it with water,' he said, still grinning.

'Kill-devil and water.'

The words hung in the air. Pyke thought about McQuillan's claim that 'kill-devil' had been some kind of code word used by Mary Edgar and Arthur Sobers.

'That's right,' Harper said, eventually. 'So what were you about to tell me?'

Pyke started with news of Mary Edgar's murder and proceeded with a summary of his investigation to date. He left nothing out, apart from Alefounder's involvement with the dead woman and the fact that the sugar trader would shortly be arriving in Falmouth. He also didn't say anything about his suspicions regarding Elizabeth Malvern or indeed about the manner of Mary Edgar's death; for now, this was something he wanted to keep to himself. When he'd said all there was to say, Pyke took a sip of the fresh glass of rum Harper had poured him then swore the newspaperman to silence.

'I didn't know Mary Edgar personally but I'm sorry she's dead. Like you said, she was a beauty.' Harper hesitated, not quite meeting Pyke's gaze. 'Do you know who killed her?'

This time it was Pyke's turn to be reticent. He

239

tried to swat a fly that had landed on his arm.

'What I meant to ask was why, given she was killed in London, have you made the trip all the way out here?'

This was also a question Pyke wasn't prepared to answer. Instead, he waited for a moment and said, 'I wonder whether Charles Malvern knows his fiancée has been murdered.'

Harper poured himself another rum. 'I publish a daily newspaper and *I* hadn't heard about it. But someone might have written him a letter, his father or sister...'

Or someone might have travelled from England to break the news to him in person...

'Tell me about the father.'

'At one time Silas Malvern was the largest slave-owner in the county. About four or five years ago, just after the first emancipation act, he decided to move to England. Perhaps he saw the writing on the wall. In any case, he sold everything but Ginger Hill and moved to England with his daughter Elizabeth.'

'And Charles stayed here?'

'That's right.'

'What kind of man is he?'

'Silas or Charles?'

'Silas.'

Harper looked at him and shrugged. 'Well, he wasn't the worst of them, not by a long way.' Then he rose to his feet and told Pyke he wanted to show him something, if Pyke had a few moments to spare.

It had already fallen dark in the short space of time they had been talking, although the air was still warm and filled with the trilling of cicadas. They walked in silence along Market Street. It was noticeably quieter, eerily so, and when Pyke mentioned this to Harper, and asked why all the shutters and windows of the houses had been boarded up, Harper assured him that all would soon become clear.

Pyke heard them before he saw them; a mob of men, white men, gathered in a semicircle around a fight or some kind of spectacle in front of the courthouse. It turned out not to be a fight, though. Harper, who for obvious reasons kept his distance, said, 'This is Jamaican justice.' A black man, stripped naked to his trousers, was lying on the ground chained to a rock. Next to him, a burly white man holding a whip was catching his breath, as were the crowd who had assembled to witness the spectacle. 'The Custos found him guilty of theft, so this is his punishment.' The next lash of the whip, when it finally came, made Pyke look away. The following made him wince; twenty-five lashes later, he wanted to be sick. The mob roared their approval at every one of them and by the end there was almost nothing left of the man's back.

'There'll be retribution later,' Harper said, as they made their way to a place that he'd euphemistically called 'the hole'. 'That's why all the shutters have been closed. Once the white folk have all gone home, they'll move in from the edge of town and untie the man you saw being whipped. You can smell the anger in the air. I wouldn't go for a walk later, if I were you.' Pyke noticed Harper had referred to the town's black population as 'they'.

In fact, the 'hole' was not as euphemistically named as Pyke had imagined. The space had been dug into the ground and was covered by a roof made of corrugated iron and bamboo. It was the only place in the town, as Harper later explained, where whites and blacks could mix without causing upset. Harper also said it served the cheapest and best rum. Pyke sat on an overturned crate while Harper bought the drinks at the counter. In spite of the late hour, the room was like a furnace and Pyke's new cotton shirt was already damp with perspiration.

'The fellow with the whip,' Harper explained, after he'd put two glasses of rum filled to the brim down on the crate between them. 'That was the Custos.' When he saw Pyke didn't understand the term, he clarified, 'The chief magistrate.'

'And the man being whipped – were the charges against him fair?'

This made the big man laugh. 'They reckon he stole two goats from a landowner near Martha Brae.' Harper sat forward, his gigantic forearms resting on the crate, so that Pyke could smell the rum on his breath. 'Actually, you know him, or know of him. Your friend Michael Pemberton made the accusation.'

They sipped their rum. It was certainly more palatable than the drink Pyke had imbibed at Samuel's place in the East End. 'What had this man *really* done?'

The newspaper proprietor considered Pyke's question. 'How much do you know about this island?'

'I know the apprenticeship system was abolished two years ago.' As Pyke understood it, this was a system introduced after slavery had been outlawed three or four years previously, mostly to appease the planters. Former slaves were 'apprenticed' to their masters for a period of time which, in effect, meant they had to work in conditions similar to slavery in order to 'earn' their freedom. Pyke had read that abuses were commonplace and the system had been almost as unpopular as slavery itself, or perhaps more so; under slavery those working on the estates had at least received medical care from trained doctors.

'And how have your newspapers reported this emancipation?' The irony was difficult to miss.

'Are you saying nothing much has changed?'

'Everything and nothing.' Harper swallowed what remained of his rum and shuddered slightly. 'You can't put a price on a man's freedom. I still remember the first day I bought my freedom; the air tasted cleaner, the sun shone more brightly, the sky was that much bluer. But the landlords still have all the power and they expect us to work on their estates for next to nothing.' His eyes were shining. 'Under slavery, they were obliged to provide housing and provision grounds so that we could grow our own food. These are places where folk have lived their entire lives, where their relatives and their ancestors are buried. Now, under this new system, the landlords are charging rents almost as high as the wages they're prepared to pay. So it's true, folk ain't happy, and rightly so. The man you saw being whipped, Isaac Webb, was trying to do something about it. He's organised a strike up at Ginger Hill – they're refusing to bring in the harvest until their wage demands have been met – and now the dispute's threatening to spread across the island.'

Harper paused to wipe his face with a handkerchief. 'You see, the cane's ripe and ready to be harvested. If it ain't cut down and pressed in the next week or so, the whole crop will be lost. Malvern's workers know this and they're holding out against going to the fields, hoping he'll buckle and agree to pay them a fair wage.' From nowhere, two more rums appeared on the table. Harper grinned.

Pyke hadn't finished the one in his hand and already felt a little drunk. 'So Malvern, Pemberton, the Custos, there's no difference between them?'

'I didn't say that.' Harper picked up the full glass of rum and drank it in a single gulp. 'The dispute started at Ginger Hill because they reckon he's a soft touch.' His eyes were a little bloodshot and his accent was stronger now, too. 'Like I said, Silas wasn't the worst of them and neither is his son.'

Pyke took a sip of the next rum. Harper watched him, smiling. 'But I heard Charles is looking to leave, sell up and join his fiancée in London, or at least that's what his plans were before...' Harper hesitated, suddenly not sure what to say. But there was a mischievous twinkle in his eyes. 'In fact that's who I thought you were, when you first walked through my door, asking questions about Pemberton and Mary Edgar.'

'Who?' Pyke asked, confused.

'A potential buyer.'

'A potential or a particular buyer?'

'Malvern's had lots of potential buyers over the past year and a half; all have pulled out. I'm told a gentleman from Antigua is expected here soon. I'm also told Malvern has high hopes for this one. He's desperate to sell the estate. I have no idea how your news will affect his plans.'

Pyke turned this information over in his mind, while Harper ordered another round of drinks. 'You know this buyer's name?' he asked when Harper returned, this time carrying four glasses of rum between his calloused fingers.

'Not off the top of my head but I can find out. Why you ask?'

'This buyer is expected here soon. And if he's coming all the way from Antigua, it isn't likely anyone's actually met him, is it?'

'Exactly what I was thinking.'

Later Pyke would wonder why the newspaper-man had been so keen for him to do what they eventually agreed upon, but at the time they were both swept up on a giddy tide of rum.

'What I still don't understand is why, if Mary was killed in London, you came all this way to Jamaica.'

Pyke noticed Harper had just called her 'Mary' but didn't comment. 'I came for the sunshine.' He upended the glass into his mouth and shuddered involuntarily. 'And the rum.'

Harper's bloodshot eyes contracted slightly and his smile curdled at the corners of his mouth. 'You don't look or act like a policeman. You should take that as a compliment, by the way.'

'I'm not, but I was hired by a policeman to try

to find out who killed Mary Edgar.'

'Why?'

Pyke went to finish the latest of his rums. He closed his eyes and the dark, unfamiliar room began to spin. 'It's a long story, but I used to be a Bow Street Runner.'

'A Bow Street Runner, eh?' Harper said it as if he knew what a Bow Street Runner was. 'So you ever had to kill another man?' As he said it, he tried to grin but the effort was stillborn.

After Harper had guided him back to Mrs Mc-Alister's guest house on Seaboard Street, Pyke sat for a while on the veranda staring out at the ocean and listening to the waves breaking over the rocks. He felt more than pleasantly drunk, and as he sat there, listening to the cicadas and watching the stars dotted across the entire night sky, he almost didn't know where he was, or what he was supposed to be doing. He also knew that sleep was beyond him and decided to walk, or stumble, along Seaboard Street as far as the courthouse. The men with torches who'd been there earlier had gone elsewhere but the man who'd been whipped, Isaac Webb, was still lying there chained to a rock. Pyke had a small bottle of rum that Harper had pressed into his hands when they'd left the hole, and he bent over Webb's battered body and brought the bottle to his lips. The smell of the rum seemed to revive the man a little. Webb was lying on his front. His back, meanwhile, was criss-crossed with a lattice of raw and just about healed scars; clearly it wasn't the first time he'd suffered such a punishment. He opened his mouth and Pyke wetted his lips with some of the rum. Just for a moment, he managed to lift up his head sufficiently to see who was doing this for him. He managed a smile and croaked, 'T'anks, man.' The smell of fresh blood, together with all the rum he'd consumed, made Pyke want to vomit. Pressing the bottle into Webb's hand, Pyke stood up and looked around him, into the darkness. He noticed something move, someone; a group of people, in fact, edging towards him from the other side of the courthouse, their faces hidden by the darkness. It was only then that he remembered Harper's warning and stepped away from Webb. He held up his hands, as though to distance himself from what had happened.

The first stone hit him squarely in the chest and after that Pyke remembered running; not in any particular direction and not to the relative safety of his guest house because the mob was blocking his path back along Seaboard Street. He just ran, and behind him he could hear shouts and the sound of people following him. He ran along one street and up another, where the row of houses came to an end. Then he followed the dirt track as it disappeared into a dense mass of unfamiliar trees and vines and went as far as the seashore, where he stopped and listened. Over his own panting he could hear the muffled sounds of his pursuers and saw that some of them were carrying machetes. Pyke quickly took off his boots and socks, pulled up his trousers and waded into the sea, navigating a path around a rocky promontory. The water was warm and the sand soft against his bare soles. He was sweating profusely but kept moving along the beach, and soon he couldn't hear anything apart from the waves gently lapping against the sand and the mosquitoes buzzing in his ear. Using the moonlight to guide him, he followed the beach as far as it took him and stopped at a rocky peninsula. There was no one following him now, and everything was perfectly still. The chase had sobered him up a little but the rum had done something to his mind; shapes shifted in and out of focus. He felt disoriented. Up above him the sky was filled with more stars than he had ever seen before in his life. Staring up at them, Pyke thought about Felix and whether he would ever see his son again.

FIFTEEN

Pemberton's office was located on the ground floor of a Georgian-style building on the corner of Victoria and Rodney Streets, across the track from the police station. The lower floor was built from stone and the upper floor from wood. The veranda, which ran along the front of the building, was supported by wooden columns and afforded the man who was sitting there a view across the ocean. Pyke called up, asking where he could find Michael Pemberton.

'You're looking at him,' the man said, standing up and leaning against the wrought-iron railing. 'And who might you be, sir?' Even from a distance, Pyke could tell he cut an imposing figure; six and a half feet tall, broad, with well-developed shoulders, a wide neck and hairy, sunburnt forearms.

Pyke held his hand up to his face, to protect his eyes from the sun. 'The name's Montgomery Squires.' He waited for it to have an effect; he didn't have to wait for too long.

Pyke had just come from a sober lunch with Harper at which the newspaper proprietor had told him everything he'd managed to dig up about Squires, which wasn't very much. It was early afternoon and another cloudless day, perhaps even hotter than it had been the day before, and Pyke felt dry-mouthed and irritable, both because of the heat and all the rum he'd consumed with Harper the previous night.

'Squires, you say?' Pemberton studied Pyke carefully from the veranda. His body was stiff with tension and his stare cold and suspicious. 'We weren't expecting you for at least another week.'

'I caught an earlier ship and the winds were more favourable than I'd expected.'

'The door's open. Let yourself in; I'll meet you in the hallway.' Pemberton disappeared from view and Pyke did as he'd been instructed. The room was cool, compared to the street, and as Pyke watched the attorney descend the stairs, one at a time, he tried to take the man's measure.

Despite his size, Pemberton moved with easy grace and possessed an air of self-confidence that suggested he was used to getting his own way. He carried himself with a quiet authority but Pyke didn't doubt he'd know how to use his fists, if the occasion presented itself. In his study, Pemberton called to his servant to bring them some fruit punch and invited Pyke to sit on one of the armchairs. He wore his shirt open at the collar, with a silk neckerchief under it. As they waited for the punch to arrive, he said he was sure they could find a way of addressing their dilemma.

'And what dilemma is that?' Pyke asked.

'You're not expected at Ginger Hill for at least another week.'

'I came here first as a courtesy but surely I don't need your permission to visit an estate that I may or may not make an offer on.'

'But if you're not expected...'

Pyke cut him off. 'Let me be blunt. The fact that I'm *not* expected is exactly what I want. Then, I can see things as they really are, not some charade put on for my benefit. If I'm to pay, let's say, ten thousand for Ginger Hill, then I want to see it, warts and all.'

Pemberton shuffled uneasily in his chair. He removed a neckerchief and went to mop his forehead. 'I quite understand, but if I could prevail upon your patience to stay in Falmouth for another night...'

'Out of the question. I've arranged the use of a horse and if you'll give me instructions, I plan to set off as soon as I'm finished here.'

'But Mr Squires...'

Pyke held up his hand. 'Call me Monty. And I'm afraid you'll find my mind's made up on this one.'

'But Monty...'

'Of course, there are others in town who'll be

able to direct me to Ginger Hill, so strictly speaking, I don't *need* to be here.'

The servant came in carrying a tray with two tall glasses filled with a red-coloured fruit punch.

'Surely decorum will stop you from calling on the great house at Ginger Hill entirely unannounced...'

Pyke stood up, took one of the glasses and drank about half. 'Delicious. Quite delicious.' He turned to Pemberton and smiled. 'When it comes to *my* money, sir, there is no such thing as decorum.'

As he let himself out of the front door, he heard Pemberton's voice. 'But it's not safe, sir, to ride unaccompanied...'

This much had struck Pyke as probably correct, given what had happened to him the night before in front of the courthouse, but he wasn't about to let Pemberton talk him around. Still, as soon as he'd ridden out of town on a track baked hard by the sun, heading due south for the village of Martha Brae, Pyke had wondered about the wisdom of what he was doing. As he quickly realised, the town belonged to the whites but the countryside – or at least those areas not part of the sugar plantations that extended from the coastal plains up into the mountains – belonged to the former slaves. Those men he rode past on the track acknowledged him with a curt nod or ignored him. Harper had assured Pyke he would probably be safe – probably – and as it turned out, he was right; no one paid him much attention.

The horse was an elderly spotted gelding, and

perhaps because of the afternoon heat, it needed plenty of encouragement to remain at a sedate canter. The flint track flattened out after a while, with fields of tall, ripe sugar cane appearing on either side which swayed gently in the breeze. Farther along, they began another ascent, but this time the track was shaded by towering guano and cotton trees and logwoods whose recently discarded blossoms had been trampled into the clay verges. The occasional cloud floated across an otherwise limitless blue sky, and apart from the gentle clip-clop of hooves and the rustling of cane leaves, all was quiet. Up above, what looked like a vulture circled effortlessly in the sky, but elsewhere the heat of the sun had killed all activity.

He barely passed a soul for the first hour and a half of the ride, but as they neared what he guessed was the boundary of the Ginger Hill estate, more faces appeared at the sides of the track; black faces, curious but unsmiling. Pyke wondered whether these were the workers who, under Webb's instruction, were refusing to harvest the ripe cane and whether Charles Malvern had, in any way, been responsible for the scene Pyke had witnessed in front of the courthouse. No one spoke a word to him, in anger or otherwise, and in light of what had happened to Webb, he understood their reticence. Labourers in England were kept under the cosh, too, but never in such an explicit manner. A few years earlier, Pyke had witnessed at first hand the working conditions experienced by the navvies building the railways, but hard as they were, those men had volunteered to do their work and were paid, albeit poorly.

Here, emancipation was just a word, as Harper had said, and nothing seemed to have changed in the years since slavery had been outlawed. Seen in this light, it was hard not to think of the island as a vast prison camp dedicated to earning its proprietors as much money as possible, with no thought spared for the lives ruined in the process.

About a mile farther along the track a stone gate guarded another, smaller path up to the Ginger Hill great house, which sat atop a steep hillock and commanded views of the surrounding terrain. It took Pyke ten minutes to ride up to it. It was a sprawling colonial-style edifice built out of stone and wood, with two wings attached to the main building. The house looked more impressive from a distance than it did close up, for although it was still an imposing building, it had fallen into a state of disrepair. Roof slates hadn't been replaced; timber window frames were rotting; vines had been allowed to crawl unchecked up walls; grass sprouted through flagstones in the courtyard and the front lawn was choked with weeds.

Pyke tied his gelding to a cotton tree and took the steps at the front of the great house two at a time. A servant had heard him approach and had opened the front door. His incurious face registered the name 'Montgomery Squires' without interest. Pyke waited in the central hall, which ran along the entire length of the building, and admired the dark wooden floor, which had been polished so vigorously he could see his reflection in it.

Malvern greeted him red faced and out of breath. His thinning blond hair was matted to his pale scalp.

'Squires?' Malvern took his hand and shook it warmly, though the handshake itself was limp, like pressing a dead fish.

'Call me Monty.'

'Charles.' Malvern let his hand go. He was flustered, 'I'm afraid I wasn't expecting you for another week.'

'I know. I hope you don't mind the intrusion. I left a little earlier than expected and my ship made better time than I could have hoped. I called in to see your attorney and he assured me you wouldn't mind me calling on you unannounced.' Pyke led the way down the hall, even though he didn't know where he was going. It was important to establish his mastery from the start. The hall led to a large reception room furnished with sofas, chairs, an ottoman, stools, a mahogany bookcase and a matching side cabinet displaying fine china.

'A bit scruffy but it'll do, I suppose,' he said, apparently to himself but loud enough so that Malvern could hear.

'You'll stay for a few nights, of course,' Malvern said, trying to come to terms with this change of plan. 'I'll send someone down to Falmouth to pick up your luggage.'

Pyke thanked him and gave him the name of Mrs McAlister's guest house; Harper had promised to furnish Pyke's suitcase with apparel appropriate for a West Indian planter.

Malvern stood, hands on hips, muttering 'Very good' over and over to himself. He was a slight, insubstantial man with hunched shoulders, pinched cheeks and a pale, almost ghostly complexion. He had very little presence or charisma, and Pyke

254

wondered about his dealings with Pemberton – which one of them really made the decisions. But the most remarkable thing about him was his lips, which were plump and almost purple in colour, as though he'd just eaten a bowlful of ripe blackberries. If Pyke had passed him in the street, he wouldn't have paid him any attention, and Pyke wondered just how much of a disappointment he'd been to the father and grandfather who between them, according to Harper, had built the Ginger Hill estate into what it was.

The details regarding the Malvern family dynasty which Harper had furnished him with were, at best, sketchy. Pyke knew that Charles Malvern's grandfather, Amos, had arrived on the island some time in the early 1770s, penniless but ambitious, but he had little idea how the man had risen from the position of bookkeeper and overseer to plantation owner in just a few years. According to Harper, Amos Malvern had been a cruel and greedy man; someone capable of doing whatever was necessary in order to further his own position. Amos found that the title of planter suited him and, although he didn't have a particularly acute business mind, in those days it was difficult *not* to make money. Slaves from Africa were cheap and plentiful, the price of sugar was kept artificially high and demand was buoyant. But from the stories that Harper had told, it seemed that Amos's limitations as a planter were more than compensated for by his insatiable sexual appetite. In wedlock, he sired two children, Silas and Phillip, before his wife

255

died from yellow fever. But though he never remarried, he'd had countless other children with numerous mistresses, white and black, and even in old age, he remained an incorrigible goat. When he'd finally passed away, fittingly from the ravages of syphilis, it was rumoured that as many as twenty of his progeny, nearly all mulattos apart from Silas and Phillip, had attended the funeral.

Silas had taken over the plantation shortly after the turn of the century and as a serious, cautious young man, entirely different from his irascible father, he was the one who'd turned it into a serious commercial prospect. Under Amos's elder son the yield of raw sugar per acre trebled, as did the profits. And while Amos had, by all accounts, acted in a highly capricious manner with his slaves, fawning over them when the mood took him and then savagely whipping them if he felt they weren't displaying sufficient devotion, Silas treated them as workers first and slaves second. Realising that a contented workforce was also a productive one, he built a new hospital on the grounds of the estate, doubled their rations of salt fish, gave them better provision grounds and allowed them additional time to work their own patches. He also instituted a system of redress whereby his slaves had a forum in which to complain to him personally about excessively harsh treatment meted out by the estate's overseers.

Silas had married well, wedding the daughter of a neighbouring estate owner, and when his father-in-law passed away, this estate and another that he had bought for cash were swallowed up into the Ginger Hill empire, making him the largest and wealthiest slave-owner in the western part of the island. His wife had given him two children; Charles, the eldest, and Elizabeth, who was, by all accounts, his favourite. Indeed, until tragedy struck, many believed that Silas, and for that matter the whole Malvern family, had been blessed by God himself.

Harper didn't know the exact details of the tragedy that had ended the life of Silas's wife. The incident had taken place some twenty years earlier and the coroner at the time had recorded the death as 'accidental'. According to his report, Bonella Malvern had fallen to her death, either down the great house's staircase or directly over the first-floor banisters. Charles and Elizabeth would have been young children at the time. Afterwards, no one, not even the house servants, talked about the tragedy, and the funeral had been a small, very private affair. According to those who knew him, Silas had never really recovered from losing his wife but took solace in his daughter's companionship. Harper didn't know what Silas thought about Charles Malvern but speculated that their relationship hadn't been a good one. Ginger Hill had been spared from the violence that had swept through much of the western part of the island following the Christmas slave uprising in 1831, but by this time Silas had already decided to sell up and make a new home in England. Harper told Pyke that many blacks believed the great house was haunted; that Bonella's spirit lived on and roamed about the rooms and corridors. Some even believed that the whole family had been cursed. Harper didn't know where or how these rumours had started but he did know people, black people, who refused to go anywhere near the great house or its grounds.

Silas had eventually sold four of the five estates that made up his total holdings on the island and shortly afterwards had left for England, together with Elizabeth, to begin a new life in London. Apparently Charles had wanted to remain in Jamaica and had persuaded his father to retain Ginger Hill, but in recent times something had happened to change Charles's mind, and for almost a year he had been trying to find a buyer for the great house and five hundred acres of land, so he could follow his father and sister to London. Harper told Pyke that Charles lacked his father's intelligence and drive and that the estate had been running at a loss for the three years since Silas's departure. Apparently there had been numerous potential buyers, some serious prospects, but no one had yet made Malvern a 'reasonable' offer. This, Harper said with a grin, meant that he was now desperate to sell. Harper also explained that one of the prospective buyers had narrowly avoided being killed – he didn't know the exact details – and another had left the estate, and the island, apparently too traumatised to speak about his experiences.

'I was born in this house, Mr Squires, and to be perfectly honest, I never believed I'd leave it, at least not of my own volition.'

They were sitting in wicker chairs on the large covered veranda that overlooked the garden below and beyond, to the cane fields and thick forest of trees that covered the low conical hills in the distance. The smell was that of a garden gone to seed; the sickly sweetness of dead flowers combined with the perfumed scent of wild jasmine and honeysuckle. The light had faded, seemingly in a matter of minutes, and now wave after wave of fireflies, brilliant purple in colour, swept down into the valley beneath them. Pyke sat, quietly taking in the view. From where they were sitting, it was difficult to believe there was another human being on the island.

'Call me Monty, please,' Pyke repeated, loosening his collar. He had bathed and was wearing a white linen shirt he'd borrowed from his host. 'Why do you want to leave, if you don't mind me asking?'

Malvern appeared not to have heard Pyke's question. 'I always used to believe there were two types of people on the island, if you didn't count the blacks,' he said, staring out into the inky blackness. 'Those of us who were born here and who love this place with a passion, and those who come here to make as much money as possible in the shortest time and never even come close to regarding it as their home.' His mood was wistful, even melancholic.

'If you love this place as you claim to, why do you want to sell it and move on?'

'Ah, the all-important question.' Malvern's expression was hidden by the darkness. 'You like to get straight to the point, don't you? It's a skill my father always tells me I don't possess.' He appeared momentarily upset by this criticism. 'To tell you the truth I'm engaged to be married. And since my beloved fiancée has declared that she wants to marry and live in London – in fact, she has already departed these shores to plan our wedding – I'm afraid my time here is coming to an end.'

'Congratulations, sir.' Pyke stared out across the valley. 'You must love her very much, if you're prepared to give up all of this.'

So Malvern didn't yet know what had happened to his fiancée, which meant that his sister, Elizabeth, hadn't arrived on the island. Briefly Pyke wondered where she was and how long it would be before she arrived and broke the news to Malvern.

Pyke had expected to dislike Charles Malvern but now, sitting in the man's company, he found himself warming to his affable manner. As a result, his knowledge of what had taken place in London sat heavily on his conscience.

'I shall be sorry to part with this place, of course, but if one truly loves another person, one must be willing to make a sacrifice.'

'You mentioned just now that your fiancée has gone ahead to London to plan your nuptials?' Pyke hesitated. 'I know very little about that city but what little I do know tells me I'd want to be certain my fiancée was well looked after.' He smiled awkwardly. 'But I'm sure you know this, sir, and will have made all the necessary arrangements to ensure her safety. A chaperone, perhaps?' He was thinking about Arthur Sobers.

'A chaperone?' The colour had risen in Malvern's cheeks. 'I made arrangements, of course, but didn't insist upon a chaperone. Do you think me neglectful?'

'Of course not,' Pyke said quickly. 'I'm certain your fiancée is safe and looking forward to you joining her soon.'

'Indeed so.' Malvern stood up, apparently mollified, and stretched his legs. 'I hope you don't mind. There will be others joining us for dinner. Pemberton, whom you've already met, and his wife, Hermione, and Billy Dalling, who's one of the bookkeepers here at Ginger Hill. It'll be a merry little gathering, I hope, but if you'll excuse me I need just a few minutes to prepare myself.'

As Pyke watched Malvern amble into the house, he tried to imagine how such a placid, unassuming man could satisfy a woman as beautiful as Mary Edgar. But he was rich and white and that was perhaps sufficient to explain the attraction. Earlier in the conversation, Malvern had tried to paint himself as one of a new breed of men forever altered by their exposure to the lush, tropical environment and by the rigours of establishing their dominance over it, but in actuality he came across as peculiarly English, belonging to a particular class of expats determined to recreate a version of 'England' in whichever environment they found themselves.

Dinner was a stiff, awkward affair in which Pemberton dominated the conversation, to the point where Pyke almost forgot that Malvern was in the room. In fact, Malvern said very little throughout the three courses; as did Dalling, the bookkeeper, who contented himself with a number of furtive glances across the table at Pemberton's young wife, Hermione. It didn't take much imagination to guess why Dalling might be interested in Hermione Pemberton; there were two very apparent and sizeable reasons staring back at him across the table and the lady didn't appear to be shy about showing them off. For his part, Dalling was attractive in a swarthy, roguish way – certainly more so than Michael Pemberton – and Pyke could easily see how the two younger members of the dining party might fall into each other's arms.

Sweating from having eaten too much of the roast pork and imbibed too much of the Madeira, Pemberton seemed oblivious to the sexual tension that sparked between Dalling and his young wife. Instead he spent the best part of the evening interrogating Pyke on the best way to make rum; whether to slake the cane juice with fresh lime in order to make it granulate. He also wanted to pick Pyke's brain about the most appropriate way to treat former slaves and how to manage the rotation of cane fields. Hermione Pemberton asked a seemingly innocuous question about the parties and society events in Antigua; to which Pyke replied that he didn't have time to socialise. That drew an approving nod from Pemberton, but across the table Dalling raised his eyebrows. 'I'd always heard that Monty Squires was the last to leave any party.' The bookkeeper waited for Pyke to look at him and then smiled. 'But people get older and change their ways, don't they?'

Pyke didn't think anything of it until a little later in the meal when the subject turned to the role of the British army in keeping the peace, and Dalling, who, as far as Pyke could tell, had once served in the army himself, asked which regiment he'd belonged to. This time he studied the bookkeeper's face more carefully. Dalling was younger than Pyke but with the same muscular build, olive skin and dark-coloured hair. But as far as Pyke was concerned that was where the similarities ended; Dalling's nose was pointy and thin, his eyes were too far apart, his forehead protruded too far over his eyebrows and his eyes were almost translucent in colour, reminding Pyke of staring into a basin of water.

The first time he asked, Pyke ignored the question and asked Pemberton how he kept order on the estate – which produced a lengthy monologue about reward and punishment, with the emphasis on the latter rather than the former.

'I'm quite sure I know a fellow in the Fourteenth Dragoons. That was your regiment, wasn't it?' Dalling ran his finger down a scar that cut his left cheek diagonally in two.

They were seated opposite one another, with Pemberton just to Dalling's right, and this time he too took an interest in the bookkeeper's question. Pyke's expression remained composed but he could feel the perspiration dripping down his back. Dalling knew something; that much was beyond doubt.

'Perhaps you do, sir, but I have a terrible memory for names and an even worse one for faces.' He looked towards Pemberton and Malvern. 'And I do find reminiscences about the old regiment terribly dull.'

After that, Hermione intervened and persuaded Dalling to join her for some air on the veranda, leaving Pyke, Pemberton and Malvern to smoke their cigars and drink the rest of the brandy. More tedious conversation about the 'nigger problem' ensued, dominated by Pemberton, and it was only after he'd risen from the table and announced he had to 'attend to' his wife that Pyke could steer the conversation back to the subject of Mary Edgar.

'When we talked before dinner, I didn't mean to imply that London was, by definition, a dangerous city. I hope I didn't cause offence. I'm sure that living here carries just as many risks...'

Malvern's hollow cheeks were flush from the Madeira and brandy he'd drunk at dinner. 'Never a truer word spoken, sir,' he muttered, before realising he'd perhaps said too much.

'Do you mean to say it *is* dangerous here?'

'Dangerous is maybe the wrong word. But please, sir, credit me with more intelligence than to believe you are entirely unaware of our current difficulties.'

'I've heard, of course, that some of the workers are striking over rates of pay.'

Malvern nodded glumly. 'It's not all the blacks' fault, of course. Some planters have been demanding extortionate rents, almost as much as they offer to pay in wages, and a few have even forced those that can't or won't pay from their homes and their provision grounds. It's poisoned the whole atmosphere and driven the blacks up into the mountains, and also these damned free villages that missionaries like Knibb have been establishing with money donated by congregations in England. In his dotage, I'm told my father has

264

corresponded with Knibb and is on good terms with him so I wouldn't want to disparage the man, but he's certainly given the blacks ideas above their station. Owning their own homes and gardens? The idea is absurd. Let them have their freedom, that's what I say, but they need to work, too.' He paused. 'Most of our workforce is refusing to harvest the cane, and unless an agreement is reached in the next few days, the whole crop will be ruined. You know, I offered them almost two and a half shillings a day but they still turned me down, demanded three. *Three* shillings per day? I'd be ruined within a week.'

'Give them three and they'd demand four.' The voice came from somewhere behind them. Startled, they both turned around and saw Pemberton standing there. He had been listening to their conversation.

'But why not compromise at two and three-quarters and at least make sure the cane is harvested?' Pyke looked at Malvern rather than Pemberton. 'Can you afford for the whole crop to be lost?'

This perception seemed to upset Malvern. He stood up quickly – too quickly perhaps, because the sudden exercise after a heavy dinner seemed to make him dizzy – and said he was going to retire and that Pemberton could answer any questions about the management of the estate. But when Pyke looked behind him for the attorney, he too had gone, and for a few moments Pyke sat there at the empty table, contemplating the scene he had just witnessed and what it suggested about the health, or otherwise, of the estate.

There was a quiet knock on Pyke's bedroom door, shortly after he had retired for the night.

Quickly buttoning up his shirt, Pyke walked across the hardwood floor and opened the door slightly. William Dalling pushed his way into the room and waited for Pyke to close the door. 'This is a nice room, this one, probably the best in the house,' he said easily, as though his opinion had been invited. 'The view of the mountains is spectacular first thing in the morning.'

'I've had a long day, sir, and am not in the mood to play games. Tell me what you want and then leave.'

Dalling didn't appear to have heard him. 'Of course, it's quite right to give the bedroom with the finest views to the guest of honour.'

'Perhaps you didn't hear me. So, this one time, I'm going to pretend you're simple rather than rude and let it pass.'

'But let's just say the guest of honour wasn't who he claimed to be? How quickly would such a man be turned out of the finest bedroom in the house?'

Pyke felt the moistness on his palms. 'I have no idea what you're talking about.'

Dalling circled around him, nodding his head, as though amused by what Pyke had said. 'What would you say if I told you I'd met Montgomery Squires? Well, maybe not met him, but I've certainly been in the same room as him.'

Pyke's expression remained composed but inside he was trying not to panic. 'I'd say that Montgomery Squires isn't such an uncommon

266

name. I'd also say that you need to be very careful about making insinuations without knowing where they might take you.'

'Oh, I know very well where they're taking me.'

'Where's that?'

'A long way from this place, that's for sure.'

'And why do you think this?'

'I can see you're not short of a penny whereas I'm always just a few steps ahead of the poorhouse. Perhaps we should both look at this as a chance to even things up a little.'

Pyke took the measure of the man circling around him. 'That sounds like a very risky strategy, not one I'd want to pursue if I were you.'

But this seemed to entertain rather than unnerve the bookkeeper. 'Oh yes? And why is that?'

'If you start making accusations about people, anything could happen.'

'Is that some kind of a threat?'

'If I were threatening you, you'd know about it. You wouldn't have to ask.'

Dalling just grinned. 'Fancy yourself as a tough one, eh?'

'I'm just trying to make you aware of the situation.'

'I appreciate the warning, so what I'm going to do is lay my cards on the table.' His Adam's apple bobbed up and down in his throat. 'Let's say a hundred pounds will ensure that not a word of this conversation will be repeated to anyone in the house.'

The situation was starting to deteriorate beyond Pyke's control and there was nothing he could do about it. 'Why would I even think of paying you this kind of figure?'

Dalling stepped into the space between them, so close Pyke could smell the stale Madeira on his breath. 'Because you don't want Pemberton to find out what I know. Because if he does, I'd say your chances of making it off this estate are next to none.'

'Why?' Pyke paused. 'What would he do?'

'If Pemberton thought you were trying to cheat him, the question is, what *wouldn't* he do.'

Pyke looked into Dalling's eyes. 'And if he thought someone was cuckolding him?'

Later, Pyke would reflect on Dalling's expression with relief and some pleasure, but he knew, just as Dalling knew, that the bookkeeper would be able to make things unbearable for him unless he paid what the man had demanded. It meant that Pyke had to make plans of his own.

SIXTEEN

The following morning Pemberton was eating his breakfast alone in the dining room. He greeted Pyke's arrival with as little enthusiasm as it was possible to muster. Pyke poured himself a cup of coffee from the silver pot and sat down opposite the attorney.

'I'm guessing that you actually run the estate,' Pyke said, after a while, his eyes never leaving Pemberton's.

'I do my job.'

'A hard job for a fixed wage.'

'I'm not complaining.' Pemberton put a pastry into his mouth and began to chew.

'But it must be hard, knowing that all your hard work and acumen are benefiting someone who is clearly not your equal.'

The lawyer continued to chew his pastry and took a sip of coffee. 'Would you have said that if Charles were sitting here?'

Pyke picked up his coffee cup and stood up. 'On that note, perhaps you could tell me where I can find Charles?'

Pemberton directed him out on to the veranda, where the young planter was slouched in a wicker chair staring blankly out at the view. The sky was absolutely clear and, for the time being, the air around them was fresh and cool. In the distance, over the buzzing of insects and the chirping of birds, Pyke could hear the flow of the river. After they had greeted one another, Pyke took a chair next to Malvern. For a while, the two of them stared in silence at the vista of green that extended as far as the eye could see.

'It's beautiful up here, isn't it?'

Malvern turned to face him. 'Imagine waking up to these views every morning. If you buy this place, you won't regret it, I assure you.'

Pyke nodded amiably. 'I was told that it was your father who built this house.'

'My grandfather, actually. Or he built the main part. My father added this veranda and the upstairs bedrooms.'

'I can certainly understand why you're so loath to let it go.'

'Loath?' Malvern put his coffee cup down and shook his head. 'Oh, I'm not loath at all.'

'But at one point you told me you'd imagined never leaving Ginger Hill, or the island.'

'Yes, I thought I might be able to live here. That's to say, we might be able to live here in peace.'

'But that didn't prove possible?'

'I thought, perhaps naively, that free from my father's disapproval, we might be accepted as equals. Mixed marriages are unusual in this part of the world, and they're certainly frowned upon, but they're not unheard of.'

'Your fiancée is black?' Pyke asked, trying to muster the appropriate level of surprise and even consternation.

'Mulatto actually.' Malvern smiled dreamily. 'I suppose you think less of me now?'

'What a man does in his private life is none of my concern.' Pyke waited for a moment. 'But you were saying something about not being accepted as equals?'

'The prejudice is as much on the blacks' side as the whites'. They wouldn't leave her in peace. Things happened. She became unsettled, frightened even.' Malvern stopped, perhaps sensing he'd said too much, especially to a prospective buyer of the estate.

'Frightened?'

'It's nothing that should concern you.' Malvern tried to smile but Pyke could tell he'd realised his mistake.

'I'm thinking about making you an offer for the estate. *Anything* and *everything* about the place concerns me.'

Malvern picked up his coffee and took another sip. 'There's this primitive slave religion called Obeah. It's superstitious nonsense, you understand; a kind of black magic. Obeah men and women are said to be able to summon the spirits of the dead. One of these figures set out to ruin the happiness I was beginning to enjoy with my fiancée. I could see that it was all in her mind, but eventually it got too much for her. They'd leave bloodied feathers, chicken legs, parrots' beaks in her bed, that kind of thing. I tried to make her see it for what it was but even though she's educated and has read more widely than I have, she told me she couldn't stay here. That's when we first talked about settling in England. I tried to talk her out of it, of course. I know the place. I was schooled at Harrow and spent much of my adolescence there; a cold, dreary country, nothing to recommend it. But she'd read about England in the novels of Jane Austen – that's what she imagined it would be like, and who was I to try to convince her otherwise?'

'And so you decided to send her ahead of you to London,' Pyke said, trying to keep his tone neutral, 'to stay with your family perhaps?' But he was thinking about what the captain of the *Island Queen*, McQuillan, had said about Mary Edgar: that she had the ability to commune with the dead. Would such a person, in turn, really be frightened of a parrot's beak or cat's paw?

This made Malvern sit up in his chair. '*My family?*' His face was damp with perspiration. 'Whatever gave you that idea?'

'I thought you told me that your father and

271

sister had relocated to England as well.' It was something Malvern had mentioned the previous night over dinner.

'Mr Squires, I mean Monty...' Blood was vivid in Malvern's cheeks. 'My father helped to build this estate into what it is today and, in the end, he earned the respect of the slaves who worked here. In turn, he came to appreciate their grudging work ethic and loyalty. But do you really think he would ever consent to me, his heir and only son, marrying a mulatto girl? Enjoy carnal relations with her, perhaps, but marry? *Never.* He'd string me up before allowing it to happen.'

Pyke considered what he'd just been told and whether it implicated Silas Malvern in Mary Edgar's murder. What if the old man had found out about the proposed marriage? What if he'd told Elizabeth and she'd tried to frighten Mary off using Jemmy Crane? What if all of that had failed?

'Then surely you're taking a risk,' Pyke said, as though the thought had just come to him, 'by planning to marry in the city where he now lives?'

'But he doesn't know about the engagement. He doesn't even know Mary is in London,' Malvern said, puzzled. 'I'm hoping that when we finally do marry, he'll come to accept us. I mean, he'll have to, won't he?' Malvern's naivety was both endearing and pathetic.

'So you've made arrangements for her to stay with friends until you're able to conclude your affairs here and join her in London?' Pyke did his best to suppress an urge to ask Malvern directly about William Alefounder, whether he'd stayed at the great house and, if so, whether he'd shown any interest in Mary.

Malvern looked at him quizzically, perhaps taken aback by the personal nature of the question. 'My godfather was happy to take her in and will look after her for as long as is required. You see, Uncle William lives on his own in a large house in Mayfair.'

Pyke took note of this detail. It explained why Mary had asked McQuillan about that part of the city but didn't begin to shed light on why she'd also taken a room at the lodging house on the Ratcliff Highway. 'I'm pleased for your sake this man is more enlightened than your father.'

'He just wants me to be happy. I wrote to him and explained the problem towards the end of last year. Indeed, it was his idea. And I know for a fact he won't say a word about it to my father.' Malvern looked over at Pyke, frowning. 'Anyway, why are you so interested in my personal affairs? They have no bearing on the status of Ginger Hill.'

Pemberton had just stepped out on to the veranda.

'If I'm buying anything – a horse, a house, an estate – I want to know *exactly* why the seller is willing to give it up,' Pyke said. 'In this instance, if my questions have been of too personal a nature, forgive me. But for my own peace of mind, I needed to ask them.' He stood up and left the two men to discuss their affairs.

Pyke found his horse at the stables. It had been fed and watered after the long ride up from the town and, having saddled it himself, he mounted the docile creature and urged it into a canter with a kick of his boots. From the stables, he followed the flint track down the hill to where a stone bridge crossed the river; there, next to the river, was the boiling house, a larger building than he'd been expecting. It looked deserted but Pyke didn't stop to check. A little farther up the hill on the other side of the river was the grinding house, a slightly smaller building, again made of stone, which was connected to the boiling house via a wedge-shaped trough. As Pyke understood it, the freshly cut cane was ground using vertical iron rollers powered by a waterwheel. The cane juice then ran down the trough into the boiling house, where it was rinsed, skimmed and emptied into copper vats; there it was boiled down into raw sugar and the skimmed molasses was turned into rum. But there was no one working in either of the buildings, and the whole place felt like a cemetery. As he rode up the hill into the fields on the plateau above the river, Pyke thought about the dilemma facing Malvern – pay a higher wage or risk losing the whole crop – and wondered why the planter hadn't compromised in the short term. It seemed Malvern had been badly advised, and Pyke wondered whether the attorney really did have his best interests at heart. He also thought about what Malvern had just told him about Mary Edgar, and how distraught the planter would be when he learned about her fate.

There were more clouds in the sky than there had been the day before and the air was more humid. Pyke had ridden deep into the cane fields and the ripe canes, seven or eight feet tall, swayed in the gentle breeze. About a mile or so farther along the track, he heard some voices and then caught sight of Pemberton slouched on his grey horse, staring idly into the distance. Pyke didn't think the attorney had seen him and climbed down from his own horse, tying the reins around a cotton tree. He hadn't seen a single field hand anywhere during his ride and was therefore surprised to see a crew of about twelve men, all black, sitting under the shade of a giant mango tree, talking freely with one another and laughing. Pyke didn't want to draw attention to his hiding place and so didn't risk getting close enough to hear what they were talking about, but in all the time he watched them, they didn't move from their spot, and Pemberton, for all his rhetoric about 'nigger knocking', didn't make them. Certainly no one seemed too interested in the ripe cane plants and, from what Pyke could see, none of the surrounding fields had been harvested.

Back at the stables, Dalling was waiting for him. He was leaning against the gate, with a blade of grass in his mouth.

'I was wondering if you'd thought any more about the conversation we had last night?'

'I don't carry that amount of money around with me.'

Dalling offered Pyke a lazy smile. 'Don't insult my intelligence. You strike me as a resourceful fellow. Go out and be resourceful.'

Briefly Pyke ran through his options, or lack of them. Dalling already knew he wasn't who he claimed to be and Pyke had as good as confirmed it. But Dalling wouldn't go to Pemberton or Malvern with his suspicions until he was absolutely convinced that he wouldn't be paid. Until then he would keep his mouth shut, which, in turn, meant Pyke could ask him a question.

'You must have known Mary Edgar, or at least you must have seen her around the great house.'

Dalling's eyes widened with surprise. 'What has she to do with anything?'

'Did you get the impression that she and Malvern were as devoted to one another as he'd have people believe?'

That drew a snort of derision. 'If you count fucking one of the field hands as devotion then maybe they were.' Dalling's nostrils were black with snuff. 'Of course, given that he used to fuck his own sister, he isn't exactly a saint, either.'

That stopped Pyke dead. 'Charles slept with Elizabeth?'

'You know her, then?' Dalling smirked. 'Well, if you want to know more, you're going to have to pay more.'

'Look, I'll get you your hundred and I'll give you another hundred on top of that if you tell me what you know about Charles, Mary and Elizabeth, the lot of them.'

'Is that why you're here?' Dalling's eyes narrowed.

Pyke's head was spinning with possibilities. 'Did Charles know that Mary was sleeping with another man?'

'Course he knew. That's why he sent her away.'

'What was the man's name?'

'I'm not that stupid. If I tell you, you won't have to pay me.'

'Two hundred for everything,' Pyke said.

276

'Gives you a thrill, does it? Imagining the brother and sister going at it under the sheets?'

'I can get the money by tomorrow night,' Pyke said, his throat dry from the heat. 'But I'll need the name of the field hand now.'

'If you try to double-cross me, I'll go straight to Pemberton. Is that understood?'

A silence hung between them. 'Well?' Pyke asked finally.

Dalling picked another stalk from the ground and made to leave. 'His name's Isaac Webb. But these days you won't find him anywhere near Ginger Hill.'

Pyke found Charles Malvern on the lawn in front of the great house, standing over what turned out to be a camera obscura and a small copperplate. Malvern called him over and proceeded to explain how the process worked; he didn't ask about Pyke's tour of the estate or the strike or whether he was still interested in making an offer. He just wanted to talk about daguerreotypes and, in that sense, he reminded Pyke of a young boy who'd just found a new hobby.

'You see,' he said, pointing at the camera's lens. 'The light pours through here and projects an image on to the copper, here. But the plate has already been soaked in iodine and in about five minutes a very faint image will begin to appear. When that happens, I'll take the plate inside and develop it over heated mercury; what happens is that the mercury amalgamates with the silver to make the image.' He stood up, apparently pleased with himself.

Pyke glanced down at the camera and concluded, from the direction it was pointing, that the image would be of the house. 'I'm surprised you're able to keep abreast of such developments here.'

'Actually I have my sister to thank for it. She's been an enthusiast ever since she read about it in a newspaper. She sent me all I needed to get started and now I import the copperplates and iodine directly from a manufacturer in London.'

Pyke tried not to show his interest. 'She sounds like a forward-thinking person.' He was thinking about her attachment to Jemmy Crane, about *his* interest in daguerreotypes, and whether the two were connected.

'She is.' Malvern stopped what he was doing and looked up. 'We used to be very close as children and our bond has remained strong. I'm not afraid to say I miss her dearly.'

Pyke looked searchingly into his face for signs that what Dalling had intimated was, in fact, true. 'Then you must look forward to being reunited with her in London.'

'Indeed,' Malvern said, as though the matter were an awkward one. 'I just wish...'

'Yes?'

'It's nothing.' He smiled weakly and turned his attention back to the camera.

'When was your sister last here at Ginger Hill?'

Malvern screwed up his face. 'A couple of years ago, I'd say.' He looked around the garden. 'Lizzy loved this place as much as I do. But she's also devoted to our father; she has been ever since our mother passed away. When he announced he planned to retire in England, I rather hoped she might stay with me at Ginger Hill but in the end she chose to settle in London. I'm sure it was the right decision.' He smiled awkwardly. 'After all, this is no place to find a husband, is it?'

'You found a wife here.'

'I did, didn't I?' Malvern looked up at Pyke, almost sounding surprised. 'And I miss her terribly.' He waited for a moment, as though distracted. 'I wish I could show you a daguerreotype of her, so you could see how attractive she is. I developed a number of images but they were stolen in a burglary earlier this year, together with some coins and bonds.'

For a moment Pyke wondered whether he was referring to Elizabeth or Mary.

'Really?' Somehow it seemed amiss: coins and bonds could be fenced, but who would want to buy a collection of copperplates?

'The Custos never did find the person responsible.' Malvern looked up and saw a servant coming towards them. 'I tried to persuade her to pose for me again but this time she refused; said something about it bringing bad luck.'

The servant, Josephine, told Malvern it was time for his afternoon sleep. She spoke with a faint French accent and later Malvern explained that she'd been born in Martinique and had looked after him ever since he was a child. Pyke might not have been there, for all she noticed him. 'Massa need his sleep now,' she said.

'Were all the daguerreotypes stolen?'

'Yes, all of them.' Malvern looked at him. 'Why do you ask?'

But Josephine had already threaded her arm

through Malvern's, and before Pyke could answer, she was leading him across the lawn to the house.

That night, Pyke ate with Malvern and Dalling as the Pembertons had been invited to dine elsewhere. The conversation was stilted and awkward. A few times Pyke tried to steer it towards the subject of Malvern's family, hoping to learn something more about the mother's death, but Malvern was morose and seemingly incapable of speaking more than a few words at a time. Dalling appeared bored without Hermione Pemberton's chest to gawp at and managed to restrict himself to a few barbed remarks about Pyke's or rather Squires' background. The first time it happened Pyke let it go; the second time, when Dalling asked him where he had grown up, Pyke announced he needed to take the air and waited for the bookkeeper to join him on the veranda.

'I thought we had an arrangement,' Pyke said, after making sure Charles was still sitting at the table.

'We do, but I'm just making sure you know I'm not to be underestimated.'

Pyke stared out across the lawn in the direction of the stone counting house. 'How do I know that what you told me about Charles and Elizabeth is the truth?'

'You don't. I don't even know whether it's true or not. I'm just telling you what I heard.'

'So it's only a rumour?'

'I'm not saying another word until you've paid me what we agreed.'

Pyke hesitated and then pointed at the counting house. 'I'll meet you there tomorrow night at seven.'

'With the money?'

'With the two hundred.'

Pyke had expected Dalling to object to this arrangement or at least argue for a more public meeting place but the bookkeeper simply said, 'I'll be there. If you're not or if you don't have the full two hundred, I'll go straight to Pemberton.'

Back at the dinner table, Charles hardly seemed to have noticed his absence and made no comment when Dalling failed to return to his place. 'I'm afraid I'm rather melancholic tonight, sir, and hence not good company. You'll excuse me if I turn in early.' He smiled. 'The servants will take good care of you.' Malvern stood up and shuffled past him, but as he did so, he turned suddenly and grabbed Pyke's arm. 'You will buy the estate, won't you? I'm not sure I could take the disappointment if you didn't. Name a sensible price, sir, and Ginger Hill will be yours. There's five hundred acres, less fifty acres of the worst farming land that my father has earmarked for other purposes. I won't haggle. I won't even ask for what I know a place like this is worth. Make me an offer, sir, that's all I ask.'

Before Pyke could answer, he had headed off across the polished floor in the direction of his bedroom, leaving Pyke to ponder the reasons for his outburst. Later, over the sound of a stiffening breeze in the trees and the shutters rattling in their fastenings, Pyke thought he could hear Malvern sobbing, but when he tried to investigate,

281

Josephine appeared suddenly from her quarters carrying a lantern. She didn't say anything and remained there until Pyke turned around and headed back to his bedroom.

He removed his shirt and took off his boots, hanging the former on a hook attached to the back of the door.

In his undergarments, he went across to the bed and pulled back the fresh white sheet.

A hot spike of bile licked the back of his throat.

It wasn't a human eyeball. From its size, it had once belonged to a goat or a sheep and it lay there like a hard-boiled egg, just the faintest trace of crimson visible on the otherwise spotless sheet.

That night the rain was like nothing Pyke had ever experienced before; bullets of water hammering into the shutters and pounding the roof until he felt certain that either the roof would fall in or the shutters be ripped from their hinges. The storm lasted for two or three hours, and during this time Pyke drifted in and out of sleep, moths throwing themselves at the glass of the whale-oil lamp next to his bed. When he woke up, his back was drenched in sweat and his throat was dry and scratchy. The rain had stopped and the air around him felt damp and cool. He lay there, disoriented, wallowing in the strangeness, and when he woke again, bright sunlight was flooding in through the shutters. It was at such timed that he missed Emily the most; when his longing for her – her company and her presence next to him – caused him a physical ache. He stood up, and tried to put the thought of her lying bleeding in his arms out of his head.

From his small balcony there was little evidence of the previous night's deluge; just a few pools of water glistening in the red clay. The sky was a piercing blue, the air smelled of jasmine and cinnamon, and the still-wet foliage of the nearby orange and mango trees sparkled with renewed vigour. Pyke dressed and went downstairs, where a pot of coffee and a plate of fresh fruit and pastries awaited him in the dining room. He ate his breakfast and drank the coffee, which was delicious and strong, then asked one of the servants where he could find Malvern, Pemberton or even Dalling. Malvern, he was told, was unavailable, while Pemberton and Dalling were attending to matters on the estate. He finished his coffee and wandered across to the counting house and, from there, to a potting shed on the other side of the overgrown lawn. He found a shovel and a pick and entered the tropical forest via a gate and a set of stone steps at one end of the lawn.

The spot he was looking for – a small clearing no more than five or six hundred yards downhill from the counting house – took him ten minutes to locate. Setting the shovel and pick down on the ground, he removed his shirt and draped it over a tree branch. It was cool and shady under the foliage of the cotton, coffee and logwood trees and in the distance he could hear the river, with the croaking of bullfrogs and buzzing of mosquitoes. Looking around, to make sure he was alone, Pyke took the pick and set to work.

It took him an hour and a half to dig a hole big enough for Dalling's body, and by the time he'd finished, a pile of red earth thick with ants sat next to him. Leaving the shovel and pick next to the hole, Pyke ventured farther into the forest, towards the river, and found a bathing pool under the shade of a large mango tree. He left his clothes on a rock and dived into the clear, cold water. Coming up for air, he looked up into the trees, and his thoughts turned to Mary Edgar; whether she, too, had swum in this spot and whether there was anyone else on the island, apart from Charles Malvern, who would mourn her death.

Lunchtime had been and gone by the time Pyke returned to the great house, but as far as he could tell it was still deserted. In fact, none of the servants appeared when he called, and he decided to take the opportunity to give the rooms a quick search. He started in Malvern's study but didn't find anything of interest in either his davenport or the chest of drawers in the corner of the room. From there, after he'd made quite certain it was unoccupied, Pyke moved to Malvern's bedroom, where he found a bundle of letters in the oak davenport: none, as far as he could to tell, from Elizabeth or Silas. There was one letter that took his interest, however. The seal, embossed in red wax, had been broken, and Pyke was about to read its contents when he heard footsteps, and so he slipped the letter and envelope into his pocket.

Outside in the passage, Josephine must have seen him come from Malvern's bedroom because she stood there, arms folded, perhaps trying to decide what to do.

She was a slight person, less than five feet tall,

and shuffled rather than walked, but her physical presence was sufficient to make Pyke jump.

'What you doing in Massa's room?'

'I went in there by accident.' He tried to smile. 'A house this size, it's easy to lose one's bearings.'

The old woman wetted her lips with her small, pink tongue. 'You going to buy Ginger Hill, be the new massa?'

'I might.' Pyke looked into her small, shrivelled eyes. 'I'm sure you could tell me quite a bit about this place.'

'I seen folk come and go.'

'Like Silas's wife, Bonella?'

Her irises, green and rimmed with circles of black, contracted slightly. 'I see you talked to folk already.'

'What happened to her?'

'Curious sort, you. Too much curiosity can be a dangerous thing.'

'I heard she fell down the stairs.' Pyke waited. 'Or was she pushed?'

'Ask a lot of questions, too.'

'You'd probably know all about Charles and Elizabeth when they were younger, wouldn't you?'

They stood there for a short while, contemplating each other's expressions. This time, she didn't answer him.

'Last night I found a sheep's eyeball in my bed. Was that your handiwork?'

Her face remained unreadable. 'Why you think that?'

'Tell me what it's supposed to mean, then.'

'Finding an eyeball?'

'Yes.'

'Maybe someone trying to conjure a bad spirit, scare you a little.'

'But why an eyeball? Why not a cat's paw or a rabbit's foot?'

'Paw, foot, eyeball. All you doing is offering a sacrifice.'

Pyke allowed a short silence to settle between them. 'What if the eyeball belonged to a human?'

Josephine looked at him and then gathered up her linen skirt. 'I should go.'

'One more question,' Pyke said, before she could get away from him. 'Why is Charles frightened of you?'

'Frightened of me?' She seemed amused by this idea. 'That boy jump at his own shadow.'

Later, in his bedroom, Pyke put on a fresh linen shirt, found the bottle of rum that Harper had given him, uncorked it and took a long swig. The fiery liquid scalded the sides of his throat. He poured some into his cupped palm and splashed it over his face and neck, to try to ward off the mosquitoes. From his window, which faced westwards over fields of sugar cane towards the conical-shaped mountains in the distance, he watched the bulbous orange sun sink down over the horizon. As the breeze picked up once more, Pyke listened to the great house creak on its foundations and thought about the secrets it held, the things that had taken place within its walls.

Somewhere out there, William Dalling would be preparing himself, too.

Pyke's linen coat was hanging from a hook on the back of the door and, when he put it on, he found his sheath knife in one of the pockets and the letter he'd taken from Malvern's bedroom in the other.

Taking the envelope to the lantern next to his bed, he turned it over and inspected the wax seal. It looked genuine enough. Pyke removed the letter and scanned the contents. The writing itself was full of old-fashioned loops and flourishes. It was short, barely even a page, and its author apparently wanted to reassure Malvern that all the arrangements – whatever these were – had been made. It was signed 'Uncle William'. Pyke looked at the top of the letter where the address had been transcribed: Norfolk Street, London.

But it wasn't this which caught his attention.

It was the name. Lord William Bedford.

SEVENTEEN

It was almost dark by the time Pyke slipped unnoticed from the house via a back door and crossed the lawn, the counting house silhouetted against the dense jungle of vegetation behind it. The night air was warm and moist and up above, the inky sky was washed with streaks of moonlight. Underfoot, cockroaches and other nocturnal scavengers feasted on the dirt. Moving quickly across the lawn, the blunt edge of his knife pressing against his skin, Pyke could hear the clucking of hens from the nearby chicken coops. Near the counting house, the smell of jasmine and honeysuckle grew stronger, and Pyke thought again about what he was going to do, whether he really could kill a man in cold blood, not because he absolutely had to but because his cover would be blown if he didn't. He could still taste the fiery sweetness of the rum; he tried to swallow but there was no moisture in his mouth. Passing the counting house, he looked around him, his eyes now adjusted to the darkness. He took a few more steps and whispered, 'Dalling?' According to his watch, it was exactly seven o'clock.

Something or someone moved out of the shadows. Pyke felt his body his stiffen, his fingers brushing against the knife in the pocket of his coat. Dalling stepped into the moonlight about ten yards in front of him. Pyke had been expecting him, of course, but the bookkeeper's sudden appearance startled him none the less. They stood there for a moment, each waiting for the other to speak. It was Dalling who broke the silence.

'Have you got my money?' he whispered, glancing up at one of the windows of the counting house.

Pyke jangled the purse in his coat pocket. In fact, there was twelve rather than two hundred pounds in it, and immediately Dalling said, 'That sounds a little light.'

Pyke took a step towards him but Dalling retreated slightly, holding his hands up in the air. 'Hold on there, sir.' He seemed jumpy and again looked up at the window of the counting house.

The sudden powder flash lit up the immediate area and the simultaneous blast shattered the tranquillity. The shot had come from the same window Dalling had been looking at and it tore a hole in his chest and sent him reeling backwards into a nearby bush. Following Dalling's gaze, Pyke had seen the barrel of a pistol poking out of another window and had luckily managed to throw himself to the ground just as a second blast ripped through the air, a ball-shot fizzing just above his head. He heard voices in the counting house: Pemberton, saying, 'Did you get him?' and a voice he didn't recognise replying, 'I reckon so. Or I saw 'im go down.' Not daring to move, Pyke waited until he heard Pemberton and the other one stumbling down the steps from the counting house, then jumped up and ran in the direction of the forest. Dalling lay unmoving in one of the flower beds. Pyke didn't need to be told he was dead.

Without the moonlight to guide him, it was almost too dark for Pyke to see, and he had to move carefully through the trees, his hands stretched out in front of him. Certainly running was out of the question at first, but after a while the shapes of the forest began to slip into focus and he could move more quickly. Behind him, he could hear voices, and in the distance he could already see the flame of torches; his pursuers wouldn't have the same difficulties negotiating their path through the darkness.

Pyke didn't know where he was heading and hadn't yet formulated a plan, apart from putting as much distance between himself and the men who'd tried to murder him as possible. Nor did he have to worry about making too much noise; they hadn't followed him immediately, choosing instead to round up help and come after him with torches and in greater numbers. Already the word would be spreading through the great house and the servants' quarters: Dalling had been shot and killed, and the man who'd done it – Montgomery Squires – was now on the run. The fact that Pyke had indeed been planning to murder Dalling was beside the point. Squires would be blamed and Pemberton would have solved two problems at once: the man who was possibly sleeping with his wife was dead and the man who wanted to buy Ginger Hill was on the run, suspected of Dalling's murder. Perhaps it was better that they'd missed him. If he had been found shot dead, too, it might have looked too suspicious. Now, in the eyes of the law, running would merely confirm Pyke's guilt.

To his right, the ground fell away sharply, and Pyke decided to follow it downhill as far as it took him; at one point the slope dipped so sharply he had to descend on his hands and backside, like a crab. After about two hundred yards the ground levelled out and he stood still for a moment and listened. The river was close by – he could hear it above the sound of the leaves rustling in the breeze – and so he set off towards it, scrambling down another rocky escarpment and only just stopping himself from tumbling into the water at the bottom of the slope.

Next to the river, the canopy of trees wasn't so thick and soft beams of moonlight easily penetrated the foliage, shimmering gently on the surface of the water. But the current was strong and the water deeper than Pyke had expected.

When he stepped off the bank, it rose first to his waist and then up his chest, and then he lost his footing in the shale and mud so that, for a short while, the current carried him downriver until he realised it was taking him back in the direction of the house. Pyke tried to swim against the current, swallowing whole mouthfuls as he did so, and a few strokes later he could touch the bottom on the other side, then he hauled himself up on to the bank and lay there panting. Above him, birds stirred in the branches of the mango and guano trees. He took a moment to empty water from his shoes, wring his socks and wrap the arms of his coat around his waist.

On the move again, he scrambled up the side of the bank, crossed the same flint track he'd ridden along the previous day and followed the line of the trees as far as the edge of the first cane field; here, he could cover more ground because the moonlight was sufficient to guide him. He ran at a pace he could maintain and every now and again he would pause, his heart thumping against his ribcage while he listened for any sign of his pursuers.

Taking care to follow the narrow, uneven paths that had been cut along the side of the cane fields, he must have covered two or three miles before he stopped for a break. Allowing himself five minutes, Pyke used the time to tend to his feet, bursting a blood blister on the sole of his left foot with the tip of his knife and wringing the sweat from his socks. Then he set off again, this time taking a path that cut between two cane fields, heading towards the mountains and, he guessed, away from the coast. In the distance the

291

same ragged, conical hills he'd seen from his bedroom window rose up from the earth, silhouetted against the inky blue of the night sky and the vast panoply of stars. He kept moving towards the hills but even an hour later, running at a steady pace, they didn't seem any closer. Pausing again, he thought for the first time about the wisdom of his actions and whether his decision to put as much distance as possible between himself and the great house had been a wise one. Around him, the air was balmy. In a few hours, the sun would rise and then he would be more visible; also by then word of the murder would have spread far and wide, so Pyke would have to stay hidden until the following night or until he could find a way of contacting Harper.

Moving northwards through what seemed to be endless fields of cane, Pyke slowed to a walk; his feet hurt too much to continue running and his whole body was exhausted. He could see a giant cotton tree somewhere in the distance and told himself he would keep walking until he reached it, but after what seemed like an hour, it didn't appear to be any closer. He was trudging now, rather than walking, and when he reached the edge of one cane field he found a small grassy verge. He sat down, took off his shoes and lay down in the tall grass. Pyke was asleep almost before his head touched the ground.

The sun seemed to grow in the clear, cloudless sky and by mid-morning there wasn't a drop of moisture in Pyke's mouth. Indeed, those parts of his body unprotected by his clothes – his face, neck and hands – were sunburnt and blistered. He had covered more ground than he realized, and it took him only another hour or so to cross the final part of the mountain plain. Then he was back into dense jungle vegetation and climbing again. He found a stream and fell to his knees, lapping up the pure, mountain water until he thought his stomach might burst. Following the stream uphill for about half a mile, Pyke came across a pool in the shade of a giant logwood tree. There, he removed his clothes and jumped into the clear water, luxuriating in the sensation of suddenly being cool, and for a while he lay on his back in the water, staring up at the vine-covered branches above him. For that moment at least, Pyke wasn't thinking about his own predicament. Rather his thoughts had turned to the letter he'd found in Charles Malvern's bedroom.

Lord William Bedford was Charles Malvern's godfather. More than that: Bedford had, at Charles Malvern's behest, taken Mary Edgar into his home, so she would've been the mistress that Morel-Roux had referred to. Now, though, Bedford and Mary Edgar were both dead, and Morel-Roux was facing trial and likely imprisonment – or even death – for the aristocrat's murder. This was what Pyke *knew*. It also made him realise that the valet had probably been telling the truth, and that Mary Edgar and Lord Bedford had, very possibly, been killed by the same person or people; their bodies left in different parts of the city to conceal the connection. For what reason could someone like Morel-Roux have had for wanting both Lord Bedford and Mary Edgar dead?

Momentarily Pyke thought about Morel-Roux rotting away in his prison cell, but then he heard a noise, the snap of a twig, and his mind was wrenched back to his present circumstances. He looked up and there was a tall, lanky, black boy staring down at him, grinning.

'I'll pay one of you a silver dollar if you'll take a message to a man called John Harper at the *Falmouth Post* newspaper.'

'What message?' A skinny man with two front teeth missing looked at the other seven or eight figures gathered around Pyke, their expressions curious rather than hostile.

The village itself was a revelation: neat, single-storey houses made of brick and timber, with garden plots at the front and rear, had been constructed along two well-maintained tracks, and at the crossroads a church was being built. The men wore trousers and shirts, not rags, and the women dresses made of linen and muslin.

'That I'm here; that I want to speak to him in person; that I want him to come to your village.'

'Take half a day for a man to walk to Falmouth and another half a day for him to walk back,' another man said.

'Two silver dollars.' Pyke held open his palm and allowed them all to see the coins.

'I'll do it,' the boy who'd first seen him in the bathing pool said.

'You'll do it, boy, but the dollars go towards the building of our church,' another man said, pointing at the timber skeleton of the new edifice.

A couple of the men argued for a while in a

294

dialect Pyke couldn't understand but finally one of them turned to him and said, 'Dis is a free village, and we all the Lord's chirren now, so we don't want no trouble here.'

'Nor do I.'

The man stared at Pyke for a few moments, his eyes narrowing. 'Man told me dis mornin a white man been killed up at the big house. You know 'bout that?'

Ignoring him, Pyke produced another coin from his pocket. 'I'll pay a dollar to anyone who will take me into their home, let me rest there and cook me a meal.'

The same man who'd scolded him shook his head, as though disappointed. 'Did the Good Samaritan ask for money to help the man beaten by robbers?'

After a meal of boiled yams and sweet potato, which he ate on his own inside the stone and timber house, Pyke tended to his blistered feet, rubbing soothing aloe which he'd been given by his host into the cuts and blisters. Afterwards, he lay on a straw mat and stared up at the thatched roof, thinking about what had happened, how Dalling seemed to have known what was going to happen. In the end, Pyke could come up with only one explanation. Dalling had gone to Pemberton and told him what he knew or suspected: that Pyke wasn't who he claimed to be. Pemberton had then made the necessary arrangements. He had probably told Dalling that Pyke would be killed, hence the bookkeeper's nervous glances towards the counting-house window. Doubtless Pemberton had failed to inform the bookkeeper of his own imminent death. That way, Pyke could be blamed for his murder and be killed in the process. Later, they could tell the magistrate that Pyke had been shot while trying to escape from the scene of the crime. If the magistrate wanted to know why Pyke had killed Dalling, Pemberton could say that Pyke was, in fact, an impostor and had killed the bookkeeper to protect his cover. Pyke didn't know whether Dalling had been sleeping with Pemberton's wife and, if so, whether Pemberton had found out about the affair, but assuming both things were true, it gave Pemberton a good reason for wanting to assassinate Dalling as well.

Pemberton clearly had his eyes set on keeping the estate. It didn't matter that Pyke actually wasn't Squires. Indeed, if Squires ever made it to the island, and heard about how his good name had been besmirched, he would put himself on the first ship back to Antigua.

'You go to England to be with your fiancée,' Pemberton would say to Malvern, 'and I'll stay here and manage the estate.'

That would give him everything he wanted.

Pyke guessed that Pemberton had been trying to run the estate into the ground to deter potential buyers. And when they weren't deterred, as in this particular instance, he had taken a more direct approach.

With his belly full and his feet rested, Pyke drifted off to sleep, and when he woke next, it was dark outside and he was still alone in the house. Standing up, he put on his shirt and went outside. He could hear noises, talking and laughing in a nearby house, but otherwise the village seemed deserted. This would have been the kind of place Mary Edgar had grown up in and it would have felt like home to her, yet she'd died on the other side of a vast ocean, alone and friendless in the very best and worst city in the world.

What had she been thinking, Pyke wondered, as someone, a man, had put their hands around her throat and squeezed? Had she thought about her home, this place, an island that seemed as alien and unknowable to him as London had doubtless seemed to her?

Pyke felt a mosquito land on his neck and went to swat it. Back inside the house, he sat down on the straw mat and thought about Felix, trying to quell a rising swell of homesickness. There was nothing to do apart from wait.

At dawn, he was woken by a rooster that insisted on crowing directly outside the house. Hot, sweaty and alone, he dressed and wandered down to the bathing pool. The cold mountain water felt glorious against his naked skin and the early morning light was soothing on his eyes. Up above, the sky was overcast and the air felt cooler, as though a change in the weather was on its way. He heard the clopping of horses' hoofs coming up the track, so climbed out of the pool and dressed quickly.

John Harper had ridden from Falmouth with a companion and was berating one of the villagers when he looked up and saw Pyke walking towards him. 'Thank the Lord, you're still here,' he said, bounding to greet Pyke, his giant legs covering the ground in just a few strides.

He embraced Pyke with a hug, as though they were old friends, and then waited for his companion to join them. 'Allow me to introduce Isaac Webb. I think you might already have met, under less pleasant circumstances.'

As they shook hands, Webb smiled and said, 'T'anks for the rum, by the way.' He was a good-looking man with smooth walnut-coloured skin, lithe, with the kind of eyelashes, cheekbones and lips a lot of women would have coveted.

'I came as soon as I got your message,' Harper said, slapping Pyke firmly on the back. 'I brought Isaac with me because no one understands Ginger Hill better than him.'

The villagers seemed to know Webb better than Harper but their welcome to both men had been muted. They brought their new arrivals fresh coffee and rum, served in pots carved from wood, but treated them warily, so when they finally left them alone, Harper tried to explain their reaction. This, he said, was a free village built on land acquired by William Knibb and the Baptist church; in return for a plot of land and the loan of sufficient money to build a house, the villagers were expected to renounce their heathen ways and embrace a new life of hard work and sobriety. When Pyke pointed out that it didn't sound as if Harper approved, the big man snorted and shook his head. 'White Baptists like Knibb might pretend to be our friends but what they're offering is just another form of slavery; be good Christian men, just like them, or clear off farther into the mountains. Knibb's a good person, in his own way, but he's never stopped to ask what *we* want.'

After they'd drunk their coffee, Harper and Webb listened, without interruption, while Pyke explained what had happened to him. When he'd finished, he looked at Harper and said, 'But, of course, you knew something like this was going to happen. Or you hoped it would. I'm right, aren't I?'

Harper took a swig of the rum and handed Webb the bottle. 'Even if that were the case, and I'm not saying it was, your injuries don't look too bad.'

'I still can't work out what was in it for you. You knew for a fact that Pemberton would try to make my life difficult, because he'd done the same thing to all of Malvern's prospective buyers. So let me guess: you were hoping I'd retaliate and do your dirty work for you in the process.'

Harper glanced over at Webb. 'Pemberton and the Custos whipped my friend here to within an inch of his life, and it wasn't the first time he'd done it, either. You blame me for trying to seize an opportunity to get back at him?'

'Using me to do it?'

The big man shrugged. 'You're alive, aren't you?'

'But even as we speak, I'm quite sure half the island is looking for me: the white half anyway. Troops, police, anyone they can round up.'

Webb handed Pyke the bottle. 'Billy Dalling's dead and a white man killed him. Dat's what the Custos think. Point is, us black folk can't be held responsible.'

Pyke took a swig of rum and contemplated what he'd just been told. He was starting to see it. 'So when Pemberton and maybe a few others turn up dead, this same white man can be blamed for those murders, too.'

Harper turned to Webb and grinned. 'I told you he was a sharp one, didn't I? Sharp as a nail.'

'Meanwhile a Mr Pyke from London – nothing to do with the trouble at Ginger Hill – will already be at sea and headin' for home.' Webb returned Harper's grin then looked at Pyke. 'We get you as far as Kingston; you make the arrangements from dere.'

'And when the real Montgomery Squires turns up?'

The big man just shrugged. 'It'll just add to the mystery. But they'll still be looking for a white man.'

'I'm glad I could play my part.'

'You went to Ginger Hill for your own reasons; no one forced you to go,' Harper said.

'That doesn't alter the fact that you used me.'

That accusation seemed to sting the newspaperman. 'I know folk who've had the soles of their feet beaten with lead, who've died still tied to the treadmill, who've been locked up for no reason and shot for no reason. That's just the folks I know. So I'm not going to get up on my soapbox and give a speech about the evil white man, but I'm also not going to apologise for doing what I need to do.'

Pyke held his stare. 'You do what you need to do, I'll do what *I* need to do. How does that sound?'

'Long as our interests don't clash, that's fine. But like my friend here said, you'd do well to leave as soon as you can.'

Coming from Harper, this sounded more like a

warning rather than a friendly piece of advice. Pyke turned to Webb. 'Did you know Mary Edgar while she was here?'

'Everyone knew Mary.'

'I heard you and she were lovers. Which is why Malvern decided to send her away.'

Webb stared at him, open mouthed, and Harper had to intervene. 'Who told you that?'

'So it's true.'

They exchanged a quick look. Harper nodded, as though giving his assent. Then Webb said, 'Yeah, man, I loved her, I did. I can't believe she dead.' He was staring down at his boots, shaking his head, but somehow his grief seemed unconvincing.

'It can't have been easy for you, after Malvern found out you'd been sleeping with Mary.'

Webb pulled up his shirt to reveal a lattice of barely healed scars on his back. 'What you saw the other night weren't nothing compared to what Busha did to me.'

'Busha?'

'Pemberton,' Harpeer explained.

'On top of that, Custos give me hundred lashes in the workhouse, made me dance the treadmill every morning and evening for a month, work in the penal gang during the day.'

'I'm sorry.'

Webb shrugged. 'Big man here told me you was looking for the man who killed her.' His stare was hard and clear.

'He also said you know everything there is to know about what goes on at Ginger Hill. Is that so?'

Webb just shrugged again.

'Do you know a sugar trader from England called William Alefounder?' He was about to explain that Alefounder had perhaps visited Ginger Hill some time during the previous year, but saw it wasn't necessary.

'He stayed up at the great house for a week, the end of last year. Took a real shine to Mary.'

Pyke studied Webb's face. 'And were these feelings in any way reciprocated?'

'Mary had one white man in love wit' her. That was enough. She didn't need this other one sniffin' around her.'

'Are you suggesting she wasn't in love with Charles Malvern?'

That drew an irritated snort from Webb. 'Rich white massa offer you the world, what's a poor black girl gonna do? Turn around and say no, Massa, I prefer workin' in the fields, holing cane?'

'So was Mary sent away to England or did she choose to go?'

'Little of both.'

'But why would she have *agreed* to go?' Pyke hesitated. 'Why not wait here for Malvern to sell Ginger Hill?'

Webb sighed. 'He made the arrangements, she just did as she was told. Didn't want to ruin a good thing, I suppose.' His bitterness was self-evident.

'And Arthur Sobers?'

They both looked at one another. 'Who?' Harper said, eyebrows raised.

'A black man who was her travelling companion. She sailed with him to London and rented a room with him once they arrived.'

'Don't know no Arthur Sobers,' Webb said. 'Maybe she met him on the boat.'

'Police in London reckon he killed her.'

'You don't agree?' Harper asked eventually.

'What bothers me,' Pyke said, looking at Webb, 'is your lack of concern that Mary might have shared a bed with another man.'

But Webb was slow to anger. 'White man like you only understand the world in terms of possessions.'

It was a good answer but Pyke wasn't quite convinced by it. 'What do you know about Elizabeth Malvern?'

This sudden change of tack caught them both off guard. 'In what sense?' Harper asked, exchanging a nervous glance with Webb.

'How would you describe her, for a start?'

'Didn't really know her. Black folk aren't often asked to dine at the great house.'

'Mary was.'

Webb licked his lips. 'That was different.'

'Different or not, I can't imagine Charles's family welcoming her with open arms.'

'I guess you're right,' Harper said.

'But you don't know what Elizabeth thought about her brother marrying Mary?' Pyke said to Webb.

'Don't imagine she cared for the idea one little bit.' He wiped perspiration from his forehead with the sleeve of his shirt. 'Why? You think she killed Mary?'

'It's possible she might have been involved.' Pyke paused. 'I heard that Charles and his sister used to be – how should I put it? – *too* close.'

Harper glanced across at Webb. 'Are you saying what I think you're saying?'

'Didn't you hear the rumour, too?' Pyke said, addressing Webb.

But Webb seemed unmoved. 'Fucking about the only thing the white man is good at.'

Harper grinned and slapped Pyke on the shoulder. Pressing the rum bottle into his hand, he said, 'Have a drink and try not to look so serious. I'll be honest with you. Like Isaac said, you should go home. Mary's dead and she ain't coming back. This is *our* struggle.'

That seemed to remind Harper of something because his expression suddenly became serious. 'When we first met, you asked me to tell you when the *Island Queen* arrived.'

'And has it?'

The big man rubbed his chin, as though contemplating some deep thought. *'That's* why you came, isn't it? There's someone on board who knows something about Mary's murder.'

A moment passed between them. Pyke's jaw clenched. 'Alefounder fled London on the *Island Queen.'*

Harper nodded, as if he'd been expecting it. 'And you think he might have killed Mary?'

Pyke shrugged. 'When did the ship dock?' he asked eventually.

'Yesterday afternoon.'

'Which means Alefounder could be on his way to Ginger Hill right now.'

Harper looked at him. 'It's possible.'

Pyke nodded. 'That's why I've got to go back there.'

'Go *back?* Are you out of your mind?' Harper shook his head. 'You weren't too wrong when you said half the island was out looking for you. On the ride up here, we were stopped by three different sets of soldiers.'

'But you know this land better than anyone,' Pyke said to Webb. 'You could show me the way back to Ginger Hill and I'll wager you wouldn't even need a road or a track.'

Webb looked at him for a while, trying to make sense of what he'd just been asked to do. 'Can I ask you a question?' He waited for Pyke to nod and then continued, 'Why are you *really* here?'

'You mean, have I really come all this way to find out who killed Mary?'

'If you like.'

'Strange as it may sound, the answer would be yes.'

Webb rubbed his eyes and sighed. 'And now you want me to take you back to Ginger Hill and risk getting killed?'

'Yes.'

Webb looked over at Harper and shook his head. 'Man either too brave or too stupid or both.'

'But you'll take me there, won't you?'

This time it was Harper who spoke. 'You'll have to wait until nightfall. Even if you cut across the cane fields, you might run into some men with dogs.' He stood up, stretched his legs, and stared at the darkening sky. 'In Falmouth they were talking about a storm heading this way. Maybe the best idea would be to stay here for a couple of days, lie low, wait for it to pass.'

'I don't have a couple of days.'

'Then you should get plenty of rest. It's a long way from here to Ginger Hill.'

EIGHTEEN

By the middle of the morning the air had grown cool and moist and the wind, coming from the north, smelled of sea salt; it blew through the village, tearing straw thatches from the roofs of houses and stripping leaves from their branches. It started to rain shortly afterwards and by lunchtime the conditions had deteriorated so much that Webb reckoned it would be safe to start their journey. No one, he assured Pyke, would be looking for them in this weather. For his part, Pyke felt inclined to agree and was just as keen as Webb to get going as soon as possible, although he did wonder about Webb's volte-face; why it was Webb rather than him who was suddenly forcing the timetable. They left after lunch, armed with rum, fruit and water, and wearing hats and boots borrowed or procured by Harper from the villagers. The track down to the cane fields was already muddy and treacherous and the wind, if anything, had picked up, so much so that by the time they made it down to the plain, some of the cane plants had been flattened. The rain continued to fall and the wind blowing through the cane made it impossible to hear what the other was saying, so they walked in silence, Webb leading the way,

Pyke following.

For a while in the middle of the afternoon the wind dropped and the rain eased. They stopped for a rest under a leafy mango tree, Webb drinking from the rum bottle before passing it to Pyke.

'You smell the salt?' he said, looking up at the sky.

Pyke nodded. 'Is that a bad sign?' He swallowed some of the rum and shuddered.

'This far up into the mountains it is.'

Pyke handed the bottle back to him and waited. 'Can I ask you a question about what we discussed earlier?'

Webb took another swig of the rum but didn't answer.

'Why do I get the impression you don't want to talk to me about Mary?'

'I answered your questions.'

Pyke stared at him. 'If I said the words "kill-devil" to you, what would they mean?'

Webb stiffened slightly. 'It's what folk sometimes call rum.'

'The captain of the ship that took Mary and Arthur Sobers to London overheard them talking, reckoned it was some kind of code.'

'A code?' Webb offered him a cool stare. 'For what?'

'That's what I'm asking you.'

Webb continued to look at him, perhaps about to speak, but something changed his mind and he replaced the bottle in his knapsack and told Pyke they needed to get going.

The rain was light and patchy for the rest of the afternoon and they trudged in silence through field after field of mature cane plants. As Harper had predicted, they didn't see anyone, and after six hours of hard walking, they crossed the Martha Brae river by the stone bridge – just downhill from the great house. It was already dark and the rain had become more persistent. The wind was beginning to howl now, and the palm trees on the track up to the great house were bent over, their fronds sometimes almost touching the ground.

'I'm afraid this is as far as I go,' Webb said, pointing at the deserted boiling house. 'I'll wait for you in there until morning. If you don't come by then, I'll take it you no longer need my help.'

They parted without shaking hands, but as Pyke continued up the track he heard Webb call out, 'Good luck,' and then, 'You'll need it.'

Pyke had read about tropical storms in books but he had never been caught up in one, nor had he ever expected to be. Still, he had to question his sanity for being outside and indeed for coming back to a place where every sentient male within a ten-mile radius doubtless wanted to hang him from the nearest tree. As he steeled himself against the blasts of wind, and from the rain which was now falling horizontally, he heard a tree trunk snap and looked behind him just in time to see a giant logwood topple on to the track where he'd just been. Farther up the track, a plank of wood whistled past his ear. A rumble of thunder and a sudden crack of lightning followed, suddenly illuminating the great house at the top of the hill. It looked like a mast-less vessel riding on the top of the tallest of waves.

Rather than approach the great house from the main track and risk being spotted, Pyke circumnavigated the hill and climbed up from the other side, so that he finally emerged near the stone counting house. There, he found the hole he'd dug a few days earlier, and the shovel and pickaxe next to it, and carried them up to the counting house. The rain now tasted of salt, as though whole swathes of the sea had been sucked up by the wind and dumped on the mountains. Still, he was a long way past caring about getting wet – he was already soaked through. The wind was now uprooting mature coffee and wild fig trees as though they were made of papier mâché, tossing tree branches on to the lawn in front of him as though they weren't any heavier than toothpicks.

The house itself had taken a terrible battering; the shutters and doors had long since been bolted and fastened but the wind had torn off parts of the roof and shale. Lead slates and even a few timber beams lay strewn across parts of the garden.

Pyke had no idea how he was going to lure Pemberton outside; if indeed he was there at all. He needed to find a way of getting to the man and knocking him unconscious. While he pondered this dilemma, the wind gathered in strength until he heard an earsplitting crack; a palm tree then snapped at its base and cannoned like a battering ram into the great house, puncturing a large hole in the stone and timber wall directly under the veranda.

It was what he'd been waiting for.

Steeling himself against the wind, he staggered out on to the lawn, trying to keep his balance.

One gust almost swept him off his feet; another carried a branch of a tree to within a few inches of his head. It took him a few minutes to clear the lawn, but eventually he made it and peered into the lower floor of the house through the hole made by the tree; then he saw a lantern coming towards him and heard footsteps. He hid from view, wrapped his hands around the wooden handle of the shovel and counted to ten. *'Busha,'* Pyke called out. It was the name the black workers used for Pemberton.

Pyke swung the shovel through the air and caught the attorney squarely in the face with the metal end. Pemberton went down without a sound. Pyke checked his pulse; his nose might have been smashed and his skull dented by the blow but it hadn't killed him. He picked up the man's lantern and carried it up a flight of steps; at the top he opened the door and, as he did so, the wind, which had blown through the hole made by the palm tree, tore into the dining room, ripping paintings from the walls, knocking wineglasses and china plates from the sideboard and almost wrenching the cut-glass chandelier from its fixing. Using his back and putting his whole body into it, Pyke just managed to push the door closed and bolt it from the inside.

He found Charles Malvern and William Alefounder in Malvern's study. Between them, they had drunk most of a bottle of brandy, and despite the foul conditions outside they seemed quite merry.

'Do tell, what was that terrible crash, Pemberton?' Malvern said, without even looking up. His cheeks were glowing from the alcohol he'd consumed. 'Are we *really* all going to perish in the storm?' Perhaps he hadn't seen or comprehended the damage the storm had done to the great house.

Malvern hadn't noticed Pyke but Alefounder had. For a moment, Pyke almost felt sorry for the man. Dripping with water, sodden, holding a shovel, Pyke must have been the very last man Alefounder had expected and wanted to see, and he reacted accordingly; his jaw went slack, his eyes bulged, and the colour fell from his cheeks. Alefounder had travelled halfway around the world to escape persecution from a man who had forced his arm into a pot of boiling liquid and now that same man had just walked into the room in the middle of perhaps the worst storm he'd ever witnessed. His teeth began to chatter, his hands trembled and his lips turned blue but in the end, he managed to stammer, '*Y...y...you,*' as though this was all that was needed.

It could have been a pleasant scene, Pyke thought as he looked around the room. Old friends getting quietly drunk while the elements wreaked havoc around them.

'Squires?' Malvern looked up at him through a fug of alcohol. 'I thought you... I thought you...' But he couldn't finish his sentence.

'That I was dead? Or that I'd been shot or arrested perhaps? Or that I no longer had any interest in buying Ginger Hill?'

Alefounder cowered in his chair like a whipped dog.

'Where's Pemberton?' Malvern wanted to know.

311

'I struck him over the head with this.' Pyke held up the shovel and said, to Alefounder, 'Have you told him yet?'

Alefounder looked over at Malvern and shook his head. He looked about as crushed as a man could be. The shutters rattled violently against their jambs but no one took any notice of them.

'Told me *what?*' Malvern put his empty glass down. 'I demand to know what is going on.'

'I'm sorry, Charles. I was going to tell you tomorrow, after the storm had passed...'

'Tell me what, for God's sake?'

'That your fiancée is dead,' Pyke interrupted. 'She was murdered in London shortly after she arrived there.' He kept his voice low and hard.

Malvern stared at him, an inane smile plastered on his face. 'Murdered?'

'She was strangled and her body dumped near the docks. Her eyeballs had been cut out.' Pyke looked across at Alefounder to see how he reacted to this last piece of news but the trader's expression remained glazed and his stare empty. Pyke placed the shovel against the wall.

'I'm sorry but I have to go...' Alefounder tried to stand up but Pyke pushed him back into his chair.

'This has to be some kind of mistake,' Malvern said, bemused, looking at Pyke as if he were still Monty Squires and the world a benevolent place. 'Who *are* you, sir?'

'I was charged with the task of finding her killer.' Pyke looked at Alefounder, but the trader made no comment.

'You mean all this time...'

'I'm afraid there's more bad news,' Pyke said, interrupting. He didn't have time for the man's histrionics. 'Your godfather, Lord William Bedford, was also murdered, in an apparently separate incident. I didn't know that Mary had stayed with him until you told me about it a few days ago. Now I'm certain the two deaths are related.'

'Uncle William?' Malvern tried to stand up but stumbled, his hands clutching the sides of his davenport. 'Did you know about this, Alefounder?'

The trader's eyelids twitched and beads of sweat broke out around his temples. 'I was going to tell you...'

'So it's true?' Malvern stared at him, a feral grunt escaping from his mouth. 'She's really dead? My Mary's dead? *And* Uncle William?' He sat there staring at nothing, tapping his closed fist on the davenport. His world had collapsed in the space of a few seconds; and it was hard not to feel sympathy for him. But Pyke had travelled more than three thousand miles for this moment and he wasn't about to let the opportunity slip from his grasp.

'Tell me something, Alefounder: when did you first fuck Mary Edgar? Was it last year when you visited Ginger Hill?'

Alefounder opened his mouth – just – but actually speaking seemed to be beyond him. Malvern stared at him, trying to make sense of the question Pyke had just put to him.

'You met her ship when it docked in London but she wasn't interested in you any more. You begged her to get into your carriage, and eventually she

313

succumbed, but it wasn't the same. *She* wasn't the same. She told you she didn't want to see you. She spurned you. In the end, you couldn't take it any more so you strangled her and then dumped her body on the Ratcliff Highway.'

'*No.*' The shout came out of Alefounder's mouth like an anguished sob.

'But the two of you were lovers. You were besotted with her, weren't you?'

Malvern stared at the trader, still trying to come to terms with what was unfolding. His fiancée had gone from merely being dead to being a harlot, but Pyke guessed that Malvern knew this already: it was why he'd sent her away in the first place. 'Did you bed her *here,* in my house?' Malvern's face was suddenly streaked with tears.

Alefounder looked at him and mouthed, 'I'm sorry.'

Without warning Malvern stood up – at first, Pyke thought, to attack Alefounder – and then charged from the room.

'You're not going to go after him?' Alefounder said, a moment later. He looked like a punctured balloon. Pyke wanted to hate him, as he had hated him in London, for his bombast and pride and the way he'd exploited his wealth and position to avoid public censure for his affair with Mary Edgar, but now he seemed like a different person – scared, alone, beaten – and Pyke felt a sudden stab of pity for him.

'And tell him what? That everyone will live happily ever after?'

'What if he decides to slit his own throat or put a pistol to his head and pull the trigger? Do you

314

want *his* blood on your hands as well?'

'I'm just playing the hand I was dealt.' But Pyke looked out of the door Malvern had just run through. 'If you leave this room, if you even move from this chair, I'll find you, I'll drag you back in here and I'll nail your hands and feet to the floor. Is that understood?'

Eventually he found Malvern downstairs in the kitchen. He was sobbing in Josephine's arms. The pots and pans were rattling in the wind and the sash windows were shaking in their frames. Josephine shot him a look of disgust. 'Can't you leave him alone to grieve?'

Back in Malvern's study, Alefounder had moved from his chair but only to fill his glass with brandy. Pyke took the bottle from him and finished it. After all the rum he'd drunk, it tasted smooth and yet a little bitter. 'I'm going to ask you some questions,' he said, wiping his mouth with his sleeve. 'This time, I want you to tell me the truth.'

Alefounder just nodded.

'Good.' Pyke hesitated. 'Did you kill Mary Edgar?'

'No. I didn't. I *swear...*'

Pyke had to fight back the sour taste of disappointment. He believed Alefounder; that was the problem. In a stroke, he'd lost his chief and, indeed, only suspect. 'So tell me who did.'

'I don't know.'

'But you *were* sleeping with her.'

This time Alefounder shook his head. There were tears in his eyes. 'We slept together once here at Ginger Hill. You're right. I *was* besotted with her. When I heard she was coming to London, I suppose I jumped to the wrong conclusion.'

'You thought she'd come to be with you?'

'I knew Charles had paid for her passage, and still expected to marry her, but...' Alefounder paused. 'I hoped I might change her mind.'

'And did you try?'

'After I met her off the ship, I suppose it was clear that she hadn't travelled across the Atlantic to rekindle our affair. I tried to insist that she stay with me, or in an apartment on The Strand I'd rented. She refused and we argued. In the end, I agreed to take her to Bedford's house in Mayfair, but only on the condition that she meet me the next day for lunch. She refused but a few days later I got a note from her asking whether I'd still be interested in giving her a tour of the city.'

Pyke searched Alefounder's face for indications he might be lying but couldn't see any. 'What happened next?'

'I picked her up in my carriage at the time we'd agreed and we spent the day together. I'd say she was a little lonely. I showed her the apartment I'd rented on The Strand. I hoped ... well, you can probably guess what I hoped.'

'And it didn't happen?'

'Not on that occasion. The next day I picked her up again but this time it was clear that she'd only used me to escape from Bedford's prying eye. She made me take her to the Tower of London and then she climbed out of the carriage and I never saw her again.'

Pyke considered what he'd just been told. 'But when you read about Bedford's murder, you must have feared the worst, surely? Why didn't you go to the police and tell them about Mary?'

The trader looked up at him and wetted his lips. It seemed as if he was considering his options for the first time. Pyke told him to think carefully before he responded.

'Because I had a visit,' he said eventually.

'From?'

'Silas Malvern. Charles's father.'

Pyke nodded. He'd expected as much. 'Do you know him well?'

'I don't know how well acquainted you are with my company but if I told you that Silas Malvern owns enough of it to make my life very difficult, would that help you to comprehend my position?'

'He told you if you didn't do exactly as he said, he'd bankrupt you.'

Alefounder shook his head. 'Nothing that explicit, I'm afraid to say. In fact he's greatly changed these days. Apart from being physically frail – he uses a wheelchair and his eyesight is fading – he's something of a religious convert. But he'll still fight tooth and claw to safeguard his family's good name. He told me that Bedford had been murdered, probably by his valet, and it would overcomplicate matters if the police found out the old man had given room and board to Charles's fiancée.' Alefounder hesitated and added, 'Of course, I asked him how Mary was, whether she was safe...'

'And what did he say?'

'He told me he'd had a long talk with her and that she'd agreed to return to Jamaica. I suspected at the time he'd paid her off. But he said

I wasn't to contact her – I was to let her go and not make a fuss.'

Pyke waited for a moment and listened to the wind roaring outside. 'So he knew about you and her?'

Alefounder shrugged. 'He never actually said so, but I suspect he knew.'

A short silence passed between them. 'Tell me what you did when you first heard that Mary was dead; that she'd been murdered.'

'Silas came to see me again. He told me there'd been a terrible tragedy. He explained that he'd put Mary up in a guest house on the Ratcliff Highway while she waited for her ship. He said he didn't know exactly *what* had happened; all he knew was that she'd been strangled and that her body had been found somewhere near by. He told me he blamed himself. He was very upset.'

Pyke made a mental note of exactly what Alefounder had said. 'And what did you think?'

'What do you mean, what did I *think?*' A slight element of frustration had crept into Alefounder's tone.

'For a start, did you believe him?'

'Why shouldn't I have believed him?'

'Two murders in a week, both victims living under the same roof. That didn't strike you as coincidental?'

'By then I knew the police had arrested the valet for Bedford's murder. I didn't see the two as being connected.'

'What you mean is that Silas Malvern ordered you to keep your mouth shut.'

'He made me see that doing nothing was in my

318

best interest. His, too. He didn't want to read about his family in the newspapers or have to answer some policeman's questions.'

Pyke considered what Alefounder had just told him. It made a certain amount of sense. Preserving one's good name was just about the most important thing a man like Malvern could do.

'So when I turned up in your office and made those accusations, you went directly to see Silas Malvern.'

Alefounder nodded. 'He told me I'd have to make a statement to the police but that he could arrange it so that the questions would be of a friendly nature. Above all, he said, I wasn't to admit ever having known or seen Mary.' He hesitated, thinking about what he'd just said. 'I was grateful to him, I suppose. For obvious reasons, I didn't want to become embroiled in the murder investigation.'

Pyke looked around the room and rubbed his eyes; he was tired from the long walk but he knew he had to remain alert. 'Did Malvern tell you that Elizabeth had sailed for the Caribbean?'

'Actually, she didn't make the journey in the end,' Alefounder said, staring down at his boots.

That stopped Pyke in his tracks. 'How do you know?'

'I received a letter from her saying that she'd intended to make the trip because she wanted to be the one who broke the news to Charles, but that she'd fallen ill at the last moment. For some reason, she didn't want her father to know that she hadn't made the journey, but she begged me to break the bad news to Charles.'

'You know Elizabeth Malvern, then?'

'She and I were acquainted at one time.' Alefounder brushed his hand against his chin, as he did when he was lying.

'*Acquainted?* Is that what they're calling it these days?' When Alefounder didn't seem to have understood Pyke's remark, he added, 'Your wife told me that Elizabeth Malvern was your mistress for about two years.'

That almost finished him. 'You've talked to *my wife?*' The sense of betrayal in his voice was hard to miss.

'She was very forthcoming about the affair.'

Alefounder shook his head as though he couldn't quite fathom what was happening to him.

'Your wife also told me about your charitable work for the Vice Society. Elizabeth's, too.' Pyke hesitated. 'Of course, given this, it seems a little obtuse that Elizabeth should be involved with a man like Jemmy Crane.'

This time the sugar trader's expression was more circumspect. 'What she does with her life is up to her.'

'I take it you don't approve of her choice of lover?'

'When we were still together, she expressed an interest in the work the society performs and I encouraged her to join.'

'And what precisely do you do for the society?'

'I sit on the board and help raise money for the society's work. As for Elizabeth, you'd have to ask her. We haven't had much contact in the past two years.'

'But you must hear of what she does?'

The trader sighed, clearly agitated, and shook his head. 'Field work, as far as I'm aware. She latched on to a man called Samuel Ticknor, I believe. I'm told he encourages fallen women to find more respectable occupations.'

'Does the name Lucy Luckins mean anything to you?'

'Luckins?' He appeared to give it some thought. 'No, I'm afraid not.'

'Her corpse was found in the Thames.'

'I hope you're not suggesting that I had something to do with it,' Alefounder said, rediscovering some of the pomposity he'd displayed in London.

Pyke shrugged. 'It's funny, isn't it, that you and Elizabeth should play any kind of role in the Vice Society when your own sexual predilections are so...'

This was almost too much for Alefounder to bear. His neck swelled with colour and his fists clenched into tight, white balls. 'I'll not be slandered in such a vile manner. I might have done wrong by not coming forward with information about Mary...'

But Pyke was not interested in Alefounder's outrage, whether it was heartfelt or not. He left the trader slumped in a chair and went to find Charles Malvern.

After an hour or so of fruitless searching, Pyke found the young planter wandering on the front lawn. He was muttering to himself, staring up into the dark void, seemingly oblivious to the torrential rain and fierce winds. Pyke tried to put his arm around him and guide him back into the house but Malvern pushed him away and continued to mutter to himself. He stumbled and fell, laughing drunkenly as he did so. Just at the last moment Pyke turned around and saw the plank of wood a fraction of a second before it cracked him around the head, so that in the end he wasn't sure whether someone had swung it at him or whether he'd become another victim of the storm. He fell to the ground and passed into unconsciousness.

NINETEEN

Pyke came around just after dawn the following morning, face down in a drainage ditch, his head throbbing with pain. The air around him was cool and clear and filled with birdsong. The clouds had passed too, and the sky was a mass of intense blue, dazzling to the naked eye. There was a soft breeze, laced with the scent of lily, ginger, jasmine and honeysuckle, and all across the lawn, and on the track leading down the hill towards the stables, pools of water created by the rains shimmered in the early morning light.

On another day it might have been the perfect morning, but the devastation wrought by the storm was apparent wherever you looked. The great house lay in ruins; part of the roof had been torn off and dumped across the surrounding land and the wall at one end of the building had buckled and collapsed. Much of the furniture lay scattered across the lawn, splintered and up-

ended; bookcases were overturned like ship-
wrecks, their contents distributed to every corner
of the gardens; tables and chairs were marooned
in flower beds, torn pictures lying face down in
pools of rainwater. The surrounding bush had
been flattened and pulped by the wind and trees
lay strewn across pathways, their roots having
pulled up massive clumps of red earth. It was a
strange, desolate scene, made even more eerie by
the near-total silence. Nothing moved and no one
answered Pyke's calls. He looked for Malvern,
Alefounder, Pemberton, Josephine and any of the
house servants, but the whole place was deserted.

Pyke eventually found Malvern and Pemberton
under a pile of brick rubble at the end of the
house that had collapsed. He checked their
pulses but didn't need to. Both were dead and
had been for a while. Pemberton's face was still
bruised from where Pyke had struck him with the
shovel, but there was nothing to indicate how
he'd died. Charles Malvern, on the other hand,
had died from a heavy blow to his skull. In both
cases there were drag marks in the brick dust.
Pyke rummaged through Malvern's pockets and
found a purse full of silver dollars, which he kept
for himself. Someone had wanted it to look like
an accident; nothing had been stolen and nothing would be. He retrieved Pemberton's pistol
and went looking for Alefounder.

The house itself would have to be knocked down
and rebuilt from scratch. Entire walls had collapsed, many of the ceilings had fallen in and large
sections of the roof were gone; as Pyke wandered
from room to room, he kept his sleeve up to his

mouth to shield it from the choking residue of plaster and brick dust. He didn't find Alefounder anywhere on the ground floor and the upper floor had been marooned by the partial collapse of the main staircase. Outside, Pyke continued his search of the grounds, including the counting house and, underneath it, the old slave dungeon, but the sugar trader was nowhere to be found.

Back up at the great house, he found Josephine hunched over Charles Malvern's body. When she finally looked at him, her eyes were watery and bloodshot and her face was streaked with tears.

'I knew 'im when he was a babe; I held 'im in my arms and sung to 'im.' She reached out and brushed some brick dust off his forehead.

'This wasn't an accident, was it?'

She wouldn't answer him and looked away.

'They told you they'd spare him, didn't they? No one's going to mourn for Pemberton, are they? Not even his wife, I suspect. But in a strange kind of way, Charles was an innocent.'

Josephine sat there staring down at Malvern's face for a while, and when she did finally look up, her expression was as hard as dried wax. 'If you want answers, ask her. Go to Accompong and ask *her*.' She spat out this last word with particular venom.

'Who?' Pyke tapped her shoulder.

'If you touch me again, you'll regret it.'

Pyke's throat tightened and his jaw clenched. 'Who do I ask for when I get to this place Accompong?'

'You threaten me?' This seemed to amuse her. 'You think I scared of you 'cos you big and white?'

Pyke looked down at her hunched, frail figure and sighed. 'I just want a name and then I'll leave you in peace.'

But Josephine had started to sing a haunting melody whose words Pyke couldn't quite grasp and whose meaning lay beyond him.

He waited until she had finished. 'Who put the eyeball in my bed?'

She gave him a proud, defiant stare. 'I don't know. I'd say one of the servants paid by Busha.'

'Why?'

'To scare you.'

'Why would he want to scare me, if he'd already decided to kill me?'

Josephine just shrugged. 'Maybe they don't know that. It's how Busha frighten off all them other buyers.'

Pyke waited for a moment. 'Who should I ask for in Accompong?'

Josephine closed her eyes and shook her head. When she opened her eyes again they were hard and black like pebbles. 'Ask for Bertha. She Mary's mother.'

Isaac Webb was waiting for Pyke at the bottom of the hill, a few hundred yards up the track from the old boiling house, where they had parted ways the previous evening.

The devastation was not as bad down there; the stable roof was still intact and Pyke could hear the snorting of horses.

'Malvern's dead. So is Pemberton.' Pyke looked up into Webb's eyes. 'But why am I telling you this? You already know.'

Webb's stare drifted over Pyke's shoulder. 'Some folk reckon the storm was the worst they ever saw.'

'The last I saw of them, Pemberton was out cold under the veranda and Malvern was wandering around on the lawn muttering to himself. This morning I found their corpses under a pile of plaster and brick rubble at the far end of the house. Someone had moved them there. You could see drag marks in the dust.' Pyke paused. 'Why did you have to kill Malvern? I mean, was it really necessary? Don't you see? Eventually his father will just sell the land to some other buyer and you'll be back where you started.'

Webb considered what Pyke had said for a while, his expression fixed in concentration. 'Can I ask you a question?'

'If you like.' They regarded each other in awkward silence.

'What will it take for you to go home and forget about everything you seen here, forget about the Malverns, Busha, the storm?'

'And Mary, too?'

Webb looked at him and shrugged.

'You loved her, didn't you?' Pyke took a step towards Webb and prodded him gently in the chest. 'And yet you're happy to see whoever killed her walk free?'

'Mary dead and there ain't nothing gonna bring her back.' He walked a few yards along the track and motioned for Pyke to accompany him.

'And what about Mary's family? Her mother? Are they happy to see her murder go unpunished?'

Webb turned around very slowly. 'Mary ain't

got family.'

Pyke nodded, as though he had expected Webb to say this, and casually removed the pistol that he'd tucked into his trousers. 'This is just to protect myself.' He registered Webb's surprise and wondered whether he'd read the situation correctly. 'You know. In case you have a notion to do to me what you did to Pemberton and Malvern.'

Webb looked down at the pistol without changing his expression. 'Those men died in the storm.'

'And Alefounder?'

'The trader?' Webb hesitated. 'I found his body in the house. Someone reckon Charles shot him. Don't know why.'

Pyke digested this news. Given what Charles Malvern had found out about the trader's designs on his fiancée, Charles certainly had sufficient reason to kill Alefounder. 'So where is his body? I did not see it when I searched the house this morning.'

'I took care of it,' Webb said, as though it wasn't important. 'Custos come here, see a man's been shot, gonna be suspicious. Suddenly he might ask questions, wonder if Busha and Malvern really did die in the storm.'

Pyke searched his eyes. Webb, perhaps under Harper's direction, was clearing up the mess, making sure that no one could link them with the deaths of two white men. Pyke didn't believe that they wanted to kill him as well but something in Webb's manner made him suspicious. It was why he was pointing the pistol in Webb's general direction.

Guessing, he said, 'You can tell Harper what you like. Tell him I escaped, tell him you killed me. But I'm going to take one of the horses and ride for Kingston. You have my word that you won't ever see me again.'

Webb looked at the pistol, frowning. 'Why you think I want to kill you?'

'I don't know for a fact that you do but I'm not taking any chances.' Pyke waited and then sighed. 'Maybe Harper thinks I'll go back to England and tell Silas Malvern what happened to his son, what really happened to his son, and about your plans for his estate. If it fell into disrepair and a buyer couldn't be found, there would be nothing to stop people from squatting on the land.'

'Harper knows you ain't a friend of the old massa.'

'But I'm white.'

Webb noted this with a nod but didn't say anything.

Pyke met his stare. 'Just now you asked what it would take for me to walk away, not say a word about this to anyone.'

'And?'

'I have a young son in London. His mother died a few years ago. If anything were to happen to me, he'll have no one. I know what that's like and I wouldn't wish it on anyone.'

Something in Webb's face softened. 'How old is he?'

'Ten.'

Webb nodded once, half closing his eyes. 'My boy's five.'

'I'm going to saddle up one of Malvern's horses and then you're going to point me in the direction of Kingston.'

'And Mary?'

Pyke took his time; he wanted Webb to think he was seriously considering his question. 'Like you just said, she's dead and nothing is going to bring her back.'

He walked up the path to the stables and emerged, a few minutes later, leading a black-and-white mare by the reins. Webb was waiting for him.

'Far as Harper thinks, you dead. Means you don't go nowhere near Falmouth.'

So he'd been right after all: the big man had wanted him dead. Perhaps it didn't mean very much; perhaps it was just a question of tying up loose ends. As if reading his thoughts, Webb shrugged and added, 'It weren't nothing personal.' It was as forthcoming as he was prepared to be.

Nodding, Pyke mounted the mare and took the reins. He didn't tell Webb that he was heading for Accompong or that he knew about Mary's mother, and briefly he wondered whether Josephine would own up to what she'd perhaps inadvertently revealed. What might Webb do if he knew Pyke wasn't planning to go home after all?

'Enough folk been killed.' Webb's eyes wrinkled at the corners. 'You follow the track down past the boiling house and the old stone bridge and keep going straight. It bring you to the village. From there, ask for Ulster Spring or Albert Town and then Mand'ville. You get to Mand'ville, Kingston's another day riding farther east. The whole thing take about three days.'

As he rode off, Pyke still half expected the shot, and it was only when he'd crossed the river and passed the boiling house that he started to relax.

The ride to Accompong took him all of that day and most of the next one; the silver dollars he'd taken from Malvern meant he had money to pay for food and shelter, for him and the horse, and the weather remained fair throughout. Currents of warm air carried John-crows effortlessly above the harsh, mountainous landscape and the lush, tropical valleys that plunged hundreds of feet down into fast-flowing rivers. The track, at times cut into the side of the mountain, took him higher and farther into unknown terrain. He kept to a slow pace, surprised to find that the damage from the storm lessened the farther inland he went, and when he stopped at tiny makeshift villages to ask for directions to Accompong, he was treated both as an oddity and with caution and respect. Along the way, he learned some of the history of his eventual destination. Together with a thousand acres of Cockpit country, Accompong had been ceded by the Crown some time in the previous century to the Maroons – runaway slaves who'd taken refuge in the mountains – after British soldiers had been ambushed and overpowered at a mountain pass. The terms of the treaty agreed at the time were still binding and as such Accompong and the surrounding land did not recognise British rule. 'Your laws don't mean nothing up dere,' one man had told Pyke, sniffing the air. 'Up dere, everyone free.'

The woman could have been sixty or she could have been a hundred. She greeted him with a limp handshake and without getting to her feet.

She sat in an old rocking chair in the shade of a mammoth cotton tree at the top of the village, her tiny wattle-and-daub hut with its straw-thatched roof and small garden just a few yards farther back down the hill. She listened carefully while Pyke explained who he was and why he'd come to see her but showed no emotion, even when he told her that her daughter, Mary, had been killed in London.

For a while, after he'd said his piece, they sat across from one another, neither of them speaking. Some children had gathered nearby to inspect him and were giggling and pointing.

'In our religion, we believe that when someone dies, their spirit returns to their homeland. But you see, we've been away from Africa too long now.' She spoke, Pyke was surprised to find out, without even the slightest trace of an accent.

'So you already knew your daughter was dead?' Pyke waited. He had been told by one of the village elders that she was a renowned myalist and hence was to be treated with the utmost reverence.

Bertha nodded. 'Mary's spirit has come home to me.'

'Do you know how she died?'

'I know men killed her.'

'Men? As in plural?'

She shrugged, as though the distinction wasn't an important one.

'She was strangled.' Pyke studied her wrinkled, beatific face and felt an irrational anger swelling within him. 'Her eyeballs were cut from her head.'

This time Bertha's expression did register dismay, and for a moment Pyke was pleased that he

331

had been able to puncture her seemingly implacable façade. But then he remembered who he was talking to and felt a sharp rush of shame; this was the woman who had brought Mary into the world and he had knowingly rubbed her face in the horror of her daughter's death.

Finally the old woman shuffled forward in the rocking chair, her legs dangling down like a child's. 'Why did you come all this way?'

'To Jamaica or Accompong?'

'Both.'

'I came to Jamaica because I thought your daughter's killer had fled here from London.'

'And were you right?'

'No.' Pyke hesitated.

'Go on.'

'Charles Malvern is now dead; so are his attorney, Pemberton, and a sugar trader from England called Alefounder. I believe it was part of a plot organised by a newspaperman, John Harper, and Mary's former lover, a man called Isaac Webb, to take control of the Ginger Hill estate. I found one of Malvern's servants, a woman called Josephine, weeping over his dead body. I think Malvern was murdered and his death blamed on the violent storms that passed across the island a few nights ago. When I asked her for an explanation, she just told me to come here and talk to you.' Pyke looked up at the old woman. 'Why would she say a thing like that?'

But the woman didn't seem unduly surprised by anything Pyke had said. 'Josephine always did love that boy too much,' she said, as though this were a mistake.

'You *know* her?'

Until this point Pyke hadn't taken seriously the idea that there might have been some communication between Falmouth, Ginger Hill and Accompong – the distances were too vast and the arduous travelling conditions necessarily precluded Bertha's involvement in the affairs at Ginger Hill – but suddenly he had to reassess this view; and as such, he wondered how safe he really was.

Bertha nodded. 'A long time ago, I used to work up at the great house at Ginger Hill as well. It's how I learned to speak the King's English.' She smiled sweetly. 'That's right; there was a king on the throne at the time.'

'What made you leave?'

Bertha sat back in her rocking chair and closed her eyes. 'You're a very impatient man. Impatient and troubled.'

'I've been shot at, chased, betrayed and almost killed again. I think I've earned the right to be impatient.'

'Very well. Since you've come all this way, and since you're trying to find the man or men who murdered my daughter, and since I sense you're a *good* man, I'll do my best to answer your questions.'

Pyke smiled, pleased by this sudden change of attitude. 'What made you leave?'

She nodded politely. 'Perhaps it would be better, or rather easier for me, if you weren't so blunt.'

Pyke acknowledged her point with a nod. 'Did you know Charles's father, Silas.'

She nodded and smiled. 'Yes, I did.'

'And did you like him?'

'Did I *like* him?' She seemed amused by the question. 'That's rather like asking a mouse whether he likes the eagle that's eating him.'

'Was he a good master?'

'I thought so – for a while.'

'What changed your mind?'

She looked at him, chewing her lips. 'I assume you already know something about the family's history. For example, that Silas's wife, Bonella, apparently fell to her death down the staircase at Ginger Hill.'

This made him sit up. 'Are you saying she didn't fall?'

'That's precisely what I'm saying.' She smiled at his reaction. 'More than that, I'm saying he had something to do with it.'

'Malvern killed his wife?'

'He wasn't a bad man, as slave-owners go. There were, still are, many far worse planters on the island. But he was a jealous man and he had a temper. He was especially jealous of his brother, Phillip. You see, Phillip was everything he wasn't: funny, warm, attractive. Phillip was also their father's favourite. So Silas's resentment towards his brother had been nurtured since childhood. But Silas was a complicated man; he wanted to do the right thing by his brother; he wanted to treat him well; and even though Silas took over the estate when their daddy passed away, he made sure there was always a place for Phillip at the great house.'

She paused, to clear her throat, and Pyke

waited for her to continue.

'I could see what was going to happen. It was all so predictable. Silas neglected Bonella terribly. During planting and harvesting, he would spend most of his time out on the estate. He was very active in that respect; he liked to get his hands dirty. Meanwhile Phillip would spend time with Bonella. So during the day, when Silas was away from the house, you could hear the two of them laughing; it was a joyful, happy sound, and when I think about those days now, they still lift my heart. But Phillip was also a terrible philanderer, just like his father, and his interest in Bonella was never innocent. She was a beautiful woman and he wanted to bed her. The fact that she was his brother's wife only made her more attractive in his eyes. I don't think he loved her; I don't think he loved anyone, not really. But I think, in the end, she loved him. I also think if Silas had merely caught the two of them in bed, he mightn't have reacted in the way he did; if it had just been the one time and hadn't meant anything. But it went on for years, or at least two years, and finally Bonella went to Silas and told him about the affair; she told him she loved Phillip and wanted to be with him. I don't know if Phillip knew she was going to do this. I don't think he did. He hated confrontations and he feared and wor-shipped his brother in equal measures.'

'And that's when Silas killed her?'

'To this day, I don't know whether Silas meant to kill her or not. We were downstairs in the kitchen. We could hear them arguing and then we heard a terrible crash. I ran to the hall and saw

335

her, Bonella, there on the floor. Then I looked up and saw him. I'll never forget his face: the fury, the terror and the sadness. Like I said, even then, I didn't think he was a *bad* man.'

'So what changed your mind?'

'After the funeral we were all sent away. No one knew why. Everyone, that is, except for Phillip.' She paused and bit her lip. 'But Phillip didn't want to face his brother on his own; he didn't know how much Bonella had told Silas before she died. So he asked me to stay. I think you can probably guess why he asked me, rather than anyone else.'

'You were in love with him?'

This time she laughed. '*Love?* How can a poor black slave ever hope to love a wealthy white man?'

'I thought Silas was the wealthy one.'

Bertha smiled. 'I suppose I did love Phillip, in a way.' Her smiled faded. 'But that night put an end to everything. I don't even know why Phillip didn't just leave; I think he wanted the chance to explain himself to Silas, to beg for his brother's forgiveness. From the veranda, I watched him walk across the lawn to the counting house. That's where Silas was waiting for him. I could hear them talking and for a while I thought everything might go back to how it was. Then the screaming started. Phillip's screams. I'd never heard a sound like it and I hope I never do again. I couldn't sit and do nothing, so I crept over there and I climbed those stone steps and I peered into that room through the open door.' Bertha paused; her eyes had suddenly filled with tears and her hands were trembling.

She looked at Pyke and offered a brave smile.

'This is hard for me. I've tried not to think about it for a very long time.'

Pyke returned the smile. He hated himself for putting her through this but he had to know. He'd come too far not to know.

'Silas was standing there in front of Phillip. He'd bound his brother's wrists and ankles to a chair.'

Pyke just nodded; his mouth was dry.

'Silas had these enormous hands, twice the size of yours. I remember looking at them, looking at his thumbs, wondering why they were dripping with blood. At first, I thought he'd cut himself.' She hesitated and then closed and opened her eyes. 'Then Silas stepped aside and I saw Phillip's face. I think I must have gasped because he looked around and he saw me. Silas, that is. All I could look at were those two thumbs, wet with Phillip's blood. Of course, Phillip couldn't see me. Where his eyes had been there were just two bloody slits.'

Queasy at the thought of what she'd described, Pyke waited until he thought she might be ready then asked, 'What did you do?'

'What did I do? What *could* I do? I turned and ran. I went back to my hut and gathered everything I could carry and I left Ginger Hill for the mountains. Later, I heard that Silas had offered a reward of ten pounds for my capture. After all, I was a runaway slave and in the eyes of the law I was his property. I walked for many, many days; I ate what I could find and I slept under the stars. Oddly enough it was the first time I'd ever felt free. I'd heard about this place and eventually I found it. I don't know if Silas knew I'd made it this far or that I've been here for the past twenty years. In recent years I've tried to stop thinking about him.'

Pyke nodded but didn't speak for a moment. 'And did you ever see Phillip again?'

Bertha looked exhausted. 'No. That was the last time I saw him; his eyes gouged out, tied to a chair in the counting house.'

'And you never heard what became of him?'

Her expression hardened. 'He's dead,' she said emphatically. 'I'm guessing he died shortly after Silas blinded him.'

'But do you know this for a fact?'

'I know it in here.' She tapped her chest and then her head. 'Just like Mary, his spirit has come back home as well.' She stared at him proudly as though expecting to be challenged.

'But this was never his home,' Pyke said, trying to determine whether she really believed what she was saying. 'And Phillip was a white man.'

That seemed to amuse her. 'Phillip was white because his daddy said so; likewise Mary was black because I was black. But he was darker than some black folk and she could pass as white. Black and white doesn't mean a thing apart from what those with money and power want them to mean.'

Pyke smiled at the truth of what she'd just said. Suddenly he knew what she'd perhaps been hinting at. 'Phillip was Mary's father, wasn't he?'

'How did you know that?' Her voice was tense.

'I didn't,' he said, trying to keep any trace of gloating from his voice. 'At least, not until just now.'

'You're a clever man,' she said, rocking back and

forth in the chair. 'Clever and arrogant. I imagine it brings its own rewards, and its hardships.'

'Did Phillip know he was Mary's father?'

Bertha shook her head.

'And what about Mary? Did she know that this white man – Silas's brother – was in fact her father?'

'Mary and I weren't what you'd call close. A product of circumstances, more than anything else.'

Pyke remained silent and waited for her to continue.

'What I'm trying to say is that after I left Ginger Hill, I never saw my daughter again.' Bertha's voice was quivering. 'She was five years of age at the time.'

Pyke didn't try to hide his scepticism. 'You mean she never came looking for you and you never sent word to her about your whereabouts?'

'Initially I was terrified about the prospect of her trying to follow me here. Silas knew Mary was my daughter and even though she was barely five at the time, he made her one of his house slaves, to keep her close. If she ever tried to run away, he would have caught and punished her, in order to punish me. So I didn't contact her or send word to her; after a while, it became normal and, much later, even after Silas had left for England, I just thought I'd left it too long.' Bertha dabbed her eyes, unconvincingly, Pyke thought. 'Of course, I'd hear things about her from time to time; I always craved to hear any piece of news about her, however small or trivial.'

'Even bad news?' Pyke asked, still not convinced by this part of the old woman's tale. Even taking into account the debilitating effects of slavery and its aftermath, how likely was it that a mother and daughter wouldn't make any effort to see one another during all this time?

'Is there any other kind of news for black folk on this island?'

'So what did you think when you heard that your daughter had agreed to marry the son of the man you despised?'

'What do you *think* I thought?' Bertha shook her head, as though the question were a stupid one.

'And yet you still did nothing; you didn't write to your daughter, to try to persuade her she was making a mistake?'

'A mistake? A rich white man who by all accounts loved her? Why on earth would I tell her not to marry him?'

'But they're cousins.'

For a while Bertha sat very still, her eyes tightly shut and her face composed. Then she smiled. 'You'll have to forgive me, sir. I'm no longer a young woman. Too much talking tires me out. I don't wish to be rude and I'd like you to stay here in the village tonight – as our guest. But I need to rest so I'm going to have to ask you to leave.'

'What if Phillip isn't dead?' Pyke persisted. 'What if he lived and at some point travelled to London?' He was thinking about the blind mud-lark who'd been seen talking with Arthur Sobers on the Ratcliff Highway. Was it simply coincidence that Phillip Malvern and this man were both blind?

'Phillip died a long time ago. I told you that already.'

'But you don't know that for a fact, do you?'

This time she stared at him with something approaching hostility and refused to answer the question.

'Did you know Mary had sailed for London?'

'I heard about it after she'd left.'

'And what did you think?'

'I've told you, I am tired and need a rest. Now I'm going to have to insist upon it.' She went to stand up and Pyke handed her the bamboo cane.

'Would you have supported her decision, if you'd known about it?'

This time she turned to face him. 'You mean, would I have sent her to her death?'

'You *knew* she was going to die?'

'I'm what folk here called a myal woman. The spirits visit me. I have certain powers of intuition.' She shrugged. 'I wouldn't expect you to believe me but I foresaw that Mary would die a very long way from home.'

'Mary had those powers, too, didn't she?' Pyke thought about what McQuillan had told him. 'Do you think she foresaw her death as well?'

But Bertha had clearly had enough and, without saying another word, she began to shuffle down the hill towards her hut.

That night, the villagers ate barbecued pork, drank rum and danced to the beat of their jam-jams and kitty-katties under the stars. It was a balmy night, and as Pyke watched the revellers shake their bodies in time to the music, he thought about his conversation with the old woman, unable to reconcile the different elements of what she had told him. Did she really believe that Phillip was long dead, and had Mary been entirely ignorant of her own parentage? Later in the evening, Bertha performed what he guessed was a traditional ritual: having sprinkled powder on her volunteer and fed him rum, she stood back while her assistant, a much younger man, danced in time to the drumbeats until the volunteer fell to the ground, apparently dead. While the beat of the jam-jams and kitty-katties echoed across the mountain, Bertha sprinkled herbs on to the 'corpse', squeezed juice into his mouth, touched his eyes with the tips of her fingers and chanted into the air. As the ring of revellers tightened around her, and the stamping and drumming became louder, she suddenly clapped her hands together and the volunteer came back to life.

It should have been easy for Pyke to dismiss the whole spectacle as nonsense, as other white men before him had done. Generally he wasn't a superstitious man, preferring to put his faith in the rigours of science and reason. But as he sat there taking it all in – the warm air, the strange sounds and smells, the fiery rum warming his stomach – Pyke found himself curiously affected by the spectacle. This hadn't been a performance for him or even for those who'd participated in it but rather for family and friends who'd suffered and died during slavery, and especially for Mary Edgar, who had been buried alone and unloved in a faraway city. This was *her* farewell, and as the dance broke up and the revellers fell to the ground, exhausted, Pyke caught the old woman's eye. She looked at him, puzzled at first, and then broke into a smile, as if to suggest her long-lost daughter had finally come home.

Later that night they came for him. Six or seven men crept up to his hut and pushed open the door. Pyke watched them from the trees on the other side of the clearing. Shortly afterwards they emerged from the hut, talking and gesticulating to one another. They looked around, not knowing what to do. Pyke withdrew behind the line of trees and stared up at the branches rustling overhead. Pyke didn't doubt that, had he stayed in the hut, he would be dead by now; there was something he'd asked the old woman about, something he'd said, something he knew that made him a threat. Harper had been the same.

Earlier, before the celebration had started, he had hidden his horse a long way from the village and had already planned his escape route. He would wait for the men to disperse and then try to retrieve his mare. By that time the sun would be up and he would start the long two-day trek towards Kingston and the steamer.

Part of him wanted to have another talk with the old woman, hold a knife to her throat and force the whole truth from her. But some of the men had congregated outside her hut, and Pyke knew he wouldn't get within fifty feet of her.

To go anywhere near her was to take a risk that he wasn't prepared to take because, right at that moment, more than anything, Pyke wanted to take Felix in his arms and hold him. It was time to go home.

PART III

London

AUGUST 1840

TWENTY

Every seat in the cavernous room had been filled, which meant that Pyke had to stand at the back of the hall and could barely see, let alone hear, the figures on the stage. He moved down the aisle through the mass of bodies and eventually found a spot just to the left of the stage.

Exeter Hall was synonymous with a loosely connected group of anti-slavery, temperance and religious movements and was hosting the first Anti-Slavery Society World Convention. As Pyke surveyed the solemn faces in the crowd, listening earnestly to the sober pronouncements of the speaker, he thought about the unforgiving doctrine that many of them subscribed to – that God helped only those who helped themselves. He wanted to take each and every one of them a few streets to the north or south, to St Giles or Alsatia, and show them the conditions that many people had to endure through no fault of their own. It wasn't their views he objected to as much as their holier-than-thou attitudes, as though God had personally selected them for his mission on earth while leaving the undeserving multitude to beg for their guidance or rot in the gutters. Emily had once tried to help other people, without a trace of the smugness and self-aggrandisement displayed by the Christian missionaries, and Pyke didn't doubt she too would have despised most of the men in this room.

A new speaker had just taken to the stage and someone next to Pyke identified the man as Reverend William Knibb – 'pastor of the Baptist mission in Falmouth, Jamaica'. Knibb was a small, unprepossessing man in his late thirties or early forties but he spoke in a loud, confident voice and soon had the rapt attention of his audience. He started his address by denouncing the popular views circulating in the colonial and metropolitan newspapers, put forward by the planters' lobby, that emancipation had created a lazy and rebellious breed of negro. Knibb went on to suggest quite the opposite; that the free villages built on land purchased as a result of the generosity of congregations in Britain had fostered godliness, morality, domestic happiness and social order. 'A place,' he added, 'of noble free peasantry where the man goes out to work and the woman, released from proper toil, tends to the home, and where there is a new Bible on every table.'

That got a thunderous ovation.

Given what Pyke had seen for himself in the mountains above Falmouth, it was hard to disagree with Knibb's argument: that former slaves lived a better life freed from the shackles of slavery, and that owning their homes and tending their own plots fostered self-sufficiency and, in turn, contentment. But he also thought about John Harper's damning indictment of the Baptists' mission in Jamaica – that, in essence, it represented another form of colonialism since its goal was to turn former slaves into versions of themselves. To amuse himself, he wondered what Knibb and others would think if he took the floor and told them about what had really happened at Ginger Hill.

Still, Pyke held his tongue and waited patiently for the reason he'd come to the meeting in the first place. It came towards the end of Knibb's address.

'To show their respect for that esteemed man Joseph Sturge,' Knibb said to a deafening cheer, 'a town was set up that bore his honoured name. As we speak a new community named after my own birthplace, Kettering, is being settled and very soon a village called Malvern will be established.' Knibb waited as Silas Malvern, perched on top of his high-chair, was carried onstage by two burly men. 'It is my very great pleasure, and honour, to present to you Mr Silas Malvern. Mr Malvern is now a resident of London but until recently he owned one of the largest sugar plantations in the western part of Jamaica.' A hushed silence fell over the room; this was the enemy right there in their midst. 'My friends, please, I can perhaps guess what you're thinking but before you rush to judgement, hear me out. Ill health prevents my brother, Mr Malvern, from addressing you in person but he wishes it to be known that he now regrets his role in the slave trade and by way of restitution he has committed to donating land to our mission for the purpose of establishing two new free villages in the parish of Trelawny, Jamaica.'

Knibb basked in the applause and Silas Malvern even managed a feeble smile from his high-chair. Knibb was preparing to bring his address to a climax. 'In the name of three hundred thousand

349

negroes in Jamaica, I return to you all the thanks which grateful hearts, happy wives and children can give.'

Many in the audience stood to applaud Knibb and Malvern and the applause continued as Malvern was carried from the stage.

Pyke found the old man sitting backstage on his high-chair, looking vaguely bemused. His porters had left him and Knibb was having what looked like an intense conversation with one of his supporters. Malvern seemed to have aged noticeably in the two and a half months since Pyke had last seen him. His shoulders were hunched, his arms like pieces of string and his eyes were sunken and rimmed by red circles.

'You once owned two thousand acres of land and kept five hundred slaves. Do you really imagine a gift of a paltry hundred acres or so will buy you a place in heaven?'

Pyke could see that the old man had heard him well enough but Malvern whispered, 'Come closer, boy, so I can see you. My eyesight isn't so good these days.'

Pyke crouched down and looked into Malvern's translucent eyes. 'I came to your house to ask you questions about Mary Edgar.'

'I remember you, sir. Reckless and rude you were. I don't forget that kind of behaviour in a hurry.' Up close, the old man's breath stank of rancid meat.

'I asked you, then, if you knew Mary Edgar or had intervened in the investigation to find her killer.'

'I remember, sir, and the moment I threatened

to call the police you slunk away like a whipped dog.'

Pyke allowed Malvern his brief moment of triumph. 'I've just returned from Jamaica.'

That made Malvern sit up in his chair.

'I had a revealing discussion with William Alefounder. He told me that you conspired with him to withhold information from the police about your family's attachment to Mary Edgar and Lord Bedford. He also told me that you forced him to flee the country, fearing he might implicate you and your family in these two murders.'

'What *rot*. Did he tell you all this?' Malvern's face momentarily lit up, as if he relished the opportunity to refute Pyke's accusations. 'I might have had a quiet chat with Alefounder, assured him of my innocence in the unfortunate affairs you've just referred to and counselled him about the wisdom of unnecessarily sullying my family's good name. As for *forcing* him, the moment that I mentioned that my daughter, Elizabeth, had sailed for Jamaica to relay the tragic news to her brother, he jumped at the chance to go.'

Pyke studied his expression and concluded that Malvern hadn't yet heard about his son or the destruction at Ginger Hill. But this didn't prevent him from leaning forward, until he was almost on top of Malvern, and whispering in his ear, 'I think you're a liar and a hypocrite. Only time will tell whether you're a murderer, too, but if you had anything to do with either death, I'll make it my mission to ruin what little of your life is left.'

351

Malvern rose in his high-chair. 'You had better get your facts straight, sir. I had nothing to do with Bedford's death. Haven't you heard? The valet was tried in a court of law according to due process and was found guilty by a jury of his peers. The evidence was heard and argued over and the man was found guilty. He killed Bedford and that's all there is to it.'

Pyke contemplated what the old man had said. He'd already heard about the trial but didn't have any faith in the verdict. 'And Mary Edgar?'

'That little harlot? She appeared one day, uninvited, at my home and announced that she was going to marry my son, Charles. Tried to rub my nose in it. I told her it was out of the question – she's a negro, after all, and she used to *serve* Charles, for God's sake. We came to an arrangement. I paid her, quite a handsome sum in fact, and arranged for her passage back to Jamaica. That's the last I saw of her. The fact she ended up being murdered has *nothing* to do with me. Probably started spending some of the money I gave her and was killed for it.' His cheeks glowed with righteous indignation.

Silence fell between them. 'How, then, do you explain the manner of Mary Edgar's death?'

This seemed to irritate Malvern further. 'The *manner* of her death? What are you talking about?'

Pyke looked into Malvern's eyes. 'I'm talking about the fact that she had her eyeballs cut out with a sharp instrument.'

Malvern turned white and some of his bluster began to ebb away. He sank back into his chair and looked around for Knibb or his porters.

'You'll have to explain yourself better, sir.'

'When I was in Jamaica,' Pyke said, 'I visited a small village in the middle of the island called Accompong. Do you know it?'

'I've heard of it.'

'I had a long chat with a woman called Bertha. She used to work for you at the great house in Ginger Hill. Do you remember her?'

'Bertha? What is this? A witch hunt? No, sir, I don't recall a woman by that name. She may have worked for me but I've had hundreds of people in my employment and I don't remember every single one.'

'That's interesting because she remembers you, and your brother Phillip. More than that, she remembers a night shortly after your wife died, when you sent the servants and your children away and...'

But Malvern wouldn't listen to any more and gesticulated wildly to Knibb and the absent porters. Knibb broke off from his conversation and was joined at the high-chair by the two red-faced porters. 'Take me home; this man is upsetting me. I didn't seek out his company; he imposed himself on me and I want him removed from the building forthwith. Is that understood?'

Knibb stared at Pyke. 'Will you do as the gentleman asks, sir?'

Pyke looked down at Malvern, who was trembling in his highchair. 'I've just returned from Jamaica. I'm afraid I have some bad news which I was trying to relay to Mr Malvern.'

Part of him wanted to stop, to turn around and leave without saying another word, but it was as if a squally wind had suddenly blown up behind him and was pushing him towards a destination irrespective of whether he wanted to go there or not.

'What bad news?' Knibb said, staring down at Malvern.

'There was a terrible storm, the worst some people on the island had ever seen. It destroyed the great house at Ginger Hill and, I'm sorry to say, it killed his son Charles. A lawyer, Michael Pemberton, and a guest called William Alefounder also perished.'

Knibb stared at him, open mouthed. Pyke had already determined that neither he nor Malvern had heard about the deaths but correspondences from Jamaica, perhaps travelling on the same steamer Pyke had caught, would soon reach them.

Turning to leave, Knibb grabbed Pyke roughly by the arm. 'Is it true, sir? Is his son really dead?'

'I'm afraid it is.'

Knibb licked his lips, still trying to come to terms with what he'd just heard. 'Just who are you, sir, and what business do you have here?'

'I've already introduced myself to Malvern. I'll let him explain everything to you.'

'Just one minute, sir...'

But from the high-chair, they both heard Malvern mutter, 'Charles? Charles can't be dead. My daughter, Elizabeth, is bringing him home.'

'You tell a father his son has died with all the compassion of delivering an order to the butcher. What kind of a man are you?' Knibb stared into his face.

Pyke brushed Knibb's hand from his arm.

354

'Perhaps you should ask yourself whether you should be accepting gifts from a man who killed his own wife.'

Knibb stared aghast at Pyke's departing figure while Malvern looked around him, like a boatman without oars.

Pyke took a few moments to assess the wreckage he'd caused, feeling no pride and little satisfaction in his handiwork. He had not only rubbed the man's nose in his son's death; he'd done so knowingly and with a degree of relish.

Outside, on the steps of the hall, he waited, exhausted. Perhaps he'd misread Silas Malvern and the situation. What the man had done years earlier, rightly or wrongly, had earned him the status of a monster in Pyke's eyes, and he had drawn on these feelings to justify confronting him in such an abrupt manner. But he had now seen the man in the flesh and was beginning to have his doubts. What if the truth was not as he'd initially imagined? What if Malvern hadn't killed his wife in the manner that Bertha had described? And what if the old man's quest for forgiveness – to atone for his sins – was, in fact, well intended? More to the point, what if Malvern had told the truth? What if he *was* wholly innocent in the matter of the two murders?

As he stumbled down the steps, Pyke thought about the sins that he imagined Malvern had committed and weighed them against the lives *he* had taken; he wondered – once again – what gave him the right to judge people who were as flawed as he was.

The first thing Pyke had done, after returning from Jamaica, was to use some of the money he'd accrued from playing cards on board the steamer to rent a stout, terraced house in a respectable street in Pentonville. He'd gone to his uncle's apartment early the next morning and surprised Felix and Jo with the news they would be moving into a new house immediately. He'd arranged for a wagon to take their possessions the mile or so to Pentonville, and later that day he had shown Jo, an excitable Felix and an even more excitable mastiff around their new lodgings. It hadn't taken Felix long to forget the reason why he'd hated Pyke and, despite some tears at having to leave Godfrey, to whom he'd become very attached, he'd quickly come around to the new arrangement. It never failed to amaze Pyke how swift children were to forgive people and not dwell on the sins committed against them. Pyke had taken the largest bedroom at the front of the property, and Felix had chosen the slightly smaller room at the rear, overlooking the yard. The only awkward moment had been when Pyke had tried to persuade Jo to take the airy bedroom next to his. Jo had considered it for a while but when he'd given her no further encouragement, she'd opted for a much pokier bedroom on the top floor. Pyke's clumsy attempt to give her enough money to hire a cook had only made matters worse and, later on, when he'd proposed taking a bottle of claret into the garden, after Felix had gone to bed, she had shaken her head and then left the room.

When Pyke arrived home after his confrontation with Silas Malvern, Jo and Felix were playing in the garden. For a while he watched them from the window, Felix squealing while Jo chased him across the yard. He thought about the news he'd just delivered to Silas Malvern. What would *he* do if someone told him that Felix had perished? It was, he recognised, one of his many failings; that he never quite saw the rich as being human and fallible in the same way that everyone else was. To distract himself from this thought, he took time to admire Jo's pale complexion and unassuming beauty and found himself wondering, not for the first time, what a life with her might be like, and whether his feelings for her were a measure or a reflection of how much Felix adored her.

When Felix saw Pyke in the window, he ran inside to greet him and they chatted for a while about the birds and insects Pyke had seen in Jamaica and what Pyke intended to cook for them later. Pyke told Felix he was going to prepare a meat stew because he didn't want the lad to see the rabbit he'd picked up and would have to skin. Jo hardly said a word throughout this conversation. Eventually Pyke managed to persuade Felix to go up to his room and begin unpacking his belongings, and when he heard Felix traipsing up the stairs, he went and joined Jo in the kitchen. She had a knife in her hand and had already started to skin the dead animal.

'I was going to do that.'

Jo turned, suddenly wrenched from her thoughts. 'You must be pleased. You've made Felix very happy.'

'Godfrey told me that the boy's behaviour was much improved during my absence.' Pyke hesitated. 'And he made no further attempts to pick old men's pockets.'

'Whatever you said to Felix before you left for Jamaica had the desired effect. I'd say he's grown up a little.' But Jo wouldn't meet Pyke's gaze and her manner with him was cold and formal.

Pyke waited for a moment. 'And yet I seem to have made you unhappy at the same time.'

Jo put the knife down on the cutting board. 'Do you want to know how I felt yesterday when we first arrived here? I felt like an old piece of your furniture being moved into your new house.'

Pyke took a step towards her, but saw her face and stopped. 'I'm clumsy. Sometimes I say the wrong things.'

'Yesterday at Godfrey's apartment, you made Copper feel more welcome than me.'

'I've missed you.'

'And that's supposed to make everything right? *You've missed me.*' She pulled a strand of hair behind her ear and shook her head.

Pyke tried again. 'I wanted to take you in my arms but I didn't want to embarrass you in front of Godfrey and Felix.'

Jo stood there, hands on her hips. 'I'm not Emily, Pyke. I'm nothing like her. No one could be. I'm also not Felix's mother. I'm just a plain red-headed girl. I'm a servant, Pyke. You pay my wages. That's how it should be.'

'I'm no better than you or anyone else.'

'But why *me?* Why not a woman who's wealthier, better looking, and more intelligent than I am?'

'You don't see your good qualities, that's all.' He wanted to say more but couldn't find the

358

right words.

'You don't even know me, Pyke. That's my point. You don't know a thing about me.'

'I don't know you? Don't be absurd. We've lived under the same roof for almost ten years.'

'As your *servant*, Pyke,' Jo said, exasperated. 'Where was I born? What are my parents' names?' She must have seen his expression because she added, quickly, 'You didn't even know they were still alive, did you?'

'So I don't know their names. I'll learn. I'll make a special trip to your birthplace. But what will that really change? I know you. That's all that counts.'

But Jo wasn't mollified. 'I'm your servant, Pyke, not your mistress. For ten years you've hardly noticed me. I'm not trying to chastise you. I'm just being truthful. So what's changed all of a sudden? Why *now*? I'm not stupid, Pyke. I have a good rapport with your son and you're just nostalgic for the way things used to be when Emily was alive.'

Pyke didn't answer her because he didn't want to concede that she might, in part, be right. But his silence seemed to make her even more angry. 'I remember what Godfrey said about you going to Jamaica. He reckoned you were chasing after a ghost – that if you found justice for this woman you would somehow find justice for Emily.'

Pyke stood there, simultaneously wanting to embrace Jo and slap her around the face. 'You think I don't know Emily's dead?'

Jo ignored him. 'Even if you do find this woman's killer...' Her face turned the colour of beetroot. 'What then?'

'It's just a job. It's what I do, Jo. What I feel for

you has *nothing* to do with Mary Edgar or indeed Emily.' But as he said it, Pyke could hear how unconvincing his voice sounded.

'And what *do* you feel for me?' Jo stared at him. There were tears in her eyes. 'Do you love me?'

There were so many ways he could have answered this question but in the end they all sounded hollow, so he said nothing.

'I think I understand my position better now.' Jo gathered up her petticoat and ran up two flights of stairs to her room.

Pyke wasn't ready to let Jo have the final word on the matter and after supper, once he'd put Felix to bed, he knocked on her door. When she didn't answer, he pushed it open and stepped into the small room. She was lying on her bed, facing the wall. A candle flickered in its holder on the mantelpiece above the fireplace. Not saying anything, Pyke crossed the room and sat on the edge of her bed. She didn't move. Gently he reached out and touched the back of her neck. When she finally turned over to face him, Pyke saw she had been crying.

'What do you want?' she said, staring up at him. She sounded weary but also hopeful.

'When you asked me just now whether I loved you...' Pyke hesitated, trying to find the right words. 'I don't know how to explain it. All I can say is that when Emily died, something inside me died as well. I can't let myself be hurt like that again.'

Pyke was going to say more but she coiled her hand around his neck and gently pulled him down towards her. That first kiss seemed to have settled any doubts Jo might have been having but then, without warning, she pulled away from him.

'I can't. Not again.' She bit her lips and looked up at Pyke, her eyes glistening in the candlelight. 'Not until I know what you think, what you feel...'

Pyke stared at her without speaking. Perhaps she was right; perhaps he had used her and was continuing to do so. But he couldn't say the words she wanted to hear.

'I've thought a lot about what happened between us, the night before you left for the West Indies...'

Pyke nodded, vaguely aware that he hadn't thought about her very much while he was away.

'I've used the time that you've been away to think about my life, what I've been doing, what I want to be in the future.'

Pyke watched her, trying to reconcile his very immediate urge to kiss her again with the sense that he was using her in some way. 'And what have you decided?'

'I didn't arrive at any decision. I couldn't.' She still wouldn't look at him. 'Not until you came back and looked straight through me...'

'I'm sorry,' Pyke said, frowning. 'I didn't mean to hurt you. I did think about you while I was away, about the night we spent together. I missed you, too.'

'Like you missed Godfrey?'

'If you'll forgive me for saying, I don't find my uncle quite as attractive...'

That made her smile.

An awkward silence settled between them. 'We can talk about this again tomorrow, Pyke. For now, I'd like to be left alone.'

TWENTY-ONE

The Bluefield lodging house was as dismal as Pyke remembered. The last time he had visited, the day had been cool and cloudy, but this time the heat was almost suffocating and the air in the sunless court was choked with dust. He had been told that it hadn't rained for a month and the ground underfoot seemed to confirm this. In the depths of winter, when the city shivered under a blanket of freezing fog, he would dream of summer days when the air would feel soft against his skin, but when these days finally arrived and brought with them dust clouds, plagues of horseflies and a pungent stink exacerbated by the searing heat, it made him long for the cool days of autumn once more. This was one of those days. Pyke's back was drenched with sweat before he'd even entered the lodging house.

Thrale recognised him immediately. They met in the kitchen and the landlord adopted a pose of exaggerated servility. 'It certainly is a hot 'un,' he said, wiping his forehead with his sleeve. 'How about stepping outside for some air?'

In the yard, where it was a little cooler, Pyke said, 'I need to find a blind man called Filthy. I think he was known to Mary Edgar and Arthur

Sobers.' The notion that Filthy might in fact be Phillip Malvern had stayed with him ever since he'd talked to Mary's mother, Bertha, in Accompong.

'You told me that already and I'll say what I said back then. I don't know him. I'd tell you if I did.'

The former bare-knuckle fighter could certainly take care of himself in a fight and Pyke didn't want to antagonise him needlessly. 'Do you mind if I question your guests, see if anyone else knew him?'

'Long as you don't upset anyone.'

'I take it you haven't seen or heard anything more about Arthur Sobers.'

That drew a frown. 'I thought you'd have heard about him.'

'Heard about what?' Pyke felt his heartbeat quicken. 'I've been out of the country.'

Thrale shuffled awkwardly from foot to foot. 'Peelers got him. Last I heard he was waiting to be tried.'

'When was this?'

'A week, maybe two weeks ago. One of the lodgers remembered him, said they'd read about it in a newspaper.'

By this time Pyke was halfway across the yard.

It was only ten in the morning but already Saggers was too drunk to get up from his seat. The first thing Pyke noticed was the wet patch around the crotch of his tweed trousers. There was a plate of gnawed chop bones on the table in front of him and five or six empty pots of ale.

'How can a man write when hunger gnaws at his tummy? Should a man of my talents be lying down in the same room as coiners and mud-larks?' He was speaking to a man whose head was resting on the table next to him. 'A man of my talents grubbing for a living when scriveners and compositors, with their sticks and frames, take home fifty shillings a week? *Fifty* shillings, I say. I used to think that making words was the noblest of all professions but now I see my reward – being denied the victuals that a man of my modest appetite requires to sustain him – and I wonder that I should ever see a bowl of stewed mutton again.' He cast a stare in Pyke's direction. 'Or a half-buck of Halnaker's venison.'

Pyke tossed a five-shilling coin down on the table. It landed among the gravy and chop bones. Saggers ordered the pot-boys to fetch him another ale and a serving of steak and kidney pudding.

'You're darker than I remember,' Saggers said, licking gravy from the coin. 'I talked to your uncle. He at least was kind enough to tell me of your departure.'

'I'm sorry I didn't tell you I was leaving. In the end I didn't have the time.'

'Luckily for you I'm the forgiving type,' Saggers said, inspecting the silver coin. 'I'll be even more forgiving if you tell me about your travels and give me something nice and juicy I can slap on to Spratt's desk.'

'One day soon I will. I promise.' Pyke waited. 'In the meantime, how's the story?'

'How's the story? he asks.' Saggers' voice boomed around the empty room. 'And what story would that be? The one you abandoned without a word to your partner-in-crime?'

'The last time we spoke, you were trying to persuade Spratt to publish the story about Lucy Luckins' corpse. What happened?'

'I found Mort, the surgeon at St Thomas's, and he confirmed, in private, what the mudlark Gilbert Meeson told us. But, for obvious reasons, he wouldn't give me the official confirmation that Spratt needed. So Spratt refused to publish the story and, since then, it has ebbed away to nothing.' Saggers' mood was momentarily lifted by the fresh pot of ale put down in front of him.

'No further developments?'

'Not from my perspective.' Saggers emptied the contents of the pot in three gulps and let out a belch. 'I had an idea there might be more bodies. I mean, if this man, whoever he is, has killed two women, why stop there? I left word with mudlarks like Gilbert Meeson to keep their eyes open for another corpse, pardon the pun. I even managed to persuade Spratt to part with ten guineas as an inducement. But I've heard nothing, and any interest that we managed to build up in the story has vanished.' He shook his head. 'We made all those boasts, Pyke; we made the police seem stupid. But who looks stupid now? The police have gone about their work quietly and methodically and now they've found this negro fellow, Sobers.'

'I heard,' Pyke said. 'What else do you know about it?'

'Just that the Peelers nabbed him a few weeks ago and now they've charged him with the murder. He's due to stand trial in a couple of days.'

'Do you know where they're holding him?'

'Newgate, I think.' Saggers looked around for some sign of the steak and kidney pudding. 'I should warn you that the Crown's lawyer is going to play up the ritual aspect of the murder. Some of the newspapers have already carried stories to this effect. Spratt has asked me for something – assuming the chap is found guilty.'

'Human ape runs amok in London because it's in his nature?'

'That kind of thing,' Spratt said, wincing a little.

Pyke shook his head but he knew such stories were inevitable. 'I need you to go back to all the mudlarks you spoke to and ask them about a blind man, goes by the name of Filthy. I want to know if they've seen him recently and if so where can I find him.' This time Pyke placed a half-crown down on the table.

Saggers swept it into his lap and considered Pyke's request, his chin wobbling slightly. 'Would it be fair to say that you've been somewhat parsimonious with the truth regarding this investigation?'

'Yes, I suppose that would be a fair comment.'

'But you see, old chap, it's never easy trying to row a boat without oars.'

'One day soon I'll tell you everything I know. I promise.'

'And until then, I'm supposed to live off your scraps?'

Pyke looked at Saggers' sprawling girth. 'From where I'm standing, it doesn't look like you've made too bad a job of it.'

An hour after Pyke had dispatched a young lad with a note to deliver to Fitzroy Tilling, the deputy commissioner of the New Police strolled into the Edinburgh Coffee House on The Strand carrying his hat. He looked older somehow, as though the job and its responsibilities had accelerated his hair loss and deepened the creases on his forehead.

'If you were a policeman, you could be dismissed for drinking on the job.' He pointed to Pyke's gin and ordered a mug of coffee for himself.

This was the first time they had met since the angry words they'd exchanged outside Mayne's chambers and the atmosphere between them was palpable.

'Then it's lucky for me that I've got a mind of my own and an aversion to taking orders from people who think police work is moving pieces of paper from one side of their desk to the other.'

It drew the thinnest of smiles. 'When I got your note, I thought twice about coming to see you. I don't owe you a thing, and if there's any ground to be made up, it's your job to do so.'

'So why did you come?'

'I suppose I was curious to know what, if anything, you managed to dig up in the West Indies.'

Short of him talking to Godfrey there was only one explanation for Tilling knowing about his trip to the West Indies. Pyke decided not to pursue the question for the moment.

'I hear you made an arrest while I was away.'

'That's right. Arthur Sobers.'

'Has he made a confession?'

'He refused to speak at his committal hearing. The trial is due to take place in a couple of days.'

Tilling took his mug of coffee from the waitress and put it down on the table. 'If he continues to say nothing, he'll be found guilty.'

'Is the case against him strong?'

'Circumstantial evidence mostly,' Tilling said.

'Has Pierce done a good job?'

'In spite of what you might think, Pyke, he's a solid investigator. Very methodical.'

Pyke bit his lip. This description applied to Tilling but not Pierce, who cared only about advancing another rung up the ladder. 'Where did they find Sobers?'

'Sniffing around at the back of a property near Hyde Park. A neighbour didn't like the look of him and fetched a constable.'

'Let me guess. Pitts Head Mews.'

Tilling looked up, unable to hide his surprise. 'How did you know?'

'The property belongs to Elizabeth Malvern, daughter of Silas Malvern. I'm told she's in the West Indies.'

'But you didn't come across her when you were out there?'

Pyke shook his head. He wanted to find and speak to Elizabeth Malvern before he divulged anything further to Tilling. According to Alefounder, she had never made the trip in the first place.

'You don't think Sobers killed her, do you?'

Tilling's question sounded genuine rather than defensive. For a moment they stared at one another, trying to appraise each other's views on the subject.

'Silas Malvern went to see Sir Richard Mayne

yesterday and Mayne talked to you. That's how you know I've just returned from Jamaica, isn't it?'

Tilling nodded. He knew it was pointless to deny the accusation. 'It would seem you didn't exactly endear yourself to the old boy at an anti-slavery meeting at Exeter Hall.'

They both looked up at a pretty woman who sat down at the table next to them. 'I think he's somehow involved in Mary Edgar's murder.'

'Any particular reason?'

Pyke thought about telling Tilling what he'd found out in Jamaica but decided to keep it to himself for the moment.

'Just so you know, and this comes directly from Mayne, Silas Malvern is not a suspect. From the beginning he's cooperated with our investigation and what he's told us has been thoroughly investigated.'

'By Pierce?'

'At the risk of offending you, let me repeat myself. Malvern is *not* a suspect. That's all you need to know.'

'Did Malvern tell you that Lord Bedford was godfather to his son Charles?'

Tilling stared at him; he understood the implication of this immediately. 'Go on.'

'Charles made a private arrangement with his godfather for Mary Edgar, his fiancée, to stay with Bedford at his Norfolk Street residence because he knew his father wouldn't approve of him marrying a mulatto.'

A brief, uncomfortable silence passed between them. 'Do you have any proof of this?'

Pyke took out the letter he'd taken from the

369

great house at Ginger Hall and handed it to Tilling.

'It makes no reference to Mary Edgar by name,' Tilling said, once he'd read it. 'And from what I gather, Charles Malvern is now dead.'

'But it establishes a link between Charles Malvern and Lord Bedford. And Malvern's engagement to Mary Edgar was common knowledge in Falmouth.'

'Falmouth?'

'A port town on the north coast of Jamaica.'

Tilling scratched his chin. 'To take this farther, I'm going to need some hard evidence. Did any of Bedford's servants know about the arrangement?'

'Bedford's butler knew. Apparently Mary Edgar stayed in a basement annexe, so as not to arouse the suspicion of the rest of the household. Morel-Roux told me he thought Bedford had a mistress.'

A frown passed across Tilling's forehead. 'When did *you* speak to him?'

Briefly Pyke told Tilling about the arrangements Godfrey had made for his visit to the valet's cell.

Tilling took a sip of his coffee and stared out of the window. Pyke could tell he was upset by what he'd just heard, even if his expression was outwardly calm. 'I'm told the evidence against Morel-Roux was overwhelming. For God's sake, the man didn't even offer a defence. The jury took only a few minutes to return a verdict of guilty.'

'In the same way that Arthur Sobers isn't, for the moment, offering a defence?'

'I can't believe you actually think we knowingly

370

seek to punish innocent men? Besides, the circumstances of these two cases are completely different.' But for the first time the extent of Tilling's unease was showing.

'Are they? Mary Edgar was staying in Bedford's house. Both Mary and Bedford were killed. How likely is it that Morel-Roux committed both murders? How likely is it that Sobers committed both murders?'

Tilling contemplated this. 'You said just now that Lord Bedford's butler knew about the arrangement with Mary?'

'I'm not saying he knew who Mary Edgar really was or that she'd been murdered. But he knew she was staying there.' Pyke took out the charcoal sketch from his pocket and handed it to Tilling. 'It probably isn't an exact likeness, but show it to the man and see if he recognises her.'

'Give me a few days,' Tilling said, folding up the drawing and putting it into his pocket. 'In the meantime, stay away from Silas Malvern.'

'I want to see Sobers,' Pyke said, hoping to take advantage of the rapprochement that seemed to be taking place between them.

'I'm afraid that's out of the question.'

'I want to see him anyway.' Pyke waited. 'If he isn't talking to anyone, what harm can it do?'

Standing up, Tilling pulled his coat on. 'I'll see what I can arrange. Where can I contact you?'

Pyke scribbled down his address on a scrap of paper and pushed it across the table. 'What date has been set for Morel-Roux's execution?'

'Just over a week.'

'That soon?'

'Once the Home Secretary turned down his appeal, the judge didn't see any reason to delay it.'

'I suppose not,' Pyke said, thinking about the crowds that would gather to watch the hanging.

'I've barely made a farthing out of the whole enterprise, dear boy, and that's the God's honest truth. Ever since the vultures in the cheap presses stripped my work of literature down to its carcass and sold it in roughly bound editions using the cheapest paper for a few pennies, I've lost a large chunk of my readership. It's robbery, m'boy, and I don't know why I should stand for it.'

Pyke relaxed into the threadbare armchair and grinned. 'Forgive me if I'm mistaken, but wasn't that exactly how you made your money for much of your career?' It was afternoon and they were sitting across from one another at the back of Godfrey's gloomy basement shop.

'A detail, dear boy. And remember that as a convert to the pursuit of artistic excellence, I have seen the error of my ways.'

Pyke looked at his uncle, amazed not only that he was still alive, given his prodigious appetite for food and wine, but also that he still had the energy to care about what he wrote and published. 'And great art can't be reproduced on cheap paper?'

'It can be printed on bum fodder for all I care, so long as I get what's owed to me.'

'You're just sour because Harrison Ainsworth's *Jack Sheppard* is still selling more copies than your book.'

'Ainsworth is a crashing bore. Have you tried to read *Jack Sheppard?* I did and found myself drowning in his turgid prose. And as for *Rook-wood*, I was asleep before I'd finished the first chapter.'

'I don't know these novelists. But I read *Oliver Twist* on the journey back from the West Indies.'

'Much better but still too much moralising. Don't tell me your heart didn't sink when the point of view changed from Fagin and Sykes to Brownlow and the Maylies.'

Pyke smiled because there was an element of truth in what his uncle had just said. But what he had liked about Dickens's work was its lack of sentimentality, at least in its depictions of the underworld. Fagin and Sykes were presented as they were, nasty and venal, not to make some kind of political point. He knew people like that. It had once been his job to arrest them.

'Didn't you once tell me that the point of *your* book was to offend the sensibilities of the middling classes? In which case, what do you care if your words have been vulgarised for the purpose of appealing to the working poor?'

'Haven't you been listening to a word I've said? The whole point of my book was to make as much money as possible.'

'And not to offend readers who expect literature to give them clear moral guidance?'

This was the nub of the debate raging in newspapers and periodicals about so-called 'Newgate' novels; that, wittingly or otherwise, they celebrated criminality by presenting their rogue protagonists in a vaguely sympathetic light, and therefore encouraged the working poor to contemplate breaking the law.

Godfrey considered this point for a moment. 'I suppose I *would* like my readers to see some of the unsavoury and immoral aspects of my hero in themselves.'

Pyke looked around the musty, untidy shop and realised that he had been going there to see his uncle for as long as he could remember. He also thought about their disagreements and their clashes over Pyke's responsibilities as a father. They had always argued and Godfrey would say things that no one else dared to, but their fights were mostly short lived.

'I'd like you to do something for me, Godfrey, but I'm afraid it involves Jemmy Crane.' Pyke looked at his uncle and waited for a reaction.

'Crane? Didn't I tell you to leave that one well alone?'

'I'd like you to persuade one of your acquaintances to play the part of a customer. Preferably the disreputable type, or at least the kind of man who wouldn't blink at the sight of bare flesh, and having seen a little, might ask for something more risque. Rich and shambling would be ideal.' Pyke waited. 'You would be perfect but Crane knows of your connection to me.'

'And you think that is the type of person I choose to associate with?' He tried to appear hurt but Pyke could tell he was secretly delighted by the idea that he might appear to be rich and shambling.

'I'm just asking that they play the part. I want them to go to Crane's shop and ask for a daguerreotype, taken from life. I want them to offer an obscene sum of money but only on the condition that the daguerreotype is particularly low and offensive.'

'How low and offensive?'

'They'll offer the usual copperplates depicting nude women but I want him to ask for something warmer and hence more expensive.'

'Warm I like, expensive I don't.'

'Then I'd like him to be more specific. That is, I want him to pretend to desire women with facial deformities.'

'Facial deformities? What is this, dear boy? You're beginning to make me feel a little queasy.'

'You don't need to know. Just tell your friend to make it clear that money is no object.'

'But money *is* an object, isn't it? Who's going to fund this enterprise of yours?'

'I was hoping I could persuade you to dip into the profits you've already accrued from the book.'

'*Profits?* God, dear boy, weren't you listening to a word I said? And now the Lord Chancellor has banned any theatre shows based on my book for fear that they might incite young boys to criminality. That Morel-Roux has a lot to answer for. His arrest and trial might have helped sales in the short term but now the authorities are terrified that others will follow his lead and turn on their masters.'

'But if Morel-Roux was shown to be innocent and he therefore wasn't executed next week as planned, that might revive interest in your book?'

'Not executed? What are you talking about? He's due to hang in just over one week.'

'He didn't kill Bedford.' Pyke didn't know this for certain – the valet could always have been paid by someone to kill his master – but, in light of what he'd found out in Jamaica, he would have bet money on the man's innocence.

Godfrey sat forward in his armchair and removed his glasses. 'Do you know that for a fact?'

'I can't prove it yet. But I'd swear on Felix's life that he didn't do it.'

'That's *terrible*. An innocent man going to the gallows. It can't be allowed to happen.'

'Will you help me or not?'

'Anything, dear boy, anything.' Godfrey wiped the perspiration from his forehead. 'But how are you going to stop the execution?'

'I don't know.'

Godfrey seemed dazed. Like everyone, he had laboured under the assumption that the valet was guilty. But now this certainty had been thrown into doubt, he didn't know what to do.

Later, as Pyke was preparing to leave, Godfrey went over to his desk and riffled through a stack of papers. 'I had a visit from one of your old acquaintances, Ned Villums, while you were away. This would have been about three weeks ago. He left me his address and asked me to tell you to contact him when you returned.' Holding up a piece of paper, Godfrey added, 'I knew I hadn't lost it.'

Pyke took the address. 'Did Ned say what he wanted?'

But Godfrey's expression had darkened. 'Field, Crane and now Villums. You're keeping illustrious company these days, aren't you, dear boy?'

TWENTY-TWO

Early the next morning, before Jo, Felix or even Copper had risen, Pyke walked from the house in Pentonville to Clerkenwell and the address Godfrey had given him. It was warm, despite the earliness of the hour, but the air felt pleasant rather than muggy. The mist that had hung over the city for the past few days seemed to have lifted and there were just a few high clouds in the otherwise clear sky. Though the shops hadn't yet pulled up their shutters, the streets were surprisingly busy; drays and barrows mostly, costermongers and other tradesmen already preparing for the new day. There was also a steady trickle of commuters heading towards the City, grabbing breakfast from the street vendors and eating it as they walked.

Pyke had known Ned Vilums for more than half his life. As the former landlord of the Old Cock Inn in Holborn, he had presided over a large gambling and bookmaking operation. He had also fed Pyke – then a Bow Street Runner – with snippets of information which had, in turn, damaged the interests of his rivals; and he had been well paid for doing so. Latterly, he had become one of the underworld's most successful receivers, largely because he was very careful about what he agreed to handle. Mostly he dealt with specialist, expensive items, often stolen to order. His success could be measured by the fact that he had never been arrested, let alone spent any time in prison. Indeed, the New Police didn't seem to know he existed. He worked with a small group of loyal associates and took as few risks as possible. That he could also be as ruthless as someone like Field was another reason for his success. Pyke had seen Villums kill a man with his bare hands then sit down to eat a meal with the corpse still at his feet.

Pyke knew that Villums was an early riser and found him in his office on the corner of St John and Compton Streets. He hadn't been there before but it was as bare as he'd expected: a wainscoted partition, a shelf or two, a large oak desk, a couple of stools, a clock on the mantelpiece above the fire and a map of London on the wall. Villums had never been one to draw attention to his wealth.

Perhaps ten years older than Pyke, Villums was slow and heavy on his feet, with a poor complexion and a hatchet-like profile. In his torn velveteen coat and corduroy trousers, he still dressed like a tavern landlord rather than a man who, when Pyke had last asked him, earned fifty thousand a year. They greeted each other warmly and Villums invited him to take one of the stools while he uncorked a bottle of whisky and poured out two generous measures. For a few minutes they talked about the old days and the people they'd once known who were now either dead or in prison.

'I suppose you're wondering why I left a message for you,' Villums said, pouring them another drink.

Pyke nodded.

'Would I be right in thinking that you've got yourself mixed up with the likes of Harold Field and Jemmy Crane?'

'How did you hear that?'

'What I'm going to tell you goes no farther than these four walls.'

Pyke gave him a hard stare. 'Of course.'

'All right. Good. So, a few months ago, I had a visit from Crane. He wanted to know whether I'd be interested in fencing a large quantity of gold.'

'What did you tell him?'

'I asked him to tell me more about the gold.'

'And?'

'He talked about bars, plenty of them. His references were quite specific. I told him I needed some time to think about it. I looked into the matter, then went back and told Crane I wasn't interested.'

'What did you find out?'

'That the gold bars are, even as we speak, being held in the bullion vault at the Bank of England.'

Pyke exhaled loudly.

'Exactly my point,' Villums said, taking another drink of whisky. 'After I told Crane I wasn't interested, I gave him my word I wouldn't tell a soul about it.'

Pyke saw the concern in his old friend's eyes. 'So what happened?'

'I also owed Harold Field a favour. Don't ask me how I got into the man's debt. It's a long story and I don't want to bore you with the details.'

'I see. So you told Field about Crane and the gold.' It was starting to make sense now. Pyke thought about Field's attempts to infiltrate

Crane's organisation.

'With hindsight it wasn't the most intelligent thing to do.' Villums shrugged. 'Crane finds out Field knows about the gold, who's he likely to blame?'

'So you went back to seek certain reassurances from Field and he told you about my involvement in the matter?'

Villums nodded. 'That's right. Look, you have my word that nothing we say here will go beyond these four walls.' He paused. 'But does Crane actually *know* about Field's interest in him?'

'He knows Field has been sniffing around him but, as far as I know, he doesn't believe that Field knows about the gold.'

Pyke watched Villums take another sip of whisky; he'd never seen the man this anxious before. It was testament to Field's reputation that even someone like Ned Villums was afraid of him. 'You'll tell me if the situation changes, won't you?' Villums asked.

'I'm as keen as you are to leave the whole mess behind.'

'Course you are.' Villums tried to smile but his eyes lacked any trace of warmth. 'If the Peelers nab you with gold bars taken from the Bank of England, they may as well lead you straight to the gallows.'

Pyke contemplated the idea. 'Are you quite sure Crane's target is the Bank of England?'

'Seems unlikely, doesn't it? I mean, how do you break into bullion vault for a start, and then make off with five hundred gold bars?'

'That many, eh?'

Villums nodded. 'No way could you try going *over* the wall, you'd be dead within minutes. The bank has its own garrison.'

'What are you suggesting?'

'I don't know. I'm at a complete loss.' He scratched his face. 'But I don't *want* to know, either.'

'Perhaps Crane has connections inside the bank?'

Villums didn't seem convinced. 'What can one man do? Like I said, the bank's vaults are guarded by a regiment sent there each night from the Tower.'

Pyke took his glass and stared down at the last drops of the amber-coloured liquid.

The offices of the Vice Society were a short walk from Villums' building but when Pyke presented himself to a clerk at the front desk and asked to speak with Samuel Ticknor, he was told that Ticknor had been called away on a family matter and wouldn't be back for a few days.

'I'm looking for information about Lucy Luckins,' Pyke said. 'One of the women you helped to find work.'

The young clerk gave him a bored look. 'Was Mr Ticknor the agent responsible for this particular woman?' It was the name Pyke had been given by Alefounder in Jamaica.

'I think so.'

'Then I'm afraid you'll have to wait until he returns.' He offered an apologetic smile. 'We don't keep records of such matters.'

'How long did you say he would be away?'

'A few days. A week at most.'

Pyke spent the rest of the morning and most of the afternoon looking for the blind mudlark on the Ratcliff Highway and along the northern bank of the river. It was a warm day and the dry weather meant the bank had become encrusted with pools of slime and raw faeces. The stink was almost unbearable and, on a few occasions, he had to take refuge near street vendors who were cooking food on hot coals to give his nostrils temporary relief.

'I know 'im,' a bone collector said. He was dressed in rags and was wearing a crushed billy-cock hat. 'Least, I talked to 'im from time to time.'

As it transpired, he hadn't seen or spoken with the man he called 'Filthy' for more than three months.

'What can you tell me about him?'

'Filthy? I didn't know 'im well but he seemed like a nice man, gentle. I'd say he 'ad a good heart.'

Pyke thought about his suspicions regarding Filthy and Phillip – that they were the same person and had somehow been involved in the mutilation of Mary Edgar's corpse. In light of this description, it didn't seem likely or even possible that Phillip was the murderer. More to the point, whether he knew it not, Mary was his daughter. But at the same time, the similarities between the manner of his blinding at the hands of his brother, Silas Malvern, and the facial mutilations suffered by Mary Edgar and Lucy Luckins were impossible to ignore.

'You talk about anything in particular?'

'He liked his women dark, if you know what I mean.'

382

'Dark as in black skinned?'

'We 'ad a conversation in a tavern, that's all. He told me what he liked and I told 'im what I liked. As far as it went.'

'Anything else?'

'Was a demon at catching rats, so he was. Preferred the sewer ones, he told me. Meaner, they were. Reckoned the landlord at the Duke of York in Saffron Hill would pay 'im threepence a rat.'

Later in the afternoon, Pyke asked for the landlord of the Duke of York at the brass-topped counter in the taproom. A few moments later, a squat, ugly man with no neck and square shoulders appeared behind the counter. He said his name was Johnny Flack. Pyke explained why he was there.

'Yeah, I know the cull. Folk called 'im Filthy but I knew 'im as Phillip. He brought me plenty of the biggest, nastiest sewer rats I ever saw. Creatures the size of small dogs with tails like leather whips. Would give even the best dog a run for its money.' The Duke of York was well known as a 'ratting' pub; twice a week, rats and dogs fought for their lives in a wooden enclosure and drinkers would bet on the outcome.

Pyke tried not to show his excitement. 'You're quite certain about his real name?' This was the confirmation he'd been looking for.

'Course I'm sure.' Flack scratched his arm. 'But I ain't seen 'im for a while. To be honest, I'm disappointed. No one brings me rats like Phillip.'

'When was the last time you saw him?'

'Two, three months ago.'

'And before that, would he come here on a regular basis?'

Flack nodded. 'At least once a week.'

Pyke considered this for a short while. 'Did he ever tell you where he found his rats?'

'He trawled the sewers, I'd say, from the smell of 'im. That's how folk came to call him Filthy.'

After he left, Pyke stood at the counter, listening to the harsh, guttural accents and the casual obscenities, and wondered whether Phillip Malvern was still in London or, more to the point, whether he was still alive.

It was just getting dark when a hackney carriage dropped Pyke off at the end of Pitts Head Mews just across from Hyde Park. The air was humid with just a hint of rain and there was barely a breath of wind. He walked along the street as far as Elizabeth Malvern's house, looked up at the drawn curtains for any sign of light or movement behind them, then knocked on the front door. No one answered. He tried again, to no avail. There was a break in the terrace about halfway along the mews and Pyke made his way around to the back of what he thought was Elizabeth's house and looked up at the windows once more. The curtains were drawn but this time what looked like a light or candle was burning in one of the upstairs rooms. He climbed over the wall and dropped down into the back yard. Waiting to be sure no one had heard him, he removed his picklocks, trying to make as little sound as possible. The lock wasn't a sophisticated one. Pyke had the door open in less than a minute and stepped into the house.

She was carrying a lantern in one hand and a pistol in the other. She moved towards him quietly and carefully, like a cat, keeping the pistol aimed at his chest. She wore a cotton print dress and her dark hair was gathered up and held by a comb. It took him a few moments to realise how beautiful she was, with her smooth complexion, the colour of milky coffee, and her dark, staring eyes, like pools of liquid.

'You're Elizabeth, aren't you?'

'Don't move a muscle, sir. Tell me your name, why you've broken into my house, and why I shouldn't shoot you here and now.' She spoke in a polished, elegant tone that put him in mind of Emily.

'My name is Pyke. I was charged with the task of finding Mary Edgar's murderer. I've just returned from Jamaica.'

It was the last piece of information which seemed to soften her resolve. She lowered the pistol and held up the lantern so she could see his face better. 'Do you often break into other people's houses?'

'Only if they persistently refuse to answer their doors.' Pyke waited. 'I came here just before I sailed for the West Indies. I think I saw you in one of the upstairs rooms at the front of the house.'

'Oh, that was you.' She seemed both curious and unmoved by this revelation.

'Can I ask why you've decided to turn yourself into a prisoner in your own house? And why you feel it's necessary to possess that thing?' He pointed at the pistol.

'I thought my father might have sent you.' She hesitated, wondering whether this explained it, and then added, 'He thinks I'm in Jamaica.'

'Why would he think that?'

'It's complicated.'

'And the pistol?'

She didn't have an answer for that one.

'You told him that you'd make the journey to break the news to your brother, Charles, about the deaths of his fiancée and his godfather.'

That seemed to amuse her. 'I see you've spoken to my father.'

'We had a conversation. It didn't end well. To be honest, it didn't start well, either. But you're right, I did talk to him. And he's under the impression you sailed for Jamaica at the beginning of May.'

'And now you must be wondering what I'm doing here.'

'The question had crossed my mind.'

'In that case, I think you and I should retire to the living room. I sense we have a lot to talk about.'

He followed her into the house, up a flight of stairs and into a large, immaculately tidy room at the front of the building. Elizabeth put the lantern on the table in the middle of the room and sat down on one of the sofas. Pyke took the other one and they sat in silence for a moment. He could smell her musk, a raw, earthy smell that made him think of whisky and put him on guard at once.

'Whatever must you think of me?' She was perched on the edge of the sofa, shaking her head. 'Hiding in my own home, not answering the door, lying to my father.'

Pyke tried not to notice the way she was looking at him. 'Why did you offer to travel to

Jamaica in the first place?'

'Did Father tell you that?' She laughed. 'Even though we live in the same city, we only seem to communicate by post these days. I received a letter from him suggesting I go to the West Indies, to break some tragic news to my brother. I wrote back saying that I'd consider it but then I fell ill and I heard that a mutual friend was making the journey out there so I persuaded him to pay a visit to Charles in my place. I detest that journey more than you'll ever know, and I fancy I saw the opportunity to stay here and hibernate from the world.' She hesitated and looked across at him. 'I know it makes me sound appallingly selfish and I can see you don't believe one word I've said but I *really* was ill for a while; I barely moved from my bed for the months of June and July.'

Pyke tried to keep his stare opaque. She was right that he didn't believe her. How likely was it that someone of her standing would shut herself away for the whole Season? And hadn't Charles told him that Elizabeth and their father enjoyed a very close relationship?

Reading his mind, Elizabeth added, 'Of course, I did have *some* help. I had to swear my oldest, most faithful servant to secrecy. Frankly, I don't know what I would have done without her. She agreed to visit my father's house in Belgravia on my behalf. That was how I first heard that William intended to sail for Jamaica...'

'Alefounder.'

She touched the top of her lip with her tongue. 'You know him?'

'I've met him, and his wife. For obvious reasons, she didn't exactly recommend you to me.'

'Oh.' Elizabeth reddened slightly. 'No, I don't imagine she would have.'

'Is that all you're going to say?'

'It happened a long time ago. We were both young and stupid.' She looked at him, clear eyed. 'But I'm quite sure an affair that went stale years ago isn't the reason you broke into my house.'

Pyke didn't know what to say. After all, he could not very well tell her the real reason for his visit.

'Did you see my brother while you were in Jamaica? Is he terribly upset? I hate to think of him sad.'

'He's dead.' He saw her face plummet and added, 'I'm sorry. He died in a storm. Part of the roof at one end of the great house at Ginger Hill collapsed.'

She began to weep, quietly at first, but then louder, as she absorbed the news. Pyke didn't take any joy from imparting this news, and when her crying turned into loud sobs, he went over to the sofa. 'I'm sorry,' he repeated as he knelt down in front of her, not sure how to comfort her or whether he should even try. But without thinking about it, she opened her arms and attached herself to him, wailing so her entire ribcage shook. He tasted the saltiness of her tears on his cheeks and lips and patted her silky hair. He didn't want to admit, to himself or her, that grief made her even more attractive but it was true; her tears human-ised her and each sob transformed her from a hardened vixen into someone much more real and complicated.

Finally she pushed him away and wiped her

eyes on the vaguely flounced sleeve of her dress. 'I'm sorry,' she said, sniffing and trying to breathe at the same time.

Pyke withdrew to his sofa and looked around the tastefully furnished room. He noticed a drawing by Blake on the wall and wondered whether it was an original.

'And William?' she whispered, trying to compose herself.

'He died, too.'

That elicited another gasp but no more tears. The street below was absolutely quiet.

'Does my father know?'

'I told him.'

'Oh God.' She shook her head and buried it in her hands. 'Poor Father. If this doesn't kill him, I don't know what will. And if you've made the journey already, he'll be expecting me home any day. What will I say to him? How will I explain I *wasn't* there? Of course, he'll assume I've already made the arrangements to have Charles's body shipped back here. I'll just have to tell him the truth, won't I?' This thought seemed to fill her with dread. 'You won't tell him about me just yet. Please, sir, I beg of you. I can tell you're a kind man. Give me a few days, that's all I ask.'

He contemplated this strange, disjointed speech; how little concern she'd displayed for her father's grief and well-being and the emphasis she'd placed on her own self-inflicted plight.

'What you choose to tell your father has nothing to do with me.'

The skin wrinkled at the edges of her eyes as she smiled. 'Thank you.' A strand of hair had fallen down over her face and she tucked it behind her ear.

'I should leave you,' Pyke said, looking at her; she seemed composed all of a sudden.

'You came here to ask about Mary, didn't you?' She hesitated. 'My father told me what had happened to her.'

He nodded. 'That was one of the reasons.'

'Father told me about her visit to the house. All it took was the mention of money for her to drop her claim on my brother. *Poor* Charles.' She paused and shook her head. 'Not that it matters much now. I suppose if I had felt that her feelings for him were at all genuine I might not have disliked her as much as I did.'

'And how much did you dislike her?'

Elizabeth looked over at Pyke, apparently shocked at his question. 'You can't actually think *I* had something to do with her death? I may have disliked her but I would never have *hurt* her.'

Pyke looked away, trying to decide on the best way of phrasing what he wanted to say. 'But it can't have been easy, the idea of welcoming her into the family.'

'What do you mean?' Her expression was unreadable.

'Before emancipation, your father used to own her. I can easily see how the idea of her marrying your brother would have caused your family difficulties.'

'Because she's black?'

Later Pyke would think about the assumption she'd made – that Mary was black or had been born to a black mother and hence could be categorised as black and that she, by contrast and without question, was white. If anything, Elizabeth was perhaps a little darker than Mary, but could claim to be white because she was Silas Malvern's child and hence people saw her as white.

'In part, yes,' he said, thinking about the rumours pertaining to her affection for her brother, Charles. 'If you've seen someone as servile for your entire life, I wonder how it's possible to suddenly imagine them as your equal.'

'My father never saw his workers as *lesser* creatures,' she said firmly. Pyke noted she had used the term workers rather than slaves.

For his part, Pyke wanted to stay and ask, among other things, about her attachment to Crane, her work for the Vice Society and her interest in daguerreotypes. But he knew that if questioned her directly, she might not be forthcoming. He needed a different strategy; he needed her to like him.

'It's late and I'm sure I've outstayed my welcome.' He took out a notepad, scribbled his address on one of the pages, tore it out and handed it to her. She let it flutter on to the Turkish carpet. 'If you remember anything at all about Mary Edgar, however insignificant it may seem, you can find me at that address.'

She followed him down the stairs and, at the bottom, said, 'You can leave through the front door, if you like.'

He turned to face her but she was closer than he expected and he tried to back away.

'Why did you really go all the way to Jamaica?' Her stare was curious.

'I thought Mary's murderer had fled there, so I

followed him.'

'You mean you thought *William* had killed her?' She even managed a little laugh.

'He lied about knowing her. I put pressure on him. He ran. Those aren't the actions of an innocent man.'

Elizabeth seemed perplexed by his answer. 'You really do seem to care who killed her, don't you?' She took a step towards him and stopped. 'Please don't misunderstand me. I don't mean to judge you or suggest that what you're doing isn't a noble enterprise.'

'But you're wondering why I, or anyone else for that matter, should give a damn about a poor, dead mulatto girl?' Pyke's armpits were damp with perspiration.

To his surprise, her gaze softened a little. 'Yes, I suppose that's exactly what I meant.'

Pyke took a step towards the door. 'It was good finally to meet you, Miss Malvern.'

He held out his hand but she ignored it and instead leaned into him and kissed him on the cheek, lingering there for a few moments before whispering, 'Please call me Elizabeth. I hope we'll meet again soon.'

Outside, Pyke stood for a while staring up at the night sky, trying to make sense of what had just happened. Had she noticed the way he had been looking at her? Had she somehow manipulated him from the start? Or had his questions caused offence to an essentially innocent person? As he walked along the street, Pyke took one final look at her house and saw her face disappear behind the curtains.

TWENTY-THREE

The window was open in the dining room and a soft breeze was blowing through the house. Felix was eating a piece of toast and marmalade. Pyke could hear Jo in the kitchen. He sat down next to Felix and ruffled his hair. Copper hopped into the room and rested his head on Pyke's lap, wagging his tail.

'Will Uncle Godfrey be coming to visit us soon?' Felix asked, his mouth full of toast.

Pyke looked up at Jo, who'd entered the room carrying a pot of coffee and a smaller jug of milk. He told her to sit down, said he would make his own breakfast, but she poured him a cup of coffee and said she was cooking them both eggs and had to get back to the range or else they would burn.

'We'll invite him round for a meal. How does that sound?'

Felix smiled. 'Can we have chicken? I like chicken.'

'Whatever you like.' Pyke waited for a moment. 'Godfrey and Jo tell me you haven't seen any-thing of Eric, the older boy who used to hang around outside Godfrey's apartment.'

Felix stiffened. 'No.' But he wouldn't look directly at Pyke.

'No, you haven't seen him?'

'I did see him one more time. He said he'd kidnap me, force me to do whatever he told me to.' Pyke expected Felix to well up or tremble at the memory but his eyes were clear and his voice steady.

'And what happened?'

Felix stared down at the table.

'Well?'

'I found out where Uncle Godfrey hid his pistol.' Felix bit his lip and then looked down at his hands. 'I borrowed it. Next time I saw Eric, I aimed the pistol at him and said if he didn't leave me alone, I'd use it.'

Pyke looked at his son, open mouthed. He tried to picture the lad waving a pistol in broad daylight and fought to reconcile two conflicting sentiments: anger, that Felix had put himself in such potential danger – if the pistol had gone off and he'd wounded or killed the older boy, he could have been facing a lengthy spell in prison or worse – and delight that he'd tried to address the problem himself.

'And what did Eric do?'

'He ran away and didn't bother me again,' Felix said, matter-of-factly.

Still reeling from this revelation, Pyke tried to imagine what Emily would have said. 'Did you tell Jo or Uncle Godfrey about what you did?'

Felix shook his head. 'I haven't told anyone. Except you.' This time he looked up at Pyke. His stare was sheepish, but also defiant.

'I want you to promise me that you'll never repeat what you did, at least not while you're living under my roof.'

Felix considered this. 'Are you angry with me?'

'If that pistol had gone off, your life would have

been finished. Do you understand? Eric was a rotten apple, but what if you'd killed him? Needlessly taking a life is the very worst thing you can do. And you're far too young to deal with the consequences.'

'It wasn't loaded.'

'How would you know whether it was loaded or not?'

'Outside in the alleyway, I pulled the trigger. Nothing happened.'

'That's beside the point. You're still too young.'

There was a brief silence. 'I thought you'd be proud of me,' Felix said, eventually, his tone more reticent than before.

'I am – proud of you putting a ruffian like Eric in his place. But you also took too much of a risk. That's what you have to learn. Judgement. Knowing what to do and when. That'll come with time.'

Felix listened to what Pyke had just said and nodded. 'If in doubt,' Pyke said, 'try to imagine what your mother might say about whatever it is you're about to do.' He hesitated. 'Or Jo.'

Jo brought in the scrambled eggs and the three of them chatted about inconsequential things for almost an hour. Their peace was disturbed by a rap on the front door and Copper's subsequent barking. Harold Field stood on the threshold, tapping the ground with a bamboo cane. Behind him, his assistant, Matthew Paxton, waited by the carriage. Field didn't wait to be invited into the house and made straight for the dining room. Copper growled but let Field walk past him. Without being asked, Field took the chair next to

Felix and showed the lad his snuff-box. Felix inspected it without much interest. Field was smartly attired in a blue frock-coat, cream waist-coat and cravat and grey trousers, and his whiskers had been buffed with a reddy-brown oil.

'Quite a delightful family you have here, Pyke,' Field said, smiling.

'Perhaps we could talk in the front room. It's quieter and more private.'

Field looked at him and then at Felix and whispered, 'I suspect I'm being quarantined. But it was nice to make your acquaintance.' He picked up his snuff-box and followed Pyke into the other room.

'I can see you've been back in the country long enough to find suitable accommodation,' Field said, casting his eye around the unfurnished room. 'But, it would appear, not long enough to pay me a visit.'

'How did you find out where I lived?'

Field wandered across to the bay window and looked down on to the street. 'I won't make a secret of it. You were seen by Paxton yesterday. He followed you back here and passed the address to me.'

Pyke considered this for a few moments and walked across to join Field at the window. On the front step, Matthew Paxton was smoking a pipe. Alerted by Pyke's presence in the bay window, he looked up. Field had brought two other men with him but they were waiting by his carriage. 'What do you want?'

Field turned around and studied Pyke, as though disappointed in him. 'I'm sorry to hear you adopting such a tone. I thought the two of us had come to some kind of understanding.'

'All I meant was that I'm surprised that a man with your responsibilities has the time to pay me a courtesy call.'

That seemed to appease him. 'I was in the area and was wondering whether you happened to have come across Elizabeth Malvern on your travels.'

Pyke's face remained composed, his voice measured. 'No, I'm afraid I didn't.'

'No?' The surprise in Field's voice seemed genuine.

'Her brother hadn't seen her for a couple of years.' Pyke hesitated. 'Either she didn't arrive...'

'Or?'

Pyke folded his arms. 'Like I said, I don't know where she is.'

'Did I suggest that you did?' Field's stare was cold and piercing. 'It's just a little strange, don't you think? Impeccable sources assured me that she had made the journey, after all.'

Pyke remained silent but turned and walked across to the fireplace. He didn't want Field to see that he was lying. 'On a different subject, did Bessie Daniels come home in the end?'

'Not as far as I'm aware.' This time, Field had to look away, apparently uneasy for the first time.

'Not as far as you're *aware?*' Pyke tried to swallow but his throat was dry. 'Do you mean you haven't actually looked into the matter?'

'I'd be very careful about the tone you take with me, Pyke.'

But this time Pyke couldn't help himself. 'You mean to tell me you paid this woman to spy on an extremely dangerous individual and you haven't made any effort to make sure she's safe?'

Field took a few steps away from the window. 'Now you're starting to talk like a dead man.'

Unable to hold his tongue, Pyke continued. 'If you're too brazen or self-interested to look out for her, perhaps I should see what I can do.' He hesitated but didn't look across at Field. 'Where does, or should I say *did*, she live? Any family?'

He saw the blood rise in Field's neck and face until even the tips of his ears were crimson. In fact Field seemed too upset to speak and for a moment Pyke feared for his safety.

'I'm sorry.' This time Pyke held up his hands, by way of an apology. 'I shouldn't have spoken to you like that. It's just I'm concerned about Bessie. I blame myself more than I blame you.'

That seemed to calm Field down a little. 'Lord, Pyke, if you hadn't just apologised I'm not sure I could have let you live.' He shook his head as though the prospect of taking Pyke's life actually bothered him.

They stared at one another without speaking. Field went back over to the window and indicated something to Paxton.

'I have to go.' He walked past Pyke but stopped at the door, his hand on the knob. 'In answer to your question, I believe it was Eliza Craddock who sold her to Crane. If you remember, I solicited the woman's assistance *after* she'd been sold to Crane.'

Pyke absorbed this statement. 'You mind if I pay her a visit, see if she's heard anything?'

'As long as you don't mention my name I don't care what you do.' Field was poised to depart. 'And if you do find Elizabeth Malvern, you will let me know, won't you?'

Pyke nodded.

On the front steps Matthew Paxton waited for Field to pass and then looked up at Pyke, a crooked smile passing across his lips.

'I remember her,' Eliza Craddock said carefully. 'Nice lass but ugly. She had this nasty hare-lip. I used to put her in the darkest room so the men wouldn't see her face and complain to me afterwards.' She was sitting at the same table where Pyke had found her before, her bulbous arms resting by her sides.

'When was the last time you saw her?'

'I'd say a few months ago now.'

'Why did she leave?'

A noise came from somewhere in the brothel and Craddock looked behind her, then turned back to face him. 'What did you say?'

'I asked why she left.'

'Can't recall.' She flashed him a toothy grin. 'Gals come and go, can't do nothing about it.'

Pyke closed his palm slightly and slapped her hard across the face. The suddenness of his actions and the force of the blow caught her unawares.

'You're an acquaintance of Jemmy Crane, aren't you?'

When she didn't answer, Pyke kicked away the table, grabbed her by the throat and pushed her back against the wall. 'You sold Bessie to him, didn't you? He wanted a girl, someone you didn't particularly need, and the two of you agreed a price.' Pyke squeezed his hand tighter around her flabby neck. 'How much was it?'

Craddock's face had turned white and her eyes had almost doubled in size. Pyke didn't just want to strangle her; he wanted to tear out her throat. But at the last moment, he let go and watched her slide down the wall on to the floor, like a pool of water, holding her throat and gasping for air.

Bending over, he slapped her hard across the cheek once more and whispered, 'Do you know where she is now?'

'No.' But this time she didn't hesitate; he could smell the fear on her rancid breath.

'Don't lie to me.'

'I'm not,' she spluttered. 'After that day, I never saw her again.'

'Do you know what Crane wanted with her?'

'Something about copperplates, I think, but I didn't ask and he didn't tell me. None of my business.'

'How much did he pay you?'

'Five guineas.' Even she seemed ashamed of the paltry fee.

It took every ounce of self-control for Pyke not to pummel her face into a bloody mess.

She watched carefully as he prepared to leave but it was only when he was halfway along the passage towards the front door that she shouted, 'You know I'll go straight to Crane, don't you? And you won't be able to knock him around like you did me. Fact is, you don't have any idea what you're getting yourself into.'

That afternoon Pyke had just returned from walking Copper on the fields to the north of Pentonville when a figure caught his attention on the other side of the street. Her hair was tied up and covered by a straw bonnet but he recognised her immediately. Elizabeth Malvern.

'I hope you don't mind me disturbing you at home,' she said, once he had crossed the street to join her. 'I was hoping we might be able to take some air and talk at the same time.' Her plain dress, although respectable, neither copied the Empire waistlines of the Regency era nor conformed to the more contemporary preference for hooped skirts and flounced sleeves. It was slim fitting and showed off her hips. Her arms were covered by a shawl.

Pyke looked up towards his house on the other side of the road and saw Jo move away from the window. 'I could spare a few minutes.' He allowed her to walk ahead of him by a few paces and then followed, Copper hopping along by his side. 'What did you want to talk about?'

'This is difficult for me to say because I know it will reflect badly on me, but I wasn't entirely honest with you last night.'

'In what sense?' Now they were out of view of the bay window, Pyke caught up with her and took his place at her side.

'You asked me what need I had for a pistol and I was evasive in my answer.'

'I noticed.'

She bowed her head and blushed slightly. 'I wasn't entirely truthful about my reasons for not travelling to Jamaica or for deceiving my...' She paused for a moment. '...my father either.'

At the crossroads, they waited for a dray and a wagon to pass and hurried across the street.

'A few months ago I had a visit from this ... this *man*.' She hesitated. 'He was more of a beggar, actually, and he wore patches over both of his eyes. He said he was blind and he used a long stick to feel his way around.' A moment passed. 'He clearly wanted to talk to me but I was frightened and I chased him away.'

'And did he go?' Pyke kept his face composed in spite of this new information.

'Initially, yes, but he came back. That's when he told me he was my uncle.'

'And what did you say to that?'

'What do you *think* I said? I told him not to be so ridiculous and to leave me alone.'

'And did he?'

Elizabeth turned to face him, her face lined with worry. 'He told me he was my father's brother, Phillip, and when I tried to say my uncle Phillip had died a long time ago, when I was still a girl, he told me that it wasn't true and then proceeded to talk about my family and about Ginger Hill in a way that no one else could possibly have done. I suppose I believed him in the end.'

'So what did you do?'

'At the time I shooed him away. It was too much for me to take in. But then I went and told my father.' She waited and bit her lip. 'I've never seen him so angry, or so scared. That's when he gave me the pistol and said if this man ever turned up on my doorstep again, I was to brandish it in his face and, if he refused to leave or tried to harm me, I was to shoot him.'

'I thought you said you only communicated via correspondence?'

Elizabeth smiled sheepishly. 'This was before...'

'Before?'

'Before this whole business.' A steeliness had crept into her tone.

Pyke nodded. 'Did he acknowledge that this man was, or at least might have been, his brother?'

'He didn't believe me at first, but then I told him about the patches over his eyes and he went very quiet.'

They walked on for a few yards and then crossed over the Regent's Canal, where fields appeared on either side of the road. Copper crouched and urinated against a fence post.

'You have to understand my father isn't well. He's old, his memory is failing him and it frustrates him. On occasion he lashes out.'

'Verbally or physically?'

Elizabeth looked out across the fields and took in a breath of air. 'He used to be such a healthy, vigorous man. It's hard for him, being confined to that chair.'

Pyke thought about the frail specimen he'd seen and wondered whether the old man was actually capable of hurting anyone except himself.

'Did you ever see this other man again – the one claiming to be your uncle?'

'No.'

'And did you have another conversation with your father about him?'

'I tried to. After...'

'After what?'

This time when she turned to face him, she looked genuinely afraid. Either that, or she was a better actress than he'd imagined. 'After I found out how Mary had been killed, her eyes cut from their sockets.'

Pyke's skin tightened across his face. 'How did you find out about that?'

'My servant heard it from one of my father's servants. She'd overheard him talking to a policeman about it.'

'Inspector Pierce?'

'I'm sorry, I don't know.' She pulled her shawl up over her shoulders and stared down at the ground.

'And what did you think?'

'What did I think about what?'

'About the way Mary's face had been mutilated.'

She walked a few paces ahead of him then turned around. 'To be honest, I didn't *want* to think about it. So I asked my father.'

'And?'

'He was angry at first and then he tried to deny any involvement in the matter.'

'But you suspect that Mary's death might have had something to do with your uncle?'

Elizabeth stood there, very quiet. 'One of the things Phillip told me was that my father had been responsible for blinding him.'

'And you thought the business with Mary might have been a case of history repeating itself?'

Tears appeared at the corners of her eyes. 'I didn't know what to think. I'm so confused I don't know my own mind.' She turned around and stared out at the open space. 'But that's the reason I've been hiding from my father; why I write to him rather than visit him in person. It's why I refused to go to the West Indies. I don't know what to say to him any more. I always adored him, even as a child. And now he's so thin and weak. I'm afraid he's going to die...'

Without thinking about it, Pyke went and stood next to her. When she looked up at him, her cheeks were stained with tears. Perhaps she was lying to him but Pyke wasn't sure; every detail of her story matched what he'd been told in Jamaica. Still, he wasn't wholly convinced by her performance. And more to the point, she was, according to Field at least, Crane's mistress.

Elizabeth looked back towards the row of houses behind them. 'Could you help me to look for him?' She untied the ribbon under her chin, removed her bonnet and allowed her long black hair to be tousled by the breeze.

'Who, Phillip?'

She nodded.

'I could always try, assuming you know where I might look for him.'

'Me?' She seemed surprised at his request.

'Perhaps he said something to you, gave you a clue as to his whereabouts?'

'I'm afraid not.' They started to walk back towards his house.

'Did you know that a man called Arthur Sobers is due to stand trial for the murder of Mary Edgar tomorrow?'

She kept on walking. 'So soon?'

'Is that all you've got to say?'

This time she stopped. 'What else do you want me to say?' But the lightness in her tone had gone.

'Well, for a start, he was Mary's companion and he was arrested just a few hundred yards from your house.'

'I heard about the arrest, of course, and I was curious...'

They stared at one another. 'He didn't pay you a visit, then?' Pyke didn't bother to hide his scepticism.

'No.'

'And you don't know what he was doing on your street?'

Elizabeth looked away first. 'No, I'm afraid I don't.'

'I'm told he hasn't spoken a word since he was arrested. If he continues to offer no defence, he'll be found guilty by default and they'll hang him for it.'

Pyke had expected some kind of reaction but not the one he got.

'It's terrible, isn't it?' she said, seemingly forgetting herself and touching his sleeve. Later he thought there had been a lingering sadness in her voice and her eyes, but even with hindsight he couldn't make any sense of it.

Godfrey was sitting in the taproom of the Crown and Anchor surrounded by empty ale pots. Underfoot the floor was damp with butcher's sawdust, mixed with the odd chop bone and oyster shell, and the air around them smelled like unwashed clothes that had been left to rot in a wardrobe.

'I'm pleased it's you, dear boy,' Godfrey said, without much enthusiasm.

'I came as soon as I got your message.' Pyke had another look at his uncle's wan face. 'Is anything wrong?'

'I'm fine, or as fine as a man can be who's had to pay money for these beastly things,' he said, removing two copperplates from his coat pocket and pushing them across the table.

Pyke took the first of the plates and studied the image. His stomach muscles clenched. The subject was Bessie Daniels; she was lying – naked – on the same sofa he'd seen her spread across and had the same stunned expression he remembered; the result of imbibing laudanum. There was little or nothing erotic about it and the overall effect was dispiriting, akin to watching a slab of meat in a butcher's window. Still, Pyke's eyes were drawn to her plump, well-shaped breasts and to the dark triangle of hair around her vagina. The ring on her finger was an indistinct smudge.

'That's not the worst one, by a long shot,' Godfrey said, making sure that no one else was looking in their direction.

The other image also featured Bessie Daniels but this time she had been joined by a naked man whose head was covered by a hood. Bessie was lying on a bed and the man was kneeling over her, like a victorious fighting dog standing over its vanquished foe. Such was the positioning of their almost intertwined bodies that Pyke couldn't see the man's penis but it was all too clear what impression the scene was intended to connote. Still, for all that Pyke found the general content of the image distasteful, it was Bessie's expression which caught his attention and made him feel sick. Although slightly blurred, she looked to be in pain; there was a haunting quality to her stare and the set position of her mouth, accentuated by her hare-lip, made her seem almost possessed. The overall impression was of a woman pleading for help. Pyke slid the copperplate into his pocket and tried to swallow. He could have done more to help her. No, that wasn't it. He *should* have done more to help her.

'That was as warm as the chap in the shop was prepared to go, even with my friend's coaxing.' Godfrey shook his head. 'Cost me ten pounds for both.'

'But did your friend get the impression there *was* more? Maybe something even worse?'

'What could possibly *be* any worse?' Godfrey took a slurp of ale. 'It was the second one that upset me most, that hooded beast kneeling over her.'

For a moment neither of them spoke.

'A terrible business,' Godfrey said, eventually. 'Do you know who she is, then?'

'Name's Bessie Daniels. She used to work at Craddock's on the Ratcliff Highway. Eliza Craddock sold the girl to Crane for five guineas. As far as I know, no one has seen her for at least a couple of months.'

'Five guineas for a human life.' Godfrey stared down into his empty pot. 'Less than my friend paid for the copperplates.'

'I'll reimburse you as soon as I can afford it.'

But Godfrey held up his hand as though a little offended. 'I wouldn't hear of it, dear boy. Just find her and give her whatever you think you owe me.'

'You've barely said two words since you got home,' Jo said, standing in the doorway, as though uncertain about whether to enter his room. She was carrying a lantern and wore a long, white nightdress. 'Is anything the matter?'

Pyke looked up and tried to smile; his face felt numb from the laudanum he'd taken. 'It's been a difficult day.' He was sitting up in his bed and moved over to make room for her. 'How's Felix?'

But Jo remained where she was, shifting awkwardly from one foot to the other. 'Do you want to talk about it?'

'Not particularly.'

Jo nodded, as if this was the answer she'd expected. 'Who was that woman who came to the house?'

'Her name's Elizabeth Malvern.'

She waited but he didn't add anything. 'So you're quite happy for me to cook, clean and look after your son, but I'm not supposed to ask questions about your work?'

'I told you I wanted you to employ a servant to cook and clean. And besides, my work doesn't concern you.'

Jo looked at him, apparently nonplussed. 'You're exactly as Emily said you were – a difficult man to live with.'

Pyke felt his jaw tighten. Jo saw it but couldn't stop herself. 'Am I not even allowed to say her name?'

Pyke closed his eyes and took a deep breath. 'Look, Jo, I said I was tired. We can talk about whatever you want to talk about in the morning.'

She took a step into the room and her voice took on a sarcastic tone. 'Good. We'll talk about the way you've put Emily up on a pedestal, your perfect dead wife, so nobody can touch her. Remember, I knew her better than anyone, Pyke. Believe me, she would have hated it up there.'

An awkward silence hung in the air, as if they both knew a line had been crossed.

'If anyone else had said that,' Pyke said, through gritted teeth, 'I would have torn out their tongue.'

'I'm not surprised,' she retorted, standing her ground. 'That sounds like the way you would deal with criticism.'

Jo left the room, slamming the door behind her.

TWENTY-FOUR

The public gallery at the Old Bailey was full by eight in the morning, even though the trial wasn't scheduled to start until ten. The fact that a black man was standing trial for murder was a curiosity in itself, but public interest in the proceedings had been further exacerbated by unconfirmed press reports that his victim, Mary Edgar, had been mutilated in a ritualistic manner. Pyke hadn't yet read the *Examiner* that morning but he had been told that Saggers had written a column describing in graphic detail the exact nature of the facial mutilations, doubtless penned in his most lurid prose.

Fitzroy Tilling met Pyke outside the Sessions House on Old Bailey at half-past eight and they passed unchallenged into the court itself. The bench where the presiding judges would sit, underneath the sword of justice, was unoccupied, as were the spaces reserved for the jury, the prosecuting lawyer, the press and the various clerks of court.

'I've managed to get you a few minutes with the accused,' Tilling had told him. 'Just try to convince the man to say *something* in his defence.'

They entered the dock and followed the rickety staircase down into an underground passageway that led from the courtroom through a number of guarded and fortified doors to the condemned block at Newgate prison and the press room where Arthur Sobers was being pinioned by an army of turnkeys. Somehow the restraints they were placing around his arms and shoulders seemed wholly inadequate for the task, and briefly Pyke imagined the big man sneezing and the leather straps flying loose from their fixings.

Because he was hunched on a chair while the turnkeys finished their job, it was hard for Pyke to get a proper sense of the man's size, but even through the leather restraints Pyke could see that his shoulders were like an ox's and his neck was thicker than Felix's waist. Sobers' general demeanour was that of a beaten man, however, and when, a few minutes later, Pyke sat down on a chair next to him and tried to elicit his attention, it was as if he were looking at someone who wasn't there.

'I want to help you, Arthur,' Pyke said, staring into the man's eyes. 'I don't believe you killed Mary Edgar.'

Sobers barely twitched and his stare remained as blank as a fresh sheet of paper.

411

'A pornographer called Jemmy Crane sent some of his men to threaten you and Mary at your lodging house on the Ratcliff Highway. Can you tell me what that was about?'

This time a flash of recognition passed across Sobers' eyes.

'In less than an hour, you'll stand trial for killing Mary Edgar. If you don't say anything, if you don't let me help, they'll find *you* guilty and men like Crane and Silas Malvern will escape punishment. Is that what you want?'

Sobers' body stiffened at the mention of Malvern's name, but when Pyke tried to press him, the big man's attention was lost once more.

'Will you at least tell me *why* you accompanied Mary Edgar from Jamaica?' When Sobers didn't answer, Pyke let his frustration show for the first time. 'Mary's dead, for Christ's sake. She's not coming back. Who are you being loyal to?'

Sobers continued to ignore him.

'If you don't try to defend yourself, they will kill you as surely as night follows day. Is that what you want?' Pyke could feel the beads of sweat prickling his forehead. 'Why were you loitering near Elizabeth Malvern's house when the police arrested you? Do you know her?'

Pyke wanted to grab the big man's shoulders and shake him but the turnkeys had made it clear he wasn't to touch the prisoner.

Finally Pyke played his last card. 'John Harper and Isaac Webb told me to pass on their regards.'

That seemed to garner a reaction; Sobers looked at him, puzzled and intrigued.

'Did they send you here?' Pyke asked immediately. 'Was it their idea that you chaperone Mary?'

But Sobers let his stare fall back to the floor. Pyke sensed he was angry at himself for revealing that he knew Harper and Webb.

'I've just returned from Jamaica. Charles Malvern is dead, so is Michael Pemberton.'

No visible reaction.

'Don't you understand? This is your last chance.' Pyke hesitated. 'What did Harper and Webb want you to do here in London? Make contact with Phillip Malvern? Was he the blind man you were seen talking to on the Ratcliff Highway?'

Very slowly Sobers raised his gaze to meet Pyke's. His face was lean and taut, despite his size, and his eyes glowed with a peculiar intensity.

'Does the term "kill-devil" mean anything to you?'

That registered too, but still Sobers refused to speak.

'I think Phillip – the man they call Filthy – is in real danger. I need to talk to him.'

Sobers wetted his lips with his fat, pink tongue but said nothing.

'He hasn't been seen for a couple of months. Do you know where I can find him?'

Sobers leaned forward in his chair and bowed his head. For a moment Pyke thought he was about to speak.

'He's a rat-catcher among other things. Roams the sewers and culverts underneath the city.'

But the next time Sobers looked up at Pyke, his face was once again devoid of expression.

In the hour they'd been gone, the courtroom had

413

filled up almost to its capacity. The jury had taken their seats to the left of the bench, as had the journalists, who sat across from them under the public gallery. The prosecuting barrister was adjusting his horsehair wig and the clerks of court were making last-minute preparations. Pyke took his place next to Saggers in the press gallery and watched Pierce stride into the room accompanied by three constables. They took their positions alongside other witnesses for the prosecution. In front of them, the two judges entered the courtroom and everyone stood up. Finally, they all watched as Arthur Sobers was led into the dock.

Pyke found the whole thing hard to swallow. The wigs, the pomp, the solemnity of the occasion led one to believe that due process was being adhered to. But the verdict was never in question. Sobers' natural or innate savagery would be given as an explanation for his murderous tendencies and so-called 'expert' witnesses would corroborate this view. There would be a flimsy chain of circumstantial evidence linking Sobers to Mary's murder. The prosecuting barrister would lead the jury through his case unchallenged – and being unchallenged, the man wouldn't have to temper his assertions. Finally, the jury would retire for a respectable amount of time – long enough to give the impression they'd considered the evidence – and the foreman would stand up and deliver a guilty verdict. The recorder would then congratulate the jury for its verdict and would pass a death sentence on Sobers. All of this would happen and the man would sit there in silence and watch it; afterwards he would have to face those like Pierce who would be slapping each other on the back and congratulating themselves on a job well done.

The assistant judge, the deputy recorder of London, dressed in his ceremonial robes and wig, waited for silence. Having read out the first part of the indictment to the whole court, he turned to Sobers.

'It is hereby presented that Arthur Sobers, late of the Ratcliff Highway in the county of Middlesex, being of evil disposition and having strayed from God's righteous path, did on the first day of May in the third year of the reign of our Sovereign Queen Victoria, and with malice aforethought, wilfully murder Mary Edgar, late of the Ratcliff Highway, by strangulation.' He looked up from the bench and waited for a few moments. 'How do you plead? Guilty or not guilty?'

All eyes in the courtroom turned to Sobers, whose giant hands were gripping the rail in front of him.

'Accused, how do you plead?'

Sobers stared back at the deputy recorder and opened his mouth. 'Guilty.'

For a moment there was consternation in the room and the recorder had to bang his gavel on the bench to restore some semblance of order.

'Could you repeat your plea for the court, accused.'

'Guilty,' Sobers said, his plea carrying right across the courtroom.

'Do you understand what you are pleading guilty to?'

Sobers nodded. 'I do.'

The deputy recorder exchanged a glance, and a

few words, with the recorder. 'Do you have anything else you wish to say to the court?'

Sobers stood there, still gripping the rail, but this time said nothing.

'A few words of contrition? A confession before God?'

Saggers leaned over and whispered, 'I didn't see that one coming, did you?'

Pyke was too stunned to speak. Even though he'd heard Sobers as clearly as everyone else he couldn't reconcile himself to what the big man had just admitted.

There was a general sense of bewilderment and even deflation in the room. People had queued for hours expecting to hear lurid descriptions of bodily mutilations and accounts of the evils of black magic and witchcraft. Now they had to be content with a guilty plea and silence. Even the recorder himself seemed affected by the mood.

'It is my duty as recorder of London to make quite sure you understand the severity of the crime that you have pleaded guilty to and the nature of the punishment that awaits you.'

'I understand perfectly, Your Honour.' Sobers spoke in a deep, flinty voice. 'I killed her and now I'm ready to face the consequences.'

'But you have nothing additional to say to this court, perhaps regarding the reasons for your actions?'

Sobers stared down at his boots and waited for the moment to pass.

'Usually the expectation that the guilty party will make an appeal to the Home Office means that it is prudent not to rush the date of the execution, but since you have pleaded guilty by your own tongue, and showed no remorse for your actions, I see no reason to delay matters,' the judge said, removing his grey wig and replacing it with a black cap. 'It is my duty to sentence you to hang by the neck at the earliest opportunity.' He banged the gavel. 'Take this man from the dock.'

On the steps of the Sessions House, Sir Richard Mayne was congratulating Pierce. It was a hot, breathless day and the sky was washed with a haze of high cloud. Tilling joined Pyke a few steps away and said what everyone was saying: that he hadn't anticipated Sobers pleading guilty, but if the man really had killed her, then justice had been served.

'He didn't do it.'

That drew a weary shake of Tilling's head.

'He's protecting someone else. He's pleaded guilty to something he didn't do to protect some-one else.'

'Who? Malvern?'

Pyke ignored Tilling's jibe and watched as Pierce wandered over to a brougham that had just pulled up outside the Sessions House. Mayne came over and joined them. He slapped Tilling on the back and gave Pyke a considered stare. 'I know we've had our differences, sir, and you have said some things to me and others you probably regret now, but I just wanted to assure you that, as far as I'm concerned, the matter is closed.'

'Thank you, Sir Richard.' Pyke bowed his head slightly but still noticed Mayne's smile. 'Now can I get down on my knees and lick your boots clean, too?'

'There's no need for that, Pyke,' Tilling said. It reminded Pyke of the distance that had opened up between them and the damage he'd done to their friendship.

Tilling and Mayne drifted away without uttering another word and Pyke took the opportunity to cross the pavement to the brougham that Pierce had climbed into.

Ignoring the footman, Pyke peered into the carriage's interior and saw Silas Malvern's ghostly visage. Pierce sat next to him on the cushioned seat and it took them a few moments to notice Pyke's presence.

'Come to eat some humble pie, Pyke?' Pierce said, his face still flush from the glory of the morning's proceedings.

'I'd like a word with Malvern in private.'

Pierce shook his head and asked whether Malvern wanted one of his officers to move Pyke along.

'No, I'll hear what the man has to say,' Malvern said, his eyes not leaving Pyke for a moment.

'Well, if you need him trodden on, tell your footman to fetch me. I'll do the job with pleasure.'

'It's all worked out well for you, hasn't it, Pierce?' Pyke said, once Pierce had climbed out of the brougham.

'Just say it, Pyke. I was right. You were wrong.'

'If we weren't in a public place, I'd hurt you. I'd do more than hurt you.' Pyke took a step in his direction and Pierce scuttled across the pavement to rejoin Mayne.

'I received a letter from the Custos in Falmouth informing me of the death of my son. It was ruled an accident, the result of a natural calamity.' Malvern's bony hands trembled as he spoke. 'It seems, sir, I have you to thank for forewarning me of this truly terrible outcome and thereby softening, albeit slightly, the blow.'

Pyke felt his antipathy for the old man weakening in the face of his self-evident grief, but remained silent.

Malvern licked his pale, flaky lips. 'The last time we met, you made an oblique reference to an episode in my past that I've always felt very deeply ashamed of.'

'Which one?' Pyke waited. 'Killing your wife or blinding your brother?'

Malvern stared at him, horrified. 'I didn't kill her, sir. I couldn't have. I *loved* her.' His voice sounded as hard and small as an acorn.

'Even though she'd been cuckolding you with your brother?'

Malvern seemed physically cowed by Pyke's words. 'Except to say I regret very deeply what I did to my brother, more deeply than you'll ever know, I won't make my excuses to you, sir.'

'Did you know your brother had come to London?'

Malvern seemed surprised, though not shocked at this claim. For a few moments he sat, his arms resting on his lap like wilting runner beans. 'Before she departed for the Caribbean, my daughter informed me that a man *claiming* to be her uncle had tried to approach her but I didn't believe her.'

Pyke waited for Malvern to look at him. 'But the idea that he *might* be in London must have unsettled you.' He stared into the old man's rheumy eyes.

'I'll admit that I was less than comfortable at first but on reflection I saw it as a chance perhaps to be reconciled with him.'

'And?'

'Nothing ever came of it. Elizabeth wrote to me confirming her passage to Jamaica and that was the last I heard of it.'

'But when you heard about the way in which Mary Edgar had been mutilated, you must have thought about your brother and what you did to him.'

This time Malvern's reaction gave little away. 'I told you before, sir, I had nothing to do with that business.'

'What about your brother?'

'What about him?' Malvern barked.

'Perhaps *he* had something to do with Mary Edgar's death.'

Malvern stared down at his withered hands. 'You'll have to excuse me, sir. I have other matters to attend to.'

Pyke presented himself at the offices of the Vice Society and was told by the same clerk he'd spoken to before that Ticknor hadn't returned but was expected at any time.

'Tomorrow perhaps?'

'Tomorrow or the next day.'

'The next day is Saturday.'

'Monday, then.' The clerk looked up at him

420

from behind the desk. 'Would you like to leave him a message, sir?'

'No, thank you. It's not urgent.'

As he left, Pyke wondered why he'd said that and why, in the face of his suspicions, he was still trying to shield Elizabeth Malvern.

With a pick handle in his hand, Pyke pushed open the door to Crane's shop and when it closed behind him, he drew the bolt across and pulled the curtains. The assistant seemed puzzled by his actions and called out from behind the counter. Turning around, Pyke raised the pick handle above his head and slammed it down on the glass display case just to one side of the counter. Not pausing for breath, he pulled the lean-to cabinet from the wall and sent it crashing to the floor together with its cargo of books. He smashed the pick handle against another glass case and then swung it against the supporting leg of shelves that ran along the middle of the shop. One swing didn't do it but a second blow loosened the fixings enough for him to push the entire edifice over and watch it topple into the path of those summoned to deal with the disturbance. Jumping over piles of books, he made his way down the passage and into the yard. From there, he went to the printing room, where a number of compositors were hunched over their machines. Pushing them to one side, he brought the pick handle down on each machine, one at a time, and then turned his attention to the printing press, tipping it up on its side and then smashing it apart with the handle and the heel of his boot. Back in the shop, Pyke drove the end of the pick handle into the face of a man trying to block his path and took an oil lamp that was burning on the counter and threw it on to the floor. The flames from the shattered lamp quickly spread to the books and in a short while the entire shop was ablaze, flames devouring the books, shelves, etchings, lithographs, everything. Outside on the street, a crowd had gathered to watch, and already other shop owners, anxious about their premises, were beginning to round up pails of water to try to dampen the blaze. From upstairs windows, as charred curls of paper floated up into the gloomy late afternoon sky, some of Crane's employees had to jump to escape the encroaching fire. It was only at this point that Pyke wondered whether Crane himself was in the building to witness the destruction.

TWENTY-FIVE

Elizabeth Malvern must have seen him coming up the mews because even before he had knocked on the front door, it swung open and she was standing in the hall to greet him. She was wearing the same dress as before but this time her hair was down, framing her slim, oval face and cascading down her back almost as far as her waist.

'I want the truth this time,' Pyke said, trying to reconcile his desire for her smooth, tanned skin with his lingering urge to destroy anything in his path.

'The truth about what?' She regarded him with a mixture of curiosity and bemusement.

'You and Jemmy Crane.'

Pyke saw at once that the name had registered in her expression. 'Jeremy used to be part of my circle of friends until I got to know him better and discovered how he makes his money.'

'I know you were Crane's mistress: maybe you still are.'

Elizabeth pulled some hair away from her face and frowned. 'Why would anybody say that?'

'So it isn't true?'

She stared at him with something approaching anger. '*No,* of course it isn't true.'

Their eyes locked and, in the end, Pyke had to look away first.

'Are you going to let me know who told you this lie?'

'Harold Field.'

She looked blankly at him. 'I don't know him.'

'He owns a slaughterhouse in Smithfield together with a dozen ginneries and taverns and half of the gaming clubs in the city.'

'And you imagine that's the kind of company I keep?' But some of her indignation had started to abate. 'Why is this man insisting I'm Crane's mistress?'

'I don't know.'

'Do you believe him?'

'I don't know what to believe.'

'Do you believe *me?*'

Pyke didn't answer.

'I don't have to justify myself to him, or to you,' Elizabeth said, eventually. 'I haven't seen Crane

423

in more than a year. That's the God's honest truth. Whether you choose to believe me or not is up to you.'

'What about Arthur Sobers?'

That drew a different reaction, one of concern rather than irritation. 'What happened at the trial?'

'Why do *you* care what happened?' Pyke studied her reaction. He could smell his own sweat, a reminder of his recent rampage through Crane's shop.

'What is this, Pyke? Why the inquisition? You know about my family's interest in the murder and the investigation. It's not a secret. I just asked whether the jury had delivered their verdict.'

'They didn't need to. He pleaded guilty.'

For a moment this news seemed to jolt her but she quickly recovered her composure.

'You knew him, didn't you? That's why he was arrested near by. He'd come to visit you, hadn't he?'

She absorbed the heat of his gaze and waited for a moment. 'I've no idea what he was doing in this street and I've never even laid eyes on the man.'

'You're not sorry he's going to hang, then?'

'If he killed her, then no, I'm not.'

Pyke studied her expression. 'I saw your father outside the Sessions House. He seemed pleased by the verdict, too.'

'Who said I was pleased? The man pleaded guilty. Surely it's just a matter of justice being served?'

Pyke took a breath and tried to gather his thoughts. He'd intended to confront her and force the truth out of her but now she was calm and *he* was floundering.

'I should go,' he said.

'But you've just got here,' she replied, puzzled.

'I've had a long day.'

She gave him an apologetic smile. 'Look, I won't offer to cook for you but I can put a glass into your hand.'

Pyke was exhausted but in truth he didn't have anywhere else to go. If he went home, the police might be waiting for him. Briefly, he wondered whether the fire had spread beyond Crane's shop and what kind of damage had been caused.

'Maybe just a quick drink.'

Elizabeth's eyes were sparkling as she led him into the house.

They sat opposite one another at her kitchen table. It was an informal arrangement, the kind he might have enjoyed with an old friend, but with her, the informality seemed contrived, as if it had been conjured solely to elicit his approval. She seemed to want him to like her, and if he was honest he found himself thinking about her more and more. But he couldn't get away from the fact that she was somehow involved in the matter he was investigating and, as such, he had to be cautious.

'It's funny, isn't it? Terrible things have happened in these last few months but I've been happier here, on my own, than I would have been enjoying the delights of the Season.'

Pyke nodded, trying to appear genial. 'I'd rather swallow a razor blade than listen to the inbred fools and their dull-witted wives chatter about the wonders of opera.'

Her laugh was throaty and, he felt, a little dirty. 'It's the women I detest more than the men. Often their opinions simply parrot their husbands'.'

'The blind leading the blind.'

She looked at him, perhaps surprised by his reference to blindness. 'You're different, Pyke. You don't seem afraid...'

'Afraid of what?'

'Saying what's on your mind, *doing* things, getting things done.' Her gaze seemed to take in his whole body. 'There's nothing predictable about you.'

'I could say the same thing about you.'

Elizabeth held his eyes. 'But I can see you still don't trust me.'

'Or you me.'

'Why wouldn't I trust you?'

'Because you think the only reason I'm here is to ask you more questions about your family.'

'I don't think that's the *only* reason you're here.'

Pyke felt his stomach tighten and knew he had to change the subject. 'Tell me about your interest in daguerreotypes.'

'Ah, back to the interrogation.' Her smile was sly and warm. 'In that case I'm going to need a drop of something to loosen my tongue.' In the pantry, she dug out a bottle and put it down on the table, together with two glasses. 'The drink I promised you. Rum from Jamaica. I have it shipped to me.'

'Kill-devil.'

This made her look up. She filled both glasses to the brim and handed one of them to Pyke. 'I haven't heard it called that for a while.'

'You don't take yours with water?'

Elizabeth picked up the glass and poured the rum down her throat. It didn't seem to affect her. 'Tell me about your time in Jamaica.'

'What do you want to know?'

'What were your impressions of the place? Where did you go? Who did you meet?'

Pyke took a sip of rum; it tasted smoother and sweeter than the spirit he'd drunk in Jamaica. 'I thought I was the one questioning you.' Ignoring his better judgement, he followed suit and downed what was in his glass in a single gulp.

She gave him a crooked smile and refilled their glasses.

For the next half an hour, they talked about Jamaica. Pyke kept his descriptions vague and didn't mention any names unless they were attached to Ginger Hill. For the most part, Elizabeth listened intently and filled their glasses when they were empty. Pyke was careful about what he said about her brother and, for some reason, she didn't press him for further information. She seemed more interested in what he'd done in Falmouth, and when he mentioned he'd ventured into the middle of the island, she wanted to know why and where he'd gone. He gave evasive answers and eventually her interest began to wane.

'But did you *like* it?' It wasn't the first time she'd asked the question.

'Yes, I suppose I did. It was much more beautiful than I'd imagined.'

'Dangerous, too.' She brushed a lash from her eye. 'You must have been frightened for your life during the storm.'

'I suppose so.' Pyke tried to remember what

he'd felt that night but couldn't put it into words.

'I was thinking about what happened to my brother and I can't help feeling that something is amiss. He would *never* have taken shelter in that part of the house. In the old days, if a storm hit, we would take refuge in the counting house or even the dungeon.'

'I don't know what to say. I wasn't privy to his decision.'

Elizabeth nodded, but seemed dissatisfied with the answer. 'But they're sure he died as a result of the storm?'

'As far as I know. I mean, why wouldn't they be?'

'I don't know. I'd hate to think foul play was involved, but he had written to me recently and told me how fractious the atmosphere at Ginger Hill had become.'

'No, I'm certain your brother's death was a consequence of the storm.'

This seemed to settle her. She fiddled with her empty glass. 'It still doesn't explain why you went all that way just to find out what happened to Mary.' She added, with a shrug, 'I hope you don't mind me prying. I'm just trying to understand you a little better.'

'Why do you want to understand me better?'

Neither of them spoke for a few moments. 'You don't think this man, Arthur Sobers, killed her, do you?' she said, trying to read his thoughts.

'Honestly? No, I don't.'

'Then why did he plead guilty?'

Pyke stared into her dark eyes and noticed tiny yellow flecks spotted around her irises. 'I think he's trying to shoulder the blame for someone else. But I don't know why.'

'Really?' She didn't flinch or turn away. 'Why would he do that?'

'Love, misplaced loyalty, who knows?'

She let his words linger between them for a few moments. 'But what are *you* hoping to gain by finding the man who really killed her?'

'Who said it was a man?'

She reached for the rum bottle and again refilled both of their glasses. 'You didn't answer my question,' she said, taking a sip of the rum.

'Are you asking me why I care about Mary's death?'

Elizabeth just nodded.

'It's a job I agreed to do. I like to see things through to the end.'

'That's it?'

'You think I should just let her rot in an unmarked grave?'

She shook her head and gave him a solemn look. 'Honestly, I think what you're doing is entirely to your credit.' It was a bland statement, in a way, but when he looked at her, there were tears in her eyes.

She reached out across the table and squeezed his hand. He let it linger there for longer than he should have. All the rum he'd drunk had left him light headed. Elizabeth, on the other hand, seemed almost sober.

'A while ago, I asked about daguerreotypes,' he said, noticing the way the curve of her neck accentuated the shape of her chin.

'Ah, back to the questions...' She withdrew her hand and offered him a good-natured smile.

'You don't mind?'

She shrugged. 'If I'm honest, I quite like the fact that you're interested in me. I've been so starved of human company...'

'Daguerreotypes.' In Jamaica, Charles Malvern had told Pyke that his interest in the new medium had been fired by his sister.

'It's a pastime. Other women like to press flowers.'

'But how did you first develop an interest in it?'

'I read about it in the newspaper. It sounded interesting.' Absentmindedly, she coiled a loose strand of hair around her finger. 'I'm not the spoiled, stupid planter's daughter you think I am.'

'Who said I thought that?' Pyke took out the copperplate of Bessie Daniels and pushed it across the table. He needed to steer their conversation back towards more neutral matters. 'I don't know what your dealings with Crane are but he's learned about daguerreotypes from someone – for some reason I suspected it might be you. While you might just take pictures of flowers and plants, you'll see he's been quick to exploit the medium for his own ends.'

She studied the image, then pushed it back across the table. The disgusted look on her face seemed genuine. 'You think I taught him how to do that?'

'I do.' Pyke waited.

She closed her eyes and shook her head. 'God, whatever must you think of me?'

Refusing to be sidetracked, Pyke added, 'Her name's Bessie Daniels. A brothel madam called Eliza Craddock sold her to Crane for five guineas.' He took the daguerreotype and put it back into his coat pocket.

'Is she...' Elizabeth couldn't bring herself to finish the question.

'Is she dead?' Pyke saw her pupils dilate slightly. 'I don't know.' He wanted to be angry at her – at anyone – but somehow he couldn't quite manage it.

'I'm sorry I ever met him.'

Suddenly she looked exhausted, but Pyke wasn't quite finished with his questions. 'And Samuel Ticknor?'

'I don't think I know him.' She smiled apologetically. 'Should I?'

'He's an agent for the Vice Society.'

'I'm still not sure,' she said, her brow furrowed in thought.

'It's not a trick question,' Pyke said, allowing his frustration to show. 'Either you know him or you don't.'

'I haven't been into the field for more than a year and I'm afraid that my memory for names isn't good. Perhaps I might recognise him.' Her expression seemed so sincere that he was disarmed.

'Do you remember meeting a woman called Lucy Luckins?'

'No. Who is she?'

'Just another girl fallen on hard times.' For some reason, Pyke didn't want to tell her that Lucy was also dead.

'I might know her. But then again I might not.' She shrugged apologetically. 'I meet so many people from all walks of life...'

'But none you actually like?' he asked, softening a little. He was beginning to sense her weariness and frustration.

'But none I actually like,' she said, repeating his line and smiling. 'Or almost none.' This time she looked directly into his eyes. 'You didn't come here *only* to ask me questions, did you?' She finished her rum and waited for Pyke to do likewise.

They were sitting across the table from one another so she couldn't see his erection. She'd answered his questions with patience and humour but he also knew that that didn't mean she'd told the truth.

'You're not married, are you?' she asked suddenly.

'My wife died five years ago.' For some reason Pyke wanted her to know this; wanted her to know the truth. In part, it felt as if they'd both been playing a game, toying with each other, and that this was the first honest thing he'd said.

'I'm sorry.' She bit her lip. 'I shouldn't have asked.'

The warmth from the rum had spread to his stomach. 'I'm glad you did.' Tentatively he put his hand out across the table.

She reached across the table and their fingers brushed together. Was he still trying to elicit information from her? To expose her as a liar? In an instant the game had changed and suddenly he was unsure of himself.

'Pyke?' Elizabeth stared at him, clear eyed, absolutely serious.

'Yes?' The word seemed to get stuck in his throat.

Their fingers coiled together. He squeezed. She squeezed. The candle that had been glowing on the table next to them flickered and then burned out. He heard her chair move and felt her pull his hand towards her. Standing, he groped for her face, touching her nose, her lips, her eyes, her hair, their mouths meeting somewhere over the middle of the table, lips, tongues, teeth urgently seeking their counterpart, each touch, each messy kiss, firing rather than satiating his need, until all he could do was climb up on to the table and pull her under him. But she seemed just as hungry as him, more so if that were possible, and she wasn't going to be dictated to; she wouldn't let him rip off her dress, and whenever his hands ventured near her back, she grunted slightly and shooed him away. Still, as she guided him into her, Pyke was too far gone to tell whether her sudden gasp was genuine or not; the intensity of the moment was almost too much for him to bear.

Later, after she had led him up to her bedroom and they had made love again, this time more slowly and somehow even more pleasurably, they lay there in silence. She was still wearing her dress and had just hitched up it while they made love, repelling all of his attempts to remove it.

'Will you stay with me tonight?'

Pyke closed his eyes, the guilt now beginning to wash over him. 'I can't.'

Next to him her body hardly moved.

'Are you angry with me, that I have to go?'

To his surprise, she laughed. 'You have your life, I have mine.'

Her face looked so beautiful and guileless. 'Elizabeth?'

'Yes, my darling?'

Pyke wanted to say something about the evening, the sex, but he couldn't find the right words. 'Nothing.'

But she squeezed his hand anyway and whispered, 'I know.'

He washed himself with soap and water at the basin in the kitchen and dressed quickly. When he returned to the bedroom, she hadn't moved. He went over to the bed and kissed her on the mouth.

'Will I see you again?' Elizabeth asked, as he prepared to leave. When he didn't answer, she waited for a moment and added, 'Whatever happens, don't think badly of me. I don't think I could bear it if you thought badly of me.'

It was late, after eleven, by the time the hackney carriage dropped him outside his house and he found Jo waiting up for him in the front room.

'Some policemen were here earlier.' She was wearing a white nightdress and a matching gown tied at the waist.

'They say what they wanted?' He was wondering whether she could sense the guilt he was feeling.

'Your friend, or he claimed to be your friend, told you to meet him tomorrow noon at Trafalgar Square, in front of the National Gallery.'

'Fitzroy Tilling?'

'That's the name he gave.'

They stood there for a while contemplating one another without speaking. Pyke could feel his perspiration.

'Is this how it's going to be?' Her arms were folded tight to her body and her face was hot with anger.

434

'Is this how what's going to be?'

'Us, *you*.' She took a step towards him and seemed to sense or smell something. 'Where have you been, Pyke?'

Pyke hesitated just a little too long. 'I've been looking for a missing prostitute.'

She stood there for a moment, not knowing whether to challenge him or not. Then she moved away and shook her head. 'This isn't going to work.'

'Look, it's late and we're both tired. Maybe we should talk in the morning.' Pyke tried to give her a hug but she saw it coming and backed away.

'I've been thinking about this for a while, Pyke. In fact, I haven't thought about much else since you returned from Jamaica.' She held up her hand to stop him from interrupting. 'Let me finish, please. If you don't, I might never say what I need to say.' For a moment, he thought she might cry. 'I'll continue here until the end of this month, while I look for another position. But I can't go on like this, not knowing what you feel for me, if it's anything more than gratitude; wondering what my place is in this house, and worrying about my future and whether I have one.'

Pyke felt a sharp stab of shame and thought about all his declarations of intent to her – and how by making them, by articulating what he thought they both wanted, he'd actually believed he could will a life for them both into existence.

'I don't know what to say, Jo. Is there any way you could be persuaded to change your mind?' He tried to imagine life without her but couldn't.

'That's just the problem, Pyke. You don't know

what to say because you don't know what you want.'

'Tell me what to say and I'll say it. For my sake and for Felix's sake. Please, Jo, I'm begging you. I'll get down on my hands and knees if I have to. Stay until the New Year and make a decision then. If we can make it until January, maybe we do have a future.'

'As nursemaid to your child or mistress in your bed?'

The bluntness of her question took him by surprise and Pyke didn't have an immediate answer.

'For me, it's simple,' she said. 'Unfortunately, I'm in love with you. I probably have been for a long, long time, but I've never dared to acknowledge it even to myself. But what happened between us before you left for Jamaica unleashed those feelings in a way I couldn't have expected.' She paused and her eyes filled with tears. 'These past few months have been the most unhappy, the most miserable, of my life, and I just can't do it any more. I can't just put my feelings back into a box and pretend they don't exist.'

Guilt, shame, affection, respect. Pyke felt all those things. He wanted to take Jo in his arms and tell her that he loved her; wipe away her tears and convince her that they had a future together. He wanted to do it for Felix's sake, of course, but also for his own. For he knew that a part of him wanted the things that she could give him: a happy, stable domestic life. But he could still feel the taste of Elizabeth Malvern's tongue in his mouth and recall the way it had made him feel, and he knew that in time he would hurt Jo more than he already had, and that he would keep on hurting her.

'I'm sorry, I really am sorry.'

That riled her. 'What exactly are you sorry about?'

He thought about Emily; how he'd been more or less faithful to her throughout their time together. 'That I don't love you in the same way.'

Perhaps Jo had been expecting it; perhaps she'd even been trying to provoke him into admitting it. But the baldness of his confession still made her gasp. She stared at him, her eyes wide open, trying to make sense of what he'd just said, before wiping her nose on the sleeve of her dress and smiling. 'Thank you,' she said quietly.

'For what?' It would have been hard for Pyke to hate himself any more than he did at that moment.

'For finally being honest with me.' As her eyes started to fill up again, she managed to say, 'Could you leave me alone now, please?'

TWENTY-SIX

As part of an attempt by planners to tear down the ancient city and construct a modern metropolis of wide avenues and open public spaces, Trafalgar Square had been envisaged as the embodiment of Britain's imperial might and as its centrepiece a column built of Portland stone upon which a statue of Nelson would one day sit was beginning to take shape. Pyke could see that, when completed, the square might be a pleasant place to pass the time, but in the middle of summer and with plumes of dust whipped up by the building work and the slow procession of omnibuses, drays, cabs, barrows and carriages moving between The Strand and the West End, it was about as disagreeable a spot as he could imagine.

While he waited, Pyke tried to think about his investigation; what he had found out and more importantly what he had missed. It pained him to realise he still didn't know who had killed Mary Edgar or even why she had been killed. Different pieces of information were still pulling him in different directions. The fact that she had been staying in Bedford's home at the behest of Charles Malvern and that Bedford, too, had been murdered suggested that the same man – or woman – had been responsible for both deaths. But there was also the question of Mary's facial mutilation and how this replicated an incident that had taken place in Jamaica many years earlier involving Silas Malvern and his brother, Phillip. That had to be significant – the coincidence was too stark – but while a familial connection between Mary and Phillip Malvern seemed to offer a partial explanation, it still didn't begin to explain why Lucy Luckins had been mutilated in a similar fashion.

Who or what linked Mary Edgar and Lucy Luckins?

The manner of their deaths was the same – they had been strangled and their eyeballs removed – but there the similarities ended. Lucy was poor, white and flirting with prostitution. Mary Edgar had good looks and a degree of security by dint of her connection to Bedford and Charles

Malvern. Desperate and afraid, Lucy had turned to prostitution as a last resort while Mary had had to beat off a number of potential suitors.

The bells of St Martin's-in-the-Field had just chimed midday when Pyke saw Tilling striding towards him, suited in black and wearing his matching stovepipe hat.

'Let's walk,' Tilling said, his expression and demeanour devoid of any warmth.

Pyke started to say something but Tilling cut him off. 'Are you out of your mind? Does the Great Fire mean anything to you? What you did was reckless and irresponsible and it put untold lives at risk – and for what? Did you achieve what you wanted or was it just to make yourself feel better?'

'At least Crane isn't going to be trading for a while.' They continued for a few steps in silence. 'Is that a problem for you?'

'The problem is you, Pyke.' Tilling turned to face him. 'And the fact you don't seem to accept that the law is the law. It's a blunt instrument, I'll grant you, but it's all that separates us from anarchy.'

'So you think what I did was wrong?'

'The sanctity of private property is the bedrock of our legal system.'

'Then arrest me,' Pyke said, half joking.

That drew an irritated chuckle. 'Oh, believe me, Mayne would like nothing better than to put you behind bars. But the only way an arrest warrant can be issued is if Crane makes an official complaint and at the moment no one seems to know where he is.'

'So I'm still a free man?'

Tilling shrugged. 'For the time being.'

As they walked down towards Haymarket, Pyke thought about Crane and the robbery he was planning. How was he planning to breach the Bank of England's impregnable security? Was it possible to countenance such an action? In less than two days, Jerome Morel-Roux would hang before an expected crowd of fifty thousand. Before he'd gone to Jamaica, Bessie Daniels had whispered the valet's name to him. Why? The only explanation Pyke could think of was that Bessie had overheard Crane mention that the robbery had been planned to coincide with the hanging. Still, he didn't know this for certain and it paid not to jump to any conclusions.

'The reason I wanted to see you is that I might have found out the whereabouts of Lord Bedford's butler.'

Stopping, Pyke turned to face his erstwhile friend. If the butler admitted to knowing about Mary Edgar and the arrangement Bedford had struck with Charles Malvern, then they might be able to insist that the investigation into both murders be reopened. In any case it might be enough temporarily to halt the execution.

'Can I come with you to talk to him?'

Tilling put his hand up to his eyes. 'I'd rather do it on my own. But come around to the house tomorrow afternoon. I'll have more news for you then.'

Pyke's thoughts switched back to the robbery that Crane was, or might be, planning. 'Can I ask you a question?' He didn't wait for an answer. 'Is

Mayne at all concerned by the prospect of fifty thousand men and women, mostly the poorest of the poor, pouring into the city on Sunday night and Monday morning?'

'Concerned in what sense?'

'I don't know.' Pyke hesitated, trying to gather his thoughts. 'That the crowd might be infiltrated by radicals intent on pursuing their own cause?'

This time Tilling's face creased with worry. 'Have you heard something to this effect?'

Pyke shrugged. 'If I were you, I'd ask the Bank of England about additional security provisions taken in light of the crowds expected to gather on Monday morning.'

That did nothing to ease Tilling's concern. 'Why the Bank of England? What *exactly* have you heard?'

'Just ask.' Pyke looked at him and waited. 'Like you said we can talk about it tomorrow afternoon at your house.'

He watched Tilling walk off in the direction of Whitehall.

About an hour later, Pyke found Samuel Ticknor in a coffee house on St John Street, just around the corner from the offices of the Vice Society. He was a timid, bald-headed man with rancid breath and a punctilious manner that put Pyke in mind of a headmaster or clergyman. Indeed, there was a well-thumbed copy of the King James Bible next to his empty plate. He didn't seem like the kind of man who'd knowingly set out to profit from the exploitation of his charges.

'Perhaps you might enlighten me as to the

precise nature of your enquiries, sir? I am a busy man.' He checked his gold pocket watch.

'You've been a difficult man to find.'

'A private matter demanded my attention in the West Country. But I'm here now, so perhaps you might be so bold as to tell me why this matter couldn't wait until next week.'

'Do you remember a woman called Lucy Luckins?'

'Luckins, you say?'

'From Shadwell.'

That seemed to make the difference. 'Ah, indeed. Lucy. If I'm not mistaken, I helped to find her work as a seamstress last year. Not the most glamorous or well-paid occupation, I'll admit, but a good deal better for her soul than walking the streets.' He gave the Bible next to him a supercilious tap. 'Why do you ask?'

'Do you know Elizabeth Malvern?'

Ticknor's expression darkened. 'I used to be acquainted with her.'

Pyke felt his throat tighten. 'What was the precise nature of your acquaintance?'

'She used to raise funds for the society and on occasion she would accompany me on field visits.'

'Did she ever accompany you when you visited Lucy Luckins?'

'I can't remember exactly.'

'Then *think*.'

'Excuse me, sir, but you're going to have to tell me the precise nature of your interest in Miss Luckins...'

Pyke cut him off. 'She's dead. She was

strangled and then both of her eyes were cut out.'

Ashen-faced, Ticknor immediately retched on to the table. A spool of saliva hung from his chin.

'I'll ask you again. Did Elizabeth Malvern accompany you when you visited her?' Ticknor stared at Pyke and nodded. 'Miss Malvern was the one who found her work as a seamstress.'

Pyke found himself gripping the edge of the table. 'Just now, you said she used to raise funds for the society?'

'Yes.'

'Not any more?'

'She was asked to leave.'

'*Why?*'

'On account of the company she kept.'

Pyke slammed his fist down on the table. 'What, precisely, do you mean by that?'

'A gentleman. A *particular* gentleman.' Ticknor's hands were trembling.

'Was his name Jemmy Crane, by any chance?'

Ticknor's mouth fell open. 'How did you know?'

'And there's no possibility you could have been mistaken about the nature of their association?'

'I saw them with my own eyes.'

'When?'

'Some time in the spring. April, perhaps.' Ticknor's stare was solid, even defiant. 'I saw them, sir. I saw them embrace.'

When Pyke arrived at Pitts Lane Mews, someone had evidently beaten him to it. The back door had been kicked open and, inside, shards of broken glass and crockery covered the downstairs floor. Upstairs, wardrobes had been overturned and sheets had been ripped off the beds. In the kitchen, he paused at the table they had sat around the previous night. The table they'd fucked on. The room, the whole house, smelled of her.

So Elizabeth Malvern *was* Jemmy Crane's mistress. It was just as Field had said. Field and Ticknor.

But what did that mean?

What if Elizabeth had put Lucy Luckins in touch with Crane rather than finding her a job as a seamstress?

And what had happened in the intervening period – from the time Elizabeth and Lucy met to the moment Lucy's strangled corpse had been hauled out of the river by Gilbert Meeson?

Why had Lucy's eyeballs been cut from their sockets just like Mary's?

Pyke's thoughts turned to Phillip Malvern. Somehow the two matters were related; they *had* to be. For a while, he sat at the kitchen table trying to remember all the bits of information about Phillip he'd come across. Eventually he came back to what the bone collector had said: *He likes his women dark.* But where would he find a black woman on the Ratcliff Highway? Pyke thought about Eliza Craddock's brothel and about Jane Shaw, who had been abandoned because she'd contracted syphilis. It was a remote possibility but it was a possibility none the less. He left the house via the front door.

At first Pyke thought that Jane Shaw was dead, but then she coughed and turned over, perhaps disturbed by the light from his lantern. Down below, in another part of the building, he heard raised voices and then a scream. He stepped into the tiny, airless room and waited. The air stank of faeces and death. Her eyes opened slightly and she tried to sit up. He thought he saw her smile but it could have been a grimace.

'You came back.' This time the disease had spread from her face to every part of her body. There was almost nothing left of her.

'How could I keep away?'

That seemed to make her laugh, but as she did so something caught in her throat and she coughed. 'If I'd known you were coming, I would have combed my hair.' She touched her bald head.

He sat down next to her and took her hand. It felt like a skeleton's. 'I wanted to ask you a question.'

'Lucky you didn't wait too much longer.' She grimaced each time she tried to move and Pyke guessed that her back was covered with sores. 'You find the one who killed the mulatto?'

'Not yet.'

'Is that why you here?'

'In part.' Pyke waited. 'When I was last here, you said you could remember the faces of all the men you'd ever slept with.'

'I 'member. So?'

'Were you ever visited by a blind man?'

'Phillip.'

Pyke didn't try to hide his excitement. 'That's right. Did you see him often?'

'While I was still working at Craddock's. He was a little mad but he was also gentle and considerate, not like most of 'em.'

'Mad in what sense?'

'He believed there were evil spirits trying to harm him.'

Pyke thought about what he'd learned about Phillip Malvern in Jamaica. 'Did he ever talk to you about what he did, where he lived?'

'He scavenged the sewers, reckoned he could make a living from it, too. That's why they called him Filthy.' She tried to smile. 'You could smell it on him, too, but I didn't mind. Better that he was gentle.'

'Did he say anything else?'

'No, not really. He wasn't much of a talker, to be honest. Is he in trouble?'

'He might be.' Pyke waited. 'I need to find him. It's important. Do you know where he lives?'

'He didn't tell me.'

'Or where he went to scavenge?' Pyke waited. 'He sold rats to a landlord in Saffron Hill.'

Jane tried to move and grimaced again. 'He did mention this sewer or tunnel he found under the City...'

'Yes?'

Jane closed her eyes. 'He told me he found a barrel of wine down there once. Said you could walk into it from the Thames at low tide underneath Dowgate Wharf.'

As he moved away, she took his hand and tried to squeeze it. 'You can't leave me like this, Pyke.'

'I have to go. I'll come back, though. I promise.'

'I meant, you can't leave me like this. I want you to finish it. I've asked other folk but they're all too afraid...' She motioned up towards the ceiling.

'Eternal damnation.'

'I was thinking you might be different.'

'I was damned a long time ago.' Pyke looked into her pale eyes. 'You want me to end your life?'

'Take my pillow, put it over my mouth. It won't take more than a few seconds. I can't go on like this any longer.'

'Is that what you really want?'

Jane nodded. 'I'm so tired, in such pain.'

'What you're asking me to do,' Pyke said, thinking about it, 'some would consider it to be a mortal sin.'

'I ain't said my prayers for years now, if that's what you're asking me.'

'And you're ready to go?'

She produced a bottle of gin from beside the mattress. 'You'll have a last drink with me, won't you?'

In the end she was so weak he had to help her hold the bottle to her lips. She sipped at the clear liquid like a suckling baby. Pyke took the bottle, put it to his mouth and drank until he needed a breath.

'The funny thing is, I used to think I'd make something of my life.' Jane looked around the dingy room and shook her head. 'Everything I had, I've bartered away or it's been stolen.'

'We come into this world with nothing, we leave it with nothing.' For some reason, Pyke found himself thinking about Felix.

She touched his hand and tried to squeeze it. 'You're a good man.'

They stared at one another for a few moments. 'Are you quite sure you're ready?'

'Living here, like this,' Jane smiled sadly, 'I been

ready for a while now.'

Pyke cupped the back of her head in his hand, pulled out her pillow and helped her lie back down on the mattress.

'You actually going to do it?' Jane seemed scared all of a sudden.

'Only if you want me to.'

Pyke sat there and watched while she considered the decision. 'I want you to,' she said, eventually. Her eyes were as dry as a tinderbox.

'You're sure?' Suddenly the pillow felt heavier than a bag of anvils.

'Either do it or leave,' she said, a hardness in her tone. She closed her eyes, took a deep breath and whispered, 'But whatever you decide, I'm ready.'

Even though she'd been expecting it, and indeed had asked for it, the moment that he forced the pillow down against her bony face, her body seemed to jolt with surprise and after that, in spite of her weakened condition, she battled, arms and legs convulsing until there was no more fight left in her.

Putting the pillow down, Pyke looked around the room. Apart from the empty gin bottle, there was nothing.

Like the Fleet, which until the thirteenth or fourteenth century had been a navigable river that cut through Alsatia, Holborn and Saffron Hill before rising in Hampstead, Walbrook had once flowed into the Thames near Southwark Bridge, having followed a path from Moorfields directly through the City of London. Pyke was told this by a mudlark who showed him to the entrance of the tunnel. The river had long since been built over and had actually been reconstructed as a sewer, in order to transport the city's soil directly into the Thames. It had served this function, of course, for as long as people had lived in the City.

The tide was out and the smell emanating from the mudbanks was horrendous but, as the mudlark gleefully informed him, it was nothing compared to the stink inside the tunnel. The two of them clambered down under Dowgate Wharf and the mudlark directed Pyke to a small, dark entrance directly under the creaking wooden edifice. 'That's you, cock,' he said, accepting the coin Pyke gave him, then added, 'You got a stick to beat off the rats?'

Alone, Pyke checked to make sure he still had his sheath knife, a handkerchief to cover his mouth, a nosegay, a lantern, a ball of twine, his jemmy and an old pair of gloves. Pinching his nostrils with the nosegay and tying the handkerchief around his mouth, he picked up the lantern and moved towards the tunnel entrance. A trickle of brown soil was emanating from the tunnel and the ground was marshy underfoot. At the entrance itself, he held up the lantern and peered inside. The walls and ceilings of the sewer had been built using bricks, and it was about as tall as he was and as wide as a brougham. He stepped into the tunnel and almost gagged, through the handkerchief, from the vileness of the stink.

'Phillip?'

He walked another few yards along the tunnel, trying to ignore both the stink and the feeling of entrapment that being in such a confined space induced, then hesitated. Holding up the lantern, he peered down at the thick soil blackening his knee-high boots. It was difficult to imagine how a man might live in such a place. Ahead, he saw his first rat, but it scuttled off in the opposite direction. The mudlark had mischievously told him that sewer rats liked to attack humans but Pyke had dismissed this as fantastical. Yet alone in this damp, foul-smelling tunnel, he found himself stepping more cautiously through the sludge, trying not to step on or disturb any vermin.

For a hundred yards, the tunnel was sufficiently tall and wide for him to walk unimpeded, but after that it became narrower and smaller, so much so that, eventually, he was forced down on to his hands and knees, the stream of piss and shit glistening in the greasy lantern light. He felt a rat scurry past his hands and leapt up, banging his head against the brick ceiling. About fifty or sixty yards farther on, the tunnel expanded again, allowing him back on to his feet, and he followed its course for another ten minutes. There was a nest of rats ahead of him and Pyke panned through the soil to find something to throw at them. In the end, he found a rusty piece of metal and hurled it at the quivering mass of fur. Shrieks momentarily filled the tunnel and then the rats scurried off deeper into the darkness.

Fifty yards farther on, the tunnel widened again, and Pyke noticed a flight of steps cut into the wall; he decided to follow them. At the top, he found himself in what looked to be some kind of underground crypt or cellar, a large room with brick walls and a high ceiling. Placing the lantern on the floor, he looked around him and spotted a make-shift bed and a rotten table and chair in one corner, with a rusty copper pot perched on some charred embers.

'Phillip?'

His voice echoed around the cavernous chamber. He waited for a response but heard nothing.

'Phillip?'

Could someone really live in such a place?

Moving towards the bed, Pyke's wellington boots squelched through the slush.

Next to the bed was an old wooden cabinet, guarded by a rusty padlock. He retrieved his jemmy and prised the door open. The cabinet was filled with a collection of glass jars, each one filled with liquid and some kind of matter. He picked up one of them and took it over to the lantern. Two eyeballs floating in water stared back at him. The shock of it almost caused him to drop the jar. As he unscrewed the lid, the smell of vinegar was unmistakable. Pyke prodded one of the eyeballs with his finger and watched it sink down to the bottom of the jar then rise up to the surface again. It looked as harmless as a hard-boiled egg. Taking the lantern across to the cabinet, he found another four jars, each with two eyeballs in them. Bile licked the back of his throat. Even the thought of what he might be looking at made Pyke feel weak. Something darted through the mud, a rat perhaps; the suddenness of the movement startled him and the jar slipped through his fingers, shattering on the ground. Bending over, Pyke picked up one of the stranded eyeballs and cupped it in his hand. It felt cold and slimy, not quite real.

'Phillip?'

He completed a brief search of the room but found nothing else of significance; he left the eyeballs where he'd found them.

Having retraced his steps down into the tunnel, he decided to push on rather than turn around, to see where the tunnel led. He didn't doubt that he'd just found Phillip Malvern's living quarters but he tried not to jump to any conclusions. Given what he had just seen, though, it was hard not to. Had Phillip Malvern killed Mary Edgar, Lucy Luckins and perhaps others? The evidence, or what he'd seen in the jars, seemed to speak for itself.

Ahead, he saw something, a large, unmoving object silhouetted against the ooze. Moving towards it, he brought the lantern up to his eyes, already fighting off a queasy feeling in his stomach.

'Phillip?'

Now he could see the outline of someone's shoulders and also their head. He also saw a swarm of rats jostling for position around the corpse. Without thinking what he was doing, he ran at the rats, shouting. They dispersed as soon as they saw him. Putting the lantern down in the soil, Pyke turned the body over, expecting to see the weather-beaten face of an old man. In fact, it was hard to tell whether the corpse was male or female, such was the extent of the decomposition. In the end, though, he decided it was a woman. What little skin remained on the face was soggy and bloated and had been gnawed by rats.

But it was the two eye sockets which drew his attention; empty holes that looked back at him where the eyeballs had once been. Removing the handkerchief from his mouth, Pyke turned away from the corpse and retched.

A while later, he summoned up the strength to give the corpse a more thorough examination. One of the hands was buried in the soil and it was only after he'd excavated it that he noticed the ring; a silver ring adorned by a dirty amethyst stone bearing a serpent motif. He'd seen the same one on Bessie Daniels's finger. He brought the lantern closer but the corpse was too decomposed for him to make a positive identification, so he turned his attention back to the ring. Without question, it was the one he'd seen Bessie Daniels wearing while she'd posed for Crane's daguerreo-types. In itself, Pyke knew that the ring wasn't conclusive proof that the corpse was, in fact, Bessie Daniels but for the moment there wasn't any other apparent explanation for the ring's presence on the corpse's finger. Now, since much of the flesh had decomposed, the ring slipped off her finger with ease.

The last time he had seen Bessie, she'd smiled at him and giggled, under the influence of laudanum. Now she looked like a carcass you might come across in Field's slaughterhouse. He'd had a chance to help her and hadn't taken it. Now she was dead. That was all he could think about as he retraced his path along the tunnel.

Back on Dowgate Hill, he took the twine, tied one end of it to a post and let it unravel as he walked northwards along the narrow street, away

453

from the river, in the direction of the Bank of England. Crossing Cannon Street, he continued towards the Bank, eventually passing Mansion House on his right before stepping out on to Cornhill. The ball of twine had nearly unravelled completely. Pyke crossed the road, walked right the way up to the Bank's outer wall and cut the twine with his teeth, letting the remnants fall to the ground. From there, he retraced his path to the river, gathering up the twine as he went.

At the mouth of the tunnel, Pyke tied one end of the twine around one of the legs of the wharf and set off in the same direction he'd headed in earlier, allowing the twine to spool through his hands as he went. It ran out before he'd reached the steps leading up to Malvern's chamber. At the exact spot where the twine ended, he inspected the brickwork above him, moving forward inch by inch, looking for any gaps or loose bricks.

It took him half an hour of painstaking scrutiny to find what he was looking for: a few loose bricks. Once he'd prised them out, he was staring at a hole almost the same size as he was.

It was four in the afternoon by the time the driver of the hackney carriage dropped Pyke outside Fitzroy Tilling's house, and already darkness was beginning to gnaw at the edges of the plum-coloured sky. It had been a cooler afternoon and there was a hint of rain in the air, the first drops since Pyke had returned from the West Indies.

Pyke had washed in a tub in the back yard of his house and had changed his clothes, but he could still smell the raw sewage on his skin and inside his nostrils.

Tilling answered the door as soon as Pyke knocked. His thinning hair was damp with perspiration and the worry lines on his forehead suggested that the news wasn't good.

In the front room, an old ginger cat was asleep on one of the chairs and it was joined by a younger cat, slim, with sleek grey fur. Shrugging apologetically, Tilling mumbled, 'You have a child, I have two cats,' as he poured them both a gin. There was something warmer about Tilling's manner, as though their recent disagreements – and the way in which Pyke had betrayed him – had, for the time being, been put to one side.

'Well?'

'I tracked down Lord Bedford's butler. He was frightened of something but eventually I managed to get the truth from him.' Tilling tipped back his gin, the spirit barely touching the sides of his throat. 'It seems you were right about Mary Edgar staying with Bedford. The butler confirmed it, after I'd threatened him with prison if he didn't cooperate.'

'But that's good news, isn't it?' Pyke said, still trying to make sense of Tilling's sombre expression.

'I found him in St Albans. I was going to bring him back to London and take him to see Mayne. But he gave me the slip before we could board the stagecoach. Said he needed to go for a piss. I looked everywhere for him but couldn't find him. He was scared of me, but he was definitely more frightened of someone else.'

'You think he knows who killed Bedford?'

'I asked him; he swore he didn't. But he knows something.'

Pyke absorbed this news, trying to work out what it could mean. 'What happens now?'

'I went to see Mayne, told him what I'd found out from the butler.'

'And?'

'My word on its own is not enough. Even with the butler's corroboration, it wouldn't be sufficient to earn Morel-Roux a reprieve. Mayne told me that unless I could find some hard evidence *proving* Morel-Roux was set up, he won't be able to intervene and take the matter to the Home Secretary.'

'So an official pardon is out of the question.'

Tilling's stare was listless. 'It looks very much that way.'

'In which case Morel-Roux will be executed first thing on Monday morning.' It was already Saturday afternoon.

Tilling stared down into the empty glass.

'Can I ask you a question?' Pyke looked directly at him. 'Do you believe Morel-Roux murdered Bedford?'

'*Me?* What I believe isn't important right now. It's what can be proved.'

Pyke nodded, as if this were the response he had been expecting. 'The question is what we're prepared to do about it.'

'What *can* we do? Our hands are tied.'

'Are they?'

Tilling lifted up the sleeping cats, sat down in the armchair and rearranged them on his lap. He motioned for Pyke to sit in the other chair. 'What do you mean by that?'

'Could you arrange a visit to Morel-Roux's cell tomorrow night, under the guise of trying to elicit a last-minute confession?'

'Isn't that the job of the ordinary?'

'What I meant to ask was whether you could get *me* into the prison so I could talk to him.'

'Out of the question.' Tilling licked his lips. 'How would I do that?'

'You could always requisition a constable's uniform for me. I could be your assistant.'

Tilling shrugged, evidently not delighted by this prospect. 'It's possible, I suppose, but what good would talking to him serve?'

'If you can get me into the prison, I'll take care of the rest.'

'The rest?' But Pyke could see that Tilling was beginning to understand what he was suggesting. 'Oh, no. God, no. They'd hang you if they caught you. Me, too, if I was stupid enough to help you.'

'If Morel-Roux did kill Bedford and Mary Edgar, I'll force a confession out of him. If he didn't, an innocent man is going to die unless we do something. I can't sit around and wait for it to happen.'

For his part, Pyke had gone over and over the evidence in his head and he couldn't see any reason why Morel-Roux would have murdered both Lord Bedford *and* Mary Edgar. And why would he have killed her in such a grotesque fashion?

'It just isn't possible to break into the prison and help a man to escape. Anyway, he'll be under constant supervision.'

'There *is* a way. There's always a way.'

'You've actually given this matter some thought, haven't you?' Tilling stared at him, incredulous.

'I won't deny it's risky. And you'll do well to come out of it with your position in the New Police still intact.'

'What about the risk you're running? You have a young lad who depends on you. I just have a couple of cats,' Tilling said, stroking the ginger one's ears. Pyke could hear it purring from across the room.

He walked over to the window and stared out towards the heath. He'd always liked the view from Tilling's front room. 'What if I could offer you something by way of recompense – something that would make you look good in the eyes of your peers?' He turned around to face Tilling.

'Such as?'

'Jemmy Crane wrapped up in a nice little box with a ribbon tied around it.'

'You'll have to be more specific.'

'All right.' Pyke took a deep breath. 'What if I told you that Crane had managed to find a way into the Bank of England's bullion vault via an old sewer tunnel that runs directly beneath it?'

That made Tilling sit up and take notice. 'That's why you asked me about the Bank of England yesterday?'

'It will happen some time tomorrow night, I'd guess, as people gather for the hanging. Certainly before the bank opens for business on Monday morning.'

'Jesus,' Tilling muttered. He stood up abruptly, spilling both of the cats and his empty glass of gin on to the floor. 'Jesus,' he said again, shaking his head. 'You'd better sit down and tell me what you've found out.'

'So you're interested?'

Tilling took out a handkerchief and wiped his forehead. 'Of course I'm interested. The question is what do we do about it.'

Pyke waited for a moment. 'You need to call a meeting of all of the guards in the governor's office first thing tomorrow morning.'

'Then what?' Tilling still seemed shocked by Pyke's revelation.

'Then you work out how you're going to set a trap for Crane and his men.'

Later that night, after he had arrived home, Pyke looked in on Felix and watched him sleep, an ache building in his gut. The idea of not being part of his life, of not seeing him grow up to be a man, made Pyke feel so ill at ease that he came within a whisker of calling off his plans.

What did he really care about the Swiss valet anyway?

As he passed in and out of sleep, his dreams took him back to Jamaica and, later, while it was still dark outside, he lay in his bed, listening to himself breathe. Images drifted through his mind like fast-moving clouds. He'd seen something in his dream; something significant. Drawing air into his lungs, he tried to relax, tried to remember what it was, but it wouldn't come to him. Lying still, he closed his eyes and let his mind go blank. Later, just as he was drifting back to sleep, he heard a voice call out to him. *Whatever happens, don't think bad of me. I don't think I could bear it if you thought badly of me.*

But there was another voice, too, and almost at once he realised it belonged to Harriet Alefounder.

I was a long way away and my eyesight isn't what it used to be but I swear there was a little of her, of the Malvern woman, in this mulatto girl.

TWENTY-SEVEN

As he was crossing the street, a carriage came to a halt in front of him, almost blocking his path. The door swung open and Pyke found Harold Field pointing a pistol at his chest. Matthew Paxton, Field's second-in-command, held a brass-cannoned blunderbuss in both hands and grinned.

Pyke had just returned from the tunnel that ran under the bullion vault at the Bank of England and his trousers and boots smelled of decomposing flesh and faeces.

'Get in, Pyke.' Putting a cigar to his lips, Field inhaled, opened his mouth slightly and let the smoke drift out through the open glass. 'Save my friend here the ignominy of having to kill you in broad daylight.'

Pyke did as he was told and sat down next to Paxton. The carriage moved forward and Field pulled up the glass.

'I was under the impression I'd paid off my debt,' Pyke said, trying to keep his tone measured.

'After your wilful destruction of Crane's shop –
which on a personal level I applaud, by the way –
I couldn't run the risk of you disrupting the
man's plans any further.'

'Why? Are the two of you partners now?'

'Reluctant ones, perhaps. Let's just say we've
arrived at a necessary agreement.' Field sniffed
the air in the carriage. 'Is that you, bringing your
stink into my domain?'

Pyke ignored the question. 'Necessary for
whom?'

'For Crane, of course. When he discovered I
had his mistress in my possession, let's just say he
was persuaded to accept my terms.'

Pyke felt his stomach jolt. 'You've got Elizabeth
Malvern?' It explained why he'd found her front
door unhinged and her house ransacked.

'I believe I might have you to thank for that,'
Field said nonchalantly, inspecting the end of his
cigar.

'You had someone follow me.'

'And you *didn't* let me down. I'm told you spent
a fair amount of time in her company.' Field blew
smoke into Pyke's face and smiled. 'I hear she
has a rather ... unusual sexual appetite – that she
likes it hard and violent. I'm very much looking
forward to satisfying her wishes.'

Pyke lunged at Field but, before he was out of
his seat, Paxton had brought the end of the
blunderbuss up to his throat.

'If you move again, my young friend here will
pull the trigger.' Field took the cigar and rammed
the burning ash down on to Pyke's knuckles.

Pyke grunted rather than screamed, even

461

though the pain was excruciating.

Field was just a few feet from his face, his oiled whiskers shining in the half-light of the carriage. 'I have to say, I'm a little disappointed in you, Pyke. I thought we understood each other perfectly.'

Pyke tried not to let the pain, and a sense of panic, affect his thinking. 'Bessie Daniels is dead. I think Crane killed her and tossed her away like a piece of rubbish.'

Field's stare was cold and lifeless. 'I'm sorry to hear that. I really am. She was a good girl. I'll make sure her family are taken care of.'

In spite of his predicament, Pyke couldn't help himself. 'That's it? Once she'd been sold to Crane, you used her, put her in even more danger than she was already in and then you sat back and let her be sacrificed?'

'She knew the risks she was taking,' Field said, smoothing his hair with the palms of his hands. 'Anyway, your misplaced sense of ethics is beginning to bore me.'

'Her blood is on your hands.' Pyke waited for a moment, contemplating the wisdom of what he was about to say. 'Your mother would be turning in her grave if she could see you now.'

Field's gaze turned to wax and, for a moment, no one in the carriage spoke. 'I did intend to allow you to live, Pyke. I really did.' He shook his head.

Leaning forward, Field tapped on the roof of the carriage and waited for the horses to come to a complete stop. He opened the door, climbed down on to the pavement, pulled down the glass and peered back into the carriage. His sense of disappointment was palpable. 'I don't care what you do,' he said to Paxton. 'I don't ever want to see or hear or read about him again. Just make him go away.'

With that, Field slammed the door and set off along the pavement, not once bothering to turn around, almost as though, in his own mind, Pyke had already ceased to exist.

As they moved off, Pyke glanced out of the window and concluded they were heading down St John's Street in the direction of Smithfield and perhaps Field's slaughterhouse.

'I'd say this is the end of the road for you,' Paxton said, as if this idea somehow pleased him. He wasn't much older than a boy but his hand wasn't trembling and his gaze remained calm, composed even. His index finger was curled around the trigger in preparation for firing. Pyke thought of the way he'd looked at the coins on the card table after Field had murdered his whist partner.

'Have you ever seen a bar of gold?' Pyke waited. 'Have you ever picked one up, felt how heavy it is?'

Paxton regarded him lazily.

'If you like, I can show you one. I might even let you keep it.' He watched Paxton's face to see his reaction. 'A bar of gold is worth about eight hundred pounds. A good receiver might give you five hundred.' He paused. 'How much did you earn last year?' Paxton didn't answer immediately, so he went on, 'I thought so. Nothing like that figure, was it?'

Paxton licked his lips. 'I ain't complaining.'

Pyke met his gaze and waited. 'You're not afraid of him, are you?'

'Everyone's afraid of Harold Field. Even you. I

saw it in your eyes after he burned you with his cigar.'

'I'm scared of the Harold Field I once knew, before you were even born. But now he's getting older and perhaps a little careless. You've seen it but you haven't said anything to him. You've just been watching, waiting, biding your time.'

'Is that so?' Paxton kept the blunderbuss pointed at Pyke's chest but his face had already betrayed his interest.

'And part of you, a little part at the back of your head, has been wondering what would happen if Field wasn't around. Who would take over?'

'You'd never get close enough to do it. He'd see you coming.'

'But he wouldn't suspect you, would he?'

Paxton shook his head and tightened his grip around the handle of the blunderbuss. 'That's as far as this conversation goes. I pull the trigger, you're a dead man.'

'But you're not going to because you're thinking about that gold bar.' Pyke looked into his face. 'How about I make it two gold bars? If you were careful, you could clear a thousand.'

For a while neither of them spoke. Through the smeared glass, Pyke could see that they were nearing Smithfield. Paxton wiped his forehead with the sleeve of his coat and finally put down the blunderbuss.

'We'll make a policeman of you yet,' Fitzroy Tilling said, when he saw Pyke in the blue, swallow-tailed frock-coat and matching trousers. The brass buttons had been done up to the top

464

and Pyke was carrying, rather than wearing, the tall stovepipe hat. He had hidden a knife, a jemmy, a cudgel, a length of chain and a padlock inside the hat and had wrapped as much rope as he could get away with around his chest and waist, before putting on the coat, which was a few sizes too large for him.

Tilling took a swig of gin straight from the bottle, wiped his mouth on his sleeve and passed it to Pyke.

'A turnkey smells that on your breath, he'll be suspicious right away.'

'You're right.' He put the bottle down and went to stroke the old ginger cat. 'You'll be all right without me, won't you, Tom?' The cat lifted its head slightly and purred but didn't move from the chair.

Pyke pulled out his watch and checked the time. 'We should get going. The service will be finished by now and they'll be taking him back to his cell.'

Morel-Roux would have been led in chains to the 'condemned' pew and forced to beg for God's forgiveness in front of other prisoners and dignitaries invited by the governor. Pyke could only begin to imagine the depths of the man's despair. He would perhaps be thinking of the moment on the gallows when the plank would be kicked away, wondering whether he'd feel pain, life and death colliding in the blink of an eye, and also perhaps whether the hangman would have to pull down on his legs to finish the job.

'Is everything in place at the Bank?'

Tilling nodded. 'The Home Office nearly

insisted the hanging take place behind closed doors. Someone's clearly worried that the crowds might be influenced by the radicals.'

'And the guards?' Pyke asked, even though he knew that Tilling had called a meeting earlier that morning involving all the soldiers responsible for guarding the Bank.

'Before I went to see the governor, the plan had been to deploy them around the outer walls in case of an attack by radicals.'

Pyke immediately understood the significance of this. It meant that the bullion vault would have been left unguarded and, as such, explained why Crane had waited until now to execute his robbery.

'In any case,' Tilling added, 'the soldiers all know what to do, and I'll be joining them, if all goes well tonight.'

Pyke didn't answer him and tried not to think about all the things that could go wrong with their plan.

'You know, I've never actually broken the law before.' Tilling looked around his living room, as though for the last time. 'Not once, in my whole life. This will be the first time.'

Pyke felt a trickle of sweat snake its way down his lower back. 'You said the other day that the law is a blunt instrument. In this instance, it's so blunt that an innocent man will die unless we do something.'

'But if I do this, how will I be different from...'

'From me?'

Tilling's forehead was thick with perspiration. 'Can I ask you a question, Pyke?'

'Of course.'

'Are you afraid?'

'Yes, of course.' He thought about it for a moment. 'I've got more to lose now than I ever did.'

'Good.' Tilling put on a brave smile. 'Because I'm absolutely petrified.'

They knocked on the door of the governor's house at half-past six and were shown into an office on the right-hand side of the passage, where a turnkey met them and took them into another room. Here Tilling signed the book for both of them, Pyke as PC William Dell, and afterwards they followed the turnkey through another door, which brought them to the lodge. Pyke recognised the collection of heavy irons fixed to the wall; it was here that one of his escape bids had floundered ten years earlier. He kept his head down and no one paid him any attention. Certainly the turnkey who acted as their guide hadn't wanted to search them or ask them to turn out their pockets, but that was to be expected. After all, Tilling was the third or fourth most senior figure in the New Police. From the lodge they passed through a heavy oak gate bound with iron and studded with nails that was guarded by another turnkey, and went down a few steps into a gloomy stone passage lit only by candles, which they followed as far as another gate that led into a narrow yard. The air smelled stale and dead, and it was hard not to be affected by the feeling of oppression and doom that seemed to seep through the thick granite walls. They crossed the paved yard and were admitted through an iron gate into a narrow passage that led to another door and eventually into the space where the condemned building was located. Pyke could feel the blood rising in his chest and his stomach begin to churn.

The press yard was a narrow, paved court with sheer granite walls protected at the top by inward-projecting iron spikes. Even a brief glance up to the top of the wall made Pyke feel dizzy. At the end of the yard, they were ushered directly into the condemned building, bypassing the press rooms where Morel-Roux would be pinioned early in the morning before his lonely walk through the prison. After following their guide along another dark passage and up a narrow staircase, they finally came upon the cells. The turnkey explained that the prisoner had been removed from the day room at about five and would be allowed a candle in his cell until ten. There were three turnkeys sitting on stools outside Morel-Roux's cell. Tilling explained that he would wait in the passage with the turnkeys while Pyke – PC Dell – questioned the condemned man. No one thought to query his judgement.

The cell was a stone dungeon, eight feet by six feet, with a wooden bench at the upper end, an iron candlestick affixed to the wall and a small, high window reinforced with a double row of iron bars. It was hard for Pyke to fathom just how much Morel-Roux had changed – or wasted away – in the two and a half months since they had last conversed. Even then he had seemed thin, but the circumstances of his trial and the imminent prospect of facing the gallows had clearly taken their toll. His arms and face were emaciated and his neck was so thin it looked as if it might slip through the noose. He barely looked up when Pyke entered the cell and his eyes were dull and unfocused. Pyke waited for the door to be closed and bolted before he took off his stovepipe hat. His hair was matted with sweat. Morel-Roux was sitting on the bench and it took him a few moments to place Pyke's face. When he did, his expression barely changed. He was resigned to his own death, and for a moment Pyke wondered how the valet would react to the hope he was offering.

'What do you want?'

Pyke took another step into the cell. 'You didn't kill Lord Bedford, did you?'

Morel-Roux gave him a puzzled stare. 'I tried to tell you that before my trial.'

'Well, this time I believe you.'

That drew a strange chuckle. 'Doesn't do me much good now, does it?'

'That's why I'm here.' Pyke hesitated. 'I'm going to get you out of here.'

Morel-Roux sat up. His face looked pasty and wan in the flickering candlelight. 'Is that right?' The tone suggested mockery.

Pyke took out a piece of paper with a roughly sketched map of the prison, indicating the route Morel-Roux would take in the morning to Debtors' Door and the scaffold.

'Have you made your confession yet?' He put the map down on the bench for Morel-Roux to look at.

'Earlier today they made me stand in this pew, painted black, and the ordinary told me to confess my sins before God.' He shook his head. 'I refused to even look at him.'

'Good.' Pyke pointed to the map and described the route. 'Just here,' he said, indicating the yard beyond the press yard. 'You're going to break down *just here* and demand the right to unburden yourself before God.' He paused. 'The governor, the sheriffs, the under-sheriffs, everyone in the procession, will want you to make your confession on the gallows. They won't want to keep the mob waiting and a confession on the gallows makes for good theatre. But you're going to have to be firm. Tell the ordinary you'll unburden yourself to him, and him alone, in the chapel. It *has* to be the chapel. Of course, they won't leave you and the ordinary alone in the chapel but insist on some kind of privacy. Make it clear that you intend to make a full and frank confession. The ordinary won't need to be convinced. There's a lot of interest in this execution and he'll be thinking about the money he could make from selling an account of your confession.'

Morel-Roux looked at the map and then at Pyke. His expression had changed. 'I think you're being serious.'

'Of course I'm being serious. I'm in your cell the night before your execution. If they find out I'm not a police officer, I'll face transportation.'

The valet's eyes went back to the map. 'But can it really be done?' He sounded dazed.

'If you do your bit, I'll take care of the rest.' Pyke pointed at the map. 'Commit it to memory and then eat it.' He turned around and banged on the door.

'Pyke?'

He put his finger to his lips and whispered, 'The chapel.'

The door swung open and Pyke stepped out into the passage. He put the hat back on his head and said, to the turnkeys as much as Tilling, 'In spite of the new evidence I presented, he still refuses to acknowledge his guilt.'

'You did your best, sir,' one of the turnkeys muttered. 'The good Lord will judge him for what he did.'

Pyke lowered his head and followed Tilling and their guide back along the passage and down the stone steps into the yard. They walked through the yard in silence and passed through the two gates. The turnkey there acknowledged them with a curt nod and muttered, 'Goodnight, sir.' Pyke glanced across at the steps leading up to the chapel, where Morel-Roux would stage his dramatic, last-minute act in the morning, but he would have to find another way to get back there. If he wasn't seen leaving the prison, his absence would be noted and the alarm raised. It didn't matter that he was a policeman, in their eyes at least. They passed through one gate, followed the passage as far as the other gate, and waited while their guide banged on the door. A few stone steps took them back up into the lodge, where the turnkey gave them an awkward nod and asked whether they needed any assistance. When Tilling told him they would be fine, he disappeared back down the steps into the bowels of the prison. The gatekeeper unlocked the door that opened on to Old Bailey. Knowing that this was his last chance, Pyke told

471

Tilling he'd left his stick in the office in the governor's house and that he'd meet him outside. The gatekeeper didn't seem overly concerned by this, and didn't try to accompany Pyke back along the passage to the room with the book. Alone, Pyke took a breath and tried another door leading off this room. To his relief it wasn't locked. He stepped into what he supposed was part of the governor's house, shut the door behind him and waited. If the gatekeeper didn't double-check that Pyke had left, he would be all right. He was at one end of a dark, gloomy passage which he followed to a door at the other end. Making as little noise as possible, he opened the door and stepped into the hallway. He could hear voices coming from one of the rooms as he tiptoed across the polished floor in the opposite direction, towards the staircase, which he mounted two steps at a time. Dripping with sweat, he paused briefly at the top of the stairs, listening for any further voices. When all appeared to be silent, he let himself into what turned out to be an unoccupied guest bedroom. He closed the door behind him and sat down on the edge of the bed. It was about eight in the evening and already people would be starting to gather outside the prison in anticipation of the hanging. He had the rest of the night to try to find his way back into the chapel.

It took Pyke a while to get his bearings. The small, grated window, although locked, had a view of Newgate Street. He knew that the chapel, and also the press yard, backed on to Newgate Street, just as he knew, or had read, that the governor's house had no windows at the front and no views over the interior of the prison. All this meant that if he went to the very top of the governor's house and found the main chimney flume he might be able to clamber up inside it and find a way on to the roof.

He found the flume in what seemed to be an unused nursery and peered up into the darkness. Perhaps a young boy might have been able to clamber up there but Pyke quickly ruled it out for himself. In the other rooms, he inspected the ceiling for a hatch leading up into the attic, if indeed the building had one. After ten or so minutes, he found what he was looking for in one of the servant's rooms and, standing on the bed, managed to pull himself up through the space. Once in the attic, he slid the hatch back into place and waited for his eyes to adjust to the darkness. There would have to be some kind of light-well or opening on to the roof. He moved carefully across the wooden beams and looked out into the cavernous space. Ahead he could see a patch of light and a few minutes later he was standing on the roof, staring out across the city – Westminster Abbey in one direction, St Paul's gargantuan dome in the other.

The roof was flat and he was able to cross it with ease and look down into the Debtors' Quadrangle beside the yard he'd walked through earlier with Tilling. There was a drop of about twenty feet on to the roof of the chapel. He lowered himself off the roof as far as he was able and jumped, landing awkwardly but without turning his ankle. Standing up, Pyke hurried over to the edge of the roof and looked down into the garden of the Royal College of Physicians, which bordered the prison. The drop was somewhere between fifty and a hundred feet. Having removed the rope from around his shoulder, he tied one end of it around a stone balustrade and let the rest of it fall down the side of the chapel as near to one of the windows as possible. Then he took the stovepipe hat, removed his swallow-tailed coat and threw both items into the garden, where he could pick them up later. More comfortable in just trousers and a shirt, he rubbed his palms dry, made sure the knife and jemmy were within reach and took the rope in his hand. Carefully he lowered himself over the edge of the roof, gripped the rope with his hands, threaded it through his ankles and shimmied down it as far as the window, which was still a drop of seventy or so yards from the ground. Clasping the rope with one hand and threading it around his feet to take his weight, he jemmied the window open and manoeuvred himself into the gap. There, Pyke gathered in the rest of the rope and let it drop down inside the building. A minute later, he was again standing on solid ground, alone in the eerie solitude of the chapel.

His pocket watch said that it was only midnight but it felt later. About that time, he mused, a wagon would pull out of the prison's main gate and come to a halt by the black-painted door on Old Bailey. There, trained workers would take the poles and boarding and begin the task of assembling the scaffold. Meanwhile, wooden barriers would be erected around the perimeter of the scaffold to prevent the crowds from getting too close. With more than eight hours to go before the execution, much of Old Bailey would already be filled with people eager to secure a good spot to witness the spectacle, and the taverns, gin-neries and beer shops in the immediate vicinity would be heaving with customers. And since the murder and the trial had attracted so much attention – an aristocrat had been killed by his servant, after all, or so people had been led to believe – the crowd would be particularly sizeable. Some might even want to cheer Morel-Roux for what he was alleged to have done.

Pyke wandered over to the condemned pew, a huge black pen, where he had sat bound and silent ten years earlier. Then, he'd been accused of murdering his mistress, but just like the valet he had held his tongue, refusing to participate in the charade and offering no confession to the ordinary.

Little had changed in the intervening years and the chapel remained a desolate place, even more so now it was silent and deserted. The bare pulpit, the sturdy altar table and the unpainted benches all stood in stark contrast to the plush appointments of many modern churches. Prisoners awaiting execution had, at one time, been forced to look down at their own coffins but such a practice had been stopped because some felt it too barbaric. Pyke had often wondered about this logic; for wasn't it also barbaric to execute people in public? Or to execute anyone at all?

A little later, he lay down on one of the hard, wooden benches and closed his eyes.

He woke about five, though in truth he hadn't

really slept, at least not the kind of deep, satisfying sleep he was used to. The air was cool and stale in the chapel and it still felt eerily quiet, even though the crowds outside the prison would now be backing up the slope towards Snow Hill and Smithfield. They would be boisterous, too, as crowds always were on such days. Boisterous, vast and sprawling. Pyke estimated, there would be forty or fifty thousand people crammed into Old Bailey and the surrounding streets.

He stood up and stretched his legs. The cudgel, jemmy, knife, chain and padlock were laid out on the bench. He put the cudgel in his pocket and took the chain and padlock over to the door that Morel-Roux, a turnkey and the ordinary would use to enter the chapel. There was just enough chain to wrap around both door handles. He practised this a few times, snapping on the padlock at the end, and once he was happy that he could perform this exercise in just a few seconds, he went over to the table by the altar and, as quietly as could, dragged it across the stone floor to the main door.

Pyke checked his pocket watch for the fourth or fifth time since he'd woken. The time was a quarter past five. He had less than three hours to wait.

At half-past seven Pyke gathered himself and took up his position by the door. By now Morel-Roux would have been pinioned and handed over to the sheriffs and under-sheriffs and the slow walk to the scaffold would soon begin. The procession would include a turnkey at the front, closely followed by the sheriffs, under-sheriffs, the governor, the ordinary and, of course, the dead man walking. It would pass by the steps leading up to the chapel before continuing its path through the prison and down into the subterranean walkway that connected the prison and the Sessions House; a passage that would eventually bring them up into a room behind Debtors' Door. Pyke hoped they wouldn't get that far.

Even in the chapel, he could feel the expectation of the masses gathered in the streets outside the prison. For his part, he could hardly breathe, and his heart was thumping against his ribcage. He went across to the window and checked the rope for the third or fourth time that morning. One way or another it would soon be over.

The last thing he did was put on a black hood so that no one would be able to identify him.

At eight Pyke listened for the chimes of St Sepulchre's bells. The procession would be moving through the press yard. Any moment now, he hoped, Morel-Roux would break down and plead for a private audience with the ordinary. That would cause some delay but there was always a chance the sheriffs wouldn't allow him to confess in the chapel. It was five minutes past eight. He could hear something now, raised voices in the yard; footsteps coming towards him up the steps to the chapel. He heard someone insert a key into the door and turn it. The lock sprang open; the door opened inwards and light flooded into the chapel. The turnkey was first, closely followed by Morel-Roux and then the ordinary. Just the three of them. Pyke waited for the ordinary to close the door and heard him say, 'Why's the table by the door?' He gripped the cudgel in his right hand, and appeared suddenly from behind the door, knocking the turnkey out with a single blow to his skull. The ordinary shouted for help. Pyke brought the cudgel down on his head and pushed the table over to block the door. It took him just a few seconds to wrap the chain through the brass door handles and snap the padlock closed. Taking out his knife, Pyke cut through the leather restraints binding Morel-Roux's arms; there was nothing he could do about the chains around his ankles.

Morel-Roux hobbled towards the window; Pyke ran. He could hear shouting from the yard. Shinning up the rope, he waited on the ledge for the valet to do the same. Precious seconds ticked by. There wasn't much strength in Morel-Roux's arms and it took longer than Pyke expected for him to reach the ledge. The shouts from the yard were louder and the banging on the door became more violent. The chain wouldn't hold for much longer; he pulled up the rope and fed it through the open window. Morel-Roux, who hadn't spoken a word, looked out of the window and down into the garden below. It was a sheer drop of about fifty feet.

'I'm terrified of heights,' he said, holding on to the wall with both hands. He was having difficulty breathing.

Pyke ignored him; he didn't take this warning seriously. 'Follow me.' He climbed out of the window and started to shimmy down the rope towards the ground. He let it slide through his hands, ignoring the pain. When the rope ran out, he prepared himself for a moment and let go, landing cleanly on flagstones in the yard. He looked up, expecting to see Morel-Roux almost at the bottom of the rope, but the valet was still up on the ledge. His whole body was shaking. He looked down at Pyke and screamed, *'I'm scared of heights.'*

'Move.'

Then Pyke saw other faces at the window, hands grabbing the valet, pulling him back into the chapel.

He ran to find the coat and hat he'd thrown from the roof and made for the gate at the far end of the wall.

Pyke didn't witness the hanging but later he read accounts of it by Thackeray and Dickens and he overheard people talk about it in taverns and ginneries; how Morel-Roux, suited in black with his shirt open and hands tied in front of him, had walked firmly across the scaffold and without being told had positioned himself under the beam; how Calcraft had put the night cap over the valet's face and head; how the plank had been kicked away from under him; how it had taken some time for Morel-Roux to die and how Calcraft had had to seize his quivering legs and pull them down until the quivering stopped. Thackeray had used his column to underline his bond with the 'gentle, good-natured' crowd, attack the debauched profligacy of those occupying the better vantage points in the upstairs of shops and public houses, affirm the 'wise laws' that encouraged forty thousand people to witness the execution, attack Dickens for his *ex parte* truth-telling about criminals and prostitutes and record his horror and shame at witnessing another man's death. Pyke preferred Boz's account: it didn't dwell on the details but mounted a coruscating assault on the evils of capital punishment and asked the question that Pyke had posed to himself: what was actually gained by watching another man die? But even this piece was dry and reflective: it didn't capture what Pyke had felt, his anger at Morel-Roux, his disgust at the law and his guilt at still being alive. He could have done more; he could have lobbied harder; he could have found out who'd *really* killed Bedford earlier; he could have acted more decisively. He should have seen it earlier; what had really happened; who was to blame. He felt weak and powerless. For weeks after it happened, he lay awake and imagined the moment when Calcraft had seized the valet's legs and pulled.

TWENTY-EIGHT

At ten thirty Pyke presented himself to one of the red-coated porters at the entrance to the Bank of England on Threadneedle Street and was escorted from there, across a small, well-kept court-yard and past the Rotunda, to the interconnecting meeting rooms occupied by the Bank's governor and directors. He found Tilling in the main saloon and saw, from the look on his old friend's face, that something had gone wrong.

'Crane and five of his accomplices have just

been moved to the City of London's chief police office at Guildhall.'

'Isn't that good news?'

Tilling waved at someone on the other side of the room and indicated he'd join the man presently. 'The soldiers didn't wait as they'd been instructed to, so Crane and the others were still in the vault.'

Pyke felt his stomach tightening. It was the one glaring weakness in his plan – that the soldiers would grow impatient and strike too soon. The hole from the sewer emerged directly outside the guards' room – which was why Crane had picked that night, when he'd been told that all the soldiers would be patrolling elsewhere. 'But they were all caught in the vault, right? That's enough to lock them away for years, isn't it? At least for treason?'

'I'm afraid it gets worse.'

'*Worse?*'

'I've just talked to the governor. He tells me he's spoken with one of his directors – a man by the name of Trevelyan, Abel Trevelyan – who reckons he was contacted by Crane about a week ago. He's ready to swear under oath that Crane came to him, in good faith, with news that an acquaintance of his, a sewer-man no less, had found a way of accessing the bullion vault from a tunnel running directly beneath it. So what happened today, at least according to Trevelyan, is nothing more than an exercise on Crane's part, as a well-intentioned citizen, to demonstrate to the directors that the vault is vulnerable to robbers. Or worse still, to radicals.'

'And they're actually prepared to believe that?'

'Trevelyan didn't tell the governor about it, didn't tell anyone about it, so he'll have to resign his post. But the governor told me he doesn't want to take the matter any further. From his point of view, it's embarrassing enough that Crane and his accomplices managed to break into the vault. If they're charged and the incident is made public, he'll become a laughing stock. The Bank's status and viability as a going concern depend on its absolute impregnability. The damage to its reputation would be incalculable if investors discovered that Crane was effectively able to walk into its most secure rooms.'

'And what do the police think?'

'I spoke with the commissioner of the City of London police a few moments ago. He'll be swayed by the governor's recommendation.'

Pyke felt the anger swelling up inside him. 'You say Crane and the others have been taken to the police office at the Guildhall?'

'That's right.'

'And the constables who took them there; you made sure they knew not to let anyone speak to or even approach Crane.'

'I made that point as firmly as I could but the New Police doesn't have any jurisdiction here.'

Pyke swore under his breath. Everything was starting to unravel. Crane might even be released in a matter of hours. 'Have you talked to this man Trevelyan?'

'The governor wouldn't let me. Apparently he's made a statement to the commissioner of the City police.'

'Surely before they actually let Crane go free,

they'll need some kind of confirmation about the sewer-man?'

Tilling nodded. 'That's where Crane's story is weakest. He says he doesn't know where this man is.'

Pyke let this remark pass without comment.

'But apparently Crane has suggested that, if and when he's located, the sewer-man could make a statement to his lawyer, in front of a witness, to corroborate his story.'

'Why not to the police?' Pyke hesitated, thinking about Phillip Malvern. 'And anyway, surely Crane's in no position to dictate terms to anyone. If he knows where the man is, he should tell someone and have done with it.'

'That's why they took him away to the cells. For now. But I'd guess that if a credible statement is produced, that will be enough to ensure Crane's release.'

Pyke gave this some thought. 'The question is, how's he going to arrange all this from inside his cell?'

'Someone will have to come to him, but for the time being no one knows where he's being held.'

'Trevelyan knows.'

Tilling contemplated what Pyke had just said. 'Go on.'

'The story about Crane performing a public service is utter tripe. We both know it. We just need to find out why Trevelyan is willing to corroborate Crane's story.'

Tilling scratched his head. 'You think he's been coerced into doing so?'

'Crane's smarter than I gave him credit for. He

planned for this, for something going wrong. You're right, I think he *knew* that Trevelyan would have to support his story.'

'And lose his position at the bank in the process?'

Pyke shrugged. 'What if he was a customer of Crane's shop? Better to lose his job than be unveiled by Crane as some kind of sexual monster.' He looked around the saloon. 'Can you point Trevelyan out to me?'

'I don't think he's here.' Tilling's gaze swept the room. 'He's been shut away in the governor's chambers all morning.'

'Can you at least describe him to me and find his address?'

That drew a heavy frown. 'I won't countenance any private action...'

The man who'd waved to Tilling earlier had returned and was loitering as if he needed to speak with Tilling as a matter of urgency.

'What if I could persuade someone close to Crane, someone he trusts *absolutely*, to go and see him and find out the whereabouts of the sewerman?'

'Could you do that?'

'I might be able to.'

Samuel Ticknor was sitting at his desk in his private office, drinking a cup of tea, when Pyke pushed open the door.

'How well did you know Elizabeth Malvern?'

Pyke's sudden appearance in his office caused Ticknor to spill his tea. He tried to mop it up with the sleeve of his coat.

'How much time did you spend in her company – when she volunteered for the Vice Society?'

This time Ticknor met his gaze. Pyke had to stop himself from jumping over the desk and grabbing the man's throat.

'I knew her well enough to see her for what she really was.'

'Enough to remember what colour her eyes were?'

Ticknor removed his spectacles and blew on to the lenses. 'Green. They were green, no question about it.'

'You're sure?'

'Quite positive, sir. Now will you tell me what this is all about?'

Pyke stood there, trying to hold himself together. Different thoughts collided with one another in his head. He saw it clearly now; suddenly everything had fallen into place – about Mary, Elizabeth, the Malvern family, even Lord Bedford.

'I presume you know there's a rotten corpse out in the yard?' Godfrey said, as soon as Pyke had stepped into his basement shop.

'There wasn't anywhere else to put it.' The previous day, he had pushed Bessie Daniels' corpse on a costermonger's wheelbarrow, hidden under a canvas tarpaulin, from Dowgate Hill to St Paul's Yard. He'd told Godfrey he needed the keys to the shop, but not *why* he needed them. Now, clearly, his uncle had found out.

'And how long were you hoping to keep it out there?'

'Another day, two at most.'

Godfrey ran his hands through his bone-white hair and sighed. 'I called at the house to see you. Jo told me the news. I don't have to tell you what I think. You're mad to let her go, a complete fool.'

'I'm not letting her go. She's leaving.'

Godfrey pushed his spectacles back up his nose and made a dismissive gesture towards Pyke. At times like this, he felt like more of a father than an uncle to him and Pyke hated disappointing him.

'So who is it? I couldn't bring myself to give it a proper look.'

'Hard to tell for certain but I think it's Bessie Daniels. I found this ring on one of her fingers.' Pyke held up the amethyst ring for his uncle to see. 'The woman in the copperplate you bought from Crane.'

Godfrey collapsed into his armchair, suddenly looking his age. 'Jesus. Poor, poor girl. And to think...'

Pyke just nodded. His uncle was momentarily lost for words.

'Who killed her?' he said, after a while. 'Crane?'

'Looks that way.' Pyke drew in a breath. 'By to-morrow her corpse will be gone, I promise. But I have to do what I have to do. I hope you under-stand.'

'To punish those responsible?'

Pyke nodded again. Godfrey stood up, walked over to the sideboard, took the decanter and poured himself a glass of claret.

'I want you to talk to anyone who's worked at Crane's shop,' Pyke told Saggers, after he'd found him in the Cole Hole on The Strand. 'Be

486

discreet but offer a financial inducement to anyone who's willing to testify in court that a man called Abel Trevelyan was a customer there.'

'How much of a financial inducement?'

'Up to fifty pounds, depending on the quality of the testimony. To be paid if and when Crane is convicted.'

Saggers whistled, seemingly taken aback at the money Pyke was prepared to offer. 'You must want this testimony a lot.'

'I don't expect you to do this for nothing, if that's what you're suggesting.'

The fat man put on a wounded expression that was so clearly feigned even he gave up on it. 'Well, I *do* remember you promising me a story a long time ago.'

'Murder, pornography, robbery.' Pyke watched Saggers' nonchalance disappear. 'Is that enough to be getting on with?'

'That sounds more than acceptable.'

'And I want you to find anyone who knew a girl called Bessie Daniels.' Pyke handed Saggers a scrap of paper with Bessie's old Whitechapel address scribbled on it. 'Anyone, that is, who can identify this as belonging to her.' He took out the amethyst ring and showed it to the penny-a-liner. 'I can't let you have it, I'm afraid. You'll just have to describe it as best you can.'

Saggers inspected the ring and handed it back to Pyke. 'So how quickly do you need all this?'

'By tomorrow.'

Abel Trevelyan lived in a Palladian mansion overlooking Regent's Park. Pyke could see how some people might have been impressed by the house's neoclassical grandeur, and its size alone meant that it was hard to miss, even from the other side of the park. But he found it too ostentatious, as though an already over-egged pudding had been doused in cream and butter. It was a square brick box with five large bay windows on each of the floors. In the middle of the building, a pair of stone columns supported a pediment. There were extensive gardens at the back of the mansion. Earlier in the afternoon Pyke had positioned himself behind a shrub, close to one of the windows, and observed the comings and goings of the household. As far as he could work out, Trevelyan had a wife – a plump, dowdy creature who wore her hair in tight ringlets – and a number of young children. There were also as many as a dozen servants, and Pyke spent some of the afternoon speculating about how damaging the loss of his position at the Bank might prove to be. Trevelyan was definitely at home; from the description Pyke had been given, he recognised the man sitting at his desk in the ground-floor study at one end of the house. Trevelyan had been there for most of the afternoon, leaving only to take an early supper with his family at about six. Still, he had returned to his study by about half-past seven, and Pyke's patience was finally rewarded. Just as it was beginning to get dark, Trevelyan stepped out on to the veranda to smoke a cigar.

From the shrub, it was maybe twenty yards to where Trevelyan was standing, and Pyke watched him for a few moments, trying to get the measure of the man and work out how best to take advantage of the situation. Trevelyan was silver haired and suave, but he suffered from the same weak chin that afflicted many men of his class. He was tall but his shoulders were hunched, and he didn't look as if he would be able to handle himself in a fight. The fact that he couldn't stand still, but kept pacing around the veranda, puffing his cigar, was the clearest indication of his unease.

Even though he was only twenty yards away, Pyke still wasn't close enough to ambush him without the prospect of Trevelyan shouting for help. So he threw a stone high into the air and waited for it to land a few yards on the other side of his target. Startled, Trevelyan turned around and looked up at the roof and then towards the trees. Pyke moved quickly and quietly across the lawn; Trevelyan saw him only at the last moment and managed a muffled shout just as Pyke clubbed him with his cudgel. He went down without uttering another sound, and Pyke dragged him across the lawn to the line of trees. Still tense, Pyke waited for a few moments, to make sure no one had seen the assault from the house.

It took a hard slap with the palm of his hand to Trevelyan's face to bring him around. Pyke had already bound and gagged him and Trevelyan struggled to make sense of his changed circumstances.

Bending down, with his knife in hand, Pyke held the blade to Trevelyan's throat and pulled down the gag. 'Any sudden movement, any attempt to shout for help, *anything* at all that makes me nervous, and I'll slice through your veins and let you bleed to death. Nod your head if you understand.'

Trevelyan nodded; the terror he felt was reflected in his eyes.

'What Jemmy Crane told the police, about being a good citizen, was a lie. I don't need you to confirm it. What I *do* need to know is why you corroborated the lie.'

Trevelyan tried to speak but words failed him. Pyke pressed the blade a little deeper into the skin of his neck.

'What hold does Crane have over you?'

The director looked up at him imploringly. *'Please.'*

'You have a choice between life or death. If you don't tell me what I want to know, I'll kill you and not give it another thought. Is that what you want?'

Trevelyan started to sob. Pyke inhaled and could almost taste the, sourness of the man's sweat. He closed his fist and slapped Trevelyan around the face once more. That brought the man around. His eyes popped open and his jaw went slack.

'You're a customer of his, aren't you,' Pyke said, a statement rather than a question.

Trevelyan simply nodded.

'Did you know about his plan to break into the bullion vault?'

'I didn't think he was serious.' It came out as a whispered croak.

'So he told you?'

Trevelyan stared down at the ground. 'He wanted to know about the deployment of guards.'

'And what did you tell him?'

'That the guardroom is manned at night with soldiers from the Tower.' He swallowed, his eyes darting around. Pyke had to kick him to make him go on. 'I also told him that the guardroom is situated next to the entrance to the bullion vault.'

'But what about the arrangements for last night?' As one of the directors of the Bank, Trevelyan would have been privy to the decision to move the soldiers from the guardroom to the outer fortifications to protect the Bank from the mob that had come to see the hanging.

Trevelyan squirmed. Pyke kicked him again, harder this time; he was starting to lose patience. He could just imagine how Crane would have courted Trevelyan, charmed him, used him. *Let me show you this one, sir. Perhaps you'd like to see something warmer, sir? Something even warmer still? Let's see what can be done.* Sickness feeding sickness. The more depraved the better, as far as Crane was concerned. It would give him greater leverage over Trevelyan, so that the banker would have no choice but to answer all of Crane's questions or risk being exposed.

Pyke pulled the knife away, grabbed the banker's throat with both hands and started to squeeze. He wanted to finish the job but, in the end, he let go and waited while the older man spluttered and gasped for air.

'What you tell me here will remain between us. I just want the truth. If you tell me that, I'll let you go back to your family. But you have to believe me when I say your life holds about as much worth to me as a pig's.'

Sensing a reprieve, Trevelyan spoke quickly. 'I bought certain items from Crane.' He licked his lips. 'One thing led to another. I couldn't run the risk of him exposing me.'

The way he said it made it seem so simple, innocent even. Perhaps he still believed that none of it was his fault.

'Daguerreotypes?'

Trevelyan looked at him, his expression betraying both surprise and resignation. 'Yes.'

'Of what?'

'Initially just bedroom scenes.' He hesitated. 'Naked women.'

'But that wasn't enough, was it?'

The banker shook his head, finally starting to sob.

'Crane offered you something warmer.'

Trevelyan nodded. The idea that it was all Crane's fault appealed to the banker.

Pyke asked, 'Did he sell you a daguerreotype featuring a woman with a hare-lip?'

The banker's eyes gave him away. He knew it, too, and didn't try to lie. He nodded but wouldn't meet Pyke's eyes.

'Have you still got the picture he sold you?'

'I came home this morning after...' His hands were trembling. 'I destroyed them, every last one.' For the first time, something approaching defiance entered his voice.

Pyke had expected as much. He thought about the daguerreotype Crane had sold Godfrey's friend. How much worse could it get?

'Her name was Bessie Daniels. She used to be a prostitute. She was sold to Crane for five guineas.' Pyke took a breath and swallowed; his throat felt uncomfortable. 'She's dead. She was strangled but I think you knew that already.'

Trevelyan wouldn't look up at him. Pyke brought the knife back to his throat and this time he nicked the skin and drew blood. 'Just her naked, lying on a sofa, wasn't enough, was it? You wanted *more.*'

The banker nodded. His head was bowed and his whole body was trembling with fear and shame.

'How much more?' One more slip of his hand and the blade would slice through Trevelyan's throat. The temptation was almost too much to bear. *'How ... much ... more?'* He spat the words out one by one.

Trevelyan didn't answer.

Pyke thought about the chairs he'd seen in the makeshift studio where Bessie Daniels had posed naked on the sofa – and had been killed. 'You were there, weren't you? You actually witnessed it. You witnessed someone strangle her.' There were tears in Pyke's eyes. 'My God, you watched her die. You sat in one of those chairs, you smoked a cigar and you watched as someone murdered her.'

Trevelyan still wouldn't look at him so Pyke spat into his ear, 'Answer me, you pathetic coward.'

'Yes,' the banker mumbled. His hands were shaking. He took a deep breath and waited. 'I was there. I saw it.' There were tears streaming down his face. 'A man called Sykes strangled her, to the point where she was dead or as good as dead. Then Crane set up the camera.' Trevelyan swallowed. The way he was telling it, he had played no role in what had happened. 'That's what he wanted to capture, as an image. The moment she actually passed away; she hardly moved. That was important. If she'd moved, the image would have been ruined. But later, when I saw the daguerreotype, it was almost as if I could see her dying.' The way he finished the sentence indicated wonder rather than revulsion.

Pyke knelt for a moment, the air rushing through his ears as Trevelyan's confession sunk in. The fact that Trevelyan still couldn't see the vileness of what he'd done only made it worse.

Kneeling over the trembling man, Pyke took his throat with both hands and began to squeeze. 'Is that working for you?' He squeezed a little harder. 'Are you aroused now? *Are you?*'

The banker tried to splutter something but Pyke's hands were clasped too tightly around the man's throat.

'She was a woman. She was just like your wife, just like your daughters will grow up to be. You might not have strangled her with your own hands but you as good as killed her. Your money as good as killed her.' Pyke felt his anger swell. 'What kind of a monster are you? Watching a man take an innocent's life as though they were performing on stage?'

'But that's just it,' Trevelyan spluttered, as Pyke relaxed his grip slightly. 'They weren't performing. It was real.'

That made Pyke squeeze even harder, and he watched as the man's face turned crimson.

'Did it excite you? Seeing her dying? Seeing them *all* dying.' Pyke felt a tear roll down his cheek. 'How many were there?'

He let go.

Perhaps if he'd squeezed for a few seconds

more Trevelyan would have died. As it was, he held his throat, gulping air.

Pyke knelt down and pressed his face against Trevelyan's. '*I said,* how many were there? Two, three?'

'Something like that.'

'Two or three or more?' He thought of Bessie Daniels and Lucy Luckins and about the eyeballs kept in glass jars deep underground.

'Four, I think.'

Pyke stood up and drew his sleeve across his mouth. More than anything, he wanted to kill the man lying at his feet. But death would be an escape, a blessing. Pyke wanted the man to live with his shame. Publicly. And he needed Trevelyan alive because the banker was the only one who could be used to trap Crane.

'How much did you pay for each daguerreotype?' When Trevelyan didn't answer, Pyke repeated the question, this time louder. 'How much for the daguerreotype and the best seats in the house?'

'A hundred.'

If Crane had bought Bessie Daniels for five, that meant a net profit of ninety-five pounds.

'Tomorrow morning you're going to go to the police office at the Guildhall and you're going to change your statement.' He knew this wouldn't happen but wanted Trevelyan to think he thought it might.

'I *can't.* If I do that, he'll drag me down with him.'

'If you don't, your life is finished. I'll tell your wife, your family and everyone at the Bank what you've just told me.'

Trevelyan began to weep again. For himself and his own predicament, Pyke supposed. But not for the dead women.

Suddenly the idea of spending another second in Trevelyan's company made Pyke feel ill. He started to walk. To get as far away as possible from the sourness of the man's sweat. If he stayed, he would kill him. He knew that much about himself.

'That's it? You're leaving?' Trevelyan sat up, dazed, as if none of it had actually taken place. 'Who are you?'

Pyke kept walking.

The tide was rising, and by the time Pyke had climbed down from Dowgate Wharf to the sludgy riverbank, water was already lapping around his ankles. A patchy mist clung to the river, and from his vantage point on the north bank, a hundred yards from Southwark Bridge, Pyke couldn't see the other bank or indeed New London Bridge, a few hundred yards farther along the river. Using the lantern, he peered into the tunnel entrance. The soil from the sewer had mixed with the rising river water and the resultant brown sludge sloshed around at the mouth of the tunnel. It was eerily quiet, and after midnight had come and gone, and there was still no sign of Field or Paxton, Pyke started to think that perhaps Field had had second thoughts, or that Paxton had told Field about his plans. All these thoughts went through his mind, but at about a quarter past midnight he heard whispered voices above him on the wharf and then Field call out, 'Crane?'

'Down here,' Pyke muttered, trying to disguise his voice. He didn't want Field to recognise him, at least not yet. Not until he was down with him on the bank.

Pyke waited; he could hear Field talking in a hard, clipped tone. But the man had shown up. That was the important thing.

Pyke looked up and saw a man's shoes and then the bottom of a pair of trousers. Field was first down the ladder. Pyke kept himself hidden from view as Field reached the bottom and looked around; he was carrying a lantern. Paxton climbed down the ladder to join him. He was armed but it didn't look as if Field was. 'Crane?' Field waited, holding up the lantern.

Pyke stepped out from behind the wooden legs of the wharf. Field's face was a mixture of surprise and resignation. In that instant, he knew. He turned to Paxton, who raised the barrel of his pistol and fired. Field fell to the ground, the ball-shot tearing a chunk out of his frock-coat but nothing more. Pyke took aim and fired, too, but Field rolled away from that one. He kept moving, and in the time it took Pyke to reload, Field had retreated into the mouth of the tunnel. Pyke went after him, but told Paxton to stay where he was.

Without the lantern, Pyke could barely see his hands, let alone Field. But he could hear him, footsteps sloshing in the soil. Field was running, Pyke following. With the rising tide, the level of the soil came almost to their knees, which made it even more difficult to run. Pyke raised the pistol and fired into the darkness. Briefly the explosion lit up the tunnel. Field was less than twenty yards ahead of him. Pyke heard a grunt, heard Field stumble, but he kept moving. Field's footsteps had slowed, became more erratic. He was wounded. Pyke could hear him wheezing. Another few steps, and Pyke heard Field stagger and fall. He was less than ten yards ahead. Panting, Pyke stood over Field's body. In the darkness, he could just about make out his face. He seemed to be smiling.

'Better you than someone else.'

Pyke crouched down and pulled Field's head up out of the soil. 'It wasn't personal. If I didn't do it you'd have killed me.' He now saw that his shot had struck Field in the middle of his back. Blood was leaking into the black ooze.

'Tell Paxton...' Field hesitated and coughed up some blood.

'Tell him what?'

But Field died before he could finish his sentence. His eyelids fluttered and his body went limp. A long-tailed rat scurried past them, heading deeper into the tunnel.

On the riverbank, Pyke found Paxton and told him that Field was dead. Paxton took this news in his stride.

'And the woman?'

Paxton was still holding his pistol and, just for a moment, Pyke thought he was going to use it. Instead he put it into his pocket and started climbing up the ladder. 'If you give me what you promised me, I'll take you to her.'

TWENTY-NINE

She was sitting at the dressing table, staring at her reflection in the looking glass. Field may have been holding her captive, but the room was comfortable and well appointed, with a proper bed and a place to read and write. She looked up as Pyke entered the room, then turned around, her lips parting and her eyes widening with surprise. He had to admit she looked fantastic. She had just combed her hair and it fell around her face and down her back. For a few moments they stared at one another, Pyke at her flawless complexion, long, slender neck and, above all, her eyes: brown with yellow flecks around the irises and rimmed with circles of black.

'I was hoping you'd come for me,' she said, a half-smile forming on her lips.

'Hello, Mary.' Pyke spoke the words boldly; even so, they sounded strange.

For a moment she stared at him, amazed. 'How did you know?'

'Elizabeth Malvern had green eyes.'

Mary Edgar remained perfectly still, perhaps trying to work out in her head what to say and how to say it. 'I always knew you'd be the one who would find me out.'

Pyke felt dizzy just looking at her. He tried to suck down some air. 'You should have killed me when you had the chance.'

'You think I could do that?' She seemed genuinely appalled.

'You've done it before.'

Mary waited for a moment before she spoke. 'Do you know what kind of a person she really was?'

Pyke's expression remained implacable.

'Elizabeth Malvern passed herself off as a virtuous woman – an upstanding member of society who volunteered her time to help others. But it was all a lie. She would find women, prostitutes mostly, for this man, Crane. When he was finished with them, he had someone kill them and throw them away.'

'I know that, Mary. And I also know that you didn't kill her because she offended your morals.'

Mary stared at him, as though caught in a lie.

'I know why you and Sobers came here from Jamaica – to kill Elizabeth and take her place. Silas isn't going to last much longer and, with him and Charles dead, the estate passes to Elizabeth.' Pyke waited and added, 'I never met Elizabeth, but Alefounder's wife saw you with her husband and remarked on your resemblance to her. You would have seen it, too, growing up in her shadow. Once you'd killed Elizabeth, all you had to do was sit tight, make a point of not seeing anyone who knew her, and wait for Silas to die and the estate to be settled.' Pyke whispered, 'Did you really think it would work?'

'No one thinks Elizabeth is dead. Soon Silas will receive a letter, posted from Jamaica, apparently written by Elizabeth. It will inform him of her decision to remain there.'

'Then why are you still here?'

She looked up at him and held his gaze. 'I wanted to see how everything turned out.'

'And how, Mary, is it supposed to turn out?'

'I don't know do I?' Mary put the comb down and turned around to face the looking glass. 'That's up to you.'

They ended up talking for over two hours, and gradually Pyke, with Mary's help, fitted all the pieces together. What Mary knew, she had discovered from Phillip: indeed, the two of them had evidently formed a close bond in a short time.

Whatever way one looked at the circumstances, it had started with Elizabeth Malvern. About the time she introduced Crane to the practice of daguerreotyping, Phillip Malvern had turned up on her doorstep. While he had initially presented himself as her uncle, he later tried to convince her that he was, in fact, her father. Elizabeth didn't believe him at first, but he was persistent and his story was persuasive: he told her about his long-standing affair with Bonella, Elizabeth's mother, about her mother's death and about Silas's vengeful act of blinding him. Elizabeth had always been close to her father, and Pyke wondered how she had dealt with this revelation.

Phillip had lived in London for up to a year before he'd summoned the courage to face his daughter. To earn a living, he had scavenged the riverbanks and sewers for rats, and, in doing so, had stumbled on the underground room that eventually became his home. An unassuming and quietly rational man, Phillip had also brought

501

with him some of the darker beliefs he'd inherited from his Jamaican Creole ancestry. As such, he was, from time to time, disturbed by visions and believed his blindness to be a punishment that could be cured by making sacrifices to the dark spirits that plagued him. He'd shown Elizabeth his underground 'kingdom', as he'd called it, and let her see his collection of animals' eyeballs. He also told her that if he could offer the 'duppies' a human eyeball as a sacrifice, they might be appeased and restore his sight. Elizabeth didn't take Phillip's hopes for a cure seriously, but she certainly pitied him, and when, a little later, Crane's experimentation with daguerreotyping meant that a few unfortunate women had to be sacrificed, she came up with a plan to suit every-one's interests. Instead of burying the corpses, she and Crane would allow Phillip to dispose of them, thereby indulging his 'fanciful' belief that his blindness could be cured with the help of human eyeballs. He could do whatever he liked with the corpses as long as he made them disappear.

When Phillip had first arrived in London – to try to initiate a reconciliation with Silas and Eliza-beth – he'd written to Bertha, his former lover, in Accompong. It was at this point that Bertha had confessed to Mary, her daughter, what Mary had always suspected; that she was related to the Malvern family by blood. Until that conversation, she had always believed that Silas, and not Phillip, was her father, because of her close physical resemblance to Elizabeth. Therefore her mother's revelation that Phillip was, in fact, her father, also threw into doubt Elizabeth's parentage – at least in Mary's mind. And when Bertha found out that Mary was going to London, she passed on the address Phillip had given her – the Bluefield lodging house – and told her to try to persuade Phillip to come back to Jamaica.

According to Mary, the fact that she and Elizabeth were half-sisters, by the same father, was an open secret amongst the estate's black population. Unsurprisingly, this had never been acknowledged by the Malverns, who saw her merely as a negro slave. Similarly, Elizabeth's incestuous affair with her brother, Charles, was never brought up, even though most of the household knew about it. Mary didn't know whether Silas ever found out but many of the black servants at Ginger Hill suspected he knew. According to some, it was the main reason he had brought forward his plans to retire to London and why he'd insisted that Elizabeth accompany him, forcing Charles to remain at Ginger Hill against his will to run the estate. It was after their departure that Charles's attention had turned, quite naturally, to Mary, who, though a little darker skinned, looked eerily like his sister.

At the time Mary had been sleeping with Isaac Webb, but it was Webb, and particularly Harper, who had pushed Mary into an affair with Charles: both men saw it as a good opportunity to exploit the Malvern family. And when, a year or so later, a besotted Charles proposed marriage to her, they had insisted that she accept.

When Charles had discovered that Mary was still sleeping with Isaac Webb, rather than confront her directly, he had decided to send her to London, where she would live with his godfather until he could arrange the sale of Ginger Hill. For Harper and Webb, the idea that Mary would be in the same city as Elizabeth Malvern – without Charles to interfere – was too good a chance to pass up. Ideas were discussed; plans were formulated. Arthur Sobers volunteered to accompany her to London – without, of course, Charles Malvern learning about their plan. Meanwhile, wanting Mary to be safe in London but away from the disapproving stares of his family, Charles had arranged for her to stay in an apartment annexed to his godfather's home in Mayfair.

The first obstacle that Mary had faced upon her arrival at the West India Docks in London was William Alefounder. He was a friend of Charles's who had visited Ginger Hill the previous year. He, too, had noticed the physical resemblance between Mary and his former lover, Elizabeth Malvern. He'd followed her around the great house and had tried to flirt with her. According to Mary, they had slept together once in Jamaica. From her point of view, it had been a mistake; she had been flattered by his attention and had succumbed one night when a little drunk. But Alefounder had fallen for her, and when Charles Malvern sent him a letter explaining that Mary was to travel ahead of him to London, the besotted trader insisted on meeting her at the quayside and escorting her to her final destination. At first Mary didn't want anything to do with him – the last thing she needed was an additional complication. But a few days later, when it became clear to her that Lord Bedford didn't intend to let her have the freedom of the city without a chaperone, she sent

Alefounder a message asking him to show her the sights. By Mary's own account, this was a cruel thing to do, because it gave the trader some encouragement. He set up an apartment on The Strand and took her there one evening. (Later Pyke would surmise that Alefounder's wife must have followed him there and seen him and Mary together.) According to her, nothing had happened between them; she didn't particularly like Alefounder or find him attractive and had merely used him as a foil in order to escape the attentions of Bedford.

Under the guise of spending the day with Alefounder, Mary had, in fact, travelled to the Bluefield lodging house on the Ratcliff Highway, where Sobers had taken a room, and had managed to find Phillip Malvern. Initially Phillip was shocked to discover that he had another daughter; Bertha had never told him that Mary was his, and since he'd disappeared into self-imposed exile after he'd been blinded by Silas, he hadn't seen her grow up. Old and fragile, it had taken him a few hours to adjust to the news, and it was only when she told him that Bertha wanted him to go back to Jamaica that he finally seemed to believe her. He admitted that Bertha had been the true love of his life. They spent the afternoon and some of the next day together. Phillip was intrigued by Sobers's claims that Mary was a myalist and begged for her assistance in summoning spirits and 'vanquishing the demons' who'd stolen his eyesight. Eventually, he took them down to his underground chamber and showed them his collection of eyeballs. By her own admission, Mary was appalled by what she'd seen and tried to force Phillip to tell her where the eyeballs had come from, and whether he had harmed any of the women. Shaken, he confessed that Elizabeth had procured the bodies for him – he said he didn't know where they'd come from and only later, when Mary confronted Elizabeth, did she find out the truth.

Mary insisted that Phillip had not been involved in the plot to kill Elizabeth Malvern. From her descriptions of him, Phillip came across as a kind, lonely, deluded old man who was grateful to Elizabeth and didn't seem to understand the full horrors of what she and Jemmy Crane were doing. Pyke surmised that, out of gratitude, Phillip had told Elizabeth about the sewer access to the bullion vault at the Bank of England. He obeyed, of course, when she swore him to absolute secrecy. Elizabeth, for her part, had no intention of keeping it a secret, and when she told Crane about it, she set in motion a chain of events that inadvertently culminated in Crane's capture and arrest. Mary swore that she didn't know what had happened to Phillip and seemed genuinely upset when Pyke told her that he believed Phillip was being held captive by Crane's accomplices somewhere in the city, and might even be dead.

'I promised my mother I'd bring him back to her,' Mary said, facing the prospect that, despite her best efforts, she might fail to make good on this pledge.

Elizabeth Malvern's fate had effectively been sealed before Mary had even left Jamaica, but the plan – hatched by Harper and Webb – was put into action when Mary went to the Malvern residence to announce that she was going to marry Charles. This drew a predictable response from Silas and she was escorted from the house. Before Mary left, she told Silas that she was not going to change her mind – such were her feelings for Charles – and that she was willing to discuss the matter only with Elizabeth. Mary had left her address at the Bluefield lodging house, with instructions that Elizabeth should meet her there. Like her father, Elizabeth had wanted Mary out of their lives and certainly didn't want her former servant marrying her beloved brother. For this reason, Elizabeth had asked Crane and his friends to go to the lodging house to try to scare Mary into abandoning her wedding plans, but they had come up against Arthur Sobers. Later, Elizabeth sent word that she would be willing to talk to Mary at her house. Mary had agreed to go because it suited her own ambitions, but only on the condition that no one else was present, not even servants. Together with Arthur Sobers, she crossed the city on a horse and cart that Sobers had acquired the previous day. Convinced that Elizabeth was alone, Mary had excused herself and slipped downstairs to let Sobers into the house via the back entrance. According to Mary, Sobers was the one who'd actually strangled Elizabeth, but she didn't deny that she'd been a willing participant, pinning her half-sister to the floor.

When Mary described the murder, Pyke tried to gauge whether she felt any guilt or remorse, but her face remained blank.

Afterwards, Mary and Sobers took off Elizabeth's clothes, removed her jewellery and laid her out on a tarpaulin. They had already decided to cover the body with quicklime – it would dissolve some of the flesh and make a positive identification difficult. The more pressing dilemma had been what to do about Elizabeth's eyes. They were emerald green and anyone who'd seen Mary and who might be required to identify the body might notice the discrepancy. They'd already decided to try to make Elizabeth's death – *Mary's* death – resemble the murders they'd heard about from Phillip. If these murders were already known to the police, they would likely assume that Mary – or rather Elizabeth – had been killed by the same man. According to Mary, she had been the one who'd cut out her half-sister's eyes with a scalpel borrowed from Phillip. Once this procedure had been completed, they carried Elizabeth's corpse to the cart, hid it under a tarpaulin and returned to the Ratcliff Highway. There, at a spot they'd found earlier, they rolled the corpse down a grassy slope and left one of Mary's dresses – the one she'd been wearing that morning at the Bluefield – nearby, together with a bottle of rum. That, and washing the body with the rum, had been her idea. The scribbled note bearing the name of the Bluefield, which was left in the dress pocket, would lead the police to the landlord, Thrale, who would, in turn, identify the corpse as Mary. The rum and the apparently ritualistic nature of the killing would underline the fact that a black or mulatto woman had been killed. No one would think the corpse belonged to a white woman. The policemen wouldn't look at the skin colour; all they would see was a body decomposing with quicklime, the missing eyeballs, the rum.

Their hope, Mary explained, was that the corpse would be identified as Mary Edgar's and any investigation – if there was an investigation – wouldn't amount to much. They also knew that Silas Malvern, if he ever learned about Mary's death, wouldn't want it investigated too much either, because he wouldn't want his family's connection to a dead mulatto to become a matter of public record.

The only problem, of course, was Lord William Bedford. A kindly old man who was devoted to his godson, he had been true to his word and, at Mary's insistence, he'd told no one about her engagement, except for his most trusted servant, the butler. If Mary's murder was publicised and Bedford, or the butler, read about it, either man might go to the police and tell them what he knew: that Mary had been a guest in his house and that she was engaged to his godson, Charles Malvern. Moreover, if she went to see him after the death, the old man would know that the victim wasn't, in fact, Mary or the woman the police believed to be Mary.

'So you had to do something about him, didn't you? You didn't have a choice in the matter.' Pyke tried to push this point.

For her part, Mary tried to convince Pyke that she'd gone back to Bedford's mansion after discarding Elizabeth Malvern's body merely to talk to him; to explain that she'd decided to return to Jamaica. This way, and assuming her death wasn't widely reported in the press, Bedford wouldn't think anything of her vanishing act.

'But didn't you just tell me that Bedford was bound to hear of the murder and go to the police?'

Mary didn't have an answer for this. Pyke asked her to describe what had happened when she visited the old aristocrat. He expected Mary to be reticent or evasive, but she spoke openly about what she had done. Yet it wasn't long before her composure, and her voice, started to crack.

That night, Mary had slipped into Bedford's house without being seen and had made it all the way to his bedroom without disturbing any of the servants. Bedford had been reading a book in bed, and when he saw her enter his room, he beckoned her over and made a place for her next to him. He asked her what she wanted, what was so urgent that it couldn't wait until the morning. She had started to tell him about her decision to return to Jamaica when he noticed the silver necklace around her neck. Elizabeth's necklace. Mary had put it on after removing it from Elizabeth's corpse, and had forgotten all about it. Bedford said he knew it was Elizabeth's necklace because he had given it to her – he'd had it made specially for her eighteenth birthday. Bedford had demanded to know how she'd acquired it, and when she didn't answer him straight away, he had threatened to call the police if she didn't explain herself.

At this point, Mary's voice cracked and her face began to crumple. 'I didn't want to do it. I didn't plan to do it. I had no choice,' she whispered. 'Kind as he was, he would have ruined everything.'

Pyke waited for her to go on but Mary couldn't

get the words out.

'And the letter opener?'

She looked at him and he saw the struggle between guilt and remorse playing itself out in her expression. In a hollow whisper, she finally muttered, 'I stabbed him. I stuck the knife into the old man's belly and left him to die.'

They had talked for hours and Mary looked exhausted; there were tears in her eyes and this final confession had taken her last drop of strength.

'It makes a nice story but I don't quite believe it. I think you went to Bedford's house with a plan to kill him already in your mind.'

'He was a kind old man.' There were tears in Mary's eyes. 'Why would I have wanted to kill him?'

'Because Bedford would have gone to the police and told them about your connection to Charles Malvern.' Pyke shrugged. 'You planned all of this too carefully to allow a loose end to upset things.'

'What are you saying?' she said in barely a whisper. 'That I murdered him in cold blood?'

'Maybe you managed to convince yourself that you were just going there to talk to him but I think, deep down, you knew you had to kill him.'

They stared at one another for what seemed like minutes.

'I have to say, I'm still bothered by some of the evidence that the police found when they arrived at Bedford's house.' Pyke was thinking about the police investigation and the trail of evidence that had, in turn, suggested Morel-Roux's guilt.

Mary sniffed and wiped her eyes on her sleeve. 'What do you mean?'

'Did you try to hide Bedford's money and his rings in the valet's quarters in order to incriminate the valet?'

Mary's eyes widened at this new accusation. 'No. I just dropped the letter opener and ran.' Pyke studied her reaction.

'And kill-devil was the code name for the operation?'

She looked at him, surprised. 'How did you know that?'

'You were overheard talking to Sobers on the *Island Queen*. I mentioned it to Sobers, and also to Webb and Harper in Jamaica. Each of them flinched at those words. I knew it meant *something*.'

Mary looked at him. 'Harper thought it was appropriate, given what we were trying to do.'

There was a short silence. 'Come on, get up.'

'What are you doing?' She was still sitting at the dressing table, her back to the looking glass. Pyke was standing over her.

'I'm taking you to the police where you'll make your full confession.'

Mary didn't move but continued to stare at her hands. 'I know what I did to Bedford was wrong. He was a kind old man who didn't deserve to die, and no matter what happens, I'll have to live with that for the rest of my life.'

Trying to restrain his anger, Pyke looked down at Mary's hunched form. 'Lord Bedford wasn't just a kind old man, Mary. He was innocent, and you killed him.' He took a breath and tried to calm himself. 'But that's not all. Another innocent man was hanged for a crime that you committed.'

Mary seemed to sink even farther into herself.

While Pyke was in no doubt that Mary had stabbed and killed Lord Bedford, he now believed that she'd fled the scene immediately after the murder. He questioned her further on the minutiae of what had happened and her answers seemed to make sense. What didn't make sense was how the apparently stolen coins had ended up in Morel-Roux's quarters. It was clear to Pyke that Morel-Roux had been set up; that the evidence that had convicted him of Bedford's murder had been fabricated – just not by Mary. But Pyke didn't know who would have wanted to see Morel-Roux hang and why.

Pyke's confusion over Morel-Roux didn't quell his anger. Pacing around the room, he spoke as calmly as he could. 'And let's not forget that you were a willing accomplice to your half-sister's murder and the mutilation of her corpse.'

'I feel *no remorse whatsoever* for what I did to Elizabeth Malvern. She deserved everything she got.'

For the first time Pyke didn't know what to say, largely because he agreed with what she'd just said.

'You might have spent a few weeks in Jamaica but you have absolutely no idea what it's like to live there, what it's always been like. Have you ever tried to walk in manacles? Do you know what it's like to be whipped with a cat-o'-nine-tails? What it's like to be bought and sold like cattle? What it's like to know that whatever someone does to you, a *white man* does to you, you have no redress under the law? Even if they rape or kill you?' Her face was hot with rage, and she pulled up her dress to show him her back. Her skin was a coarse lattice of half-healed scars. 'I got those seven years ago and they'll *never* go away.'

Pyke felt his own anger abating in the face of hers.

'Now you want to pity me,' she said, still burning with indignation. 'I can see it in your eyes. But I don't want your pity, Pyke. None of us wants your pity. Harper, Webb, Sobers, *none* of us.' Mary stood up and stared directly into his face. 'Tell me something, Pyke. What would you have done if you'd been in our shoes? Would you have simply taken the punishment doled out by men like Pemberton without trying to do anything about it?'

'I can't say,' Pyke replied quietly.

'We decided to do something, to act. To see what was possible. To see what we could carve out for ourselves.' She spat these last words. 'I didn't come all this way just because Harper or Webb told me to. I came because I wanted to; because I didn't want to be a victim any longer. If there was a chance, just a tiny chance, that we could make this happen, then it would all be worth it.' Softening, she took his hand. 'When Silas dies, as he soon will, everything will pass to Elizabeth. Now do you see how close we are?'

'And I'm somehow meant to ignore the small fact that innocent lives have been taken in the process?'

Mary let go of his hand and folded her arms. 'You're talking to me about innocent lives? I've read your book. I know what kind of a man you are.'

Pyke thought about all the ways he could respond but none seemed appropriate. In the end it came down to a simple truth: he'd killed people for good and bad reasons – and had avoided the noose.

'If I told you that what's in my uncle's book in no way corresponds to the truth, would it make a difference?'

But she wasn't prepared to let the subject drop. 'Just answer me this: have you killed a man who hasn't deserved to die?'

He lowered his face and whispered, 'Yes.'

Mary reached out and touched his cheek. It was a simple act and he wanted to somehow reciprocate but couldn't bring himself to.

'When I first broke into Elizabeth's house that night,' he said tentatively, 'why didn't you just throw me out or fire the pistol at me?'

'I knew who you were, of course. That you were investigating the murder. I'd tried to follow your progress. At the time, I was lonely and a little frightened. Arthur had been arrested and then you showed up.' She cleared her throat and tried to swallow. 'And you seemed so full of a desire to find justice for Mary.'

It was true that he'd felt an affinity with her from the start. Now he didn't know what to think; whether to feel foolish or grateful that it wasn't Mary who'd been buried in that grave in Limehouse.

'Look, Mary. I'm a detective. Perhaps not in title but it's what I do; and I do it well. I could let you go, of course, but it wouldn't come naturally to me. I don't care about the law or justice but I agreed to do a job and I won't be able to sleep at night if I feel I haven't finished it.'

Mary stepped into the space between them and, in spite of everything, he still felt a stirring in his groin. 'When those men broke into the house and dragged me here, I thought it was over. That man, Field, told me why he'd brought me here, that he would return me to Crane in exchange for something he wouldn't divulge. I knew then that it was finished. If Crane didn't make the deal, Field said he'd kill me, and I believed him. If Crane did make the deal, he'd see right away that I wasn't his mistress and *he'd* kill me. So when I saw you walk into the room a few hours ago, I swore to myself I'd tell you the truth and put my fate in your hands. Does that make any sense?'

'What if I don't want that kind of responsibility?' But Pyke could feel his heart beating against his ribcage.

'You're here and I don't have anything left in my arsenal. What else can I do but throw myself at your mercy?'

Pyke looked at her plump, velvety lips and long lashes. He had to take a long breath. 'And now I don't know what I think or feel.'

'But you do feel something for me, don't you?' Mary stared directly into his eyes. 'I'm saying that, Pyke, because I feel something for you.'

That afternoon Pyke took Mary Edgar back to his house and introduced her to Jo and Felix. Jo was polite but cold; she told him of her plans to depart the following afternoon and left them in the front room. They talked about inconsequential things.

Mary didn't seem interested in the idea of running away. She relaxed, even laughed with Felix. That night she slept in the guest room and the next morning she was still there when Pyke brought her a cup of tea. She said she had slept well. He said he had, too, even though he had lain awake for most of the night. Laudanum hadn't helped, either.

When he suggested that she play Elizabeth one last time, and explained what he wanted her to do and why, she said she'd do it.

Even when he introduced her outside the Guildhall police office to Fitzroy Tilling, as Elizabeth Malvern rather than Mary Edgar, she didn't seem overawed. They went over the plan another time. She asked whether Jemmy Crane would actually see her. Tilling assured her that she wouldn't have to confront Crane directly and her face would remain hidden. As long as he believed she was who she claimed to be, that was all that mattered. She was introduced to the police sergeant who would take her down to the cells. Pyke watched as she and the sergeant disappeared into the building.

Pyke looked up at the Guildhall and they waited for a horse and cart to rattle past. 'I was thinking about Trevelyan.'

'And?'

'And you could always take some police constables to his house and search the study.'

'Why does it sound like you already know what they might find?'

'Trevelyan bought daguerreotypes from Crane of dead and dying women. Do you think he should be given the benefit of the doubt?'

Tilling's stare remained impassive. 'Anywhere in particular they should look?'

'Any loose floorboards would be a good place to start.' Pyke found himself looking at the entrance to the police office. 'Mind if you ever manage to find Bedford's butler again it's my guess he'll tell you that it was Pierce, acting for Silas Malvern, who fabricated the evidence that convicted Morel-Roux.'

Tilling turned to face him, his expression suddenly hardening. 'That's a very, *very* grave allegation.'

'Morel-Roux didn't kill Bedford. The evidence suggested he did.'

'But if *he* didn't kill Bedford, who did?' Tilling's frown deepened. 'And who killed Mary Edgar?'

'Arthur Sobers.'

'Both?'

Pyke shrugged.

Tilling reddened and shook his head. 'What aren't you telling me, Pyke?'

But just at that moment Mary Edgar appeared in the entrance. She looked up, walked towards them and waited for them to ask the question.

'Well?' Pyke beat Tilling to it.

'Crane had Phillip killed, once he was no longer useful to him. He wanted me to find a scavenger, *any* scavenger, put words into his mouth and bring him back here to this office.' A solitary tear snaked down her cheek.

Tilling looked at both of them and took a few steps backwards. 'I'll be over here if you need me.'

Pyke took her hand and squeezed it. 'I'm sorry.'

When she looked up at him, her eyes were wet with tears. 'So what have you decided? Should I give myself up?'

THIRTY

The following morning, half a dozen police constables attached to the 'A' or Whitehall Division, acting under the orders of Fitzroy Tilling, conducted a search of Abel Trevelyan's Regent's Park mansion. One of the party, Constable Henry Steggles, came across a loose floorboard in the study and, having lifted it up, found a daguerreotype depicting a naked woman sprawled out on a bed, staring into the camera, a hooded man standing over her. An amethyst ring with a serpent motif was also found and, later, as a result of testimony provided by former neighbours, it was identified as having belonged to Bessie Daniels, the woman in the daguerreotype. Meanwhile, after an anonymous tip-off a decomposed corpse was excavated from Trevelyan's garden. Though the body couldn't be positively identified, the police were happy to conclude that it was the woman in the daguerreotype, especially once Saggers had submitted the testimony regarding the ring. The banker was taken to the watch-house at Scotland Yard. There, it was established, via statements made by two former employees of a pornographer's shop on Holywell Street (again procured by Saggers), that Trevelyan had been a customer at

Crane's shop for a number of years. Presented with all this evidence, Trevelyan (who had, of course, strenuously objected to the police's search of his property and had denied all knowledge of both the daguerreotype and the body) was persuaded to change the statement he'd made to the City police regarding the break-in at the Bank of England. Additionally, and in exchange for the promise of judicial leniency over the matter of his ownership of obscene materials, he put his name to a deposition naming Crane – and three accomplices including a man called Sykes – as central figures in a conspiracy to profit from the lives and deaths of a number of 'low' women. In the end, although the corpse was found on his property, and despite the presence of Bessie's amethyst ring under the floorboards, no one could say with absolute certainty either that it was Bessie Daniels or that Trevelyan had killed her.

With their collective defence regarding the break-in at the Bank of England in tatters, and facing the likelihood of transportation for life and possibly even the gallows (depending on whether the robbery was interpreted as treason or not), Crane's accomplices willingly turned on him and named him as the leader of the plot. For his part, Crane threatened to name names and expose men who'd been his long-standing customers unless all charges against him were dropped, but his threats fell on deaf ears. Since Tilling couldn't cajole Crane and Sykes into turning on each other, however, the police weren't able to charge the two of them with the murders of Bessie Daniels, Lucy Luckins and as many as five other 'low' women.

This was the one glaring failure of the action Pyke had mounted against the pornographer, and it meant that, officially at least, the deaths of these women went unpunished. Still, at his trial for the attempted robbery of the Bank of England, the Crown played on Crane's former associations with radical thinkers and rabble-rousers and presented the robbery as a treasonous action intended to destabilise the national economy. Crane and his six accomplices were found guilty; Crane, as the leader, was sentenced to hang, while the others, including Sykes were transported to Australia for life.

On a cool, autumnal morning, Pyke joined the large crowd that watched Crane walk on to the scaffold in front of Newgate prison and wait as the hangman put the noose around his neck. When the block was kicked away from under him and he fell to his death, Pyke tried to think of the last, and only, time he'd seen Bessie Daniels alive. As the hangman pulled down on Crane's legs to finish the job, he thought of the manner of the transaction whereby Bessie had been sold to Crane by Eliza Craddock, and about Silas Malvern, who had accrued a vast fortune using exactly the same process: hard currency in exchange for a human life. But as Pyke watched Crane die, he didn't feel any satisfaction, not did he try to convince himself that justice had been served.

A month earlier, Arthur Sobers had made the same short trek from Debtors' Door to the scaffold, this time in front of a much smaller crowd. Pyke hadn't attended this execution because he didn't want to have to ask himself the difficult

521

question: was it right to punish an essentially good man for taking another's life? In the small hours of the morning, Pyke asked himself the same question and found himself thinking about Peter Hunt, the son of the former governor of Newgate prison who had tried and failed to avenge his father's death. Pyke knew that the law and justice were very different creatures, but often he would wake up, unable to silence the screams of the men he'd killed.

Phillip Malvern's body was never found.

The governor and directors of the Bank of England sought to limit the damage to the Bank's reputation as a result of the failed robbery and to distance themselves from their former friend and colleague, Abel Trevelyan, who was sentenced to three years' imprisonment for the possession of lewd and obscene materials. Their efforts to 'contain' the story were thrown into disarray, however, by a series of columns in the *Examiner* by 'staff writer' Edmund Saggers, in which he laid bare the link between Trevelyan and Crane and between pornography, the unexplained deaths of at least two women and the failed attempt to empty the bullion vault under the Bank of England. No mention was made of Harold Field; nor was his disappearance mourned. As far as Pyke knew, Matthew Paxton stepped into the dead man's shoes without too much guilt.

About a week after the body of Lord William Bedford's former butler was discovered floating in a lake near St Albans, Pyke found himself waiting in Scotland Yard for Pierce, who had just been promoted to the rank of superintendent.

'I'd say congratulations, but that would suggest you earned our promotion rather than buying it with the blood of an innocent.'

Pierce removed his hat and smoothed his hair. 'Your preference for the melodramatic is well known but tedious.'

'An innocent man went to the gallows because you took the thirty pieces of silver that Silas Malvern offered you, to keep his family's name out of the investigation.'

Pierce seemed amused rather than upset by this accusation. 'You want to know something, Pyke?' he said, picking his teeth. 'We never did apprehend the fellow who tried to help Morel-Roux escape from Newgate.'

'I hope you see Morel-Roux's face when you're lying in your bed late at night, trying to forget about what you've done.'

'I sleep perfectly well.' Pierce looked around the yard and put on his hat. 'It's quite clear you don't. That should tell you something.'

'Yes, it tells me I've got a conscience.'

Pierce appeared to be on the verge of saying something but at the last moment shook his head, as though it wasn't worth the effort.

'I'm not scared of you, Pyke, and I'm not even remotely concerned by your low opinion of me. In fact, the notion that you – of *all* people – think you're somehow more ethical than I am greatly amuses me.'

Pierce walked off and left Pyke to his thoughts. It took every ounce of self-control on Pyke's part not to follow him.

A few weeks after Jo had moved out to take up a nursemaid's post in a household in Bloomsbury, she came to visit Felix. After a long and tearful reunion with her former charge, she came to find Pyke and sat with him in the front room.

'You look well.' He meant it, too.

'I wish I could say the same about you.' She said this, he thought later, not to crow but simply to point out what was self-evident: he hadn't washed or trimmed his whiskers for days and he'd been surviving on a diet of laudanum and baked potatoes.

'And your visitor? I never did find out her name.'

Pyke couldn't bring himself to look at her. 'She's gone.'

'Oh.' Jo's expression was measured, her voice composed.

For a while neither of them spoke. The rattle of wood and iron wheels across cobbles temporarily filled the room.

'I saw the way you looked at her and I recognised it. It was the same way I used to look at you.' When he didn't respond, Jo offered a gentle smile.

Pyke fumbled around in his pocket and produced an envelope. 'I'd like you to have this as a token of my appreciation for all the work you did for my family.'

Jo took it, peered into the envelope and tried to hand it back to him. 'I couldn't possibly accept it, as generous as it is.'

'Don't think of it as coming from me. Think of it as a gift from Emily. I'd say you were her best, and most loved, friend. Or think of it as a gift from Felix if that makes you feel any better.' Pyke looked away suddenly because he didn't want her to see his expression.

She held out the envelope for him again but he wouldn't take it. 'Please, keep it. I'd like to think I've done at least one right thing with respect to you.'

Jo sat there for a while contemplating what he'd said and finally put the envelope into her shawl.

'Will you come and visit Felix again?'

On the front steps, they shook hands and, as their fingers parted, Pyke had to rein in a sudden desire to take her hand and ask her to reconsider. Tying her bonnet under her chin, she turned around and looked at him. 'Try not to be too hard on yourself, Pyke. For some reason, and I hope you take this as a compliment, self-loathing doesn't suit you.'

The same night Mary had found out that her father had been killed by Crane, she had come to Pyke's room. She wore a cotton nightdress that clung to her figure and revealed just enough of her firm, plump calves to elicit his attention. He had been sitting up in bed reading. She had stood by the door and even when he had invited her into the room, and had cleared a space for her next to him on the bed, she had remained where she was.

'I'm scared, Pyke.' She stood there unmoving. 'I'm scared that all this, all that we've done, all the lives that have been damaged – that it's all been for nothing.'

'I'm not sure what you want me to say. Do you expect me to tell you that everything is going to be all right?'

'Not at all,' she said, staring towards the window.

'What did you mean, then?'

Mary wiped a strand of hair from her eye and took a tentative step into the room. Pyke looked down at the book he'd been reading, trying to ignore his groin and the hammering of his heart.

'If you'd asked me a month ago, I would have told you how much I longed to be back in Jamaica. To feel the warmth of the sun on my skin, see my old friends.'

'And now?' His gaze followed the curve of her cheekbones down to the smoothness of her neck.

'Now I don't know what I feel.' She took another step into the room, and was almost close enough for him to reach out and touch her. 'Do you know?'

'What about?' He tried to swallow but couldn't.

'About what happened between you and me.'

She stared at him. But in saying it, in calling attention to what had happened, it was as if some kind of spell had been broken. This time, when Pyke patted the place for her on the bed, she sat down next to him.

'I've been thinking a lot about the few weeks that I spent in Jamaica.' He hesitated. 'At the time, it didn't make sense to me why no one seemed much interested in helping me to find your murderer.'

'You didn't ever suspect what we'd done?'

Pyke shrugged. 'Perhaps I did. Perhaps I didn't. It's hard to remember with any degree of certainty what I thought. But that's not what I'm trying to say.'

'I'm sorry.'

'You don't have to apologise. It's just...' Pyke hesitated. 'I was just thinking about a conversation I had with Isaac Webb.' He looked over at her, but her expression remained blank. 'I'm sure, looking back on it, he'd been told to kill me. I was becoming a nuisance. If I'd been allowed to return to London, I might've discovered the truth and threatened everything. It wasn't personal – in fact, I think Harper and Webb liked me for some reason. In any case, I pre-empted Webb – I knew what he was going to do and I pulled my pistol on him instead. Thinking about it now, I'm certain he could have followed me and finished the job. I told him that my place was here, with my son. He told me about his son and in the end, I think he let me go because he didn't want any more blood to be spilled. But as I rode away I remember thinking about home, about London, and how I didn't belong there in Jamaica.'

Her jaw tightened a little. 'And by that you mean I don't belong here?'

'I didn't mean that. I just meant that Webb and I seemed to come to an accommodation. Over there was his place.'

'But it isn't his place. Isn't that the whole point? It belongs to Silas Malvern, and when he dies it will be sold to another white planter. It will never be our place unless we're prepared to do something about it.'

Pyke absorbed the heat of her gaze but his silence seemed to make her angrier. 'Here in this room, in this house, what you have is all yours.

You can do as you please. You have no idea how lucky you are and how many things you take for granted.'

Pyke nodded, to concede the point. He knew what he had to say but the words seemed to catch in his throat. 'There's a ...' He hesitated and tried to swallow. 'There's a steamer leaving from Southampton in two days. I've booked your passage as far as Kingston.' He couldn't bring himself to look at her but he sensed her body going rigid.

'Just like that?' There was still a small spark of hope in her voice. She reached out and touched his hand and he had to bite back an urge to pull her towards him.

'I'll accompany you as far as Southampton, to make sure you take up your cabin.'

That drew a hollow laugh. 'A cage with golden bars.'

'Better that than a prison cell here in London.'

'And Silas Malvern?' She gave him a hollow look. 'What will you tell him?'

'I'll tell him the truth.' This time he looked directly at her and sighed. 'That's all I can do.'

Picking up the half-full bottle, Fitzroy Tilling leaned across the table and poured them both a glass of claret.

'You know what I think?' he said, chewing a piece of bread. 'I think, in the end, there isn't a great deal that separates us. I'd even go as far as to say there could be a place for you in the New Police if you wanted it. The political winds are shifting. There'll be an election within the year and Peel will win it. The current Liberal administration is a spent force. I've talked to Peel about your ideas vis-à-vis detection, rather than just prevention, of crime. He seems keen on the idea of a detective bureau and I think he might offer you a position. What would you say to that?'

'Me? A police officer?' Pyke started to laugh.

'A detective. And remember you were once a Bow Street Runner.'

Pyke took a sip of claret. He would have to think about Tilling's offer, but it was true that he enjoyed the work. Sitting back in his chair, he looked at the man across from him and wondered about their similarities.

'Did anyone ever connect you with the attempt to break Morel-Roux out of Newgate?'

Tilling looked up from his food, a grilled lamb chop, and shrugged. 'They investigated, of course, and found that a PC William Dell and I left the prison through the main gate at a quarter to ten.'

'You know, I got him as far as the chapel window. All he had to do was climb down the rope. But he froze. He was terrified of heights.'

Tilling put down his cutlery and exhaled. 'We did all we could, Pyke.'

'Do you really believe that?' Pyke could tell that Tilling was still troubled.

'If I had the chance to do it again, to try to rescue Morel-Roux, I wouldn't. The law's the law. It's the only thing that separates us from beasts.'

'But the law is also the means by which men like Silas Malvern have accrued their fortunes.'

Tilling chewed a piece of meat and washed it down with a mouthful of claret. He didn't have an answer. One of the things Pyke liked best about

Tilling was that they disagreed so fundamentally on so many different things but somehow managed to keep those disagreements at bay. He wondered what this said about their friendship.

'I had lunch with the governor of the Bank of England today,' Tilling said, breaking the silence.

'Oh?'

'In light of what happened, they've just completed an audit of their bullion reserves.'

'And?' Pyke pretended to concentrate on what was on his plate.

'Twenty gold bars have gone missing.'

'Just twenty?'

'Indeed, given what *might* have happened, he seemed rather relieved.'

'Could've been a lot worse.'

'And he knows he has you to thank for that.' Tilling wetted his lips. 'You were the one who foiled Crane's plans, after all.'

Pyke accepted the compliment. 'What's he going to do?'

'Any more than twenty, I'd say he would have called in the City of London police.'

'But a man in his position wouldn't want to advertise that even one single gold bar had gone missing, would he?'

Tilling pushed a piece of meat around his plate with a fork. 'The hole leading up from the sewer came out directly in front of the guard room. To get in and out of the bullion vault, someone would have had to be fairly sure that no guards would be present. That's what Crane was counting on. But what if someone knew, for example, that on the Sunday morning before the robbery, a meeting had been called in the governor's chamber, involving all the soldiers, and hence the entrance to the bullion vault would have been left unguarded for at least half an hour?'

Pyke took a sip of wine and held Tilling's stare. 'That's quite an elaborate story. But I don't know what it's got to do with me.'

Tilling's eyes narrowed. 'It pleases me to hear you say that. Because if I thought you'd used me, I'd do my utmost to see you prosecuted to the fullest extent of the law.'

Pyke said nothing.

'Listen, I mentioned this idea of the detective bureau earlier because I think you're the most tenacious, gifted investigator I've ever known. I think you enjoy it, too. But these are changed times. Any slip-ups, any vague flirtations with criminality, and Peel won't touch you with a ten-foot stick.'

Pyke assured Tilling that he would think about what he'd said.

That afternoon, Pyke collected Felix from God-frey's shop and took him back to the house, where they rescued Copper from the back yard. They walked to the fields just to the north of their street. It was a warm, late summer day and, away from the maw of the city, the air smelled clean and refreshing. The sky was an unbroken panoply of blue, and the ground underfoot had been baked hard by the sun. Copper limped contentedly by their side and, as they walked, Felix discussed the good and bad points of the new nanny, mostly in terms of how she was and wasn't like Jo.

The field to their right had been portioned up into allotments and Pyke had taken one of the plots and had started to plant his own vegetables. He liked the idea of working a small patch of land and showing Felix how particular foods arrived on his plate. There was a small shed in one corner of the allotment from which Pyke collected a shovel before digging down into recently cultivated earth. Felix and Copper looked on without much interest. Eventually, the end of the shovel struck the top of the trunk. Pyke cleared a space around it and invited Felix to join him in the hole.

'I want you to see something,' Pyke said, putting his arm around Felix's shoulder. 'I was hoping you could open up the trunk for me.'

'Why? What's inside?'

'Why don't you open it and see for yourself.' Pyke stood back while Felix unfastened the catch and lifted up the lid.

The eighteen gold bars were just as he'd left them. The reflection from the sun made it hard to look at them for any length of time.

For days, Pyke had agonised over whether to tell Felix about the bars or show them to him. The risk of doing so was great: Felix might turn against him or, worse still, denounce him as a common criminal. That said, considering the way Felix had dealt with Eric, the pickpocket, Pyke had seen something in his son, an indifference to the finer points of the law, and it was something he liked. That suggested to him it might be time to trust the lad a little more, show him something of the world Pyke actually inhabited. Let him be proud of his father; proud of his rougher edges and daring, rather than of his willingness to serve the very letter of the law.

Felix didn't know what to do. 'Are they real?' he asked, afraid to reach out and touch them.

'Try lifting one up. You'll need both hands.'

Felix did as Pyke suggested and tottered unconvincingly under the weight of one of the bars before letting it drop back on to the pile. 'Where have they come from?' he asked eventually, still adjusting to the wonder of it all.

'That doesn't matter. What matters is they're ours. Yours and mine. This is our secret. I want you to shake my hand; then we'll both swear we'll never tell another living soul about it.'

They shook hands and made the pledge. Pyke lifted one of the bars out of the trunk and put it in a satchel he'd brought with him. The market price was something in the region of eight hundred pounds; Ned Villums had offered to pay him half that. But it would be more than enough to settle his debts and pay his bills for the foreseeable future.

'What are we going to do with them all?'

Pyke smiled at the speed with which his son had accepted his ownership of the bars. 'Keep them here. From time to time I might sell one. But this is our future. I promised I'd try harder. This is the start of it.'

'But what if someone else comes and digs them up?'

'No one else knows about them. As long as we don't tell anyone else, they'll be more than safe right here.'

Later, as they walked back towards the house,

the sun was setting in the west and the entire sky was washed with streaks of orange and gold. Copper trotted ahead on his three good legs and Felix walked next to Pyke holding his hand.

It took Pyke another month after he had seen Mary on to the steamer at Southampton to summon the necessary fortitude to face Silas Malvern in his own home. He was ushered in by the same butler into the same greenhouse he had visited three or four months earlier. This time, though, Malvern almost seemed pleased to see him and even made the butler fetch two glasses of his best cognac. He also ordered the man to bring a chair for Pyke and put it close by so that they could talk without being interrupted. He seemed to be in good spirits and, if anything, his health had improved slightly since Pyke had last seen him outside the Sessions House.

'Now, sir, to what do I owe the dubious honour of this visit?' he asked, once the butler had returned with the chair and the brandies.

'You once expressed a desire to be reunited with your brother, Phillip. I'm sorry to tell you he's dead.'

Malvern's expression crumpled and his top lip began to quiver. 'I see.' He tried to regain control of his mouth. 'Can I ask where and how he died...' Closing his eyes, he went on, 'and what has become of his body? I should like to honour him in death in a manner I wasn't able to in life.'

'He fell in with the wrong people. It's likely his body will never be found.'

'Will you at least tell me about the circumstances of his death and the identity of these people you refer to?'

'On certain conditions.'

Malvern licked his lips. 'Such as?'

'I want you to own up to what you did. An innocent man was sacrificed to preserve your family's good name.'

Malvern paused and then nodded his head slowly, as though acknowledging the truth of what Pyke had just said. With a lazy movement he waved his hand, as though swatting an imaginary fly. 'What would be the purpose of raking over old ground?'

The almost casual manner with which Malvern had admitted to his part in the plot to fabricate the evidence against Morel-Roux took Pyke's breath away.

'You've clung on to your honour and fortune and Pierce has been promoted to the rank of superintendent. But a good man is dead for no other reason than he was poor and foreign and therefore expendable. Is that something you want to take to your grave?'

'If I ever felt the need to confess my sins, I'd do so in the presence of a priest, not a common thief.'

'I'm not talking about making a statement before the Church or even the law. I know you'd never do it. I just want you to admit what you did to *me*.'

'Why?' This time Malvern seemed genuinely curious. 'You already seem to have made up your mind anyway.'

'Because I want to hear the words come from your lips.'

The idea of exacting his own justice had crossed Pyke's mind, but such an act would only play into the hands of the Jamaican conspirators. He wondered what he had really hoped to achieve by confronting the old man.

When Malvern didn't answer, Pyke added, 'I realise that some vague information about a brother you haven't seen in more than twenty years is perhaps insufficient inducement here, so I'm prepared to sweeten my offer.'

'Sweeten in what sense?'

'I also have some information about your daughter.'

That made him sit up straighter. 'What do you mean? What information do you have about my Elizabeth?'

Pyke pretended not to have heard him. 'But you see, I've changed my mind. I'll tell you what I know only if you'll agree to make a confession in front of Sir Richard Mayne and Fitzroy Tilling.'

He sat back and watched the old man's bewilderment, enjoying it until he considered his own motivations for doing what he was about to do. Until now it hadn't been clear to him, but suddenly it was: he wanted to ruin Pierce and break Malvern. Any hint of wrongdoing on Pierce's part would bring about his dismissal and the truth about Elizabeth Malvern would surely send the old man to his grave. What Pyke was doing had nothing to do with justice, with avenging the Swiss valet's death.

'I've just received a letter from my daughter.' Malvern stared at him with ill-concealed hostility. 'It would appear she's decided to remain in

Jamaica for the time being and she's quite adamant that I'm not to sanction the sale of Ginger Hill.' Pyke couldn't tell whether he welcomed this move or not.

He thought about Mary Edgar and the way the skin around her eyes creased when she smiled. But he also thought about what she and Webb and Harper and Bertha and Sobers had done, or tried to do, and how close they were to realising their ambitions. He'd thought about little else in the month or so since Mary had departed on the steamer bound for Kingston.

'It would appear we've reached an impasse, sir,' Malvern said, sipping his cognac. 'You see, I'm sufficiently curious about this new information you claim to have acquired regarding my daughter to at least consider your request, even if it comes at great personal cost to myself.'

'But?'

'But I can't agree to honouring this agreement until I know more about the specific nature of your information.'

Pyke felt his stomach tighten. 'Perhaps I could ask you a question, in the meantime?'

Malvern nodded.

'What's become of your intention to donate a tranche of land at Ginger Hill to Knibb's church?'

'I signed the papers before Knibb sailed for Jamaica.'

'A hundred acres?'

Malvern hesitated, his eyes narrowing slightly. 'More like fifty.'

'*Like* fifty, or fifty?'

'Forty perhaps. No, definitely forty.'

537

Pyke contemplated what he'd just been told. 'But the estate at Ginger Hill encompasses more than five hundred acres.'

'That's correct, sir.'

'And you think that donating a paltry forty acres is enough to make up for the profits your family has accrued from the forced labour of slaves? *That* is your expression of remorse – forty acres?'

Malvern pulled his blanket up over his knees and took another sip of brandy. 'I know you've visited the island, sir, and know a little of the challenges faced by planters and negroes alike. But you can't simply tear down one system and replace it with another overnight. That takes time. Little by little change will come, and if the negroes show themselves capable and worthy of adjusting to their new circumstances as citizens of the Crown, more opportunities will come their way. But they will have to prove themselves first. Even Knibb would tell you the same thing.'

Pyke thought about Webb and Harper, but most of all about Mary Edgar. Had they proved themselves?

'I'm afraid you'll have to excuse me, sir. I've had a change of heart.' Pyke stood up and looked down at Malvern's face.

'What do you mean, a change of heart?'

'If you were to be seized by a sudden desire to unburden yourself to Mayne or Tilling, I for one would welcome it. But I see no further reason for continuing this conversation.'

He started to walk towards the door. Malvern tried to climb up from his chair but the act was beyond him. 'What about your news of Elizabeth? What's happened to her? You can't leave me like this. Sir, I beg you.'

On the steps outside Malvern's house, Pyke steadied himself against the stone column and watched a milkmaid pass by on the pavement, two metal churns balancing on either side of a wooden yoke. It was a cool, overcast day and the air smelled of wet leaves, but Pyke's thoughts were not of the imminent change of season, nor even about the conversation he'd just had with a frail old man. Rather, he thought of a place high in the mountains where people grew their own food and lived in their own houses, and whether it was possible to commit terrible acts in the name of a general good – and still be able to face your own reflection without hating what you saw.

ACKNOWLEDGEMENTS

This book is dedicated to Debbie Lisle, who has tirelessly read, scribbled all over and commented on countless versions of it, at each stage of the writing process. My gratitude and love go to her.

I would also like to thank Helen Garnons-Williams and Kirsty Dunseath, my editors at Weidenfeld & Nicolson, for their detailed, imaginative and thoughtful advice and their general good sense. Thanks also to Luigi Bonomi, my agent, Dave Torrens at No Alibis in Belfast and David and Daniel at Goldsboro Books for all their support. The initial idea for this novel came from reading Thackeray's 'Going to see a man hanged' about the execution of Courvoisier for the murder of Lord William Russell, and from finding an account on the Bank of England Museum website about a sewer-man who, in 1836, accessed the bullion vault via an underground tunnel. In terms of my research, James Parrent, of Falmouth Heritage Renewal, pushed me in the right direction while visiting Falmouth, but my guides were mostly books, and those that deserve particular mention include Matthew Lewis's *Journal of a West India Planter*, *A Narrative of Events, Since the First of August 1834, by James Williams, an Apprenticed*

Labourer in Jamaica, Jean Rhys's *Wide Sargasso Sea,* Richard Hughes's *A High Wind in Jamaica,* Peta Jensen's *The Last Colonials: The Slog of Two European Families in Jamaica* and, for its general context, Catherine Hall's *Civilising Subjects: Metropole and Colony in the English Imagination, 1830-1867.* Details of Knibb's speech at the Anti-Slavery Society meeting in London (which I doctored slightly for my purposes) were gleaned from Madhavi Kale's essay in *Empire and Others: British Encounters with Indigenous Peoples, 1600-1850.* Ed Glinert's *East End Chronicles* and Watts Phillips's *The Wild Tribes of London* were particularly helpful for their accounts of life in and around London's docks and the Ratcliff Highway, while Lynda Nead's *Victorian Babylon* offered an excellent introduction to the murky world of Victorian pornography. Suffice to say all of the mistakes, and the really nasty bits in the book, are mine.

The publishers hope that this book has given you enjoyable reading. Large Print Books are especially designed to be as easy to see and hold as possible. If you wish a complete list of our books please ask at your local library or write directly to:

Magna Large Print Books
Magna House, Long Preston,
Skipton, North Yorkshire.
BD23 4ND